AFTERSHOCKS

AFTERSHOCKS

Richard S. Wheeler

A TOM DOHERTY ASSOCIATES BOOK

NEW YORK

This is a work of fiction. All the characters and events portrayed in this novel are either fictitious or are used fictitiously.

AFTERSHOCKS

This book is printed on acid-free paper.

A Forge Book
Published by Tom Doherty Associates, Inc.
175 Fifth Avenue
New York, NY 10010

Forge® is a registered trademark of Tom Doherty Associates, Inc.

Library of Congress Cataloging-in-Publication Data

Wheeler, Richard S.
    Aftershocks / Richard S. Wheeler.—1st ed.
        p.   cm.
    "A Tom Doherty Associates book."
    ISBN 0-312-86527-9
    1. Earthquakes—California—San Francisco—History—
20th century—Fiction.   I. Title.
PS3573.H4345A68   1999
813'.54—dc21   98-45339
                                                     CIP

First Edition: January 1999

Printed in the United States of America

0 9 8 7 6 5 4 3 2 1

To my publisher, Tom Doherty,
and his gifted staff

AFTERSHOCKS

CHAPTER 1

. . . .

The four-poster bucked Harrison Barnes White to the hardwood floor and then attacked him. White dodged the bed by rolling away, spinning himself into his bedclothes like a crêpe suzette. But the four-poster reared like a stallion, landed like a wrecking ball, and pinned him to the floor, which gave way under him and then delivered an uppercut to his flailing body.

After that the floor lurched sideways, like a rocking cradle, heaving him this way and that. He felt sheets tear under him. He heard glass shattering and the tinkle of shards on the maple flooring. A strange, unearthly thunder rose from the bowels of the earth, the sound of a thousand cataracts, punctuated with cannon and rifle shots. The humping of the floor slowed, and the rhythm seemed almost predictable, except when it wasn't, and another unseen fist poked him in the gut.

Then the thunderous noise retreated outside, but he heard it echoing over the peninsula as if it had come from the core of the earth. The spacious house bounced and its members groaned and creaked and snapped as the unseen force toyed with its two thousand nails. He could not believe what he had experienced and knew he could never describe it because no words, in any tongue, existed to convey it to any other mortal. The house returned to its foundations, and rocked gently, the rhythm a memory of the previous moments, and then settled into resignation. Bits of plaster landed on him. He felt the night air, cool and fresh off the Pacific, eddy through the room. A predawn light filled the heavens. He reckoned it was about five, and a unique way to begin an April day.

9

She was laughing. My God, how could he have ignored her? He hadn't, really; scarcely a minute had passed since he had been tossed out of bed, and that minute contained a dozen lifetimes within it. Where was she? He tried to free himself, but a blanket, sheet, and coverlet encased him like a straitjacket.

"Marcia?"

"Really, Harrison, I know you're a lusty man, but now you've gone too far." She laughed, but it sounded just as much like sobbing.

He heard the soft giggles from the other side of the four-poster, which stood akimbo, jammed against one gray wainscot. He wrestled with his cocoon, at first unable to free himself. But finally he worked an arm free, and then wrenched himself loose of the bedclothes. He clambered to his hands and knees, and then stood, only to tumble again. The floor was heaving like the teak deck of a schooner in heavy seas. That struck him as funny, mostly because she was laughing and her humor was infectious.

He waited a few moments while the planet settled into sobriety, and then found her pinioned between the wall and the mahogany four-poster. He levered the bed away, inch by inch. She didn't get up but lay on the polished hardwood. She may have been laughing, but he saw tears in her eyes.

He knelt.

"Marcia? Are you all right?"

She reached for him. He held her a moment and then helped her stand up.

The earth-gods cooperated. No more whimsy. She stood. He stood. He admired her a moment in the dim dawn light. Her cheeks glistened. Her glossy dark hair fell loose over her white cotton nightgown.

They heard wailing.

"Oh, darlings," she said, bestirring herself for the first time.

She walked tentatively. The floor did not buck.

The sea breeze penetrated shattered windows. The odd roar outside had not entirely abated. They walked gingerly, barefooted, through fields of shattered glass, into the wide hall, and across to the children's rooms. By some unspoken understanding, Marcia headed for Daisy's lemon-yellow room, while Harrison headed for the bold blue room of his son and namesake.

The house trembled, and the roar outside rose out of the throat of the earth. The door frame jarred Harrison, and then it was over. A final hiccup. His son, the Third, stared solemnly. Something had cut his cheek just enough to wet it with blood. The boy was rubbing his finger in the blood and staring at it.

"I'm afraid," he said.

"Big quake. It's over, Harry. Maybe some aftershocks, but those aren't so bad. We're alive. We have our nice house, and we'll repair it. Wasn't that something to remember?"

"I don't want to live here anymore."

Harrison didn't reply. He loved San Francisco more than any other place on earth. He heard weeping from the other bedroom. Daisy, two years younger, wasn't so stoic.

Suddenly Harrison knew there were things he must do, and fast.

"Get dressed. Don't cut your feet on the glass," he said.

Heeding his own advice, he gingerly maneuvered to the great gray bedroom of his wedlock, found his slippers, and plunged down the broad stairs.

He smelled the gas and heard it hiss. He peered about wildly, wondering how to venture into the darkened basement to turn the cock. He dared not try the electric light switch. It would arc—if there was electricity at all. He fumbled his way down the basement stairs. Hadn't he designed this house? Wouldn't he know where to go, light or dark? He maneuvered across a pitch-black basement in the general direction of the gas pipe. The concrete under him swayed. The basement reeked of coal gas, the product of one of several suppliers in San Francisco. He found the pipe, ran his hand along it, found the cock, and turned it until it was perpendicular. He heard nothing, but knew the hissing in the kitchen had stopped. He retreated swiftly toward the dim cone of light at the stair, fearful of asphyxiating himself if he stayed down there.

He swore the railing leaped as he climbed up to the first floor, but he knew that was his imagination. The slightest dizziness or misstep seemed like another tremor. He acknowledged he was not far from terror himself.

The kitchen was a shambles. The cupboards had vomited everything, and most of it lay shattered. In the dining room, every piece of china and cut glass in the hutch lay in pieces on the floor. So, too, was his library—books everywhere, including his architectural journals. The parlor looked like it had been vandalized. There wasn't a painting on a wall. The seven-day clock had sailed from the mantel to the leather wingchair and was still ticking, the glass intact. It reported 5:22. Outside, the dawn was chattering like the rattle of Maxim guns, the oddest sound Harrison had ever heard. It shot chills through him.

He had insurance but didn't know whether it covered earthquakes. Maybe it excluded acts of God. No matter. He'd be rich. Ruined cities needed architects. That odd thought snagged in his stream of consciousness, hung there. Yes, it was true. Because of this, he would soon be rich and important.

The thought spurred him to his bedroom. Marcia was still with the children. He could hear her with them, and didn't know whether the sobbing was hers or Daisy's or Harry's. He needed to get out and into the real world. He pulled the chest of drawers around so he could ransack it, found underdrawers and stockings, a shirt lying on the floor, his trousers in a heap, two matched wing-tip shoes at opposite ends of the room. He debated whether or not to shave. He had never roamed the streets unshaven, and didn't wish to do so now. He would shave. Yes, he must shave. He must act the gentleman, the man of parts. He hastened to the lavatory, a place with every modern convenience including an oak commode, pedestal washbasin, clawfoot tub, and gas-fired water heater. The water would still be hot.

His shaving mug, straightedge, and brush were nowhere to be found. Frantically he poked around in the dim light, and located them beneath the tub, against the wall. But he couldn't find the soap. No matter. He would scrape his face.

He turned the faucet, and it dripped once, twice. No water. An odd thing, no water. But of course they would have it on soon. A main had broken somewhere. They had shut the valves. It irritated him. He would have to venture into the dawn looking like a bum. He suddenly wanted a drink, coffee, liquid in him after the long night.

"There's no water," he said, but Marcia was with the children. Irritably, he dressed. Maybe no one would notice his blond stubble. That was it. He would make his tour and be back at the big house on Pacific before the mobs were out. There were things he must see. He tied his cravat, straightened his collar, and stood before the looking glass. A lean, handsome, square-jawed architect, twenty-eight, and this would be his day of triumph.

"I'm going out," he said.

"How about straightening the furniture first?"

"I can't. I've important things to do. There's no water. Don't push a light switch. You can clean up while I'm out. I'll take care of the heavy pieces when I get back."

"But Harrison—"

She wasn't smiling now. The children stared numbly. "This is my day," he said.

"I need you."

She looked so angry. What was the matter with her, anyway? Why couldn't she be strong like him? Why couldn't the children settle down and begin the day? He felt a moment of guilt, but set it aside.

"Just an hour or two," he said, knowing it would be much more than that. "Marcia, you can't imagine how important this is."

She started laughing again. "I should've known," she said.

Female logic. It annoyed him. "You're my sweethearts," he said, smiling. Then he beat a retreat. The front door didn't open easily. It had been sprung. He rammed it with his shoulder, and found himself catapulted onto the veranda. The house had been situated with views toward the Golden Gate, and east, toward Telegraph Hill and the vast blue bay, which lay subdued, purple, in the thickening light. No lamplight glowed anywhere. The white city lay somnolent but not quiet. An odd chatter permeated the air, and his architect's instinct told him it consisted of falling brick and mortar, cornices, beams, and trusses groaning under new weight, the forces of gravity everywhere tearing at damaged buildings. Several columns of smoke rose into the windless air, illumined by the rose of predawn light. The fires were south of the Slot, mostly—a residential tinderbox on man-made land. The fire department would have its hands full. Might be opportunity there. He had some ideas about how the area south of Market Street could be beautified. Maybe, if enough blocks burned, it could be the chance of a lifetime.

There would be no hack. He would walk a half hour to get to his destination. He hastened eastward on Pacific, feeling a little bit bothered about abandoning his family. They would be all right, of course. But this was important. This was the test of everything: who he was, the level of his skills, his vision as an architect and engineer and city planner, his future—and a firm of his own rather than his current position as a junior in Wolper and Demaris, having to fight for everything new among older, more timid men.

He hadn't designed the Claus Spreckels Building, eighteen floors built of steel I-beams, but he wished he had. He had been employed on the Chronicle Building, twelve stories, steel construction; the Fairmount Hotel, not yet finished; the Monadnock Building, almost done. That was his, that one. He was the primary architect. And that was where he was heading. If it stood undamaged, he would be famous. There was nothing like a quake to make an architect's reputation.

CHAPTER 2

atharine Steinmetz awakened early. Some dogs were howling. She had not known there were so many dogs in the neighborhood. Some were baying like wolves. That was odd.

She liked to get up early and watch the dawn brighten in the east from her bay window overlooking the city. Light always woke her up. She loved light, understood it, made good use of it. By mid-morning her flat would be wreathed in it, and she would enjoy its faint warmth upon her wrinkled flesh.

Emil would sleep until ten if she let him. Light didn't affect him. That was good. It gave her some hours to be alone with herself. She wrapped an ancient white robe about her thick body, and struggled to her feet. She stood, feeling the familiar stab of pain in her arthritic knees. She would have a good hour, and then the wear of the day would start the swollen knees to throbbing again. Each day, it seemed, walking came harder.

She studied the somnolent city from her window on the east flank of Russian Hill, not far from the corner of Taylor and Vallejo. She and Emil Wolff had shared this place for six years, but now she wondered if they could hang on. The future filled her with foreboding. Emil lived and worked in a rickety wheelchair; she would soon not be able to walk and would end up in a chair like his. Who would take care of her and her lover? Sometimes, in recent months, they had been late with their rent—once over a week. How could they hang on?

They needed a place on flat ground. She no longer had the strength to wheel Emil uphill, or worse, downhill. Several times she had almost lost control. But who would move them and where would they go? Maybe to Columbus Avenue. That wasn't so far, and she liked those Italian neighborhoods.

The city lay velvet and soft and mysterious in the predawn glow. She had studied the dawns and knew she could never catch them. Sunsets she could capture, but not dawns. They were different, different light. Maybe scientists would laugh and say it was all the same light, but she knew better, and her camera said so, too. She could not capture the dawn, but she would keep trying.

The foreboding was sharp in her this morning. She delayed starting a pot of coffee on her gas stove so that she could feel this new and gritty sensation that was affecting her. Maybe it was money. Emil's sales hadn't been good, and hers had been worse. But that wasn't it, at least not all of it. She didn't know how she could take care of Emil, get his etchings to galleries, cook for them both, clean, buy his chemicals and copper plates, pursue her own photographic goals, take her own prints to market, collect money, wheel Emil up and down slopes that were becoming impossible, and live—that was it—just plain live, with aches so deep and terrible in both knees that she often stopped mid-step and fought back tears. She was getting old. That was it. Her heavy body was breaking down—and there was no one to help.

Emil, too. Once, not many years before, Emil Wolff was regarded as the best engraver in the West. He had more work than he could handle, rendering plates for magazines and newspapers, plates of such uncommon beauty and clarity that publishers flocked to him. And not all of them were in San Francisco, either. *Harper's Monthly* bought everything he could produce. The checks rolled in; they had been more than enough. But now most magazines were using lithographed photos on their pages, and Emil's engraving trade had withered. He had turned to etchings, saying he preferred art to commerce. He made beautiful etchings, often working from her photographs. But they didn't sell very well. Or maybe she just lacked the time and energy—and freedom from pain—to market them.

He had changed, too. He said he was doing what he wanted now, exquisite etchings of San Francisco buildings and scenes—and yet he had darkened, grown short with her, often cross, always frustrated by his immobility. The thank-yous had long since vanished, along with endearments, affectionate pats and hugs. His legs had been wasted since youth, but the rest of him had always been strong and manly, and he had been a robust lover, a man with a wild mane of black hair, a high forehead, burning brown eyes, a muscled torso, powerful biceps—and the gentlest hands a woman could ever experience. But that was the past. Emil Wolff was a husk.

She ground some roasted M. J. Brandenstein coffee and started it brewing in an ancient speckled blue pot. This had been her dawn ritual for as long as she could remember. Then she would sip two cups and watch the light rise in the east, spending a quiet hour in her old wrapper before facing the pain of the day. They occupied a ground-floor flat, but the duplex had been notched into a slope and the lower flat afforded almost as fine a view of the bay, and its ship traffic, as the flat above. She might lose that view if they had to move, and she knew they did. She needed level ground, where she could wheel Emil to doctors, or out for air.

She felt besieged with worry this morning.

Her photography was not earning her a living, not even for one person, much less Emil. She wondered bleakly whether to leave him. They had the thinnest of relationships now, crabbiness and old familiarity replacing what once had been support and affection. Never love. She had never loved in her life. And he was not capable of it, self-centered monster that he was. They had used each other, mostly for comfort and companionship, and now he was using her in more desperate ways.

She sipped, loving the coffee, feeling it energize her body, enjoying its aroma. For a little while each morning, the smell of fresh coffee overpowered the other odors in the apartment, the sour odors of her developer and stop bath and fixer, and the violent and acrid odors of his mordants, usually hydrochloric acid but sometimes nitric, which ate furiously at his copper plates wherever he had scraped away his beeswax and resin and bitumen ground, ultimately incising the copper into a plate with which he could print exquisite images. He had a gift. The flat always reeked, and it was a wonder that their landlady, Madame Foucault, tolerated it. Worse, occasional spills, especially when Wolff splattered acid into the hardwood floor, had damaged the place. She wondered whether their landlady would bill them for the damage if they moved.

He worked in an alcove off the parlor; she had converted the pantry into a darkroom. Sometimes, when they were both processing their work, the fumes intermingled and bred new and vile odors that required fresh air.

This Wednesday she wanted to get away from Emil and take pictures. But she didn't know where to go. Before her knees became so inflamed, she could always find subjects. But now she could walk only a few blocks, toting her camera equipment, unless she got a costly hack. She liked to photograph people—not portraits, but people at work, or at play, or doing their humble tasks. Sometimes she had gone to the produce market at dawn, catching blurred images of the bargaining and toting and hauling there. But now that was too far—the other side of town. Maybe she would go to Union Square today, and photograph workmen, or the swells at the Bohemian Club, or matrons with their babies in perambulators. Yes, she would do that.

Maybe what she did wouldn't win acceptance in the famous New York 291 gallery of the Photo-Secession, or with all those young men like Alfred Steiglitz or Edward Steichen, but she had her own skills, and no one was better than she at using blurred images to catch motion. She had never won an award or even gained entry to their New York salons, but it didn't matter much. She kept up with all of that by reading their club journal, *Camera Notes,* and sometimes she learned things from them.

But that was all art. Her need was for money. Sometimes they interlocked, sometimes not. Union Square. Matrons with babies. That resolved, she began to plan her day. First she would load cut film into glass plate holders. She preferred cut film to roll film, which always curled, or to glass plates, which were heavy and fragile. She could tote a bag full of cut film in its holders. Her camera of choice was a small Kodet, which yielded five-by-seven-inch negatives. Even with a tripod, it was relatively light. It was a mahogany box with polished brass fittings. Its hinged front panel, or bed, dropped down and formed the floor for the black bellows. It had a Bausch & Lomb lens and shutter, which gave her the focus and light sensitivity she needed. It was no heavier than a large lunch box, and did not require a heavy tripod, either. Some of the larger cameras, the eight-by-tens, or eleven-by-fourteens, could weigh ninety pounds with their tripods, and were utterly beyond her.

It was time to take a cup of coffee to Emil. He would drink it, but lounge in bed until midmorning. She always brewed enough for them both, but she never awakened him until she had enjoyed her precious private dawn. She rose, and the floor dropped from under her. She careened downward, astonished, and landed hard. Fiery pain shot through her arthritic knees. The floor catapulted her upward now, and then sideways, rolling her about, stabbing her with new pain every time her knees buckled. She didn't know what was happening; only that the world had gone berserk. She heard a roar now, something sinister, from the devil's throat. Glass shattered. Windows popped and broke, letting in air and an incredible racket, like the chattering of ten thousand monkeys.

Acrid smells reached her nostrils, and she knew her bottles of developer and fixer had shattered, and Emil's flasks of acid had fallen and broken, releasing the vicious mordants. The parlor heaved under her, and she heard the beams of the building creak and protest, and the nails howl. In the space of thirty or forty seconds her flat had been devastated. Kitchen things rolled and crashed, furniture slid into walls, lamps stabbed at her, an old sofa rumbled toward her and jammed into her knees. She heard her enlarger tip over and fall to the floor.

She screamed. Then she heard Emil, howling in the bedroom, something hysterical in his voice. She had to help him. Get him dressed. Get him into his wheelchair. Get him out of there before the building folded. This wasn't just an earthquake; this was maybe the end of the world.

The earth paused. She stood, her knees howling, and stepped tentatively toward the bedroom. And then she was thrown into it, another convulsion of the foundations of the world, throwing her toward the bed with indescribable force. She felt like a feather in a hurricane. She tumbled into the disheveled bed, but Emil wasn't there. She lay upon the quaking mattress, feeling it depart from her in sickening lurches, and then it stopped. The bed quieted; the beast within it had fled. She heard a strange wail from the shattered windows. The whole world wailed. She heard things dropping, thunderous roars when walls and cornices and roofs caved in. But her building stood. Indeed, its flexible wooden frame hadn't been damaged much, as far as she could see. She stood, tentatively, half expecting to be slammed into the floor again. But nothing happened.

She found Emil pushed against a wall, and she helped him up and into his wheelchair, which had careened into a corner. He looked like a frightened puppy, slumping helplessly there, sucking air in spurts, as if his body could never get enough oxygen.

"Quake," she said. "Bad."

"God," he said.

"Your acid's all over. I'll have to dilute it before it eats up the house."

"Acid? The flask broke? Ach! Why didn't you tell me? Pour soda. Make a mixture of baking soda and water," he said.

"I will in a minute. Are you all right?"

"Am I ever all right?" His glare was intended to wither her. She ignored it.

"You can dress yourself," she said, mercilessly.

"Where's my coffee?"

"All over the floor, along with acid, developer, fixer, and a lot of other things."

"I want coffee now, not ten minutes."

"Emil—"

"Now!"

She limped to the kitchen, pain lancing her, and hunted around for the old pot, and the tin of coffee beans, and the grinder. The beans were scattered all over, soaking up developer from the pantry. But she salvaged a few and looked for the grinder, finding it under the stove. She rescued the pot and started in. But the tap yielded no water. The stove would not ignite. And the smell of chemicals was dizzying her.

She retreated to the bedroom to dress.

"You won't get any coffee this morning," she said.

CHAPTER 3

There were really two of Carl Lubbich. The one abed now, just before dawn on Wednesday, April 18, 1906, was city engineer of San Francisco, a quiet industrious young man appointed by Mayor Eugene Schmitz to oversee the city's water and sewer systems, and occasionally deal with other matters, such as bridges and tunnels and public buildings. This version of Lubbich lived sedately in the Mission District, in a redbrick home of modest proportions, solid masonry in a wooden city and a sign of the engineer's substantial, if a bit stolid, tastes. There, in that four-bedroom brickpile, he and his wife of twelve years, Rosemary, raised two children, Carl Jr. and Gretchen, and busied themselves with friends and neighbors, schooling and health—Carl Jr., was asthmatic, and Gretchen had been born with a cleft palate, much to the sorrow of her parents.

The other Carl Lubbich was unknown to his wife and children. They only knew that their husband and father seemed to be very busy and rarely present at the massive oak dining table of the Lubbich residence. City business, of course. The city engineer was always on call, dealing with problems. And that is what he told them.

The other Carl Lubbich received a brown envelope once a week from the man who really ran San Francisco, the mysterious and almost reclusive Abe Ruef. Each envelope contained a hundred dollars in small bills, and was payment for services rendered. The city's engineering office was charged with certain matters of great interest to Ruef, such as reviewing and approving or modifying construction contracts; overseeing the city's water utility, the Spring Valley Water Company; preparing and reviewing reports that dealt with water and sewage utilities, bridges, streets and trestles, and municipal buildings. It was within the discretion of the city engineer's office to alter contracts, set performance and construction standards, impose building schedules, determine whether engineering met basic criteria for public safety and health, and so forth. Carl Lubbich had learned to be flexible, and was steadily rewarded for it.

He had become a man about town, a habitue of the best restaurants, a man to be found in unusual company most any evening except Sunday, which he always devoted to his family.

Lubbich had done yeoman service in the fall of 1905, when a report from the National Board of Fire Underwriters had put a lot of heat on City Hall as well as the Spring Valley Water Company. After noting that the city's water supply was woefully inadequate, it concluded that "San Francisco has violated all underwriting traditions and precedents by not burning up. That it has not already done so is largely due to the vigilance of the Fire Department, which cannot be relied upon indefinitely to stave off disaster."

Of course Lubbich had been called in, and immediately examined the entire utility system and pronounced it sound. There were really three interlocking systems, he explained. One massive line delivered water from the San Andreas Reservoir, down the peninsula, to the city. Another was the Crystal Springs line, which supplied the business district and drew its water from the springs off to the south as well as sources in Alameda County across the bay. And the third system supplied water from the Pilarcitos Reservoir west of Hillsborough to the west side, and included Lake Merced, a vast reservoir with abundant water, easily piped into the city. All were doing what they were built to do. That quieted the matter. The water company profits and dividends were not diminished by new expenses; the expert opinion of the city engineer had concluded that the fire underwriters were profiteering alarmists wanting extraordinary protection to lower their risk.

But it hadn't stopped there, actually. Dennis Sullivan, chief of the city's fire department, had sided with the underwriters and had sought to rebuild numerous cisterns under the business district to hold emergency water, and also to build an emergency saltwater backup system that would pump seawater into the mains if necessary to fight a conflagration. That, of course, would cost money, and while Mayor Eugene Schmitz and the gray eminence behind him, Abe Ruef, were not averse to spending money—to the benefit of themselves and those around them—they simply had other, more urgent priorities. So once again, City Engineer Lubbich came to the rescue, diplomatically commending Sullivan's diligence while vaguely indicating that the backup water system could be phased in over a twenty-year construction program.

Thus did Carl Lubbich earn the bills in his brown envelopes. But of this Rosemary had no knowledge, nor did anyone else save for Abe Ruef and the mayor. And it was this boodle that Lubbich spent flamboyantly in his other life, which he walled away from his home in the Mission District.

Such as last night, which he had spent at the Grand Opera House enjoying *Carmen*, the second offering of the New York Metropolitan Opera in its visit to the city. None other than the great tenor Enrico Caruso had played Don Jose, and had sung the role gloriously, backed by such formidable singers as the basso Antonio Scotti, and Olive Fremstad, the Wagnerian soprano. But Caruso had stolen the opera, and wave after wave of ecstatic applause had washed over him at the conclusion. Carl Lubbich didn't quite understand all that. He preferred a good Viennese waltz, or maybe a polka. But then, what would an engineer know about the arts? He preferred serious things, such as politics, science in all its branches, social justice, and the seething social reform movements of central Europe.

The lady at Lubbich's side that evening was not his wife. She was blond and statuesque, with smoldering blue eyes and ill-concealed passions, and a lugubrious wit that was comic because it always misfired. She called herself Helene, and had no visible means of support. But her invisible means were considerable. Helene had been Carl's companion for several months. He had inherited her from a certain Spring Valley Water Company magnate, whose gaze was forever roaming. Like Carl, she didn't really enjoy opera, all those screeching Italians. But it was the thing to do that Tuesday evening in San Francisco.

Carl had gotten home at one, after chewing on some Sen-Sen to deaden the scent of Veuve Cliquot sufficiently to fool Rosemary, who could be easily fooled because her world didn't extend far beyond the brick home, *Century* magazine, and Golden Gate Park. He had left his tuxedo, boiled shirt, bow tie, and patent leather shoes in Helene's closet. After the opera he and Helene had joined City Hall friends at one of the "French restaurants" of notorious repute and excellent cuisine. This time he had stayed on the first floor, where the food was served. On other occasions he and Helene had taken their meal on the second floor, in one of the private chambers containing a small dining table and oversized sofa. One could, in such an establishment, bring one's own company to those rooms, or employ one of the demimondaines whose residence was on the third and top floor. These French restaurants owed their existence to the broad-mindedness of Eugene Schmitz's City Hall—and boodle. Eugene Schmitz, tall, personable, a musician and strong trade unionist, had been a popular mayor with a penchant for letting things alone. Very alone.

Such as the bubonic plague that lurked under the streets of San Francisco, carried by the tens of thousands of rats that made a home of the ramshackle sewage system. The plague had arrived in Chinatown in 1900, along with the Chinese slave girls steadily being smuggled into the city as if the Thirteenth Amendment didn't exist. Bubonic plague was bad for business, so the Schmitz administration denied that it existed, even though it had killed a hundred and thirteen people between March 1900 and February 1904. City Hall's policemen had even arrested a federal health officer, and the administration had attempted to oust some of the members of the Board of Health who were insisting that plague lived in the sewers. The mayor had refused to publish vital statistics. A state bacteriologist had found the plague germs, and as a result lost his job.

The ever-pliant Lubbich publicly insisted that the sewage system was just fine, and was not the breeding ground of thousands of rats, although he cautiously said he couldn't vouch for the system underlying Chinatown, which was the work of its inscrutable denizens. Lubbich doubted that plague persisted, even if there had been a few deaths among the Chinese. There were too many hysterical reformers around. Besides, he argued, ridding the city of its few rats would require awesome sums of tax money devoted to poisoning rats, rebuilding sewers, pouring concrete into pestilential cisterns and tunnels and holes, all of which simply couldn't be justified to cope with what was, after all, only a rumor about some medieval disease. He loved to make a great joke of all the clamor especially in male company, over cigars and a glass of port. What white man, after all, had died of it?

And so the city engineer slumbered into the dawn of an April day, until the earth lifted and dropped his solid brick house, lifted it, bounced it, shook it, swayed it, and let it plummet a few feet—and then the rear wall crumbled and the roof fell in. He was, actually, slow to wake up, having only recently retired, and at first he was immersed in a dream in which he rocked in a cradle. But the roar, the grinding and groaning, Rosemary's whimpers, the ominous reports—like cannons being fired—emanating from his brick house, awakened him into a world of dark terror. Window glass snapped and flew, shattering everywhere. An unearthly roar pounded his ears, a roar he not only heard but felt, as it vibrated through his skull.

His bed shot into a wall, then lurched downslope into the center of the room, then bounced up and down. Lubbich couldn't even get out of it, much less escape anywhere. He and Rosemary lay abed, plastered there by giant forces. Then, with a terrible roar, the west wall of the house collapsed, the floor tilted crazily, and the roof slowly sagged and groaned downward into the void. All this Lubbich experienced without so much as getting out of bed. He rose, shakily, walked a few tentative steps, cut his foot on glass, and then found himself hammered to the floor by another convulsion that left him dizzy and nauseous. Rosemary wailed.

He waited, but this time the quake had apparently spent itself, and he was able to stand up and survey the ruin of his home. The shattered windows let in predawn light. He rattled the bedroom door. It would not yield. He could not open it because the sagging roof had come to rest on the partition, and had warped it. He and Rosemary were trapped. They could not reach the children. He heard nothing but the rattle of falling brick, and the groaning of beams and rafters and joists. He had to find the children. He pushed hard, but the stubborn door was jammed into place. Panic ate at him. What about the gas? What about the electricity?

He returned to the bed bewildered, his mind refusing to function. He eyed Rosemary, but couldn't think of anything to say. He sat on the tilted bed, swaying, clutching his arms about him, listening to a dying city. Someone on the street was shouting. He should call for help, but words failed him. He couldn't fathom what was happening. An earthquake, yes. An earthquake. It didn't make sense.

Rosemary stirred, wept now, stared at Carl as if awaiting his leadership. He was the man of the family.

"Oh, my God. Aren't you going to get dressed?" she asked.

"We had an earthquake."

"Yes. We must get dressed."

That brought him out of his daze. He stood, slipped gingerly downslope to the dresser and closet, dodged window glass, and slowly assembled his wardrobe. Everything seemed so hard. He struggled with everything. He had to lean against a wall to put on his drawers, sit on the floor to tie his shoes.

"What about you?" he said. She clung to the tilted bed, still in her nightgown.

"They're dead," she said.

"What?"

"The children. I know."

"Don't be hysterical."

"We would hear," she insisted.

He struggled up to the bedroom door and shoved. It didn't yield. So he skidded down to the window, toothed with broken glass, and stared down. The street was rubble.

"I'll get us out," he said, but he didn't know how. He saw a few people moving on the street, some half dressed. "For God's sake, get us out," he yelled. "We're trapped."

A man stared up, face white in the murky light.

Lubbich heard noises, talk, the sound of an ax on his door. Rosemary cowered under the covers, modestly drawing the blanket to her chin. The center of the four-panel door caved in. Two men stood there.

"Better hurry. This building's tumbling," one said.

Lubbich stared through the shattered door, onto what had been the upstairs hall, which was now a void. There were no bedrooms across the way, only space. Far below, under a tumble of brick and rafters and shingles, were Carl Jr. and Gretchen.

"We've got to dig them out!" he cried.

"Who?" asked a man.

"My children!"

The man stared into the rubble and shook his head.

CHAPTER 4

The upheaval came to Ginger Severance while she was reading the Book of Isaiah by the glow of a coal oil lamp while the dawn gathered light outside her window. She read a chapter of each Testament every morning, and had completed the entire Bible several times over, committing much of it to memory.

Her evenings rarely ended before ten or eleven, and yet she was up, in her robe, reading by five every morning, for it was all part of her mission and her work. Although her boardinghouse stood in a seedy neighborhood not far from the Barbary Coast, Chinatown, and the waterfront, she had made her room pleasant and kept it thoroughly clean. She needed no more, and the locale placed her close to her vineyards, as she called the neighborhood.

The first convulsion lifted her chair upward, as if she were on one of those electric elevators, and then the floor fell away from under her.

The lamp careened on the table, chattered a moment and slid to the rough plank floor ragged over with old rugs, and shattered. The kerosene spread through a rug, ignited, and swiftly created a circle of flame. She tried to rise, but a series of twisting shocks spun her to the floor, rolled her close to the flame, and then against the small iron bed where she had slept. She pushed away from the bed and rolled up the rug, in the process snuffing the fire. But the smoke choked her and she fell back, coughing. Her sole window shattered as the sleazy building rocked and twisted around her. Air rushed in and she was able to breathe without searing her throat. She crawled through shattered glass to the rug, lifted it and pitched it outside, and then sank into her bed, coughing.

Was this the judgment of God? Only a few minutes earlier, she had read of it in Isaiah.

> The city of confusion is broken down; every house is shut up,
>   that no man may come in.
> There is a crying for wine in the streets; all joy is darkened, the
>   mirth of the land is gone.
> In the city is left desolation, and the gate is smitten with
>   destruction.

Her iron cot lurched under her, a mad beast chattering on the floor to the tune of the groaning building. Then it stopped.

She waited for it to start again. She heard a strange cacophony outside, a rumble from the earth, the crash of falling brick and cornices, the rattle of outraged beams and joists and joints snapping and cracking. And the screams of mortals.

But it didn't start again. At least for the moment. But she was certain more would follow: fire, pestilence, disease, homelessness, and maybe many more shocks. Had this been foretold? Was this the end of the world? Was this the time of the great judgment, or the Second Coming of Christ? She didn't know. Could God be the author of things so terrible?

She needed to dress and then go out onto the streets. Maybe people needed help or comforting. That was a part of her calling, and now she felt the need to bring the Good News to people. But she sat, paralyzed, unable to function, the violence of the earthquake shattering will and purpose.

She had lost nothing significant. She had no possessions to speak of; everything had gone into her mission, save for a few small comforts she allowed herself. The Lord didn't want her to starve, or live in discomfort, or wear rags. She didn't need much of anything to pursue her work.

Her room wasn't particularly chaotic, even after the wild shaking it had received, and she found all she needed. She wished to wash, but the cold water tap—the room, with its lavatory alcove, lacked hot water—yielded only a trickle. It was enough to wet her face. Who needed more? She dressed swiftly, listening, listening to the injured world, listening to the death of buildings, the cries of the tormented—those people were sorely afraid—and a strange rumble that sounded like a barrage of cannons. What was a city without water? A plain of ashes and rubble. God gave Living Water.

She wondered what was happening on the Barbary Coast; whether its denizens were too drunk or stupefied with opiates, or too worn from their diseases to help themselves. Surely that place would disgorge its cargo of the wretched onto the hard, cold streets of dawn. She had often proselytized just outside of the district, sometimes by day, but often in the evening, by the light of a lantern she would take with her.

It had always been frightening, but nothing would separate her from doing the will of God. Men wanted to drag her to brothels, or drive her away with rocks, or cut her to ribbons or break her bones. Sometimes they stood and mocked or shouted obscenities. She knew them all, every vile thing that might issue from the human mouth. Once a mob of merchant seamen had torn her white dress from her very body. But she had always passed through unscathed, and always would. And even if God chose to let her suffer in their hands, she would see it as an opportunity to bring her message of love and redemption to her captors or tormenters.

Though she rarely penetrated to the heart of the Barbary Coast, she knew it well. In its dark saloons, drifters and whores drank rotgut for a nickel a pint. The Living Flea, the Red Rooster, and other establishments trafficked in flesh. In between the bawdy houses were crimping joints, where men were drugged and shanghaied, fandango places, pawn shops, dance halls where men paid to do the Chicken Glide and Pony Boy and Bunny Hug, erotic theaters such as Canterbury Hall and Opera Comique, and all those dark corners, Dead Man's Alley, Murder Point, Bull Run Alley, where the traffic consisted of bodies live and dead, money, spirits, and drugs. That was her parish, and these her congregation.

It had been a strange life, this four years of a personal ministry, but not an unrewarding one. She had boldly chosen to minister to the most desperate and vicious of all, those most in need of God. And she had rescued a dozen girls from wickedness, and lifted drunks out of their debauched life, and quieted the vicious, and stopped a murder, and prevented several shanghais. But most of all she had given them union with her Lord and Christ. Now the Barbary Coast knew her, and now they usually respected her, even those who hated her presence on the edge of the most vicious district in the nation. She regarded each triumph as a white rose she could lay before the Throne of God. She had brought Him several fragrant roses.

She usually dressed in white, and this Wednesday was no exception. She knew she was a great beauty, with a lovely oval face framed by rich auburn hair, her figure tall and willowy, her limbs slender and graceful. Her handsomeness was one of the Lord's many gifts, and she employed it to draw her street-corner audiences. If the preaching of a beautiful twenty-eight-year-old woman was what drew men—and sometimes women—to her corner, then for God's sake she would make full use of her assets.

This strange and stricken morning she wore a white dress with a high neck and fitted bodice and bouffant sleeves, and plain white shoes to match. She decided not to take her large leather-bound King James with her so she might devote both hands to nursing and comforting, but she did slip a tiny Testament into a pocket in her full skirt. She added a dozen or so Bible Society tracts. They might comfort people in their hour of need. She had cartons of them, seven different texts. She selected the ones on Deliverance, thin pamphlets of tight text jammed onto pulpy newsprint.

Then she was ready. She glanced about the room, and then placed herself in the hands of God. The door had sprung, and opened readily into a dank hall that always smelled of cabbage. The building had survived shock, bending with each blow, but probably would succumb to fire. She sensed that much of the great wicked city would burn this day.

She didn't want to go out there. She wanted only to crawl back into her bed, and forget the earthquake. She paused at the door, debating, yearning to stay in her small, safe warren. But duty called. She was one of God's soldiers, and she must do what was required of her. She rebuked herself and her self-indulgence, and stepped out.

Even in the few minutes between the shocks and her appearance on the street, the night had fled. Her shabby workmen's neighborhood didn't look much different from what it had always been, crowded, dirty, paintless, odoriferous, and decaying. But glass carpeted the brick street. Everywhere, half-dressed or almost undressed people wandered, their faces blank, their minds unfocused, their ability to fend for themselves or care for others utterly gone. That seemed strange to Ginger. She had not experienced fear or terror; the knowledge that she was safe with God had sufficed. But she saw at once that these people were deranged, and their every act betrayed their shock. One man kept trying to tie a shoe that didn't exist on his foot. Another was laughing. A woman in a nightgown had curled into a ball and was softly weeping, oblivious of the passing world.

No one was helping her so Ginger decided she would. "Let's get you to your rooms and dressed. You'll feel better," she said.

The woman didn't move, except to clutch herself tighter.

"It's over," Ginger said. "Now is the time to trust in God. He will deliver you from all evil. You must have hope . . ."

The woman glanced sharply at Ginger, her face a mask.

"Do you speak English?"

"Trust in God! Why is my little girl dead? Her dresser fell on her. And you tell me to trust in God!"

Ginger felt sorrow flood through her. "That is a terrible thing, but not the work of God," she said gently. "I'm sorry. Maybe she's not dead. Let's see. What's her name?"

"You ever seen a bashed-in skull?"

Ginger absorbed that somberly. "Where's your husband?"

"I have none."

"I have a beautiful, joyous gift to give you. I have a comforting message about Deliverance here—"

"I don't want your help. Leave me be."

"At least let me help you dress."

"I don't want to go back in there."

"But you need to dress."

"Just go away."

"But I'm here to help—"

"I'm doing my weeping, can't you see?"

Horrified, Ginger retreated. Reluctantly she abandoned the woman to her grief, and turned to the rest. Some of them were talking and laughing, gripped by some manic frenzy. But most stared silently, dazed, uncertain.

She approached a man wearing only his underdrawers. "You need help. It's going to be all right," she said. "I have good news, the best news . . ."

He stood in the street, mumbling.

"It's all over now. You need to cover your body."

He didn't respond.

"Show me where you live," she said. "We'll go there. You can get dressed and I'll bundle up some food. You'll need it—and a blanket. And water, if you have any. And I have a joyous message for you, which you can read anytime. The Lord is your hope and salvation in a time of trouble."

"Doomsday," the man said. "It'll come again. It'll shake us like a terrier shakes a rat."

"This is not Doomsday," she said, a little uncertainly. "You're alive. We'll go to your rooms and find what you need."

"I'm all right," he said. "Help someone else. I don't need help."

She offered him the Deliverance tract, but he would not take it.

Reluctantly she turned away. There was so much trouble, and people were so paralyzed. She passed a caved-in frame building—the first wreckage she had spotted in this neighborhood—and was horrified to hear the sounds of sobbing from within the rubble.

She stumbled over planks and plaster, window frames and shingles and debris. "Where, where?" she cried.

"Help me, for God's sake," came the voice from down in the midst of that ruin.

"I've got to get help. Help is coming. Just hang on!"

She raced to the nearest group of men. "There's a woman in there. We've got to help her!"

They stared. "Help me," she cried.

Silently they followed her to the ruin and studied the pile of rubble, heavy joists sticking upward, caved-in floors collapsed into massive layers. It had been a three-floor rooming house, ruptured by the quake and crushed by its own weight.

"She's under there," Ginger cried, pointing to where she had heard the faint sobbing.

"Lady, we got no tools," one man said.

"But she needs help."

She raced into the wreckage, dislodging something that sent a shower of lath and plaster over her.

"Where are you?" she cried.

There was no answer.

"Answer me. Where are you? Please, just make a noise."

But there was no noise.

"She's gone," said a man. "All we coulda done is shoot her, if we had a gun."

Shaken, Ginger stood helplessly, witnessing the murderous force of the quake. Doubt flooded through her: was this God's punishment upon a wicked city? Was he destroying San Francisco as he had destroyed Sodom and Gomorrah?

CHAPTER 5

. . . .

The Spreckels Building stood. Harrison White peered up at its eighteen floors, feverish with delight. A few cracked windows, some damaged masonry, some cornices lost, but it stood! The rising sun blazed its eastern facade, while plunging the rest into deep shadow. He studied it closely from several angles, and then entered its dark lobby, eerie with silence, and hiked up a few floors since the elevators were not working. He tried the fourth floor, entering a dark foyer. The swaying had stressed some plaster, leaving debris on the polished floors. It was all right; everything was all right. It was a triumph of his firm's architectural genius over the worst nature could throw at it. He poked about the darkened building, looking for signs of serious trouble, but found none. He was elated.

He retreated swiftly to the grim rubble-filled streets, eager to examine the next and the next. People wandered about, dazed, fearful, but he ignored them. It was merely an earthquake; why were they behaving as if some disaster had visited them? The Call Building stood. The Examiner Building. The Chronicle Building, twelve stories, almost undamaged.

He turned at last to his own unfinished Monadnock Building on Market, and examined it inside and out. The brick cladding, bright now in the early sun, had been damaged but not beyond repair. No matter. It could be redone. The interior was intact, save for some glass. The building stood, relatively undamaged, its steel frame strong enough for any shock. He stared admiringly at his work. This was his! He had won! He was not yet thirty, but this would be his ticket to fame! He walked around the structure once again, admiring it from every angle before he moved on. Mark Wolper and Peter Demaris would be proud of him. They would give him a raise, better assignments, and tout him to clients, the fair-haired boy.

The whole city still seemed to groan. Stressed beams and timbers protested; rubble continued to drop to the earth with startling crashes. Fearsome humps and hollows pocked the streets. Street-car rails had been twisted and corkscrewed. Power lines lay about, no longer arcing. The ferocious kinetic forces had demolished masonry buildings, which lay in rubble, a haze of dust lying over them. Ruined brick and stone walls stood precariously, unsupported by anything. Others lay in rubble, heaped mortar and rock and brick. Sheared walls revealed offices, apartments, hallways, furniture hanging crazily, all naked to the eye. Rubble filtered downward, occasionally in alarming bursts. He felt the shock and desolation of the wounded city, knowing it would be years before it could rebuild itself.

But his buildings had survived. He felt an odd upwelling of power and exhilaration, a sense that he and his colleagues had bested nature; that with proper engineering, a city could rise anywhere and be a wonder of the world. Now the city could be rebuilt the way it should, with planning by architects trained to do the job, with strength, and especially with beauty. The whole of San Francisco had been laid out carelessly, a helter-skelter jumble of buildings without aesthetic purpose or design. Opportunity! He would make San Francisco the most daring and beautiful city in the world.

Only in the last few years had the technology been available to build practical high-rise buildings. The perfection of the elevator, for one, each cage marvelously counterbalanced and operated by electric motors. Internal combustion engines, for another, which were needed on location to hoist the heavy steel I-beams into place. And the new technology of cladding the steel members in tile or brick had been crucial because steel begins to lose its strength at four hundred degrees centigrade. In the event of a fire, the masonry cladding kept the steel frame sufficiently cool to maintain its integrity. There had been other major problems to work out: the weight of a skyscraper required new types of foundations, usually sunk down to bedrock, and the sheer exposure to wind required diagonal trussing riveted to the frame, and other measures. But all these problems had been surmounted, and now cities could erupt upward, saving valuable real estate, and announcing their dominion over the surrounding lands.

The whole profession owed much to William Le Baron Jenney, who had developed these techniques in Chicago, building one breathtaking building after another from rolled steel beams riveted together. White had never met Jenney, but revered the man as the pioneer of the future city and the most fruitful and seminal thinker in his profession. White had ventured to Chicago just to see the work of Jenney and his followers: the Home Insurance Company Building, the Manhattan Building, the Old Colony Building, the Ludington Building, the Stock Exchange Building, the Fair Store, and others. He had visited a few of the Chicago architects, too, and come away a true believer in a whole new world his professors at MIT had scarcely begun to grasp. His professors at the Ecole de Beaux Arts in Paris had yet to understand any of it. The steel-frame skyscraper was an American invention, and perfectly expressive of a robust and daring young nation.

He knew he should return to Pacific Avenue and help Marcia with the debris, and calm the children, but he couldn't bear to do that. This was more important. This sort of thing came once in a lifetime. He was here, amid the ruins of a quake, his eyes gulping impressions, his mind making notes, his intuition leading him toward epiphany. He would walk away from these ruins, this mad day, equipped to conquer the world. And besides, Marcia needed no help. Her maid would come soon. What was there to do but clean up? Tack a little pasteboard over broken windows? He wished he had insured his home and what it held for its full value, but it was too late for that.

But none of these rationalizations assuaged the gloom he was feeling about leaving her to her own devices in a moment of crisis. His morning was turning sour. The streets were filling with people now, some half-dressed, others bizarrely clad, not entirely in control of their faculties. How odd. He was entirely in control of his. He found one stooped old man in a nightshirt, and decided to admonish the fellow.

"Why not go home and dress, man? You'll be wanting to see to your food and water."

"I have no home to go to," the man said. "My wife—she's gone."

"I'm sorry. Where do you live? We'll find some neighbors."

"I don't live anywhere."

Impatiently, White abandoned the old fellow. Horse-drawn red-enameled fire wagons rattled across Market Street, some of them manned by only one or two firemen. Chief Sullivan's finest. They were the best in the world, and they'd lick that blaze that even now was belching smoke in a great column south of Market Street, its eastern side dazzled by the rising sun. Well, that was a teeming tenement, and made to burn. The whole city had known that for years, and the ruin of a few blocks would be greeted with a shrug. But the flames wouldn't get beyond Market, which was broad and lined with solid, fire-resistant buildings.

Or would it? Another column of smoke was boiling up north and east of where he stood on Market Street. Uneasily, White eyed it, knowing it could spread through the whole business district unless it was stopped fast. They would have to get the water going, and then it would be all right. He had read the insurance underwriters' report and knew that the city's water works were inadequate to deal with a conflagration. Why wasn't anyone doing anything?

He hiked toward City Hall, and discovered one reason: it no longer existed. The new, seven-million-dollar structure had been shaken down to its ribs. Its masonry had formed a mountain of rubble under the naked girders. The sight shocked and enraged him. The construction of the huge, domed, ornate City Hall building had obviously been shoddy, no doubt because that impossible Schmitz regime, along with that miserable Ruef, had built it that way and skinned every nickel they could from it. Mayor Eugene Schmitz, musician, bon vivant, hapless window dressing for the worst four-flushers on the West Coast, didn't have the brains or courage to lead a stricken city out of its crisis. No wonder there weren't any police or firemen about!

He knew he should return to his home; there wasn't the slightest doubt about it. He was a husband and father. And yet he couldn't. He had to see it all. He could not return until he had examined every building in the district. He couldn't explain it. He was a perfectly sober, responsible person, and yet now a demon had possessed him along with pure curiosity. He would hike, he would examine until he couldn't walk another step.

And so he walked. The Grand Opera House stood, but severely damaged. The United States Mint looked untouched. He examined the damaged Grant, Parrott, and Flood Buildings. The Crocker Building. The Phelan Building. The Rialto. The Merchants Exchange Building was in ruins. The Union Trust Building. The Casserly Building. The Orpheum, Majestic, and Columbia theaters in ruins. The Terminal Hotel down, its guests huddled about the rubble. Wellman, Peck and Company, heavily damaged. The Ferry Building standing, comforting, offering escape. And the massive post office. Ah, yes, and the redoubtable Palace Hotel stood, its massive walls and fireproof construction ensuring its safety. An American flag flew from the staff on its roof, a proud symbol of triumph. The Palace wouldn't fall. Nor the mint. A well-built building wouldn't die, no matter what furies nature threw at it.

He continued through the district, wandering toward Union Square. Yes, the St. Francis stood, and by God, he could see people eating breakfast in its dining room. The square was filling with people, some of them carrying bizarre things, a parrot on a stand, a set of china plates, an ornate clock that told White it was already after eight. One man had built a fire out of heaven-knows-what and was boiling something in a pot.

Now at last White saw a few policemen, although they seemed as dazed and aimless as the rest of the mob. They were obviously without direction, doing little more than showing the blue. Now, too, he witnessed death and injury. A woman lay on the square sobbing and holding her arm, which was apparently broken. A man lay near her, his head swathed in bloody bandages. A corner of the square had been turned into a morgue. White stared at a row of inert forms, old people, children, bloodied, battered, half-dressed—and dead. White counted fourteen. There would be many more found this day. Nearby a harassed doctor was assisting the injured, but there was obviously little he could do except bandage wounds. A merchant's delivery wagon was hauling the worst cases to the Mechanics' Pavilion, near City Hall, where an emergency hospital was being set up.

In all of his morning's tour, White had scarcely thought about people, but now their plight caught his attention. He had been looking for injuries to buildings, not mortals. He was struck by the tragedy he was witnessing. The square teemed with people, who were making a refuge of it because it was a safe place, away from crumbling buildings. Almost as the thought occurred to him, a sharp upheaval nearly unbalanced him, and he knew the quakes were not yet over; the giant forces beneath his feet weren't spent. He pulled out his silver pocket watch. It read 8:14. Around him people moaned.

"It is the wrath of God," cried a man. "We are doomed."

"It's all over the country! New York's ablaze, and Baltimore's collapsed," a youth announced. "And a tidal wave has swept New Orleans into the sea. This is the Day of Judgment, mark my words."

White doubted that. But he was increasingly troubled by the smoke billowing up south of Market Street, boiling white in the sunlight, patched with black, eerie light flashing through it like sun inside thunderclouds. That area would burn to the ground. Much of it lay on land reclaimed from the bay, built on a city's refuse. He thought he could hear the roar of the conflagration, an ominous throbbing, pulsing thunder in the background. But he smelled nothing of the smoke, nor did any ash filter down, because a sea breeze took the smoke away.

Why didn't they get the water mains operating again? It slowly dawned on him that maybe they couldn't, and maybe San Francisco was doomed. The thought wrought anguish in him. Had his Monadnock Building survived, had all the other steel-framed buildings survived, only to be demolished by fire?

CHAPTER 6

o it happened again. He was gone. Marcia Devereaux White stared at the chaos in her house, knowing that she would never be more to Harrison than a domestic servant. Harrison lived for his career, not his family, and not his wife.

She was past bitterness, having wrestled with all that many times, and had come to a wait-and-see perspective. She had often thought about divorcing him, but divorces were hard on children, and it would be a scandal. And there probably weren't adequate grounds. The law said you couldn't just divorce a man who merely ignored you.

But maybe she would find a way. This time he really shocked her, speeding off in a time of trouble so he could examine buildings, or whatever he did. She instructed Harrison III and Daisy to dress, and then they would see about putting their house back together. She followed her own counsel, throwing on a warm woolen dress because there would be no heat and the house would be chill. She rattled around her bedroom, dodging window glass, digging through clothes that had been flipped off hangers. She couldn't locate the shoes she wanted, black pumps, but found some brown ones that would do.

A dozen times, while she bustled about, she swore she felt the earth lurch under her, some malignant monster under San Francisco still toying with its people. She had mostly gotten past the fear, but not quite. She had survived the worst, but what would come next? Everything solid that she had trusted in had vanished. Maybe the sun wouldn't come up tomorrow, or San Francisco would sink into the sea, or she would step outside and find everyone dead. This fear, this helplessness, were new to her. Especially the helplessness, the sense that there was utterly nothing she could do to stay this monster under her feet, or protect her children, or guard her house, or set her life into an orderly orbit ever again.

And then there was the Harrison problem. Her husband was a dodger. She should have a "Wanted" poster made. A ten-dollar reward for information leading to the capture and arrest. . . . No, that was too high. A one-cent reward. She laughed. She had always had the knack of turning her miseries into comedy, and that trait, inherited from her wacky family, had blessed her all her life.

She found her children awaiting her in the upstairs hall, wide-eyed and solemn, and she accompanied them down the curved stairs, guarded by a white balustrade, into the foyer below. And there, on the main floor, the chaos was frightful. Not a picture hung, not a stick of furniture rested in its proper place, and shards of glass carpeted everything.

"We will have to make do with odd food this morning," she said. "I'll find something to eat, and then we'll clean the kitchen. We'll do that first, so we can eat."

"I'm thirsty," Daisy said.

"We'll find you something," Marcia replied. She led them into the kitchen—they needed leading this morning, and clung to her skirts, afraid to take a step away from her.

If the parlor was chaos, the kitchen was madness. She could not wade across the floor amid the wreckage of crockery and glass, kitchen utensils, half-emptied tins of flour and rice and sugar, silverware, dish towels, and even curtains. A moist cold wind filtered through the gaping window.

"Does this mean we're bad?" asked Harry.

"Now there's a good question. I'd like to tell whoever did this that no one's perfect," she replied, something comic in her tone. "No, dear, this isn't anyone's fault."

The golden oak icebox stood, but angled against the wall. She wondered whether she could open the door, and what she would find within.

"Help me push it," she said.

She and the children patiently rocked it around a little, until she could work the door handle. Within the dim interior she could make out a jumble, including a bottle of milk that had survived.

"If we can find glasses, I'll give you some milk," she said. "Look around, but don't cut yourself."

Daisy and Harrison swiftly discovered three unbroken tumblers on a shelf, along with a tin measuring cup on the floor. Marcia shook the milk bottle for a moment to mix in the cream, pulled the pasteboard cap off of the bottle, and poured a glass for each child and herself. It was a small triumph, something nourishing after the monsters of the earth had destroyed their food. She wished for coffee, but there was no water, and no way to heat it, and the tin of coffee beans had burst on the floor, scattering the roasted beans through the muck. She put the milk bottle back, realizing that for a day or so they would have ice enough to keep food cool. And water, too. They could drink the meltwater that collected in the pan under the block of ice.

She discovered the bread box on the floor and rescued it. "I'll give you bread this morning," she said. "Maybe I can even butter it."

"Are we going to die?" her son asked.

She stared at the poor dear, aware of how deeply this catastrophe had pierced him. "No, I think we will be all right. But maybe we can move someplace that doesn't have earthquakes."

"Can we move now?" Daisy asked.

Marcia didn't answer a moment. She was, actually, thinking of a little apartment of her own, far from here and Harrison. "Not just now," she said. "Maybe some day."

She peered into the morning light—the whole eastern sky had whitened—and saw the city stretching eastward. Gray columns of smoke rose from several places, slowly rotating and drifting. Of course there would be fires, she thought. The firemen would be busy this morning. She looked sharply for nearby smoke, and found none. Pacific Avenue dozed in the golden dawn. The fires disturbed her, though; the torment of this city was not yet complete. She hoped they had water there to fight the fires. If they didn't . . . She banished the thought. This was a moment for quiet courage, not a moment to harbor apocalyptic visions.

"It's cold," said Daisy.

"Find a sweater, dear. And you, too, Harry. It'll be many days before we can get glass for the windows or start up the gas burners."

She watched the children pick their way through the debris, and sat down. She knew she should be doing something. Making emergency plans. Water, food, blankets, a place to go—and yet she couldn't. Something paralyzing had settled on her, robbing her of her ability to act. One moment she felt like weeping, the next like laughing, the next she relived the terror of those violent convulsions under her, the mystery of nature, the helpless feeling of being thrown out of her warm sanctuary, her very bed, and then jammed into a wall by that lurching bed. She lived it and relived it, over and over, unable to let go of it and begin the necessary tasks.

"What's the matter, Mama?" Daisy asked.

Marcia started. "Nothing, nothing. It's all right, dear."

But it wasn't. It might never be. How could anyone go on living here, waiting for the next quake? How could one plan a life, or want to equip a gracious home, while waiting for the next one?

"Why don't you go sit outside on the porch?" she asked.

"It's cold."

"Well, it's cold in here. And it's safer there. Nothing will fall down on you there."

"Will the sky fall down now?" Harry asked.

She was wondering that herself. What more could happen. "I don't think so," she said.

"I want to be with you," Daisy said.

Marcia understood. These two wouldn't budge from her side. She was the only normal thing in their lives just now.

"All right. We will clean up together."

They nodded.

But she sat, numbly, not wanting to begin. She couldn't imagine why she didn't just stand up and start in. Sweep up glass. Salvage what wasn't broken. Put things back on shelves. Organize. Why on earth couldn't she?

But she couldn't. Maybe it would all tumble down again.

The children settled beside her. She smoothed Harry's hair. How were they going to bathe? What would the next days bring? How could she explain to them that their secure world wasn't?

She was annoyed at herself because she didn't want to start in. She had more spine than that. She had been brought up to take care of things, to stand on her own two feet. The Devereaux family were not social register people—her father scorned that sort of snobbery—but they didn't lack funds. She herself had declined to be a debutante when she had been invited, back there in Cleveland. The family preferred, instead, to cultivate the gardens of their minds and hearts, each in his own way. Her father was a lecturer at Western Reserve University, but the household did not depend on his academic stipend. An old canal fortune undergirded the family. The entire family was gifted. Her mother was a pianist of note but better known for a barbed wit; her brothers were in medicine, rhetoric, history, various sciences, and her sister was a harpsichordist and flutist. Marcia had started as a classicist specializing in Greece, turned to painting—she met Harrison at the Ecole des Beaux Arts in Paris—and now was a little of everything including battle-ax. She laughed. Even in bad moments, her self-deprecating humor cropped up. Marcia Battle-ax White.

She felt homesick. The foundations of the earth didn't convulse along the banks of the Cuyahoga River. Maybe she would go back for a while. Maybe stay, divorced or not. Maybe this was the last straw. She wondered when she would see Harrison again, or whether he would help her if he did show up, and not just prattle on about ruins, and standing buildings, as if the children he had sired in the sweet darkness of the night didn't count. As if Marcia Devereaux White, his lawful wedded wife, didn't either.

She found courage, and decided she would try to tidy the house. She had to. Two little innocents depended on her. A third innocent did, too. She suddenly felt far more worldly and sophisticated than her straying husband.

She stood, aware of people in the streets, aware of excited conversations drifting through her gaping windows, neighbors beginning the ritual of recounting the terror, the dawn's war stories that would be embroidered with each retelling, adding a little until the story outpaced reality.

She didn't feel like talking. So much needed doing. She tried the faucets and found not the slightest trickle. Water was going to be precious, and one of the first things she might do would be to find some milk bottles—if any were left—and fill them with meltwater from the icebox. Not that even that would last long.

She wandered about, racking her brains to figure out what to do, and finally decided just to pick up. That was it. Just pick things up and put them back, comforting herself with the restoration of each item. Order meant everything. Put the demented world in order. She did that for a while, as the children watched solemnly. The pots and kettles, the frying pan, the dish towels, the cans of tomato paste and beans, the spatula and tongs and wire mesh strainer, the malevolent cutlery, each back into its slot.

She swore the earth trembled under her again, and peered out upon Pacific Avenue. But no one was shouting. She wearied of the cleanup after a bit. What good did it do? It'd all come tumbling down.

This time, she stepped outside into a fine chill April day, and stared at the city around her. Little had changed, except for the broken windows.

A stranger accosted her. She wasn't used to that. But this one came right up to her, an excited man with a walrus mustache, a pot belly, and a silk hat. He wore two different shoes: one brown, the other white.

"Prepare, madam," he said. "Prepare for the worst."

She nodded.

"The whole city is going to burn, burn, burn," he said. "Not a bit of water. The firemen have nothing but axes to halt the infernos. The lines from the reservoirs down the peninsula are cracked plumb into pieces. The pumps don't pump. The mains under the streets are sieves. They say giant fountains of water rise from the Crystal Springs line and drain toward the bay. Right over the fault, you know. Right smack over the fault. Terrible engineering. Not a drop in the city, except for a few cisterns. Fires everywhere, and all will go. Chinatown soon, everything south of Market, Telegraph Hill, Mission District—all going up. Nothing to stop them. By tomorrow, madam, this'll be ashes."

CHAPTER 7

Pain shot fire through Katharine Steinmetz's legs, but she ignored it as much as she could. She would take all the photographs she could. Never again would there be anything like this. The business district, with all its great buildings, was beyond her reach. Other photographers could shoot noble ruins and shock the world. She could roam only a few blocks, even with her light Kodet and tripod. But she, too, would find memorable things for her lens this day.

It was half past seven in the morning of a bright day. She had frantically tried to put the flat in some sort of order and take care of Emil. But how could she mop up all those chemicals and acids when there was no water? In the end, she had let the mop blot up as much as it could. There was nothing more she could do. The acids would eat at the floor and ruin it.

She had dressed Emil, while he grumbled the whole while, and found him some bread and leftover pie in the safe. He was thirsty, but she could give him nothing except beer. A case of brown glass bottles had survived. So had some wine. There would be a little water in the icebox, once the ice melted. Enough liquid for the moment.

"I'm going out," she said.

"No! I will die here. The fumes. Fire, robbers."

But she knew what she had to do.

"You'll be all right. Fresh air's coming through every window. I'll tuck a blanket around you. I'm going to load film and go out. This morning I will take the best photographs in my life," she said. "Maybe I can sell some."

He offered no argument to that. Money had become a torment and obsession with them. She could take memorable photos, once-in-a-lifetime photos. She had plenty of dry chemicals with which to develop the plates, assuming she could find water—which loomed as a question mark now. She had twenty holders, most of them empty, so she filled the rest with cut film. Working in total darkness, she loaded five-by-seven sheets into the holders and slid them shut, sealing the film from light. That took time; everything this morning took too much time.

"Back around noon," she said.

"And leave me to die from these fumes."

"Emil!"

She hiked east, down the hill, lugging her mahogany camera and a heavy bag full of plates. She saw smoke billowing to the south, below Market, and in the east, too. If there was no water, the firemen would not be able to put them out. But there would be water. Someone was fixing the mains.

The district she traversed consisted of small shops and multistory residences packed tightly together on the land-starved peninsula. Most of them were wood. They were all tinder, she thought.

When she reached Columbus Avenue, she knew at once she would do her work there. It had become a street of refugees, people carrying everything they could manage on their backs, or dragging trunks behind them. She saw lots of people, most of them looking shocked, self-absorbed, fearful. A few men laughed and boasted, but most were tight-lipped.

She wouldn't even need to wander. She could set up her Kodet and wait. The world in all its oddity would trundle by, and she would capture the faces of people in the midst of terror and despair. They looked like refugees from war, a stream of humanity fleeing cannon, mortars, bayonets. These people were all dressed. They had gotten themselves into street attire, some of it jaunty. Some men even wore spats. She saw no women in wrappers or nightgowns, or men in nightshirts, as she had earlier from her shattered windows. They were carrying the oddest things, and not much of what they toted had anything to do with survival. One carried a lamp with a base of Chinese porcelain. Another hauled an armload of books. A few led dogs. They didn't even know where they were going; only that they had to go somewhere safe.

She could ask for nothing better. She found a dispirited family, a boy and girl sitting on portmanteaus too heavy for them to carry; the mother grimly trying to persuade them to continue. She was carrying blankets. Her mustached, nervous husband lugged a sack full of food and a canary in a cage.

Ah, what a photo, the faces pinched with fear and exhaustion, the children fretting and sullen, the mother frantic. Swiftly, Katharine set up her tripod. They stared stolidly, not much caring. She dropped the bed, pulled out the bellows, and focused her lens, moving the tripod left a bit to catch the group in a way that opened them to her. Then she pressed the shutter. She knew she had something unforgettable.

For the next little while—she didn't register the passage of time—she photographed one refugee after another. A man whose face was wrapped in bloody bandage. A crippled man, hobbling along with a gnarled cane for support. A tiny trim woman carrying nothing at all, not even a handbag, her eyes as vacant as the eyes of a morphine addict. A child crying. A boy in knickers, excited and shouting, his face revealing unbearable excitement.

"Lookit the smoke!" he cried, dancing about, jabbing his fingers at ominous black clouds billowing to the south, the east, and now the north, too. She caught that gesture, knowing the blurred arm would convey the youth's wild excitement, while the black clouds loomed behind his sunlit pimpled face.

She marveled. These were plates that would record something much more than ruins; plates that might make life good for Emil and herself, open doors, sell widely.

Then a new phenomenon appeared. Marching briskly down Columbus Avenue were soldiers, four abreast, in their mustard-colored uniforms, boots thrashing pavement, puttees, ammunition pouches—and wicked-looking rifles with bayonets attached. They sent a chill through her. What were soldiers doing here? Taking over the city? Who sent them? Where were they from? The Presidio? Fort Mason? They marched squarely down the center of the street, scattering weary refugees, stopping for nothing, their leader an aging sergeant, his field uniform as plain and ugly as those of the rest of the blank-faced enlisted men.

"Water," cried an old woman to the soldiers. "Get us water. We have nothing to drink."

The column marched by, ignoring her.

"We need water!" she bellowed, edging close to the rank.

A corporal marching beside the column blew a whistle and then hustled her away. She stood quietly.

"I have water," said a civilian man. He proffered her what looked to be a bottle of wine. She took it to her lips only to have the corporal dash the bottle to the ground, where it shattered.

"What? What?" the man bawled. "What are you doing?"

"No liquor. We're confiscating all wine, spirits, and beer," the corporal said. "That's orders."

"That was water!"

"That was a wine bottle."

"Soldier, I don't know what your authority is—"

The corporal lowered his rifle until the bayonet leveled at the man. The civilian fled. The rest backed away in a hurry.

Katharine swung her camera around, focused, shot swiftly, caught the last of it. Then she shot the column, knowing a hundred boots would blur, but she would catch the thrust of force and death and naked bayonets in the middle of an American city. She shot again, this time when they bore down on her, unswerving. She yanked her tripod back only an instant before it would have been smashed to the ground by the vanguard. Fear choked her a moment. The sergeant looked like he would pounce on her camera and smash it, but he didn't, and the column passed, and suddenly the street wasn't the same anymore. After that, the refugees from quake and fire stuck close to the gutters, as if the center of the street had been ripped away from them.

She trembled. What would become of her? Maybe the soldiers would stop the looting, and that was all there was to it; Mayor Schmitz had summoned help. Yes, surely. The soldiers would protect persons and property. She thought it, but didn't believe it, and wondered why. Some sort of intuition told her it would not work out that way.

She had had enough. Her knees could bear no more abuse, and she feared she could not even walk to the flat, or climb that last terrible hill. She grew aware of noise. Something as low as a growl, as deep as thunder, filled the heavens and earth. She thought she was hearing fire. Not one now, but dozens. From where she stood she could see several distinct plumes. She felt odd drafts of air eddying by, sometimes cold air off the ocean as the infernos sucked air, heated it and shot it a thousand feet into the sky. She could scarcely see blue sky now; only billowing white, with black underbellies.

She had three plates left, but decided she had taken enough; in any case, she wanted to save the rest in the event of something that begged to be photographed. She pushed the bellows and lens back into the box and closed the bed, and then started back, worried about Emil, about the helpless people on the streets who seemed too numb to prepare themselves for apocalypse.

Yes, that was it. Apocalypse. She felt another chill, and suddenly became aware of her vulnerability, her smallness, her helplessness. How could a woman with arthritic knees escape a conflagration? And a man in a rickety wheelchair?

There was no point worrying about it. She lugged her equipment back, block after block, resting frequently, fiercely ignoring the howl of her knees, and finally reached her flat. She deposited her gear and collapsed into a chair near Emil.

For once he didn't scold her. His gaze seemed riveted to the ominous columns of smoke that filled every horizon. She sank into her chair while her heart settled and the hot torment of her knees lessened a little.

"Emil, we have to make plans. We have to go somewhere if the fire comes. They have no water."

"Where?" he asked.

"Maybe Golden Gate Park. The panhandle. Or the ferry. Maybe we can go to Oakland. But that's where all the fires are. Market Street. How would we get to the Ferry Building? Someone would have to push both of us. I can't walk another step."

"Who?"

"We will have to start, and hope someone will help."

"Ha! Help! It's dog-eat-dog now."

"People are good. Today I saw many good things. People helped each other. A stranger helped a woman wheel a baby buggy full of things. I saw people raiding a grocery, and the grocer just let them. He didn't fight, even when they didn't pay. A man gave water to a woman . . ."

She told him about the soldiers.

"They shouldn't be here," he said.

"They must have gotten permission. Maybe Schmitz asked them . . ."

"You go ahead and save yourself if fire comes. I know what I'll do. Just leave me be."

"Emil—"

"Leave me."

The harshness in his voice surprised her. "We will get help," she said. "Besides, the fires are a long way away. And I saw firemen today. A fire wagon went by. They are fighting the fires."

He wheeled suddenly toward the bedroom, maneuvering around glass and debris. The wheels picked up acid, and it soaked his hands as he tugged the wheels around.

"My God," he cried, but didn't slow down. She was too tired to follow, but when he returned, she saw he had his old revolver resting in his lap. And he sat there shaking his hands, wiping them on his trousers, spitting on them, cursing softly.

"You see, if I move—acid on the wheels, it eats up my hands," he said. "But now I'm ready."

CHAPTER 8

Carl Lubbich stood in the middle of Guerrero Street watching his house die piece by piece. The ruins had a will of their own, convulsing every few moments as additional segments of wall and floor gave way with a roar, dumping more brick and rubble onto the growing heap and shooting up clouds of dust. Two walls stood precariously, but they were decaying with each aftershock.

Rosemary stood beside him, sobbing and mumbling things he couldn't grasp. "My babies, Gretchen, Carl," she mumbled, and slid into a deep wail that was torn out of her soul and cast upon the unfeeling world. "They're dead, dead. What have I done? What sin deserved this? Why were we spared? Why them and not us?"

Lubbich couldn't answer such questions. He wept as well, standing helplessly while he watched neighbors in nightshirts and long johns tear at the rubble, helpless before the amassed weight of the brick and twisted roof.

Rosemary trembled, convulsed, and clutched madly at him, berserk with loss and death. Gloomy predawn light filtered through the neighborhood, turning the rubble grotesque and sinister. It had been better in the dark when they could see so little. The sight seared his soul. How many tons of brick had crushed their babies? How long had it taken for their children to die in unspeakable torment? Rosemary knew. The hand of Fate had tortured her children for long moments before murdering them. She clutched Lubbich, her face buried in his chest, her hands clenching and unclenching his shirt.

Helplessness engulfed him. An aftershock rattled the ruin, driving brick to earth, endangering the weary rescuers. They shouted, dodged, pulled back a while, and waited until they could safely resume. But Fate had decreed that their small fierce efforts would count for nothing. Both bodies were deep in the basement, covered with mountains of debris.

The light thickened, and Carl Lubbich noticed the debris elsewhere, the ruins of masonry walls, the collapsed roofs. But his ruined house mesmerized him. He felt the choked sobs of his wife as she wept her soul away against his chest.

The neighbors, the Bierstadts, gently took Rosemary into their un-damaged frame house, but Lubbich couldn't bear to be inside. The sur-rounding wooden houses had weathered the quake, but his brick one had died that morning, and now a silent crowd stood before it. The neighbors slowed their excavating, and finally surrendered in silence, although any sign of life, so much as a whimper, would have stirred that crowd to frenzied digging. Carl Jr. and Gretchen were dead.

People consoled him, but he barely listened, and didn't know who they were. He didn't know what to do or where to take Rosemary. The day quickened, and sunlight found its way into the neighborhood. The street was passable on foot but littered with debris. He wondered what the streets looked like elsewhere, or whether God had chosen his house, his small refuge, to reveal his wrath. Maybe this was the end of the world. People were telling him that Baltimore and Detroit lay in ru-ins, Chicago was burning, and a tidal wave hand engulfed New York City. Who could say?

A touring car chattered toward him, its goggled driver apparently looking for something, and then stopped before what had been the Lubbich home.

"Is he dead?" the driver asked. "Lubbich?"

"I am Lubbich."

"Get in. Mayor Schmitz wants you. The city's burning and you've got to fix the mains."

"Fix the mains? Me?"

"You're the city engineer, ain't ya?"

"But I've lost—my children are dead."

The driver paused. "I'm sorry. But you're the one knows the mains, and they're busted in a thousand places and there ain't water."

The crowd of half-dressed people stared.

Lubbich nodded and opened the half-door opposite the driver and settled into the leather seat.

"Tell Rosemary I'll be gone a while," he said to a neighbor. "I have no choice. She won't understand, but tell her."

The driver advanced the spark and tugged the accelerator lever down, and the auto lurched forward. The man dodged brick, eased over enormous cracks and ruptures in the macadamized pavement, drove over a lawn to avoid a fallen utility pole, all at breakneck speed.

Lubbich wondered what had gone wrong with the water system, and where he would find some repair crews and equipment. It was a task for the utility company, not the city engineer.

"Town's burning down," the driver said. "Schmitz, he ain't got a city hall, so he's getting his people together at the Hall of Justice. He's taken over the basement there. So we're heading for Portsmouth Square."

"You've been pressed into service?"

"Yeah, ain't many autos around, and they snatched me. I like it, helping big shots, if this old Bessy holds up."

"Will you take me and a crew to wherever the trouble is?"

"Well, I gotta see what they want."

Lubbich realized suddenly he hadn't had a bite to eat, or coffee. "Any chance of finding some breakfast?"

"Ha!"

Mission Street was blocked by a chasm across it, and the driver dodged this way and that, miraculously finding passage when there seemed none. At one point he and Lubbich climbed out to push a fallen timber aside. The damage appalled Lubbich, but even more appalling were the black clouds of smoke boiling up to the east, blackening the whole skyline to the south of Market, and rapidly filling the northern skyline as well. Without water . . . they were depending on him to rescue San Francisco.

He swallowed. His schemata of the water mains were in the ruined City Hall, along with feasibility studies, cost estimates, specifications, site investigation reports, designs and blueprints, construction schedules, contracts, and advice on bids, but much of the system resided in his skull—except for the gates. He didn't remember their locales. He hoped the mayor would have a crew ready for him, some trucks, fifty men, and replacement mains. He knew he wouldn't.

The touring car pierced into the devastated Market Street area, the sights so appalling to Lubbich that they rattled him. He saw his first body, a woman, sprawled on a curb, her head crushed in from a falling cornice. He wanted to vomit.

"St. Luke's Hospital fell in, and the City Emergency Hospital is lying under the ruins of City Hall," the driver said. "They got the Mechanics' Pavilion for a hospital and a morgue now."

"Go up to Union Square," he yelled. "I want to stop at the water company. They might have diagrams."

The driver looked irritated, but agreed. The Spring Valley Water Company maintained executive and engineering offices on the top floor of the five-story building that housed the City of Paris department store on Geary and Stockton, and ran its Service and Meter Department from the basement. This was their problem, not his.

He clambered out when the auto chugged to a halt before the darkened building, tried doors, pushed in, raced upward five flights of stairs, dodging plaster and glass, only to find the doors locked tight. Then he raced downstairs, his heart hammering, and found not a soul in the service department, its door locked. It angered him. The water supply was their responsibility! The company had a yard on Bryant

Street, and maybe its men were gathering there, where they could load spare mains, gates, and other supplies.

He hoped so. A city lay dying. He burst out, and climbed into the automobile. His driver adjusted his goggles and off they went, this time to Portsmouth Square, passing ruin upon ruin, dodging teetering cliffs of brick and stone as they went.

Lubbich saw some men digging furiously in the rubble, trying to free the trapped, while other people stared, in some sort of paralysis. A wave of despair and helplessness engulfed him. How was he supposed to repair a wrecked water system?

Miraculously, the driver delivered him to Portsmouth Square, where he swiftly found his way into the basement bunker that was serving as City Hall.

"There you are," said Schmitz. "You've got to get the water going or the whole city'll burn."

"It's the utility's problem."

Schmitz glared. "It is our problem. Get busy."

"With what?"

Schmitz turned to the police chief, Jeremiah Dinan. "Can you get some men? Press them into service?"

"We'll do what we must, fast as men come in. I'm rounding them up."

Lubbich intervened. "I mean, where, with what equipment, and replacement mains? It all belongs to the utility, not the city."

"Find their men. I'm putting you in charge."

"I'll do everything I can. I checked their offices on the way here. No one there."

"Go find out where they are and report as soon as possible. Begin immediate repairs, Carl. The future of San Francisco is in your hands."

"Where's Sullivan? What's he doing about the fires?"

"Dennis Sullivan's wounded. Hit in the head by falling brick. He won't make it, they tell me. John Dougherty's taken over. General Funston's sent in the army."

A worn, sixty-nine-year-old veteran was commanding the entire fire department in the hour of the city's death throes.

"Well, don't just stand there, Carl. Find that driver and find out where the trouble is," Schmitz said. "Get the crews together. Put the city's own men on it."

The crisp command surprised Lubbich. Schmitz was showing some spine that no one had ever imagined lay within the man whose real objective from the day he took office had been genteel graft. That was something that Lubbich knew about.

He climbed up to street level and was instantly engulfed in smoke, which seared his lungs and started him coughing. The driver—a bewhiskered old man—was waiting patiently beside his machine, polishing the headlamps.

"Are you up to a good-sized trip—gasoline, tires?"

"We'll make it if I don't blow a tire. I have some patches, but that takes time."

"All right. We're going to Bryant Street and then have a look at the whole system."

"That's a mighty trip, take hours. By the way, I'm Paisley, like in a cravat."

"I'm Lubbich, city engineer."

"I know who you are. Mister, you're carrying a cross on your back as heavy as a big city. But I'm here to help."

Paisley cranked, the touring car vibrated and came to life, and Lubbich found himself being driven through the bleeding city, once again dodging rubble, working around ruptured streets, bent rails poking the sky, and increasing mobs of people, blank-faced, oddly calm in the face of mounting calamity. Lubbich stared at them, the homeless, the babies, mothers, grandparents, sick and helpless, all without water. One man in a fine black broadcloth suit and silk cravat waved money at the driver and begged to be taken down the peninsula.

"City business!" Paisley bawled.

"Monkey business! No water! Schmitz's criminals!" the man roared, as Lubbich's driver veered past.

The encounter shook Carl Lubbich. *Criminals.*

They were depending on Carl Lubbich for water now, water to stay the conflagration that could turn San Francisco into a charred wasteland. This morning he had lost two children, and now, unless he performed a miracle, he would lose a city, a reputation, and a bright future.

His thoughts twisted to Helene, up there on Jackson, she of the twisted lips and lascivious blue eyes. He had spent too much time with her. The hearings, the court hearings after this—they would find out all about her and every way the Spring Valley Water Company had cut corners and delayed construction, with the connivance of the city engineer. The Spring Valley Water Company was the great teat around which a city of over four hundred thousand had clamped its thirsty lips.

Everywhere now, he saw people milling in the streets, most of them well-dressed, vacant-eyed, rudderless, sightseeing because what else was there to do? And no doubt a veritable fleshpot of rumors, such as all those end-of-the-world ones he had heard on the pavement of Guerrero Street at dawn. A mob, capable of lynching men responsible for the city water supply. He shivered.

The utility's yards lay far out of town, near the cemeteries, and as Paisley maneuvered and dodged his way south and west, Lubbich wondered what the point was, and what a city engineer could do. But the mayor had given him a task, and he would do it. At the Bryant Street yard, he did find Spring Valley men. A few had drifted in, including an assistant superintendent named Ed Wilsall.

"What's being done? The mayor sent me," Lubbich said.

Wilsall eyed him patiently. "Inspecting. Walking the lines. We have to find the trouble before we can repair it."

"How long'll that take?"

"I already have line walkers out, but we haven't started on the city mains. As soon as a crew comes . . ."

"I have an auto at my disposal. Perhaps we could inspect together, you for the company and I for the city. The mayor desperately needs a report—information for his firemen."

"Well, I already know some things, and they won't make him happy. The forty-four-inch line from Crystal Springs—west of San Mateo—was thrown off its trestle just south of South San Francisco and won't be in service for days. About five hundred feet of it is lying in mudflats. The thirty-seven-and-a-half-inch and the thirty-inch lines from the San Andreas Reservoir were also ruptured, near here, at the end of the Baden trestle near the Holy Cross Cemetery. They're so bad we may have to forget them for a week or two."

"The rest?"

He shrugged. "Pilarcitos Reservoir. Out there near Half Moon Bay. That's a thirty-inch gravity line, and it's so badly damaged we're going to have to abandon it. Maybe start over. I just heard from the line walker. There's a place called Knowles Gulch where it crossed a trestle, hundred fifty feet, and the line broke into two chunks, both thrown upstream, and the trestle was thrown downstream.

"Here's one good thing: both the Crystal Springs and the San Andreas dams were built within a hundred yards of the fault, and they survived even though the ground shifted six or eight feet. Good, solid, clay-filled dams designed by our chief engineer, Herman Schussler. We have water; the trick is to get it into town."

That was the trick.

"What are you doing about it?"

"Closing gates. We won't get pressure anywhere until we seal off the leaking lines. After that we open each section, under pressure, and see where the leaks are. I've sent men out to close gates everywhere. That's a big job. I've also requested livestock and feed so we can start moving pipe. Hard to get so many animals so fast. When we get some teams, we can begin hauling some pipe into place. Meanwhile, all we can do is close gates."

"What about the Alameda water?"

"Don't know yet. It feeds into the ruptured Crystal Springs line, which feeds downtown San Francisco, North Beach, Pacific Heights, Russian Hill, Clarendon Heights, and most of the area south of Market and some of the Mission District. I doubt that we'll get water there for days."

"The business district!"

The man shrugged.

Lubbich knew there would be hellish accusations. That line ran directly over the San Andreas Fault. And so did other lines. But maybe the Alameda County water would rescue them. That water, rising from the Sunol filter beds, was conveyed to the bay in a thirty-six-inch line, and then traversed the bottom of the bay in two sixteen-inch and two twenty-two-inch bell-and-socket-joint galvanized wrought-iron lines covered with asphaltum. They reached the peninsula at Ravenswood, and that water was then pumped into a thirty-six-inch line that connected to the Crystal Springs line at Burlingame.

"And Lake Merced?"

"Don't know yet. It'll depend on whether the Lake Merced pumps are working. Should know soon. That's our only good bet and I'm banking on it."

"Anything else?"

"No. We've no telephone so I don't know. I haven't the faintest idea how much water's in the reservoirs."

"Do you want to go look? I need to make a complete report to the mayor."

"Someone has to stay here and direct this. I guess that's me. But if you do go, I would like a report as soon as possible."

"I'll need a man who can tell me what I'm seeing. I can't just walk up to a reservoir and know whether it's full or empty."

"I've got men out, and can't spare another. Sorry."

"Have you got a schematic of the system I could use? Nothing's left of City Hall and our files."

"Spring Valley Engineering Office, maybe, if it's not burned up."

"It wasn't when I drove by earlier. But that was hours ago. But I couldn't get in."

"Look, I've got an emergency here—"

"I understand. I'll tell the mayor where you stand."

"Yeah. Maybe Lake Merced. Nothing else for days."

Lubbich settled into Paisley's touring machine and directed the oldster to head for the Hall of Justice—if that's where the mayor was still ensconced. He hoped he would not encounter a lynch mob asking the big question: why didn't the Schmitz administration build the salt-water backup system the underwriters and fire chief and others insisted was necessary?

Lubbich didn't know the real reasons, which were locked in the heads of the mayor and his gray eminence. But he knew that Ruef had expected him to smooth it over. Which he had done, without knowing he was putting his neck in a noose.

CHAPTER 9

G inger Severance toiled in her vineyards all morning but grew disheartened. She was offering deliverance and comfort, triumph over all the terrors of the world, and yet no one seemed the slightest bit interested in her message, or in her tracts. People weren't seeking the gifts of God, even in the midst of devastation. She had wandered willy-nilly through the rubble-strewn streets, hoping to comfort the terrified and grief-stricken, but no one would even listen.

The ruins of buildings didn't interest her. At times people had shouted her away from teetering walls, decaying cliffs of brick, fractures in the streets, and half-hidden pits. Acrid fumes eddied through the streets, and sometimes the sun vanished under the glowering umbrella of smoke that lay over the dying city. She had no eye for all this, seeing only the miserable people milling about like sheep without their shepherd, people who would find comfort and purpose and hope if only they would pause to read her tracts.

Nothing she said had any effect.

"This is the will of God," one man told her. "Doomsday."

"Don't libel God," she retorted. "Don't make God a butcher and murderer and thief. I am here to tell you just the opposite. He is your everlasting help in a time of need."

But the man had only shaken his head, wanting to believe this earthquake was the vengeance of an angry God, and drifted away.

If she handed out Bible Society tracts, people tossed them to the ground. "Crazy woman," one muttered. "We need water and food and shelter, and you hand out propaganda."

She thanked God for the wound, and retrieved the precious tracts.

She tried every tack she could thing of. "Don't be afraid. You are not alone, and the Lord is right at your side," she said to one bewildered woman, handing her the tract titled "Confidence."

"I want to get to the Oakland Ferry," the woman replied.

"I am speaking of your spirit and soul."

"Excuse me. My mortal body needs help," the woman retorted.

Ginger spotted looters running into a ruined haberdashery, and chastised them when they emerged with armloads of hats.

"Shame, shame, shame," she cried. "The Commandment says—"

One of them slammed into her, bowling her over. They all scattered. Ruefully she picked herself up from the grimy street, lamenting the dark smears on her snowy dress. She had just the tract for them, "Overcoming Temptation."

She saw two men squatting over something in a ruin on Bush Street, and headed toward them. They whirled as she approached, and steel glinted in the hand of one. The other held a sausage—no, not that, a severed finger that bore a gold ring.

"You—you are robbing corpses," she cried. "Surely you will face the judgment of God."

The one with the knife laughed and ignored her.

"Let us pray for the dead," she said resolutely.

They worked the ring loose, tossed the bloody finger at her, and walked away. She fought back the nausea building in her, and fled.

She discovered a mob at a grocery, swiftly manhandling every item in the place out the door. Two rough men clamped the chubby grocer between them.

"You're stealing," she cried.

"Lady, who's stealing what? What do you know, anyway? This crook tripled the price of everything, trying to make a killing. You know what he wanted for a potato? A goddamned quarter. We should string him up."

"You're still stealing!"

"He deserves it."

"There's a better way," she said. "Let me give you a pamphlet about temptation."

The ruddy man laughed.

She lost track of time and place, wandering the streets, dodging rubble, crawling over debris. She drifted along the edge of heathen Chinatown, seeing no one—the place seemed to sleep. She angled north again, toward her own neighborhood, and saw flames boiling into the sky several blocks distant, great, fierce billowing curtains of fire eating at the ruined wooden houses and shops.

Here she saw soldiers dressed in mustard uniforms, armed with rifles with wicked bayonets on them. They functioned in pairs or squads, patrolling the streets, driving people away from the flames. Maybe that was good, she thought. They would stop the evil. She wanted to give the soldiers a tract.

She heard a deep report, like cannon firing, and saw a distant building fly apart, sail upward, and settle with a roar. What was all that about? Were they blowing things up? What on earth did they do that for?

She reached her own Montague Place, and started for her room, but soldiers blocked the way.

"I need to get to my room," she said.

"Lady, you can't go there."

"But I just need to get something." What she really needed was to use the water closet. And to pick up something, anything, to eat and drink.

"You heard us. Get out of here. You take one more step and you're in trouble."

"The fire's not here yet. I'm going. I'll be back shortly." She started toward her half-ruined building, only to smack into the hard barrel of the rifle, which slapped across her waist, knocking her back. One of the soldiers laughed.

"What's a pretty thing like you robbing rooms, for, eh?" asked one. "Seems like you aren't content to get your hand in a man's pockets."

Angrily she turned away, and then remembered her mission. "God forgive you," she said. "I have a tract for you." She pulled out two, not caring which ones. Neither accepted one. "This will comfort you in your hour of grief."

They were grinning.

She fled, but her energies deserted her. She was in the middle of a crowd meandering helplessly about. She needed to closet herself. Thirst tormented her. She felt dizzy with hunger.

She saw a man carrying a crockery jug.

"May I have some?" she whispered.

He grinned and handed it to her. She brought it to her lips and swallowed—a fiery liquid, which she spat out, tears welling up.

"Oh!" she cried.

"Better get it while you can. Schmitz made it illegal. They're putting signs up, got the soldiers smashing up bottles in the liquor stores—what they don't steal first for themselves."

"Where can I get water?"

"Bay's full of it."

"Here," she said, handing him a tract.

He eyed it, eyed her, and chuckled.

Bitterly, Ginger retreated. She would find an empty building and use its privacy. She headed for one, only to have two well-meaning men stop her.

"Don't go in there, lady. It's not safe."

"I need to for a moment."

"No, little lady, you'd better not. The soldiers find you in there, they'd shoot first and ask questions later."

"I need to find a necessary room."

"Talk to some women, then."

She retreated up Varennes Street, slipped into a small fenced yard next to a frame house, and found a corner for herself, feeling mortified by the demands of her own body. When she arranged her skirts, she discovered a beetle-browed woman staring from a window above.

"I'm sorry," she mumbled, and started to escape. But she paused. "Do you have water?" she asked. "Food?"

The woman said something in a tongue Ginger didn't understand. "Water?" she asked, pantomiming a drink.

"Vino?" She smiled and shrugged.

Ginger summoned her Latin. "Aqua?"

"Aqua, I give."

Moments later the woman, an elderly matron with hair tightly braided, emerged from a door and handed Ginger a glass of water, which she drank as if it were nectar from heaven. She felt better at once. Her body stopped crying out to her.

"Oh, thank you," she said. "Thank you."

The woman said something, retreated, and a moment later returned with the butt of a loaf of bread. She handed it to Ginger, smiling, her gestures plain: eat it.

Ginger tore a piece loose and chewed it, drinking once again, while the woman watched intently. Ginger ate every last crumb, and felt her body relax into peacefulness. The woman continued to watch, asking questions that Ginger couldn't answer. The woman finally touched her bosom, where an elaborate black and gold crucifix lay, and Ginger caught words that made her believe the woman was blessing her.

The papist was nurturing her. She was grateful, but that rankled a little. She wished that her succor had come from a good strong Baptist or something. She pulled one of her tracts from her pocket and laid it upon the woman's palm. The old woman studied it and looked up, her eyes neutral, and nodded.

"Thank you. I must go now," Ginger said, retreating through the gate.

She hadn't gone a block before the weariness returned, stealing through limbs, settling into her shoulders, hurting her feet. Where was she going? What would happen this April day? She tried to summon faith and courage, but those things came hard to a young woman with nothing but the clothes she wore, and nowhere to go. She wanted to live a purely spiritual life, but her body kept interfering. Oh! If she could just escape it, and live as an angel.

When she reached Washington Square she found it crowded with refugees, most of whom had settled on the ground and were awaiting word, or instruction, or help. Lost sheep. No one tending the flock, she thought. Families were lounging on blankets. Some had picnic baskets of food. Single people, like herself, looked miserable and isolated, with no one to share the calamity. She would help if she could, but just then she wanted only to rest, to watch the smoke gray the heavens, smell the ash and fumes, and follow the seagulls as they swept over the park, ignoring the disaster below them.

She needed to let her family know she was safe. She needed to let her Bible Society know, too. She wondered how to do that; how to send a wire when she hadn't a penny, and couldn't even buy a stamp and some paper. But they would worry about her, there in the Ohio foothills of the Alleghenies where her parents and brothers still lived. She would rest, and then ask. Surely there would be some way to send a message.

Her head ached. All this was too much for her body, and now she was paying the price. She clamped her eyelids tightly shut to drive out light, and tried some spiritual exercises. Thank God for all things, St. Paul had written. Thank God for the earthquake. Thank God for the test of her faith. Thank God for the chance to be of service.

She tried all that, and they seemed to allay the other thing that was building within her, the terror that she couldn't quite push out of mind.

She watched a squad of soldiers gather on the east side of the square. And then some corporal made an announcement she couldn't hear, but people slowly began standing, lifting their burdens, folding blankets, and shuffling wearily away. The soldiers were clearing the square.

"What was the soldier saying?" she asked a burdened man.

"That we have to leave," he said.

"Where are we going?"

"Who knows?"

"Why must we leave? It's not burning."

"They said it will, soon enough."

"What if we don't?"

He stared a moment at her. "I saw them kill a man who resisted them. He wanted to get some food and water out of his house. They shot him and left him on the street."

"Maybe he was stealing."

"No," the man said. "He was rich. He would have found the soldiers ransacking his house."

CHAPTER 10

. . . .

Sergeant Major Jack Deal, United States Coast Artillery, knew how to turn something to his advantage. Like surplus puttees or blankets, or discarded rifles, or old ammunition, or mildewed haversacks, or a company clerk caught pilfering petty change, or a poker game in the latrine after hours. Or an earthquake and fire. How often did a sharp man get a chance like that? The Coast Artillery and the Twenty-second Regiment, United States Infantry, were going to make war on the thugs of San Francisco. And all the rest of the population, he thought, but didn't voice an opinion like that.

Old Freddy Funston had started the game right after the quake by running the troops into the burg. Up there on Nob Hill, where he sipped tea with the rich folks, old Funston saw the fires, knew there wasn't a lick of water, and decided to take over. That's how the story went, anyway. Deal had gotten it from Larken, the officer of the day at the Presidio, and got still more of it from the CO's aide-de-camp.

What happened, according to Deal's sources, was that Funston had commandeered a shavetail lieutenant over at the army stables in town, and sent him galloping out to the Presidio with orders to bring in the troops and take over the whole bloomin' city. The Presidio's commanding officer, Colonel Charles Morris of the Coast Artillery, popped his cork. He thought Funston was nuts, and only the president of the old U.S. of A. could order armed troops into an American city. The Constitution got in the way, or something like that. So he tossed the shavetail out on his ear, but Lieutenant Long went ahead on his own, had the bugler sound the call to arms, and soon was marching the whole command into the city by fours, every man armed for combat—against American citizens.

Pretty good stuff. It paid to have a pipeline. The Corps of Engineers were coming in from Fort Mason, too. That meant the entire command in the area was taking over. In addition to the Twenty-second Regiment, Infantry, the Presidio was manned by ten companies of Coast Artillery, three troops from the Fourteenth Cavalry, three batteries of Field Artillery, and B Company, Hospital Corps.

That oughta keep a lid on the slugs, he thought. But not a lid on Jack Deal and a few men who'd go along and make a little boodle this fine April day when the earth under them bounced and bobbed and cracked apart like a bucking whore.

The army was blessed with numerous fine, combat-tested sergeants, straight-arrow men worth their weight in diamonds. Deal had been one of them until it dawned on him that he was grossly underpaid for risking his life to defend the U.S. of A. Also, he realized that he knew twice as much as any well-paid peachfuzz officer out of West Point, and was more valuable. After that, he went his own way, carefully and discreetly, all the more powerful because he knew how to pull the levers. Some officers feared him, and that was useful to him.

He and his men marched smartly through town and reported to Mayor Schmitz at the Hall of Justice on Portsmouth Square, but that was a joke, too. What they did, really, was tell the mayor they were taking over, martial law in fact if not legal nicety. They dressed it all up with fancy words like *consulted,* but Deal wasn't fooled. This was Funston's royal flush, and Schmitz and his City Hall cronies had a busted hand.

Even so, His Honor was showing some feistiness there in the street in front of the massive Hall of Justice barely two hours after the quake. He'd heard that Eugene Schmitz was sort of a patsy, easy-times guy, a pushover for anyone with some cash in his britches. But this stern Mayor Schmitz surprised him. The man was taking command.

"All right, men, we're glad you're here. We have only a small fraction of our police at present, but others are reporting. We want you to shut down the saloons. Confiscate the stuff or destroy it if they won't close their doors. Break every bottle you see on the streets. Drunks would be a danger to the community in these circumstances. Stop anyone who's drinking," the mayor announced.

That sounded mighty fine to Sergeant Deal. He knew just where to stash a little hooch. There was an old abandoned ammunition bunker on the Presidio grounds, and only he had a key. The muckety-mucks didn't know it existed.

"I've issued a proclamation that looters are to be shot on sight. We're printing up some copies and they'll be posted around the city. The police under Captain Dinan will enforce it; you men will, too. As a last resort, use deadly force. But only as a last resort, and only when you're sure you're seeing looters and not people trying to retrieve their own possessions."

Shoot on sight. Rough stuff, all just fine with Jack Deal.

"And you're to prevent price gouging by grocers, riots, disorders. Close liquor stores and keep people away. You're to confiscate stolen groceries to prevent hoarding, and wagon them out to the Presidio. The army will distribute all food fairly to the thousands of victims we'll be helping. You're to provide such water as is available to thirsty people. You're to clear people out of the fire areas. Your mission is to protect people and property. There are now over twenty blazes out of control, and no means to stop them. We're looking for dynamite so your artillerymen and engineers can create a firebreak. We need to move the public out of all such areas."

That appealed to Jack Deal as much as the rest. He nudged Walt and Wayne beside him, and elbowed Nils and smiled at Joey. They'd all gotten the message.

"Help people leave the endangered areas. We need all the manpower we can get. Encourage people to take food and water with them. In many cases you'll be working with our police. We're going to set up relief at Golden Gate Park, the panhandle, and maybe the Presidio itself."

Schmitz had plenty more to say, but Deal was already doing some swift calculating. He didn't want to work with city cops. He wanted a squad if he could get one. But that would be easy. They'd leave it to him to detail the men. And he wanted to put a few reliables, old fellows from the Philippines campaign in each squad. They'd know what to do, and they'd owe Sergeant Major Jack Deal plenty when all the dust settled. He liked that. Debts and favors, that's how to shape up a bunch of rummies.

There was a lot more, but then the shavetails assigned Deal to cover the North Side, and Deal began allocating his men, saving his picked ones for his own squad. He had been in the artillery a long time, and he knew just what to do, and how to deal with civilian turkeys.

Briskly he snapped out commands, set territories, and watched his regiment fragment and march off to war on hooligans. The shavetails liked that. Leave it to an old top sergeant, that was what they'd learned in a hurry the day they began active duty. Then everything went right. Deal knew how to make everything go wrong for a shavetail until Junior learned who runs the army.

Deal thought that was all just fine. He led his men, all of them armed with .30-caliber Krag-Jorgensen six-shot bolt-action rifles slung over their shoulders, ready for use against the nefarious slugs pawing through the rubble trying to cut ring fingers off corpses. Miserable drunks raiding liquor stores. Panicky galoots tearing grocery stores to pieces.

That was fine, but what he needed was a fire. He didn't have far to go before he found one, a wall of flames billowing through a dozen frame houses close to the Barbary Coast. Even from a hundred yards, the heat lanced his face and hands. This conflagration, feeding on wooden structures packed cheek to jowl, was doing nicely, rolling his way in spite of a pack of helpless firemen who were trying to cut a firebreak with their axes. Fat chance!

He approached a sweating man with chevrons on his arm. "You want us to clear the neighborhood, right?" he yelled over the thunder of the fire.

"Yeah, get 'em clear of here. Door to door."

That pleased Deal. Door to door.

"All right, door to door. Clear civilians out," he said to his squad. "Get 'em packing, right now, no excuses. Out! Bust down any locked door, see what's in there.

"Clear out the next two blocks west and north, and then we'll regroup."

The places were mostly deserted. He didn't expect to find much of any interest. Not here in an area full of seedy rooming houses and sailors' rest homes. But this little old fire was heading for Nob, or maybe Russian Hill, and there things would get interesting.

He led the assault on a decaying three-story building, taking a pair of his buddies with him. He hammered on the first door with the butt of his .45-caliber automatic, an officer's sidearm he'd latched onto. No response, so he kicked in the flimsy door and found the place empty. Swiftly the three shook out the mattress, hunted the crannies, and found nothing.

"The hell with it," Deal said.

They found some coins and a few bills in the next room, and a bottle of rotgut in the third. They all had a good swig and then threw the half-full bottle through the window.

The whole joint yielded hardly ten bucks and a gold crucifix. They gave all the stuff to him, and he stuffed it in his ammo pouch. They weren't going to take anything big or heavy; no place for it, and anyway that was the way to get into trouble. They didn't need to. Jewels, coin, gold, silverware, currency, stuff like that was what they wanted. They could collect thousands of dollars of it and it would all fit into their ammo pouches.

In the next dump they busted open a door on some old merchant seaman, varicose veins lacing his face, sleeping off drink.

"What the hell is this?" he yelled, bolting up.

"Get out. Fire's coming," Deal bellowed.

"And who the hell are you?"

Deal pulled his semi-automatic and pointed the bore at the seaman's head. "We're a forty-five caliber bullet," he said.

The seaman blanched. "What is this anyway?"

"Goddammit, get out."

The man was dressed; he had stumbled into bed without so much as pulling off his shoes. They shoved him out the door.

"Sonofabitch's so drunk he didn't even know about the quake," Joey said.

"Screw this. There's not a dime in here," Deal said.

They cleaned out the block, evicting a squawking fat lady with lard hanging from her arms and rings lining her chubby little fingers. But

Deal took one look at her, decided the rings were gold-plated, and nodded the boys away. There were better goods, and he didn't want witnesses, nor did he want to leave bullet-ridden corpses around.

The fires were a long way off, three blocks, but that didn't deter Deal. The more time, the better. They barged into a mob whirling around an ice-cream parlor. They'd busted in the door and were helping themselves to ice cream, phosphate drinks, and whatnot.

Deal blew his whistle, which shrilled them to a halt.

"Stealin' are ya? Out!" he bellowed.

"It's liquid. We need water," someone retorted. "Our children—"

"Out!" He nodded to Joey and Walt. They lowered the Krags until the bayonets pointed straight into the crowd, which was mostly young people, some children. One little girl clung to her mother, weeping.

One by one, the bunch retreated out the door and into the smoky street. Joey dashed a bottle from one man's hand with a deft thrust of his bayonet.

"Stealin' that's what it is," Deal said. "Get outta here. Fire's coming. Get out to Golden Gate Park. Old Uncle Sam, he'll feed ya."

The glum people withered away while the infantry watched.

"Well, this is thirsty work. You men want some ice cream before it all melts?" he asked.

CHAPTER 11

ella Clapp was pregnant before and after the quake. She wished she weren't so. She had hoped that all that bouncing and violence and roar and fear would have wrought a miscarriage, a swift trip to the lavatory, a moment's pain, and release.

But it didn't happen. The quake rattled the Wedgwood china, made the silverware clang, banged pots, cracked plaster in her maid's quarters, trundled her iron bed around like a carnival ride, evoked mighty squeals from her—she hadn't experienced such turmoil since, well, since that night with that treacherous Jeremy—but not all the forces pent up beneath Nob Hill had altered her condition one iota. Not even when the armoire tipped over with an awful crash, startling her out of her wits, had anything very helpful resulted. She stared glumly at her belly, ruing her fine health and twenty-year-old bloom. Why couldn't she be pale, anemic, given to spells and fits?

No luck.

Jeremy was the perfidious young master she had been trying to interest in her womanly charms. She had felt herself destined for a better life than maid. Pretty? She made the word sound barren. She was beautiful, blond, rosy-cheeked, with eyes of Delft blue, bee-stung lips, and all the right curves where they counted. But she had always known that someone of Jeremy's station would want more than breathtaking beauty. So she stopped biting her nails, learned how to walk and talk at charm school, got herself a mail-order diploma certifying she had passed the twelfth grade, studied fashion with a keen eye, blotting up style whenever she served guests in the parlor or dining room, examining *Godey's* and *Harper's* and other magazines devoted to cultivation and refinement, and took instructions in manners, elocution, piano playing, dance, and spiritualism, about which she was enthused after reading an article by Arthur Conan Doyle.

In between, she read romances, and memorized love stories, until she had a great fund of knowledge of the ways of a man with a woman. Except, of course, for certain blanks she was eager to fill in when the time seemed appropriate. She believed in happy endings. Her object was wedlock, followed by yachts, parties, croquet, steamship travel, social prominence, and maybe one or two little darlings in the nursery, cared for, of course, by a nanny and wet nurse and maid.

She had been all too successful.

Not that Jeremy wouldn't marry her if she pressed the issue. But she had not raised it with him for fear that she would be out of a job, and his formidable parents would send her packing within minutes of her revelation. Her body had betrayed her. What she really intended was to drive Jeremy mad, accept his proposal, and let him deal with his parents. But instead, that rat, that bounder, that cad, had taken her to his suite in the back of the second floor, and offered to show her the ways of the world, and once his lips had locked on hers, she not only couldn't say no, she didn't want to. A few blissful weeks later she found out how it went, and calculated what she must do before time ran out. The novels didn't say much about that.

Maybe she should accuse him of seducing her and get some cash out of it. She was working on that when the quake rattled Nob Hill and she thought the stone mansion would slide right off and down to Union Square, with her in it.

This Wednesday morning, wandering through the household debris, she lacked direction. Her employer, the Honorable Edvard Sanchez-Groppi, Argentine consul, and his American-born wife, Annelise, were visiting some Brazilians who lived on the Monterey Peninsula, so Nella was without instruction in this catastrophic moment. Sr. Sanchez-Groppi had made a killing in Argentine and Chilean railroad debentures and had himself appointed Argentine consul so he could invite grand personages to his bountiful table and hold great entertainments and stay close to American capitalists.

Miss Clapp had been his faithful employee for almost two years, rising to the position of top female domestic, and second only to the butler.

She supposed she would have to clean up the debris. But not today. Maybe tomorrow. Maybe they would wire her instructions. She retreated, over a rainbow of broken stained glass from the windows, red shards of Ming vases, around an ebony grandfather clock that lay like an alligator across a threshold, and up to her private quarters at the rear of the Hyde Street manse. There she doffed her ermine-necked wrapper and examined herself minutely. Surely the earthquake had done some sort of irreparable damage to her rosy flesh. Surely she would find something—black spots, or a withered elbow, or cracks between her toes, indicating that she had undergone the most alarming and horrible experience any woman could endure. She examined her lush breasts, certain they would never give milk, but they looked just the same as they had before. With her looking glass she checked her back, wondering if there would be new humps or bumps, but it all seemed quite what it had been. She started to examine her loins, and then decided not to. Traitorous part of her anatomy that she had known little about. They had a will of their own. All the rest of her passed muster, too. How could anyone know she had just suffered an earthquake when there wasn't a blemish on her?

But ah, that was it. The blemish was within. She would never be the same. Her eyes would never shine so brightly as they had on Tuesday. Her lips would never form into a ready smile, her gaze never be so direct and honest, after being visited by the Beast from under the earth. Yes, the baby would be marked, too, forever afraid, its little unformed soul savaged by the thunderous and threatening roar, the violent thrusts, the sobbing of the mother. Not even a womb was safe from an earthquake. Yes, that was truly it. The poor dear infant had suffered, just as she, Nella Clapp, had forever lost joy and happiness and innocence this day of the quake.

She dressed fitfully, pawing underthings from tilting dressers, until at least she had made herself presentable. She didn't know what she would do. Conrad, the butler, had accompanied the Sanchez-Groppis, and she doubted that any of the daymaids or the cook would show up. She needed big men just to put the furniture upright and back in place. She wandered helplessly through the parlor, music room, smoking room, library, observatory, billiard room, sunroom, dining room, kitchen, pantry, and laundry, not knowing where to start, bewildered by such chaos. Yet she had to start somewhere so she picked the kitchen. Broken crockery lay everywhere, along with silver, pots and pans, tins of food, cans, sacks, and a few undamaged bottles. She decided she would scrounge a breakfast first, and plunge in.

While she was thus engaged in feeding herself with a stray loaf and an orange, Jeremy stalked in, a frown on his pale face, his dress disheveled. She had not been alone with him since their night together, simply because the Sanchez-Groppi menagerie was always well populated.

"Where is the coffee?" he asked.

"Jeremy! Sir. That was so terrible. I'm still frightened." She smiled at the dashing young man.

"Make some coffee pronto, por favor. Who is here?"

"Just me."

"Well, the breakfast please make. Cream of Wheat, eggs Benedict, and herring."

She didn't reply. If he had eyes, he would see.

"You are not in uniform," he said.

"It's in an armoire that overturned."

"Well, that is what fate brings. Now you must clean this up."

"I'll need help. Would you lift things?"

"Do not be impertinent."

"I need help. Just help me lift things, like the grandfather clock. What else do you have to do on a day like this?"

"Visit people. This is a day to remember. Where is breakfast?"

"On the floor."

"Coffee, senõrita."

She noted the edge in his voice, plucked up a speckled blue pot and attempted to fill it with water, but none flowed from the tap.

"No water," she said.

"There must be water." He took the pot from her and tried the tap himself. "Incompetent. It is the fault of the city. I will go out. Clean this up before I am back, si?"

She had him alone at last, and decided to make use of the moment. "Jeremy? I need to talk to you about something."

"I am busy."

"We made a baby."

He paused, his liquid brown eyes focusing on her. "It is not so."

"You are the father."

He turned petulant. "You tell me this when the house is in ruins?"

"It is the first time we've been alone since . . ."

"Since what?"

"Since we did it."

"I do not know what you are talking about."

She suspected it would come to this and knew better than to remind him of that impetuous, sweet and fragrant night. "You have an obligation," she said.

"First earthquakes, then this. I will not hear it."

"Jeremy, my dear, the child needs support. I will not be able to work because I will have to take care of it. It is your child."

He drew into himself, his face hard, his eyes darting, as if he were weighing a thousand things. She wondered what she had seen in him, apart from riches and a handsome Argentine face, and a haughty profile, and a dashing way about him in the presence of women. Something calculating filled his features, and she knew he was swiftly inventorying his options.

"I know nothing of this. The Sanchez-Groppi family cannot have an immoral servant on the premises," he said.

"You cannot make a baby go away. If you're a good man you will help me. Your parents would help me."

"You will not talk to them."

"I'll ask for help if I must. They owe me that much. Oh, Jeremy, don't be like this."

He drew himself up, imperiously. "They won't come back soon. Why should they come back to a ruin? It will be months. I will tell them to stay away until order is restored and the house is prepared for them. You will not see them, and you will not stay here."

"I am two and a half months along. It's going to be a boy like you."

"You are making this up to get money from us."

"We will find a doctor together, and see."

"Getting money. That was your purpose all along, but this earthquake changed everything and now you are desperate."

"I thought maybe you cared about me. You acted like it. Stupid, wasn't it?"

"Fantasies! ¡Basta! ¡basta! Pack and leave and don't steal the silver."

"Where will I go? You owe me half a month."

"This is extortion. You will leave at once or I will throw you out."

She saw how it was going. Well, she didn't want him anyway. So much for dreams. She nodded, returned to her maid's quarters while he dogged her every step to make sure she didn't steal so much as a serviette. Slowly she packed her things while he hovered over her like a warden. Some of her clothing was in the overturned armoire, but she couldn't budge it and he didn't offer to help.

"Your key," he said.

"It is in my uniform in the armoire."

"Show me what is in your pockets."

"I will not!"

"It is as I thought."

Angrily she pulled her pockets out and showed him. Minutes later she stepped into a smoky outdoors toting an unbearably heavy portmanteau, and picked her way along a rubble-strewn street amid a ruined city, not knowing where her next meal, or drink of water, or bed would come from. Her luggage was too burdensome, and she realized, that young April day, that she could not even keep the gowns she had saved so long to buy. She opened it, pulled out a shawl, and walked away.

C H A P T E R   1 2

arrison Barnes White—he preferred to use his middle name—sauntered to the Palace Hotel, the greatest hostelry in the West, intending to see how the famous place survived, and maybe hobnob with its distinguished guests as well.

Nothing would destroy the Palace. It was the safest hotel in the world. No expense had been spared to strengthen it against earthquake and fire. It's two-foot-thick brick walls were reinforced by double iron straps every four feet, all bolted together. It stood on huge pillars twelve feet deep. Its private reservoirs in the basement and on the roof supplied water to every floor and every room. Its seven roof reservoirs held 130,000 gallons and fed sprinklers that would extinguish roof blazes, drench cinders from neighboring fires. There were three hundred fifty outlets in the hotel, to which thousands of feet of fire hose were attached. Its rooms contained sensors that detected heat and notified the operations office. Three powerful pumps in the basement provided water pressure at a hundred pounds per square inch for the fire hoses.

White had seen all these precautions several times in the course of his architectural business, and marveled at them.

The great hotel not only housed the world's notables when they came to town, but provided unparalleled security and comfort. Even now, Enrico Caruso occupied a suite there, along with his entourage, and others of the New York Opera. Plainly, though, the hotel would be under siege from the fires sweeping the nearby flats south of Market, close to the hotel. He intended to stay and watch, because those crackling, towering fires racing through the lower districts would pounce on the hotel within an hour unless the city found water somewhere. Of course the hotel would survive. How could it burn when it possessed such formidable sprinklers?

He surveyed the exterior, finding minimal damage even though brick was not the preferred choice to resist quakes. But this was not ordinary masonry because it had been reinforced by so much iron, and it was as thick as a fortress. Disheveled people stared at it, stared at the flag flying proudly on its roof, a symbol of its defiance of all the forces of nature.

White meandered in, finding little amiss in the great central court of the hotel. Things seemed to hum along very nicely, save for a few guests who were hurriedly checking out. The skylight above the court provided ample light, making it seem almost normal. He looked about, hoping to spot the great tenor, but saw no one he recognized as a celebrity. The dining room was in operation, as if nothing much had happened. White stared—undamaged crystal glasses stood on linen-covered tables, china place settings were ready for guests, and waiters with white napkins over their arms were serving hot foods to customers or pouring steaming coffee from pewter pots. Imagine!

It occurred to White that he hadn't eaten and should do so. He could catch up on the gossip while he did. What fun! It was all because of the virtue of the architects, of course. They had designed a hotel that could serve food in the midst of crisis, put out its own fires, resist the worst that nature could throw at it.

He discovered no maître d'hôtel, and finally just sat down. In moments an elderly waiter in a black dinner jacket was pouring fragrant coffee in his monogrammed cup. Ah, paradise!

"We're a bit shy of some items, sir. No deliveries this morning, you know. And ice. The iceman didn't come. Now what can we do for you?"

White ordered oatmeal, toast and jams, eggs, orange juice, and bacon. "Now how are you going to cook it?" he asked.

"We have several ranges, sir. One's coal-fired, and it is serving nicely this morning."

"Will the hotel burn?"

"They say not, sir, but I confess, most of the guests are checking out."

"Caruso?"

"He's magnificent, sir. You know what he did? He sang this morning, and it gladdened the souls of everyone. Yes, just a phrase or so, but that voice, so true and sweet, why, I'll remember it for as long as I am in service."

The waiter vanished into the kitchen, and White surveyed the other guests. They didn't look calm, and the peacefulness of the dining room was illusory. Smoke eddied through the magnificent dining room now and then, and he could see it hanging in layers in the great central court. The registration area was a tumult of people, sweating porters, unhappy customers who had been forced to descend by stairwell because the elevators didn't function, and pacing men. He saw a dozen or so men walking furiously, like trapped animals, and wondered what was in their minds.

"No paper this morning, blast it," the man at the next table grumbled. "I'd like to separate fact from rumor. All I hear is Judgment Day, Doomsday. Go out in the streets and they're saying the world's coming to an end, New York's plunged into the sea, volcanoes are erupting everywhere, the sky has blackened, the sun is expiring, and it is too late to repent."

"The human mind conjures up terrors," White replied. "But it's only nature at work. That's what I deal with every day. I'm an architect, sir. I designed the office building up a block or so, and it's fine—if the fires don't reach it. It's on the other side of Market, so I think it's safe."

"Well, whoever built this brickpile did a job of it. Hardly a broken window. But the blasted ones in my room did crack. Bad luck, eh?"

"Are you checking out?"

"Only if I have to."

"Where'll you go?"

"Catch the ferry, of course. The world's not ending out in the bay. Just in town. The bay's quite level and full of water and the sun is shining upon it and it is not burning, and the ferries will deposit me at the Oakland Terminal, where I shall embark for Cleveland on the next express. Ferry Building's in fine shape and a few blocks away. So what's the worry, eh?"

A series of booms rattled the room.

"Dynamite, sounds like. They finally found some. More's the luck," the Cleveland man said. "The Palace will lose the rest of its windows, but there'll be a good firebreak between us and the inferno."

The waiter arrived, and deposited the oatmeal, eggs, bacon, toast and butter and jams, a glass of juice, and a small pitcher of cream for the oatmeal, as well as a sugar bowl. Then he refilled White's cup.

"They say, sir," the waiter said, "that we may have to close up shortly. Our apologies, of course, but they do expect the fire to arrive here within a half hour, and want our guests to be comfortable and out of danger. We regret the inconvenience."

White chuckled, and dug in. The eggs were perfectly scrambled, the oatmeal just the right moist consistency, the bacon dry and lightly done, and the famous Palace Hotel coffee was better than ever. He wished that Marcia could join him. But it would be a grand tale to tell her, how he had a handsome breakfast in the Palace Hotel this desperate morning. Oh, how she'd envy him!

He ate leisurely, not intending to be pushed about by a lackey, all the while watching the mounting chaos at the front desk, which he could see through the double doors. A new eddy of air drew acrid smoke into the building, this time alarming the guests. But the inner court rose as high as the hotel, and the smoke swiftly lifted toward the glass roof far above. He masticated his bacon and watched a man who looked like Caruso, or at least resembled the many photos White had seen of the tenor. This one wasn't a bit calm, and was howling at his manservant, pacing about like a caged lion, and gesturing in a fine Neapolitan style. Yes, it was the singer for sure. As volcanic as Vesuvius. Another delightful anecdote to tell Marcia!

More shocks rattled the building, and he knew the dynamiters were knocking down buildings right and left, making a barrier that would stay the inferno to the south. Of course they would preserve the hotel, a great landmark. What other city in America could boast of such a place, with its individually styled rooms all bearing the Palace monogram.

The waiter appeared. "I regret, sir, the inconvenience, but we're requesting that you finish up, now. Five minutes." He placed the tab, encased in its discreet leather folder, on the table. White was done anyway. He dabbed at his lips with his napkin—took a long, precautionary drink of icy water—and left some bills on the table. He thought the waiter had been a bit rude, but that was to be tolerated, given the excitement.

He drifted outside, and into a different world. Here smoke bit at him and stung his eyes. Heat rolled past him, tidal waves of it, though the fires were still a block away. Soldiers herded people to the west, away from the Ferry Building where they might escape, saying the heat and smoke made passage to the terminal impossible.

People were behaving oddly, some laughing, some panic-stricken, some paralyzed even when prodded by the bayonets of soldiers. He saw a wall of flame now, glowering, ruby, orange, yellow, black, rocketing upward, subsiding, dancing to and fro, rumbling and roaring and crackling and hammering all at once, the noise as fearsome as the heat and choking smoke. This was no ordinary fire. It towered as high as he could see, like the plume of an erupting volcano, sucking air into it below and discharging it thousands of feet up. Fear stole through him. This blaze was demonic and murderous, and far beyond the power of mere mortals to contain. Suddenly the Palace, with all its resources, didn't seem so formidable.

Now the sweating soldiers were herding him, along with the rest. To resist was to impale one's self on a bayonet, and White resented it. Who were these barbarians, pushing citizens about? He retreated, looking for a way to dodge north, but they were channeling everyone straight up Market. Fires raged on both sides of the broad avenue, their growth shocking to him. Just a few hours earlier they had been minor blazes; how they were conflagrations, and it was not yet ten in the morning.

A new round of explosions cracked behind him, the percussions so violent that they bowled some people over, and hammered him until he staggered. He felt he had been clubbed. A wave of heat followed, searing past him, scorching his lungs. The firefighters had demolished something large. He tried to see what it was amid the smoke and ash and air that made things dance and waver, and then he saw it, a giant heap of rubble, twisted steel, brick, and wood, under a towering column of dust. They had blown up his new Monadnock Building. His own building! And for what?

CHAPTER 13

Harrison White ducked north as soon as the army quit shoving, and headed toward Union Square. Then he cut over to Post, and back toward the fire area. He had to see the Monadnock Building—or what was left of it after those stupid barbarians had blown it up.

He was in a rage. What had they done that for? It was a steel-framed, brick-clad building that could have been repaired. It had survived the quake almost intact. It was anything but a tinderbox. Where had the dynamite come from, and who was using it? Probably gross incompetents. He already knew what they would tell him: they were trying to run a firebreak along Market, and also along some north-south line in that area. He snorted at that. Blowing up the downtown instead of running a line through cheaper structures, warehouses, small shops, old residences. What sort of idiots were running San Francisco? Schmitz and Ruef!

He hurried toward the conflagrations ahead. There were several, all eating whole blocks and yet not joined to one another. Heat waves shocked him. Sudden downdrafts layered choking smoke into the street. Ash settled downward, silver-dollar–sized flakes that dirtied his hair and face. He encountered two blue-clad city patrolmen, who accosted him.

"You can't go in there, fella," one said.

"That's my building. I'm the architect. I need to see—"

"What's that got to do with it?"

"I'm an architect. I am an engineer." Rage bubbled through him. He wanted to grab their nightsticks and hammer their thick skulls.

The two coppers, one skinny with muttonchops, the other pot-bellied, stared dubiously, not knowing what to make of it.

"Look," White said, trying to phrase his argument for idiot minds, "an architect understands structure, and how it should be dynamited. I need to see how my building was reduced. I can advise—"

One copper shrugged. "Don't touch nothing," he said. "Looters get shot on sight. Also, you get hurt, don't say we didn't try to get you out."

"Who's dynamiting?"

"Army. And some fire crews. They got some from the railroad."

"Has anyone been trained to use it?"

"Can't say," the potbellied one said.

"What are they trying to do?"

"Make a firebreak, north up Kearny."

"But Chinatown's burning. The Mission District's burning—"

"Say, architect, you just have solutions for everything, I see."

"Well, who's in charge?"

"Who knows? All we know is, City Hall tumbled down and the mayor's set up headquarters in the Hall of Justice, and all them big shots are coming in and out of there. He's got a lot of chiefs and no Indians."

"I'll volunteer. They could use a man with my background."

The skinny one coughed as a new blast of acrid smoke filtered through. "You better look fast before you're fried meat, fella. Then take my advice and beat it."

Relieved, White raced past them, cursing the stupidity of the whole human race. He penetrated another two blocks, amazed by the radiant heat that pummeled him even from distant fires. He finally angled onto Market, which was alive now with firemen. The Monadnock's steel frame stood gauntly, its upper members vanishing into smoke. The rest was rubble.

Beyond stood the Palace, dauntless, solid, defiant, the Stars and Stripes still waving languidly from its roof. The sprinklers, the 130,000 gallons of water up there, were saving the building. White made a mental note to study the whole setup after the holocaust. Raging flames almost surrounded the Palace, licking ominously at the majestic hotel. Only its Market Street side remained unthreatened, largely because the street was a broad boulevard.

A series of shattering booms rocked the area, and White watched a line of smaller mercantiles fly to pieces, rise, and collapse in a haze of white dust. He stared as firemen scurried to the next demolition area.

What on earth purpose did it serve? They needed to start a fireline well west, giving themselves enough time to do a job.

He edged toward the Palace again, passing a quake-damaged building that had housed a liquor store and tobacconist below, and offices above. Three corpses sprawled grotesquely on the pavement. The sight sickened White. Each had been shot, one of them in the back twice, the head once, and a thigh once, reddening the man's clothing. None had died from the quake or fire. He hastened forward, braving heat, feeling it suck his body moisture from him. There, at the corner, stood a nattily dressed man, a carnation in his pinstriped double-breasted suit, an umbrella in hand, and his homburg perched precisely on his well-trimmed brown hair. White could barely imagine such an apparition there at that time.

"It makes one want to sing the 'Star-Spangled Banner,' eh?" he said as White drew up. The onlooker was referring to the American flag still waving over the Palace. "Fort Sumpter all over again. 'By the dawn's early light the flag was still there.' " He smiled sadly. "But it won't last long. The reservoirs are about empty. And when that happens . . ."

"How do you know that, sir?"

"I managed it, for the late Mr. Sharon."

"I'm glad he's not here to see this. That was my building across the street—the Monadnock. Ah, I designed it."

"And Funston's soldiers blew it up. It took them two charges and they hardly dented it. But they didn't touch the Palace. Dynamite wouldn't level a structure like that. There, sir, was the best hotel in the world. You know who stayed there? President Grant. General Sherman. Queen Victoria's daughter. Oscar Wilde. Mrs. Patrick Campbell. Sarah Bernhardt, Lillie Langtry. Oh, my friend, I could go on and on . . . They loved this place because it answered their every desire of heart and soul. That, sir, is a hotel."

They stared, spellbound, as the flag waved, smoke boiled, ravenous fires flattened the surrounding buildings, which capsized in showers of sparks. And then, ominously, the upper windows of the Palace Hotel shown orange, and smoke eddied from the grand hotel itself.

The manager doffed his hat and held it over his heart, doing all he could to stem the tears collecting in his reddened eyes. One by one the windows lit up, dark eyes turning bright with a feverish inner light. The flag vanished now and then, veiled by smoke, only to emerge bravely, still flying. And now everyone paused, even the exhausted firemen, watching the slow death of the building that would never burn. Harrison White thought that it was worse than watching an execution, for in this death was the humbling of modern man, his technology, his genius, his prudence, his vast and costly preparations to stay just this sort of disaster. And not least, they were watching the demise of a seven-million-dollar investment.

Then the Stars and Stripes caught fire. It blackened, and malevolent orange flame ate it. The manager sang in a quiet baritone: "O, say can you see, by the dawn's early light, What so proudly we hailed, in the twilight's last gleaming . . ."

White stared, then joined the man. It was more than the national anthem. It had become mankind's anthem. They sang it and then the flag was gone, and the Palace, too.

White stayed until flames drove him back. The fire was eating San Francisco, block by block, and the sappers trying to create a firebreak were never ahead, and their charges were utterly useless. Weary, and desperate for water, he retreated from the mesmerizing devastation, and headed back to Pacific Avenue. His pocket watch shocked him. It read four o'clock in the afternoon. How could that be?

He passed through Union Square, which had turned into a temporary refuge where people were resting away from precarious walls and rubble. He begged water but no one had any, not even the enterprising families that had started cookfires and were somehow preparing a meal. All this was doomed. Nothing stood between the square and its great buildings, including the St. Francis Hotel, and the raging fires north, east, south, and southwest of it. Infants squalled. The injured had largely been evacuated to the Mechanics' Pavilion, only to be moved again because of the Hayes Valley fire. The dead lay in rows, avoided by all except those searching for lost loved ones. One woman sat beside a corpse, numb and silent. White wondered what the death toll was. Certainly many hundreds, and rising every moment. Where would these people sleep? How long would it be before the lack of sanitation brought them all down with dysentery, typhoid, or worse?

Wearily he climbed the precipitous slope of Powell Street, struggling with every step, wondering why he had tarried so long in the fire district. By the time he reached Pacific, he was so done in he could traverse only a few yards at a time. But twenty minutes later he reached his darkened home, staggered in, and collapsed in his chair. But it wasn't where it should be. The room hadn't been straightened, which irked him. It seemed dark and hostile and somehow gloomy.

Marcia and the children appeared at once from the kitchen.

"Water," he said.

Wordlessly, his wife retreated and returned with a tumbler of water that looked less than pure. He drank it anyway and gestured for another glass.

"What is it?" he asked.

"Meltwater from the icebox."

"Did you boil it?"

She laughed sardonically.

"The city health officials—Ward and Ragan—have posted notices all over town that all water's to be boiled. I would think you'd know that."

"Boil it with what?" she retorted.

Two glasses didn't quench his thirst, but this time he stumbled into the kitchen and dipped the glass into the drain pan. That bit of water was all that stood between his family and grave trouble. There remained some unmelted ice, though.

"I was here taking care of your children. They don't post notices on quiet streets. Where were you?" she asked flatly.

"What a day! With my own eyes I saw my building in ruins, blown up by the army. My building! I knew every rivet, every hall, every cubbyhole. Gone because the stupid army decided it was in the way. And the Palace burned. Can you imagine it? Two and a half acres, two feet of brick held together by three thousand tons of iron—and it burned, hour upon hour, until the flames caught the flag. That was a sight. The flag defied the flames until the last, Marcia, fought the flames until finally it simply vanished. And everyone watching—well, I saw some tears."

Marcia nodded and settled herself across from him. She turned to the children. "Please go clean your rooms before it is too dark."

"I don't want to go," said Daisy. "It'll come again."

"You must go. You, too, Harry."

Reluctantly the children withdrew, walking fearfully over fields of glass.

"You've prepared for our safety," Marcia said, a touch of acid in her voice. "Food and water, transportation—where did you decide we should go, Harrison? What will protect us from vandals this night?"

Annoyed, White dismissed her worries. "I expected you to do that. You're perfectly capable. I happened to be busy with business. Tomorrow I'm going to the Hall of Justice and volunteer my services. They'll need an engineer."

"We have no sanitary—we have no toilets. You can imagine what the lavatory's like. You'll need to dig—"

"I can't do that. Get a man off the street to do it."

"There's not much food—at least that's edible. I can't cook anything. Would you find some firewood? Maybe we can camp."

"They don't allow fires except in parks, designated places. You'd likely be arrested."

Marcia said nothing, and then sighed slightly. He wondered what was bothering her. Women always took these things too hard.

"Did you think about our future?" she asked.

"Yes, dear, every moment. I was gathering information that'll be helpful. I know a great deal. Schmitz is forming a committee of fifty prominent men and they're going to divide into groups, and each group will tackle a problem—feeding the people, strengthening the police, getting the water system working. Things like that. I'm planning to volunteer in the morning."

"And leave us."

"The children are in good hands."

"Yes, they are," she said. "All right. That's how it's going to be. Maybe we'll get out the watercolors and paint the flames, or feed the ducks before they're fried, or go to the library while there are books, or have a soda before the police shut the ice-cream parlors down, or bow to the dragons coming out of the cracks in the ground and hope they don't eat us."

He was glad she was so accommodating.

CHAPTER 14

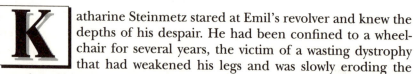

atharine Steinmetz stared at Emil's revolver and knew the depths of his despair. He had been confined to a wheelchair for several years, the victim of a wasting dystrophy that had weakened his legs and was slowly eroding the muscles of his arms and neck and torso as well. Even when she had first known Emil he walked with a cane, and seemed barely able to control his fragile body. The doctors had argued about it, but most of them said it was Lévy-Roussy syndrome. All agreed that it was neuromuscular and that it was degenerative. The miracle and paradox was that he had become a distinguished engraver, an art that required him to discipline his hands and arms.

Nowadays he etched, and each of his exquisite etchings wrought wonder in her. He did amazing portraits, shadow and highlight portrayed entirely in fine lines, sometimes thin and tender, sometimes bold, coarse, powerful. A Wolff portrait graced many a wall of the cognoscenti in San Francisco. He usually did them from photographs she brought to him, but occasionally she wheeled him out to a hack, which took him to a sitting where he sketched with pencil and studied his subject's face with a fierce and piercing gaze.

He glared at her, his thoughts dark in his eyes.

"Emil, we'll get help. Put that away."

"What help? There is none. Everyone's looking out for himself. You can't walk and I can't handle this two-wheeled hearse I'm trapped in, up or down hills."

"The police will be by sooner or later."

"Police! Ha! They will line their pockets and ignore us."

"The world isn't like that, Emil. Today I saw many people helping other people. A man offered some precious water to someone . . ."

"I am cursed with weakness. I can't help myself. Others walk and run. Not Emil Wolff. Not anymore. I'm better off dead."

She had not heard him talk like that before. Sometimes, when he was low, he had wondered what would become of him and how he could survive. Other times she had detected envy in him, especially when he talked about the young. He had a jaundiced eye for youth, and berated them all for being happy, for not knowing what was in store for them when their bodies began to betray them. He hated young people so much he would not use them for subjects or even deal with them. She knew why he hated them.

She stared through the broken windows. The breezes were their salvation, sweeping away the noxious fumes generated by the spilled engraving and photographic chemicals, which had fizzed into seething and evil puddles on the floor.

The day was peaceful. The sun beat down, offering scant heat but driving off the chill. The rumbling had almost stopped. The fires were all distant, abstract, harmless. Yes, the city was ablaze and smoke walled off the whole south half of town, but no harm would come to this peaceful slope of Russian Hill. She watched the plumes curl slowly and dissipate into the azure sky. It was the sort of day one always cherished in California.

"I admire your courage, Emil," she said. "You've had to fight to have a life, while life came easily to others. You have not let your disease conquer you, so don't let up now."

"A lot of good it did, fighting. When have I ever been happy? Answer that."

"I would like to think of the times you held me quietly in the night. You seemed happy."

He didn't respond to that at first. Then, "That's the past. Now I am stuck. The fire will kill me if the fumes and the police don't first. And what happens if you get me out of here? Where'll I go? What'll I do? Who needs a wheelchair man?"

"Emil—"

"Get my gloves." He waved his reddened hands at her.

Wordlessly she rose, found the gloves in a bureau drawer, and handed them to him.

"Look at these hands! They burn. My wheels run over acid, my hands turn the wheels. Pretty soon my flesh will fall away."

Painfully she lumbered into the kitchen. The box of baking soda was still where it always had been. She took it, and opened one of his bottles of beer. She returned to the parlor.

"Cup your hands and wash them," she said.

He did, and she poured some beer into them.

"Now I'm going to cover them with baking soda. That's the best I can do without water."

He smoothed the soda into his hands, wincing. "It won't do any good," he grumbled.

"I think most of the acid on the floor is used up anyway," she added. She hoped so. The fumes had given her a fierce headache.

He pulled the gloves on. "I'll never etch again," he said.

She wheeled him toward a window where they both could get fresh air. "Look," she said. "The fires are so far away. Like in another world. We must think about what to do." She reached into his lap and removed the revolver. He didn't stop her. She knew his moods. She could lift his spirits with some caring and attention. Whenever he felt helpless, trapped by his weakening body, he either sank into a terrible depression or got testy, berating her and everything else within range. This morning he had bottomed into melancholia.

He stared moodily, his attention caught by the ominous curling smoke to the east and south. "I should be dead," he said. "Then you wouldn't have to worry about me."

"It is my pleasure to worry about you. We have had good years together. I think so, anyway. You were here, in this home, to help me, talk, eat together. Does anyone ever think how good it is to eat with someone? There's no one I would rather share bread with than you, sweetheart."

She wasn't sure she was doing much good. He seemed to gaze into space, lost in some private world. She knew that rescuing them would be up to her. He could not cope with something as calamitous as an earthquake, fire, loss of water and power, uncertain food supplies, and the prospect of homeless wandering.

"Emil, you sit right there. I'm going to take a photo of you. I've been meaning to for a long time. I have three plates left. You're going to have to pose for me. If the world is going to see the engraver and artist Emil Wolff on the day of the earthquake, it'll be up to you to show what you're made of."

He smiled suddenly; a good sign. Hastily she gathered her equipment, set up her Kodet on its tripod, wheeled Emil close to the window where the light was good and she wouldn't have to expose the plate too long, and then fussed over him, smoothing his hair, adjusting his disheveled shirt and sweater.

"Don't make me pretty. Make it true. Make it me," he said, vigor in his voice. "I'm an artist, so don't make me look like William Sharon or Mark Hopkins."

"That's not anything to worry about," she said dryly. The movement was tormenting her.

She focused the Bausch & Lomb lens, studied the image of her lover in the ground glass, and decided she was ready. She would take it using the natural window light, which would highlight the crags and planes in his aged face. It would also catch the sharp gleam in his eye, that penetrating hawkish look as he stared directly into the lens. Good! She tripped the shutter, which whirred and clicked softly.

"That was good," she said. "You will like it."

She slid the cut film holder out, and slipped in another, and waited while he settled himself. His entire mood had changed because of the photographs, and he seemed to shed fear, despair, and age all at the same time. By the time she used up her three plates, he was almost cheerful.

"Now they'll see what Emil Wolff looked like on the worst day of his life," he said. "Maybe I'll die, but a photo is immortality. Don't you lose those plates."

"That's the last thing I'd do. Those plates, and the ones I took on Columbus Avenue this morning, go with us wherever we go, in my canvas satchel."

Emil smiled. She had lifted him out of his despair—for the moment. She ran an arthritic hand softly through his wiry hair, and sat down heavily.

She ached to draw a hot bath and soak her inflamed knees, which hurt so much she could think of little else. She lacked even the means to apply hot towels to them. It was plain, as she sat in the ruined room amid a foreboding silence, that help would not knock on their door. She had to go out. She stood, fighting back the sharp pain in her legs.

"I am going to get help. I think there must be a policeman somewhere. Maybe I can hire someone with a wagon."

"They'll charge more than you're worth," he said.

It might be true, but she had trained herself to look on the good side of things, and esteem all people unless they proved unworthy of that esteem.

She hobbled to the door, grabbing a shawl against the April chill. "I will be back soon," she said. "You have beer, and I'll make a meal later. Something, anyway."

She hobbled down the steep slope, one step at a time, trying to ignore the pain that could not be ignored. It took a long time, each moment metered by pain, to reach the intersection. She intended to stay right there and let the world come to her.

She stopped at the corner, next to a police call station, and surveyed the passing crowd, looking for some young man who was mobile, strong, and able.

"Sir," she said to one, "could you help a lame woman?"

He paused, shook his head, and continued on.

She tried a different tack with a middle-aged couple that was dragging suitcases on ropes behind them.

"Could you tell me where to get help?" she asked.

The plump man smiled apologetically. "On your own, I guess," he said. "They're saying Golden Gate Park or the Presidio. Army's setting up a camp. Don't know what we'll eat or where the water's coming from."

"Aren't they repairing the water?"

"I haven't heard a word. People working on it, I suppose."

"What's Mr. Schmitz doing?"

"Mayor's got proclamations posted—they'll shoot vandals and looters on sight, confiscate liquor. Also, no cooking fires until chimneys have been inspected, turn off the gas, boil your water, and that's about it. Oh, yes. Dig sanitary trenches. They don't explain how to boil your drinking water when you can't have a cookfire. He's got all the bigwigs running around. He got in the army and they're all over, getting people out of the path of the fires, and drinking that confiscated liquor. I hear they've shot a few looters. There's been some grocery riots, too, which they've busted up. Scheming grocers charging ten times what everything's worth. But those bayonets cure a grocer of greed in a hurry. The army's dynamiting a firebreak, one building after another, blowing up everything including themselves. But I hear it's useless. The whole city's doomed unless it rains."

"That's why I'm here," she said. "I'm lame and my husband's in a wheelchair up the hill. Would you send some patrolmen to help us? We lack water. We need to be moved in a hack or a wagon."

"If I see one, I'll give him the word, lady."

The man seemed eager to be off. His nervous wife was tugging his arm.

"Our lives may depend on it," she said, but she was speaking to the man's back. She sighed. Everything was up to her. She would have to be Emil's legs. And keep him from despair. And there weren't any miracles lying around.

CHAPTER 15

ll the way back to the Hall of Justice, Carl Lubbich's mind chewed furiously on the problem: how to shift the blame elsewhere. Paisley's attempt at speed was finally defeated in the Mission District, where rubble punctured a tire and Paisley had to patch the tube. Lubbich paced and fretted while Paisley toiled and passersby offered hundreds of dollars, gold rings, diamonds, pearls, watches, and shares of stock for transportation out of the city—which Paisley righteously refused.

"City business," he snapped.

Smoke eddied past, the scent of Hades on the breezes. San Francisco was dying. But Lubbich was preoccupied with other things: he had known that the utility's water lines ran across the San Andreas Fault, one on a trestle, the other lying in a shallow ditch. The reports were in his files at City Hall. Maybe they had burned. There should have been a backup line and cross connections.

He intended to deny that he knew anything about the water company's lines. Who knew? Mayor Schmitz and Abe Ruef knew, but they would keep quiet or deny that it had been the city's responsibility. Yes, that was it. Deny everything. He had come in with the Schmitz administration; how was he to know how the utility had run its lines? It had all been built before his tenure.

Except that it wasn't quite that foolproof. He had written several reports for the mayor, recommending lateral ties among the Spring Valley and Pilarcitos and San Andreas lines precisely to deal with earthquake damage along any of those vital arteries. He had also recommended a backup line along a low route well east of the existing lines and away from the San Andreas Fault. That was, indeed, a tacit admission that he knew about the vulnerability of the existing lines. But those reports would have died with City Hall—unless some were in private hands. Did Ruef and Schmitz have copies in their homes? He would have to talk with both men, and urge them to destroy all copies.

But the fact was, he *knew*, and that was the thing he faced. He and the mayor and the others had done nothing, not even when the acidulous underwriters' report landed on their desks. Well, it wasn't his fault. The utility had no money for things like that and the city would have had trouble enforcing its will on the utility. Blame it on the rich, those smug, heartless millionaires who had cornered the city's water supply and collected vast sums from their monopoly. Yes, blame the owners. One by one he recited their names. When the scandal finally broke, he knew just what he would say: blame the rich, heedless owners.

Every time Paisley paused or slowed to work his way around rubble, he was besieged by people waving money. Once they were stopped by soldiers who forbade them to go into the fire zone.

"City business," snarled Paisley.

"We're taking your car. Army needs it. You'll haul dynamite," one sergeant bellowed. "We need every auto in the city."

"I'm the city engineer. I'm trying to repair the mains so you can have water," Lubbich snapped. "You stop me or steal this car from me, and there'll be no repairs."

That buffaloed the sergeant, and he reluctantly waved the touring machine through.

They finally made the Hall of Justice, which now was threatened by fires on three sides. The temporary city hall was doomed.

"Wait for me, and don't let them take your car," Lubbich bellowed, and ducked into the building and down the basement stairs. He discovered all the big shots there—men he recognized, like Schmitz's mayoral opponent James Phelan; the mayor's caustic critic Rudolph Spreckels; Herbert Law, owner of the Monadnock Building; Charles Sutro; Joseph Tobin; Rufus Jennings; M. H. de Young, owner of the *Chronicle*; Downey Harvey; Henry Crocker; Bishop William Nichols; John McNaught; and more of the city's elite—including the owners of the Spring Valley Water Company.

Schmitz spotted him. "Ah! It's you, Lubbich. Give us a report. Gents, this is our city engineer. I sent him out to look at the mains."

Swift silence ensued. The fate of this city lay in his words: and his own fate, the fate of this administration, and the fate of those who owned the water company.

He stood, sweating, terror in him. These powerful men, with falcon's eyes, seemed to read his mind and plumb his darkest secrets.

"The Crystal Springs, Pilarcitos, and San Andreas Reservoir lines have all been destroyed," he began. "There is hope that the Lake Merced pumping station will soon be able to supply some water to the west side. But the mains throughout the city are cracked, in hundreds, maybe thousands, of places. I have not yet examined the reservoirs and pumping stations. The Spring Valley utility is gathering information and shutting gates. Its managers don't yet know what to do, and can't do much until they have the facts in hand," he said.

"There's no backup?" Spreckels asked.

"I'm the city engineer, not the water company's engineer," Lubbich replied evasively.

Spreckels turned to Homer Book, president of the water company. "Well?" he asked smartly.

"We had long-term plans, of course," Book said. "That sort of thing's costly and would have forced us to raise rates radically. We've always had our customers in mind. We've some major rebuilding to do now."

"Have you pipe in your yards?"

"Quite a bit. Enough to jury-rig a system."

"You'll need men," Lubbich said.

"Where's your department roster?" Schmitz asked his public works chief, Bassett.

"Buried in City Hall."

"You know most of them anyway. Draw up a list and we'll send messengers. We have to repair the pipe. That's the most important thing we have before us." He turned to a weathered army lieutenant. "I want the Corps of Engineers out there, helping the Spring Valley company. I want all the men it takes, plus equipment, plus night lighting."

"I'll ask General Funston, sir," the officer replied.

"There's no time! Get the men, on the double!"

"But, sir, I can't just order— It's a private company. The army can't legally supply labor for—"

"Do it," Schmitz roared.

The lieutenant fled.

Lubbich again marveled at Schmitz, the relaxed musician whose brisk command was flabbergasting everyone in the room.

"What sort of equipment have we in the city yards?" he asked. "Take what you need. Lend it to the utility. We'll get wagons and trucks for you. Get men."

"They lack drays, sir. That's the worst problem. Livestock and feed."

"Get to work on that," Schmitz said to one of his committee.

"Just a minute, Mr. Lubbich," said Phelan. "You said these water company lines ran right over the San Andreas Fault? Without special engineering?"

Lubbich nodded.

"Did you know that?"

"No, I wasn't familiar—the city engineer just oversees the company—"

"You didn't know these lines were improperly installed."

"I don't recollect—"

"Did you read the underwriters' report?"

"Ah, I may have—"

"—which said that it was a miracle this city hadn't burned to the ground because of its precarious water supply?"

"Is that what it said?"

"Did you read Dennis Sullivan's reports insisting on a saltwater backup in case of a major fire or quake? And full, usable cisterns around town in the event the mains were destroyed?"

"Well, I may have."

"And how did you respond?"

"I don't recollect."

"I'll recollect for you. The city didn't do a thing. Did it?"

"Ah . . ." Lubbich sweated until his armpits were soaked. Phelan was torturing him in front of the most powerful men in San Francisco. He had had all he could endure. "Sir, I lost my children today. My house caved in."

"Lost your children?" Schmitz asked, stunned.

"Both gone, Mr. Mayor, from the first quake. I would like to be excused. I've done what you asked. Reported . . ."

Swift silence enveloped the room.

"We're all very sorry, Carl. Terribly sorry. Your children—Carl Jr. and the, ah, little girl?"

Lubbich nodded miserably.

Schmitz straightened. "Carl, normally I'd say, Go home and comfort Mrs. Lubbich—Rosemary. But this desperate hour, the whole city depends on you—on the knowledge contained in your head. Hundreds of thousands of desperate people depend on you. I'll send a minister—ah, clergyman to Mrs. Lubbich, if that would help."

"That would be kind, sir." Lubbich relaxed slightly. At least there would be no more grilling him. He saw pity in the faces of his auditors. His ordeal was suspended—for the moment. He didn't doubt he faced terrible trouble a few days hence.

"Well, you're our hero, then, Carl." Schmitz turned to Police Chief Dinan. "Get a list of municipal workmen and track them down. Have them bring their tools. Find out who's a steamfitter or boiler man or pipefitter. And get me a hundred laborers. Young single men. Conscript them if you must. Get them out there to the Spring Valley yard and put them in the service of the utility."

Dinan whirled away, heading upstairs to his headquarters.

"I know some men," said Sutro. "Engineers, construction men."

"Send them out there, then."

"I'll pay them," said Rudolph Spreckels.

The mayor turned to Lubbich. "All right, Carl. I know this terrible day is an ordeal. But you're the man of the hour. Look at the reservoirs and pumping stations and report to us. We have to know everything. I'm giving you a pass, you and the driver. It'll get you past army and police." Swiftly he scribbled something on a notepad and handed it to the city engineer.

It read, "Pass the bearer through all lines," and was signed "E. E. Schmitz."

Lubbich fled, his legs rubbery from the ordeal. It had gone worse than he expected. That damned Phelan! Making politics out of a crisis! He longed for food—coffee, sweets, anything to fill his portly stomach.

He fell exhausted into the touring car. "City Hall," he announced to Paisley.

"That's rubble, sir. Fire's licking at it."

"Need some records." *And certain damning documents.*

The driver shrugged, cranked, jumped in, and jerked the horse-less carriage around until it faced south. They hit a police barrier en route, but the mayor's pass permitted passage. City Hall, what was left of it, was an impenetrable mountain of rubble, and some of it was burning. Major fires were two blocks distant. That was reassuring—for the moment.

"Union Square," he said. "The water company."

Paisley eased the machine around and made his way to Union Square, again fighting off hundreds of shouting people who wanted to hire the conveyance. "City business," he bellowed.

They arrived in Union Square, and were mobbed by scores of people waving cash and valuables. Women knelt and pleaded. Men demanded and harangued. He directed his driver to the St. Francis. "Wait here, Paisley. I'll be awhile. Don't let anyone steal your machine."

Carl Lubbich knew he had a little time and he intended to take it. The St. Francis was still serving—to anyone who could afford its stiff price. He'd heard that several times that day.

He entered the majestic lobby with its vaulting ceiling, and made his way to the red velvet–draped restaurant, finding it jammed and manned by too few waiters.

"I want a table right now," he announced to the exhausted maître d'hôtel.

"Impossible. See for yourself. It's a three-hour wait."

"City business," Lubbich said, brandishing his pass.

"I don't care if it's General Funston's business," the insolent man said.

"Make me a basket. Coffee, hotcakes, syrup, fruit, butter, cheese—and don't forget a serviette and some silver."

"Impossible."

Lubbich always carried something persuasive with him. Something that would buy him service in a crowded French restaurant or a choice pair of seats at a vaudeville theater, or the fairest lady on the third floor. In this case, he slid five double eagles from his purse and placed them in the man's palm.

"Bribery," the man announced. "Goddamned bribery. All right. I'll get you something myself, but it won't be what you asked. You make a man hate himself."

"Enough for two," Lubbich yelled. It would pay to keep Paisley happy.

CHAPTER 16

Night loomed. Ginger Severance feared it. She had always feared the night, when bad dreams uncoiled in her mind, and people sinned, and death visited.

She had wandered all afternoon, scarcely knowing where she was drifting, far from her familiar haunts, strange streets, stranger people, milling, retreating, going who-knows-where? The evening ocean breeze chilled her; she ached for a shawl, a blanket, a coat, but had only the white cotton dress.

Sometime that afternoon she had stopped handing out tracts. She rebuked herself for stopping, but in truth she had lost the stomach for it, and now she simply drifted, her mind as numb as her body. She craved water, fruit juice, a nice ice-cream phosphate, anything to nourish her tormented body.

She hailed a man carrying a bottle. "I need water badly," she said.

He thrust the bottle to her, and she sipped. Beer. She spat it out. "I don't drink," she mumbled.

"Suit yourself. All anyone has is beer."

She had sworn the temperance oath, that spirits would never pass her lips, and she wouldn't violate her pledge now. She had grown increasingly dizzy for want of food and water, and now the hills hemmed her. She could not manage those terrible slopes. She had lost track, didn't know what hills defeated her. San Francisco was nothing but hills, each a proud mountain that subdued those who wrestled with it.

She finally stopped wandering, too weary to walk another step, her feet sore, her legs aching. She stood on the brick pavement and watched people drift. A burdened young woman approached.

"Water," she begged.

"I need it for my children," the woman said, not stopping.

"Have you a spare shawl? A sweater? I'll pay you back."

The woman hurried away, her shoes clicking on the brick.

Ginger saw a policeman and approached. "I'm desperate for water," she said.

"So are we all, lady. Army's setting up relief in the panhandle. Take Market to Fell, and go out there."

"Where am I now?"

"You all right, lady?"

She nodded.

"You're on Washington. Say, you just go west until you hit Lafayette Square. Lots of people there."

"Which way is that?"

He stared, annoyed, and pointed.

"But it's so steep," she mumbled. She stood stock-still, driving away dizziness, and then started up a gentle grade. The copper watched uncertainly, and then drifted away.

She tried to pray but words deserted her. She tried to remember verses, "Mount up with the wings of eagles," things like that, and they didn't strengthen her. She did not know this place, but it had been stricken, just as her neighborhood had been stricken, by the demons under her feet.

Her heart raced. She did not know what to do. She wished for her father. He would help her. He would bring water. That's what he did; he was a well-driver and driller. That's what they needed here, a man who would make a well. Then she would have water. Her father was good at finding it. He didn't believe in dowsing, which he said was ungodly, but he almost always found water for farmers and merchants and people building houses. He just knew where to sink the well. Sometimes he hammered the pipe down, segment by segment, ramming the sand point deeper into the earth. Sometimes he dug a well with a shovel, farther and farther down, bracing the sides of his shaft so it didn't cave in. He wasn't afraid to dig down to water.

If only he were here! He would dig a well right here, save the city and give its people something to drink. But he was in Ohio, so far away. Joseph Severance could not come here in time to help her or the stricken city. Her father would know what to do. Her mother, Mary, knew what was what, except when her husband overruled her. Her younger brothers would know what to do, too, because they were boys. Her father liked to say that well-digging built character. It took patience, courage, strength, knowledge, and optimism to bring up water. He was always quick to point out that the profession killed the foolhardy and impatient, the ones who neglected to shore up the sides of a shaft and then died in a cave-in.

Ginger struggled on Washington, dreading the night, past the homes of the rich. There would be no streetlights to guide her this night. But at last, at dusk, she did reach Lafayette Square and beheld fires and people gathered around them cooking. Many people, constantly moving, knotting together, parting, seething.

She drifted through the crowds, families, old men hunched in the grass, women snuggling children to them, children dragging blankets, shop girls in showy coats, men in suits and cravats, workmen in denims. Maybe someone would help her find drink and food and warmth. She prayed that they would.

She edged toward a bright fire that shot wavering orange light into the gloom. The radiant warmth reached her, soothed her, filtered to her icy flesh. This fire was eating furniture and wood salvaged from the rubble; the people had gathered a great stack of it, and no copper was telling them to put it out.

She sank to the grass, so grateful for the fire. No one paid her much heed, though she sometimes felt she was in a forest of legs and feet and pants and skirts. She wished her father would come and bring her water. But how could he? He was probably sitting at the dining table at their spacious clapboard home, cream and white, beside the Muskingum River, worrying about her.

Well-digging had earned him a comfortable living. Almost everyone in Washington County called on him, and sometimes he was gone from Marietta for weeks at a time. When she was little, her father took her sometimes, and had her haul up buckets of dirt and then lower the bucket to him. But she tired too easily, and he said it was boys' work. But then when he was digging a well for the grindstone company, he rigged up a windlass so she could crank the buckets up and empty them, but he wished she were a boy so she could empty a five-gallon bucket instead of a two-gallon one. She was sorry she was only a girl, and she promised him she would be good, and make him happy by being just the daughter he wanted. But she wasn't really sure he wanted a daughter. He needed more sons to haul the dirt and rock up, and break up boulders with a sledgehammer, and help him drive a well, or lift heavy pipe, or set up the equipment he used to hammer pipe into the hard earth.

She knew he was disappointed, but he never said so, and always talked gravely to her about how good it was to have a young lady in the family to help her mother and tidy the big, happy house. That was how she grew up, and neither her mother nor her father ever imagined that she would take a Bible society correspondence course for a year and become a street missionary. They weren't any more or less religious Baptists than their neighbors, and they never quite understood their oldest child.

She ignored the hubbub around her, wrapped her arms tightly about herself to stay warm, and hoped they wouldn't let the fire die. She watched the daylight leach out of the night sky, and then it was dark and she could see stars and smell smoke. She needed once again to find a necessary room, and knew there would be none. What did people do? She forced herself to sit up, and then stand, shocked by her weariness. Then she wandered, dodging knots of people, women humming lullabies to fretting infants, and stumbled at last upon a place her nose told her was the right one. A planting of azaleas shielded what proved to be a trench that had been hastily hacked into the hard, dry clay. The shadowy presence of a man nearby, and the splatter of his urine, froze her and she waited until he had vanished into the dark. She found the whole business a torment and indignity, and fled back to her fire—or what she thought was hers. In the confusion she couldn't tell one fire from another. It didn't matter. She tumbled to earth, still parched, and huddled there in the inadequate heat of a dwindling flame. She was alone, even in the crowd. Where was God?

She huddled in a ball, her body shivering, trying to still its quaking. She knew little except that these weren't the same people and no one would tell her what to do or where to go. No one had a well, so she couldn't find water. Once in a while someone would feed the flames with wood salvaged from the ruins around them, and then she would feel momentarily warm.

Then a man stooped over her.

"Madam, are you all right?" he asked.

"Water."

Much to her surprise, the man summoned a woman in a nursing uniform and they lifted her up and gave her a tin cup filled with icy water. She drank it slowly because her throat was swollen, and they gave her a second glass. She peered at her benefactor in the waving dull light, and discovered a graying man in a baggy suit, exhaustion stamped on his face, his shirt open at the neck.

"Have you a blanket, madam?"

"No."

"Have you eaten?"

"No. More water."

They gave her another tumbler. He talked while she drank.

"I'm a doctor. We've organized relief teams to visit these places. We can help you."

She nodded and emptied the tin cup.

"Now, who am I addressing?"

"I'm Miss Severance."

"I'm Dr. Hotchkiss. Well, Miss Severance, have you anyone here? Are you missing relatives?"

"I have God."

"Ah, friends, family, neighbors?"

She shook her head.

"You're trembling. May I check some things?"

He seemed so kind. Like her father. "Yes," she said.

He clamped a hand on her wrist. "Elevated pulse," he said. "But that could be dehydration." He pressed a hand to her forehead. She felt that kind hand and knew he was seeking fever.

"You are sent by God," she said.

He chuckled. "Anyway, the mayor's committee. We're working in pairs, doctor and nurse, along with a few volunteers we've dragooned into carrying stuff. We have some bean soup—not much, not tasty, but it'll help."

"I'm not hungry."

He frowned. "Fever, I think. We need to move you to an infirmary. Unfortunately, we're a little crowded in that department. The Presidio General Hospital's reserved for serious cases and surgeries. St. Mary's is doomed and they're looking for some place to move patients. St. Luke's collapsed and the Mechanics' Pavilion was evacuated this afternoon. The other hospitals are gone."

"I'm all right—if I could have a blanket."

"I admire your fortitude, Miss Severance, but you're unable to stop the tremors."

"I'm cold. I need a blanket."

"Of course." He nodded to the nurse, who produced a gray army blanket of thick, coarse wool. The nurse wrapped it around Ginger. "We don't have very many of these," he said. "Mrs. Funston talked the quartermasters into emptying the shelves."

The blanket felt very good, and Ginger drew it about her as if it were a queen's ermine robe.

"We need to move you, but the wagon's always behind. There are so many. If you can walk, we'll take you to a staging area. We're taking people there who need help."

"You're like my father," she said. "He always knew what to do."

"This is Nurse Laura Arsenio. She will write your name, and how to reach your next of kin, if you would give her that information. I must go now; there are so many . . ."

He stood, wearily, his face ashen in the yellow light. "These fellows here'll help you get to the staging area. It's right here in the square, Miss Severance."

Then he was gone, his sharp eye studying each person he came across.

She told the nurse about her parents, and then the men helped her walk to a dark place where there were sick people huddled on the grass. She sat, drew the blanket around her, and waited in the dark for salvation, all the while thanking her Lord.

CHAPTER 17

. . . .

In the cold dawn Marcia watched Harrison extract precious meltwater from the icebox and shave himself carefully. Then he used the water for a spit-bath, dressed in his nattiest attire, rummaged through the kitchen for something to eat, and pat the owly and unhappy children on the head as if they were dogs. She withheld the acid comments that kept rising to tongue, knowing they wouldn't help much. Harrison seemed to brim with uncanny good cheer, somehow wildly inappropriate for the moment. She wondered whether she knew him at all; whether years of marriage had acquainted her with this stranger.

They had spent a cold night with a sheet tacked over a shattered bedroom window to stay the wind. The children would not sleep in their own rooms and insisted on being with their parents. The night had been eerie, damp, and wakeful. The stench of the lavatory drifted through the upstairs, even though broken windows let in the Pacific breezes. The relentless fires to the east lit the sky and cast wavering orange light across the room where she and her family huddled and suffered.

She hadn't slept much, her mind fitfully seeking escapes, comforts, help. But Harrison had, and somehow she resented his cheer. She felt worn and afraid of their collapsing world, and worried about their fate.

He headed for the door, but she detained him.

"Where are you going?"

"To find the mayor's committee. This is the chance of a lifetime."

"I can't imagine why."

"This is the one moment I'll be able to make business connections easily. The top men in town. The money. The city will need to be rebuilt. I'm an architect." He spoke to her in a way that suggested she was dense.

"I thought you were a father," she retorted.

He smiled, patiently. "We'll be on easy street the rest of our lives. My father used to say, when opportunity comes, don't just take it; expand it, form it, put it to work for you, because you may never have another chance. And look at him. He made it in four fields, always active, never passive. He practically pioneered title insurance. He saw a need—"

She had heard that story too many times and headed it off. "You used almost the last of the water. What will we do?"

"Why, once I connect with these people—Spreckels, Phelan, and all, I'll have all the answers. Inside information. They're going to know how to do everything. I'll ask about the water—where it is and how to get some—and get back to you."

"Before your two children suffer?"

"What do you take me for?" he asked, petulance in his tone.

"And what are we to do here?"

"Clean up, of course. Organize the food."

"And when will we see you?"

He smiled. "I'll be looking after you, believe me. By the time I return, I'll have the word on everything: what's being done, where we can find food and water, where to go if we must, what parts of the city are endangered. Some of those men on the committee—Herbert Law for one—already know me. I just have to find Law. I designed his building for him. It stood, you know. That's a gold star for me. Find Law, and pretty soon we'll be sitting pretty. He and his brother control the Fairmont Hotel, and I'm thinking he'll let us move there if we have to."

"And if we should be driven from here by the police, or soldiers, or fire—where will we meet?"

"Oh, heavens, Marcia, don't worry about that. You can always find me, wherever City Hall is. Just ask."

"Where will we meet?"

"I'll send word. I'm sure you'll do the right thing. For now, I'll be at Portsmouth Square."

He pecked her on the cheek, which she endured. She watched him trot off, jaunty, impeccable, somehow as clean and groomed as if it were another normal day, and vanish down the avenue.

Well, that was Harrison Barnes White, scion of White the First, father of White the Third. The senior Whites tended to confuse themselves with God. She drifted to the kitchen, feeling blue, found two or three cups of meltwater remaining in the icebox drain pan, and the last of the ice gone. The water would not last the day.

Smoke hung in the air. An easterly breeze was driving it and the fires west and north. She could see the columns of flame curling upward. They were much closer than they had been last evening.

The children were staring at her, and she knew she must attend to their needs. They were subdued. Blackness smudged the hollows under their eyes. Daisy's hair was ratty and needed washing. Harry looked ready to cry.

"Get dressed," she said. "When you're dressed, I'll give you each some water and Cream of Wheat."

She hoped the cereal would absorb a little water without being boiled. It was all she could do.

"I'm thirsty," Daisy said.

Marcia filled a cup of the meltwater and handed it to her. The remaining water was discolored.

Daisy stared at it, shook her head, and handed the cup back. "I want nice water," she said.

Marcia didn't argue. She would hunt for some as soon as she could. It would be hours—all day probably—before she would hear from her husband. "Now get dressed!" she snapped.

Reluctantly they turned away and drifted upstairs. They were too silent, too solemn.

She found three bowls, poured Cream of Wheat into each, added cold water, and stirred the mixture into a thick mush. Then she drank half of the remaining cup of water.

In her room she dressed, feeling filthy and uncomfortable. The children had vanished into their gloomy rooms. She tried to comb her dirty hair, gave up, and fled downstairs. She rattled around the kitchen, picking things up, her mind furiously chewing on her dilemmas. The children. Their fears. Water and food. Blankets and comfort. Disease. Fire. Escape. . . .

If Harrison wouldn't help her, she would help herself. The children appeared, looking awful, and she thrust spoons at them. They toyed with the cold cereal, ate a few mouthfuls and abandoned the rest.

"Let me add a little salt," she said, sprinkling the salt into the cold cereal. But they weren't interested, so she ate it. She needed the moisture and strength.

"Is the fire going to burn us up?" Harrison asked.

"No. But we might have to leave our house. The fire's much closer this morning."

"We're going to die," her son persisted.

"No, but we will have some bad times. We all must be strong. Aren't you a strong young man?"

"Did God do this?"

"No, God loves his people." She wondered how she might explain some of the most difficult things. "When we suffer, we learn to call on Him. We learn to be strong," she said.

"Where's Daddy?"

Marcia thrust back the bitterness. "He's looking after our future. That's what he says."

Daisy said, "I wish he was here now."

Marcia nodded. They needed him. "As long as he's not, we'll find out how to take care of ourselves. Would you like to go out?"

They nodded dubiously.

"All right. We'll go ask people where to find food and water and whatever we need."

Once they escaped the damaged house and reached the streets, warming in the tender April sun, they all felt better. The streets were dry and comfortable except for the acrid smoke; the house was dank, dark, dismal.

They discovered a steady flow of refugees, almost all trudging west, carrying as much as they could. Women had stuffed perambulators full of food and blankets. Men carried or dragged valises or pillow cases or sacks of needed things. Some men rode by on burdened bicycles. One elderly woman pushed a loaded tea cart on castors down the street. A group of young men wrestled a burdened wagon up and down slopes. Ever westward.

The view from the street told a different story from what she had discerned in her home. In the house she had seen the fires to the east, towering columns of gray smoke that blotted out the sky. But from the heights of Pacific Avenue, she discovered that the whole southern horizon was a mass of boiling smoke, even west of where she stood. The sight sickened her. Where was safety? West! Passage to the Ferry building and Oakland had no doubt been cut off. The southern fires were consuming the Mission District. How could anyone flee south, down the peninsula? West! To the Presidio, Golden Gate Park, stretches of lawn that could not burn, home of the U.S. Army, which had means to help people. West!

Where was Harrison? Fraternizing with the enemy, that's what. She laughed. Every once in a while she came up with something wry, a little mental needling she had garnered from her acid-tongued mother. Laughter had always been her true fortress and refuge, the solvent that dissolved her troubles.

Just by stepping into the street she had learned much, but now she needed more. From her vantage point, she thought that Portsmouth Square was ablaze. Where had the mayor's committee gone?

"Excuse me," she said to a man shepherding a large family. "Where are people going?"

"Don't know, ma'am. Away from the fires."

"Are they stopping the fires?"

"No water."

"We're out of water—where is some?"

"Many folks have wine and beer—but don't let the soldiers or police see it. And remember, spirits dehydrate you, too."

Wine. She and Harrison had a rack of it, the bottles undamaged in their nests. But she needed something for the children.

The man and his family drifted by. She learned a little from others, but her observations told her much. Perambulators were ideal. She could carry much in the one she had in her house. Blankets, sheets, awning for a tent, warm clothing, soap, food that could be eaten without a fire—how little there was of it—tins of anything, against the time they could use it. The next best conveyance was a wheelbarrow, but she lacked that.

She talked to dozens more, garnering wild rumors, end of the world, but very little solid information. These people stank but she supposed she did also. One piece of advice threaded through the encounters. Stay clear of the soldiers; they shot and killed, looted, confiscated, and destroyed. They had been sent to preserve order, and at least a few of them had become a murderous mob marching victoriously through a war-shattered city.

Out of all of her talk, she got no water for herself, but one man gave a drink from a flask to Daisy and Harrison Jr. She received no food, but she had at least acquired some sense of how things were going. This neighborhood would burn this evening unless the winds switched; her home, her nest, her shelter, would vanish this day; her life would change forever this day. There was no good way out. Money would buy nothing. Banks were closed anyway. The railroads weren't running because the rails had been bent and twisted as if they were baling wire. The grocery stores and bakeries had all been looted. And unless Harrison returned in an hour or two, she would be separated from him. Maybe that wasn't so bad, she thought grimly.

She led her silent children back to the dank house, dug out the perambulator from storage, loaded it with blankets and cans of tomatoes, hid two bottles of wine and a corkscrew in the bottom under some sheets, and then waited for her wayward man. She would stay as long as she could for the World's Greatest Architect.

She laughed at that, and knew she shouldn't.

CHAPTER 18

Nella Clapp decided to go to Oakland. If she had to go anywhere, it might as well be there. She sailed down Nob Hill, negotiated the mobs around Union Square, smiled at a few men, and marched toward Market as if she were on a shopping expedition.

The smoke grew thicker, and radiant heat from newly burned buildings scorched her. Ahead, the street vanished into haze and smoke. But at the end would be the Ferry building, if it still stood, and maybe passage to a safer world. Her coin purse held a few dollars; enough to get across the shimmering bay and into Oakland.

But then she encountered six soldiers, their uniforms begrimed,

their faces red and their expressions dour. They held mean-looking rifles with those sword-things attached.

"Where are you going, lady?" asked one with two of those little
stripes on his arm.

"I'm going to Oakland."

"No, miss, not now. Whole area around the Ferry Building's in
flames, firemen trying to save it so's they can start shipping out people.
Market Street's so hot you'd scorch your feet."

"Well, where can I go, then? I guess you'd know, soldier."

He shrugged. "The Presidio or Golden Gate Park. That's what I
hear."

They were all admiring her and she enjoyed that. She smiled and
took a deep breath, knowing they would admire her all the more.
"Well, you're just a sweetheart, Captain. It's so hard for a lady to get
information."

The soldier grinned and rested on his rifle as if it were a staff.

"I'm so thirsty," she said. "Where can I get some water?"

Within seconds, three canteens were thrust at her. She smiled. "Oh,
my! I'll have a little of each so no one has to go without."

She drank daintily from the first one, handed to her by a thin dark
one. Then she swallowed more from another, handed her by a man
with a bulgy belly, and still more from a big blond galoot.

"Oh, that was nice. I was so thirsty. What are your names?"

The one with two of those things on his arm did the introducing.
"Private Conrad, there, Bagliani there, Horsmann there. I'm Corporal
Stengel."

"Oh, a corporal. I'm Nella Clapp; just call me by my first name and
that'd be fine. Do you know where I could get something to eat? I'm
just starved."

Stengel looked at Conrad and nodded. The private lowered a
musette bag and extracted a wheel of cheese. With his bayonet he
sliced off a huge piece and handed it to her.

"Oh, I'm so thankful. You have generous hearts. I suppose you're at
the Presidio."

"Twenty-second Regiment, miss."

"Well, I'll remember you forever, almost."

"We have dances sometimes," said the corporal. "Anyone's
welcome."

She smiled, patted him gently on the sleeve, and said she'd remember. They all grinned. She thanked them and retreated from the chaos
of Market Street. She would have to go out to the Presidio, and she
hardly knew how to get there. She didn't want to go to Golden Gate
Park. The closer she got to soldiers, the better off she would be.

She munched cheese as she hiked back to O'Farrell and headed west, uncertain how to get there but sticking to the least hilly passage. It wasn't long before the smoke lessened and she discovered a balmy April day that made her very happy. After she had eaten her fill, she tucked the cheese into her kerchief and carried it in her hand. People were so nice. Except maybe Jeremy Sanchez-Groppi. That lobster! But that was all over.

She fell in with three well-dressed gents who looked like clerks or maybe bankers. They all were young, and looking her over; she smiled at them. They would be good company.

"How does a lady get to the Presidio?" she asked the blue-eyed man.

"Oh, just head toward the Golden Gate," he said. "We're going to the park ourselves."

"What's at the park?"

He shrugged. "They say to go there. At least there's nothing to burn down."

"I wanted to go to the ferry but they wouldn't let me."

"It wouldn't do any good. Oakland's in ruins. Everything east is in ruins, too."

"It is? Where did you hear that?"

"It's common knowledge. Chicago, Baltimore, and New York are on fire; Washington D.C.'s tumbled down. I've heard that Vesuvius exploded—it's covered Italy with three feet of ash."

Fear slid on cat's feet through Nella. "Well, how about south toward Monterey?"

"It's a dead land, destroyed by the quake, and there's nowhere to go."

Another of the men addressed her gravely: "This is the apocalypse of prophecy. Famine, war, sickness, death . . . we all know it's coming, even if we make our puny efforts to survive a bit longer. It's coming, this hour, the next, tomorrow, next week. The end. *Finis.*"

"Are you sure?"

"I am very sure. It's all in Scripture. But even the blind can see it happening."

"You mean I won't live?"

"Well, we think God will rescue his chosen, his anointed. Sixty-six thousand. We hope we'll be among them. We're all fasting and seeking his blessing."

"Sixty-six thousand? That's a lot."

"It's nothing. If you've lived a sweet, pure life, miss, maybe you'll be elected."

That left her out. She clutched the cheese to her stomach. "How do I know this?" she said, fearfully.

"You will know it in your soul."

They dodged the rubble of a brick apartment building. A wrinkled woman in a shabby wrapper stood beside it, begging for food and water.

"Here!" Nella said, thrusting the cheese at the hapless creature. The woman snatched it and began weeping as she gnawed on cheese.

"It's too late," said one of her companions. "God isn't mocked by last-ditch acts of kindness."

"Well, who are you to say?" She didn't like that one. "Who says being nice doesn't count?"

He stared at her from opaque eyes. "I knew this was coming before it happened. I saw it all. I was given the gift. I know who will be the elect and who won't."

"You did? You do?"

"I foresaw everything. This is the Doomsday written in the Book of Life. This is the day that the heavens will open and the Lord in his chariot will descend to earth."

"What hope is there for me?" she asked in a small voice.

"Many are called, few are chosen," he replied.

"Is this really Doomsday?"

"You have eyes to see, ears to hear, a nose to smell the smoke. You have seen the earth riven in two and tossed about. You have seen man's mightiest works tumble as if they were houses of cards. You have seen water vanish, fire consume, and soon you will see illness fell the multitudes, and the armies will march. The Four Horses of the Apocalypse. Your own senses tell you what day in the entire history of the world is this day. This is the time of Judgment. Prepare yourself, miss."

It all made sense. God was ending it for everyone who'd ever sinned, even once. Her thoughts flew back to those ecstatic moments with Jeremy and she knew her fate. Straight to hell. It desolated her. She was going to die and then be banished to some terrible place she had hardly even thought about. She wished she had studied the Bible more and heeded it. But she had read romances and those had inflamed her. She sighed, hiding her despair from these three men. Then she needed to be alone, so she smiled at them, turned aside on Van Ness and headed toward the comforting mansions of the rich. They scarcely remarked her departure from them.

She wandered up the broad, sunny avenue, past huge, solid, ornate homes. But she knew they were all doomed, the homes and every living person within them. Crowds walked this street, too, but none of them knew this was Judgment Day. She sat on a stone embankment that contained a sloping lawn, just to rest a moment and think about the world coming to an end. Moments later a handsome man reeled down beside her, smiled gracefully, surveyed her with knowing eyes, and patted her on the knee, an amazing liberty.

"We're doomed," she said.

"I'm drunk," he said. "And I'll stay that way until we get past doom." He thrust his hand in his suit coat and extracted a large silver flask. "Here. Have some. I have an infinite supply, by virtue of a key to a friend's home and wine cellar."

She smiled and took it. She had sampled spirits before, but not very much, and this would be an adventure. She tilted the warm flask and felt fiery liquid burn her throat. "Oh!" she cried.

He recovered his flask, guzzled a moment, screwed the cap and restored it to its nest. She could smell the spirits on his breath.

"I'm Nella. Who are you?" she asked, enjoying him.

"God in heaven. Can there be any creature on earth who doesn't recognize the visage, the brow, the noble nose?"

"I don't know what this has to do with Doomsday."

"Enchanting. On this, of all days, I have found my nemesis—and my salvation." He eyed her. "I like this. Call me John. Yes, plain, simple, John. One of the Apostles."

"Well, John, you're pretty snookered. I guess you don't care that this is Doomsday."

He eyed her. "If they bury more, it'll not be Barrymore," he said sonorously.

"They'll bury a lot, me included," she said. "All I did was fool around a little."

"Why would they bury you? Good Lord, it'd be a crime to bury you. An offense against nature."

"Well, John, we're all facing Judgment. Could I have some more of that stuff?"

"Stuff? Stuff? Brandy, dear. Good, mellow, aged brandy. My first bottle was gotten illicitly from the Bohemian Club. Then I retired from there to here, to while away my time in hiding. I am engaged in a one-man conspiracy, you know. They have me booked for Sydney, and I'll be damned if I'll go. Miserable company. And so I hide and drink and hide, and take the air, and when this is over I'll make a few pence publishing my memoirs. My, but aren't you pretty."

"Well, John, I'd like some. It sort of makes me glow."

"I'll make you glow, child. I know exactly how to make a nubile young woman glow. You are in good hands."

John was slurring his words. But at least this was fun, not like those three who told her the sky was falling down.

She took a swig. The brandy scorched its way down her throat and lit fires in her stomach. She hoped the baby would like it.

"How can you go to Sydney if the world's coming to an end?" she asked.

"A good question that requires rhetoric. The world came to an end prior to its coming to an end, that's why."

"Uh, John, you've had a lot to drink, haven't you?"

"Not half enough. *The Dictator* was abysmal, but now every last set and script and ticket is up in smoke. There is a just God. I live over there." He waved an arm languidly. "Would you care to share Doomsday with me?"

"Have you some food and water?"

"No, I have wine and lust."

She dimpled up. "Mr. John, I'm not that kind of lady."

"Well, for heaven's sake, that's nothing to hold against you. Let me help you to become one."

She laughed. This flamboyant man was funny.

He produced his silver flask and pumped some more brandy into the cap and handed it to her. She took it, smiling, and swallowed a dainty amount.

"Now, how about sharing some fruit? Grapefruit, melons, pears, oranges. Even crab apples in a pinch. I'm partial to them all."

"You have fruit?"

"We both do. Let's go sample them."

She knew where this was leading. The man was a bounder like Jeremy. "You're leading me astray on Doomsday. That's what this is. Some men explained it to me. No, I don't think so. I have to prepare."

He thrust the flask at her again.

"I've had enough," she said.

"You can't meet the Devil sober," he retorted.

CHAPTER 19

arrison White hurried toward Portsmouth Square only to discover it no longer existed.

"That's burnt up. You can't go there," some soldiers told him. "You gotta turn around or you're in trouble."

"The Hall of Justice?"

"Gone. Cinders."

"Where's the city government?"

A soldier shrugged. "They beat it out of there yesterday evening."

"Fairmont Hotel," said another. "In the ballroom. Old Freddie was there late last night talking to 'em."

"Freddie?"

"Funston. He's given them their marching orders."

White retreated, walking through stinging smoke that hurt his eyes. He saw few people, except for pairs of police, or patrols of soldiers going in and out of buildings.

Now and then he heard sharp booms as the dynamiters continued to work. He wondered if either the army or the firemen had the faintest idea how to use dynamite, or how to drop a building effectively. He doubted it. They needed engineers and architects to tell them where to place the charges, what the load-bearing members were. Well, every demolished building meant one more lot for Harrison White to build on. It was a pity, though. The sappers would do more damage than the fire, the way they were blowing up property.

From a high intersection he could see that Union Square was besieged and wouldn't last long. It had been a refuge the first day; now it was an empty flat awaiting execution by fire. Even the St. Francis looked dead, empty, ready to surrender. Why did they suppose the Fairmont and Nob Hill would escape? Didn't Mayor Schmitz have a brain?

He hurried up the slopes, winded by his exertion. Wherever the city government was hiding, he would find it. The stakes were the highest in his young life. He intended to make himself useful to the Committee of Fifty—and establish himself once and for all in the city's elite. Given what the rebuilding of the city would bring him in the next decade, he could retire young and rich.

The Fairmont was operated by Herbert and Hartland Law. White had designed the Monadnock for Herbert. He would be among influential friends there. That was perfect. He paused on the higher reaches of Nob Hill to catch his wind. Below him the city burned, north, south, southwest, and east, dying hour by hour under a black cloud of ash and smoke that blocked the sun and towered an infinity above. He eyed the southwestern fires nervously; these could complete the circle and trap him and others.

The majestic hotel stood atop the hill, lording over a lesser world below. White made his way through the gilded, darkened lobby to the mezzanine ballroom and discovered a throbbing enclave of government there. Scores, hundreds of men were swirling about. He needed to find Herbert Law, but first he reconnoitered. Mayor Schmitz operated from a dais, looking every bit the orchestra conductor he was. The man was imposing in a way, White thought, but soft-faced, as if he lacked character. White saw no sign of Abe Ruef, the gray eminence of the Schmitz political machine, and that made sense. Ruef wouldn't dare show his face among men such as these.

White walked quietly among them, a dapper young man blotting up what he could. He recognized San Francisco's leading lights. Some he had seen in the flesh; others he recognized from the plates in the newspapers. A few he guessed at. Over there was the mustached Rudolph Spreckels, sugar king; yonder was James D. Phelan, urbane, exceedingly rich, and influential. Here, close at hand, was Charles Sutro, and beyond, the *Chronicle's* publisher M. H. de Young. And yes, there was Bishop Nichols and Archbishop Montgomery. He spotted the dark visage of Ben Wheeler, and Henry Crocker, Claus Spreckels, and David Mahoney. Great men, worth collectively hundreds of millions. Men who would hire architects and planners to rebuild a mighty city, even though they had lost millions in this catastrophe. The vision made White almost giddy.

They had organized themselves. Tables stood about, each marked with a crayoned sign: Relief of the Hungry, Housing the Homeless, Relief of Sick and Wounded, Auxiliary Fire Department, Restoration of Water Supply, Transportation of Refugees, Relief of Chinese, Resumption of Civil Government, Restoration of Light and Telephones, Citizens Police, Auxiliary Fire Department, Drugs and Medical Supplies, Sanitation . . . White discovered nineteen subcommittees in all. He studied them, wondering which would be most opportune. Maybe Resumption of Retail Trade. Yes, that would be a good one for an architect. Design some new commercial buildings, maybe even a skyscraper. But he wanted something more dramatic, more showy. Housing the Homeless, maybe. Maybe Auxiliary Fire Department. He could advise the dynamiters. Certainly not Finance, or Relief of Chinese, or History and Statistics.

While thus absorbed he happened upon Herbert Law himself.

"Herbert!" he exclaimed.

"White! What are you doing here?"

"I came to help out. Pity about our building, Herbert. But she stood. I walked to her after the quake and she stood. She'd be there now but for the fires."

"Yes, well, no time for that. I don't know what you can do here. This is an emergency government."

"I came to volunteer."

Law smiled. "I'm not sure we need an architect. We have sick and hungry and cold and homeless people, little food and water, no sanitation, spotty medical help, no transportation—"

"I'll help wherever you assign me, Herbert."

Law sighed. "Go on over to Schmitz. He's recruiting a thousand citizen police to patrol against looters. He'll give you a pass that will identify you to police and military."

"Patrol? Me?"

"You're young and up to it."

"But I'm an architect. A professional."

"Well, I'm sure you'll find some way to be of service, White. Excuse me. I'm hosting this little party and I need to keep my crew on its toes—what little crew I have."

Law wheeled away.

Bad start.

White headed toward the table marked Relief of the Hungry. The younger Spreckels was there, so White approached.

"Mr. Spreckels, how may I help?"

Rudolph Spreckels stared. "Who are you?"

"Harrison White. Architect. I designed the Monadnock Building, which withstood the quake."

"I don't need architects."

"What do you need, then? I'm here to help out."

"I need to collect and move food enough to feed three or four hundred thousand people each and every day—by water from Oakland and the northern counties, and wagon because the rails up the peninsula are ruined." He raised an eyebrow into a question mark.

"Maybe I could help you find where food is—grains and things—and send people there."

"With the wires down? I tell you what you can do. Go out and locate bakers. We've got wheat coming in and it needs to be baked into loaves and given to people. Go find bakers and check the bakeries and make sure they have working ovens, wood or coal, water, and tell them flour is coming. What was your name again?"

"White, sir. I, ah, thought I might be useful here. I'm a planner. That's part of what I do."

"I need someone to go out and get information." Spreckels turned away.

White shrugged. He examined the Restoration of Abattoirs table and decided slaughtering wasn't his meat. But the Relief of Sick and Wounded table interested him. He surveyed it, not finding any of the town's leading lights there except a bishop or two, so he moved on to Finance. Here indeed, a large group of men knotted close, and many of them he knew on sight.

"How may I help?" he asked Downey Harvey, one of the city's richest men.

"Donate," Harvey said. "Food and shelter cost money."

"I can keep books."

"We have more bookkeepers than we know what to do with. Who are you?"

"Harrison White, with the firm—"

"All right, I need someone to get over to the Southern Pacific, if it's still there, and tell them to transfer—who are you, again?"

"Architect. I designed the Monadnock Building for the Laws."

"Maybe the mayor needs you."

White decided maybe there was something in it. The mayor and his pal Ruef would be needing his services. City planner. Designer of public buildings. Yes, let Schmitz know that an architect with training at the Ecole des Beaux Arts was available to help turn San Francisco into the most sublime regional capital in the world. With a little twisting of a few streets, he could do for San Francisco what Pierre-Charles L'Enfant had done for the nation's capital. Ah, to be the L'Enfant of San Francisco! His name would live forever. He headed across the smoky ballroom, smelling sweat and char and fear, and mounted the dais, where the mayor held court. People simply stood in line to see the man, so White waited his turn. He felt thirsty and the smoke had turned his throat raw.

Ahead of him he could see the towering mayor listen, cut off people who spoke too long, make abrupt decisions, and command instant action from a corps of assistants and police. This Schmitz was certainly in command. One man proposed to turn ships into temporary hotels. Another man had a plan to commandeer all automobiles and send them down the peninsula for food. Another wanted a marriage license. A marriage license! Oddly, Schmitz listened a moment, broke off the pleading, directed the man to a clerk, and said he could get his marriage license.

A marriage license! White marveled.

At last his turn came. Schmitz looked weary, his eyes burning from black hollows, his hair astray. "Yes?" he asked, his weariness economizing his civility.

"I'm Harrison White, architect, sir. I know you're busy with relief, but I just want thirty seconds. You could become the most influential mayor in our history. I've studied city planning. I've looked at Burnham's plans for this city and wish to expand them. What I'd like sir, is to begin work—"

"Not now. Later. We have four hundred thousand people to feed and move away from trouble."

"Yes, sir, but it's not too soon to be thinking of the City Beautiful, and also the city safe and strong. Remember, it'll be too late to change anything the moment people start rebuilding."

Schmitz absorbed that. "White, I'll have you leave your name with my clerk, Joseph Perigault. Maybe I'll get back to you. Thank you."

"I'll submit plans within a fortnight. A whole new San Francisco."

Schmitz sighed and turned to the next man. White thought it hadn't gone badly. The mayor would remember, and call on him when the time came. He was probably the only architect to present himself to the city fathers and the Committee of Fifty. Yes, not bad.

White threaded his way to the clerk's table. "The mayor told me to consult with you about replanning the city," he said. "I've volunteered my services as a city planner. You may not need me just now, when the city's burning, but once the rebuilding starts . . ."

"Name?" said Perigault.

"Harrison Barnes White, sir. I'll be available in my home—office's vanished, you know—on Pacific Avenue and Gough. I'm turning it into a center for redevelopment. I'll have some preliminary sketches for the mayor in forty-eight hours. And also a draft of a structural code for multistory commercial buildings. We'll make this a shockproof city, eh?"

The clerk nodded and turned to another man waiting behind White. The clerk certainly was abrupt, but under the circumstances White could forgive him. This was a coup. He had put himself on the inside track. He'd leave Wolper and Demaris, of course, and start on his own. He already knew what he would do: Market would remain the main thoroughfare, but he would cut a mall north to Union Square and put the new City Hall there, on the site of the old Bohemian Club. And then he would create broad avenues that would radiate away from the mall, very like L'Enfant's plan for the capital . . .

He spent another hour making valuable contacts. He wished he had some business cards, but they had all gone up in smoke, along with the office. In the next hours, not only did he meet everyone important and less important, but he now had a good idea where to get food, water, shelter, medicine, and a ticket out. Inside information. All you had to do was ask. They would remember Harrison Barnes White.

CHAPTER 20

Sergeant Major Jack Deal didn't much like what the old captain was telling him.

"Sergeant, we're putting you in charge of the day command, and setting up a headquarters post in the Fairmont Hotel. You'll be responsible for allocating men to fire areas, setting up a medical evacuation route, making sure the men have field rations and water, and handling problems for the city government. You'll have about five hundred men on the day side, and we're putting Lieutenant Fox in charge of the night tour, also with five hundred men. All right?"

"Well, sir, may I respectfully make some suggestions?"

The captain nodded.

"I'm thinking you'll need your most experienced noncoms on night duty, sir, when the looters are working. It'll be dark, and some of our men might shoot people who aren't looting. That's where seasoned men are needed. I'll volunteer for night duty, sir. Keep a lid on the town proper."

"We considered that, sergeant, and put officers on the night side for that reason. We'll have some lieutenants out in the field, or the streets. We want you to do what you're best at, making it all work. Do this well, and there'll be some commendations. I'll put in a word with the general."

Deal didn't like that at all. But there were a thousand ways to undermine authority. "Sir, all right. But I'll need permission to go out and look things over. Hard to see what's happening from behind a desk."

"You may employ broad discretion, Sergeant. If there's a problem, go there and resolve it. These are American citizens, and there's some question whether we should be on the streets. Martial law has not been proclaimed. Technically, we're simply supporting the civil government. So proceed carefully. If you go, keep your command post staffed to handle all personnel matters and civilian complaints. If you need help from the command, call on us at once."

That was more like it. Deal saluted smartly. The captain, who had commandeered a civilian touring car and driver, climbed in and the machine rattled off. The sergeant sighed. He wanted the night tour, and he wanted to be out in the streets. He had too much rank. A sergeant major was more a senior administrator than an enlisted man.

Well, there were ways, and ways, and ways. He put Walt and Joey in charge of squads, told them he would be at the Fairmont, and left them to their devices. They would know what to do. So would others, like Nils. Maybe this was good. From the command post he could divert a wagon or truck and make good use of it. Maybe, just maybe, he could turn a small-time deal into a big one. That munitions bunker behind the azalea bushes could hold a bonanza.

At the Fairmont he found a two-room command post. A pair of lieutenants occupied one. Their mission was to deal with City Hall. A half dozen noncoms awaited him in the other. He knew four; the others were from Fort Mason. Old hands, good men. None of them had his ambitions, but that was all right. Best that they didn't. They would serve his purposes all the better.

There were no lights; no electricity. A carbide lantern illumined each room. The hotel had provided some tables and chairs. The rooms were cold, and the men in pullover sweaters.

"What have we got?" he asked Dawkins, a veteran master sergeant who had been in Cuba.

"Roster or equipment?"

"Equipment."

"One horse-drawn ambulance."

"No motor trucks?"

"Nothing like that. They're all hauling food."

"Field rations?"

"None here except what the men are carrying. Lots more coming in, enough to feed us and civilians."

"Water?"

"Plenty at the Presidio, but not here."

"Get some here. Scrounge some drums. Any sick or injured men?"

"Yeah, three injured in the dynamite crews; one burned. Another broke an arm. Rubble hit him. Two drunk and one puking his guts out. Ambulance taking them out to Presidio. The drunks'll be disciplined. The wagon's supposed to bring back a barrel of drinking water. They should be back any moment."

"And trouble with civilians?"

Dawkins nodded. "Plenty. The lieutenants are handling it. Taking some of it to the little gen'ral."

"Let me see the roster," Deal said.

He studied the list. A mixed bag of coastal artillery, engineers, cavalry, but only a handful of infantry. A glance at the night-duty roster showed more infantry, but no engineers.

"The Fort Mason crowd get the easy detail," he said.

"The gen'ral's set up headquarters there," Dawkins said.

That was a good plan, actually. Fort Mason stood at the north end of Van Ness Street, perfectly positioned for a war against San Francisco, which is how Deal was viewing it with a certain amusement. Funston loved wars, and was making one all on his own.

"When'll we get burned out of here?"

"They're saying tonight."

"Where'll City Hall go?"

The master sergeant shrugged.

"I want some dynamite and blasting caps."

"Corps of Engineers has it. What do we need it for?"

"I just want some on hand. Go talk to the lieutenants."

Dawkins headed into the hall.

Dynamite could do a lot of things. It could open safes, or bury certain things under rubble, such as bodies with bullet holes in them.

"All right, Carville, is Union Square burning?"

"Not yet, but it's so hot it's making the varnish on the St. Francis bubble. We've cleared out everyone."

"Bohemian Club burning?"

"Who knows?"

"Get down there on the double. Grab a squad. Get anything of value out of the Bohemian Club. Silver, paintings, stuff like that. When the ambulance gets back I'll send it down there."

"Maybe too late."

"On the double, Carville."

The buck sergeant hastened out the door.

Minutes later the ambulance corps men showed up. "Go down to Union Square and pick up a load there from Carville," he said.

"Sergeant, those drays are done for. They can't bring a load up this hill anymore."

"Don't bring it here. Take it out to the Presidio and put it in the officers' mess. Tell 'em I said so."

"Isn't Union Square burning?"

"Go find out."

"You got water?"

"On the double."

The two men fled. Not a bad idea, stowing stuff, art, silver, in the officers' mess, right under their noses. Not bad at all. Deal knew a thing or two.

Two more injured showed up, both with angry-looking burns. A flash fire had boiled up yards from them.

"You'll have to wait a few hours; ambulance is busy," Deal said. "Maybe we can get a civilian automobile."

He sent a corporal over to the ballroom to see about a vehicle. This was going just fine. Maybe he didn't need to hit the streets. He had more resources here. He stepped outside and rolled a cigarette, studying the city. Nob Hill would go soon, and so would the Fairmont. Fires boiling up south and southwest, east and northeast. He studied the mansions on the neighboring streets with interest. Not a bad deal. Chase out the rich people in an hour or two, get Walt and his squad over here. Half the wealth of San Francisco lay within yards of him.

On the crown of the hill stood the Mark Hopkins mansion, repository of a major art collection. Even as Deal watched, University of California students were attempting to salvage the art. He'd offer to help them soon, take the stuff out to the Presidio. He had heard about that Hopkins place with its ornate rooms: the Palace of the Doges drawing room, the English oak dining room, the master bedroom full of ivory and inset jewels. A man with a bayonet could make quick work of it.

Leland Stanford's palace stood next door, a marble monster with an East Indies room. There would be plenty in there to rescue. Nearby was Collis P. Huntington's chateau, and he'd check that one out, too. And across the street was Charles Crocker's pile of carved wood, full of art and fancy stuff. Pretty good for an old army sergeant. He eyed the fires, and figured that sometime before the next dawn, Nob Hill would be ash. He rather enjoyed the idea. A few million dollars of snobbery done to toast.

He needed more than the ambulance with broken-down drays, and stepped back to the hotel to talk with the officers. There was only one on hand, a pimply-faced bozo, a new-minted lieutenant from the Coast Artillery, Harold Oglesby.

"I need ten trucks," he said.

"What for?"

"Hauling. Injured men out, food and water in. I've got burned men. That's what fires do."

"Every army truck in the area's bringing grain up the peninsula."

"I got to have vehicles. Get me a mess of civilian cars. Talk to the mayor."

"You'll have to do without, Sergeant Major. You have an ambulance."

"The nags are worn out. Lieutenant, sir, have you some artillery drays, some caissons, and some limbers?"

"By gad, I think we do."

Deal smiled. "That's the man," he said.

"I'll get them over here," Oglesby said, awash with pleasure.

Things were falling into place. Getting pulled off the streets turned out to be the best thing that happened to him. God bless the army. Even the damned artillery. God bless Freddie Funston. Any other soft-bottomed chief would still be trying to reach Washington.

This fire was a dandy. Pretty soon it would roll toward Van Ness, where the rest of the moguls lived. Then he'd have a crack at more loot. Blow up the rich. Share the wealth. Leave no evidence. What better deal could a man ask for? As soon as he cleaned out a building, it burned to ashes.

From what he'd seen, the dynamiters were knocking down a good chunk of the city. He wouldn't mind blowing up a few houses himself if that's what it took. He'd gotten a Funston Hunting License, and he thought he'd just take all the game around. This was a war, all right, and old Jack Deal was a profiteer.

. . . .

atharine Steinmetz stood on the corner until she could stand no more. The arthritic pain took over her mind; she could think of nothing else, and couldn't even remember what she had come there for.

Of course. To get help. But help seemed unimportant compared to the pain searing her knees, driving up her legs to explode in her head. Still, she persevered. Most people didn't pause long enough for her to tell them what she needed. Some responded amiably—and moved on. Sympathetic words came cheap; real help was too dear for them. But she understood that. Each of them was trapped in a crisis like hers, and preoccupied with survival and comfort.

At last a column of weary soldiers appeared, apparently returning to Fort Mason. Now she would get help. She waved at the corporal who was leading them.

"Sir," she cried. "Sir, we need help."

The corporal turned a smoke-begrimed face to her but didn't stop. "A word, sir!"

But the ten men didn't pause. She watched them go. They looked to be as weary as she, disheveled and dirty, thinking only of washing up, mess, bunks, and another hard shift twelve hours hence. She watched them march into a smoky haze, and knew that help was a million miles away.

Tears formed unbidden. She hated her weakness, hated crying, hated the pain that consumed her. But the soldiers had been the last hope. The streets were deserted. She turned, wondering how she could reach her flat. It wasn't far, but it was high above where she stood, and her legs would betray her.

She walked anyway, each step shooting hot agony through her body. One step at a time, rest, one more step, rest, wait for the pain to settle and step again. She had never known pain like this. Heat radiated from her knees. They felt like furnaces. And yet she took steps, and measured her progress in inches. Little steps, inches and inches. She came to a masonry retaining wall and sat on it, but the pain didn't go away. She surveyed the city and saw pain. Smoke became pain. The orange lick of fire in the distance meant pain. The dull thuds of the dynamiters signaled pain. Pain was all she knew or understood.

She stood, triggering more pain, and pained her way forward, one pain at a time, little pains and big pains, pains in her knees, pains in her feet, pains in her brain. And yet she traversed another fifty yards before she stopped, and marveled that she could endure so much pain without falling to the pavement and curling into a ball.

Then, miraculously, she overcame pain. It did not go away, but she triumphed over it and walked resolutely the last fifty yards to her flat, and up its steep steps, and into the gloomy, rank rooms. It amazed her that she had, for one fleeting minute, triumphed over the pain. She collapsed into the worn chair, opposite her silent lover.

She couldn't speak.

He held a brown bottle of beer in his hand and glowered at her. "Just like I said. No help," he muttered.

She didn't argue. Her knee-pain was taking its revenge, capturing her whole body. Her arthritis was torturing her chest, her shoulders, her head, her thighs, her neck and eyes and back. The arthritis was telling her she could not win against it. The arthritis was punishing her for even trying. She had made it to the flat, a moment of spirit over body.

"Katharine," he said. "You are very brave. You did that for me."

That unexpected gentleness from Emil unhinged her, and she wept. Just when she had thought Emil had turned bitter and beyond tenderness, he had become tender. He loved her. He knew she had borne that pain for him. So she sagged into the old chair and let her eyes fill with tears, and didn't try to hide them. She hurt too much to be happy, but half a dozen words from Emil had given meaning to all she had suffered this Wednesday, April 18, 1906.

They sat in the thickening twilight for a long time. She could not move. Damp ocean breezes sliced through the rooms, piercing broken windows. She felt cold and wanted to draw a blanket about her, but she couldn't even stand. Then Emil wheeled into the gloom and returned bearing her ancient sweater. She hurt too much to put it on, but drew it about her and sighed. What Emil was this, who would do such a thing? A long-ago Emil.

Time ebbed by, marked only by the clock of pain, but then, in full dark, she grew aware. From the windows she could see walls of smoke, columns of flame, shocking in their closeness. The fires were marching while she was experiencing only pain. The southern horizons were aglow. The buildings on the lower slopes of Nob Hill were silhouetted by the eerie yellow light beyond them. She saw the jagged teeth of the skyline etched by fires, many fires, hundreds of fires. She could not tell how close the fires were; everything was surreal and the eye was tricked. She wished she could photograph them, or paint them in their true color, a smoky yellow full of death. How could she paint death? How could she photograph it?

She watched Emil wheel his chair over broken glass to the kitchen, and heard the pop of a cork. Another beer. Maybe that was it. Emil wasn't being tender; he was just being drunk.

"You want one?" he asked from the darkness.

"Yes." She surprised herself. Maybe the alcohol would tame her pain a tiny bit.

He wheeled back and handed her one. The beer tasted oddly good, almost like nectar. She had always been indifferent to it but not now. "Thank you, Wolff," she said. She called him Wolff when she loved him most, and he knew it. She hadn't called him that for a while.

The Pilsner satisfied her. The Torturer within her set aside his whips. She stared through the cracked windows at the spectacle below her, as if it were a Fourth of July display. She realized the acrid stench of the chemicals had vanished. Maybe they could tack up sheets to foil the breezes. Her spirits lifted.

"The soldiers will find us," she said.

"That's what I'm afraid of," Emil retorted.

"They're clearing out buildings ahead of the fires. When they come we'll be helped."

Emil lifted his brown bottle and sucked hard, not answering. "Armies take lives, not save them," he said. "What do you think they're for? What are bullets and bayonets for?"

"Emil—"

"Do you know who goes into the peacetime army? You don't. Well you'll see who goes into the army."

She ignored him. He had never seen any good in an army. He used to tell her about armies marching through his parents' village in the Ukraine, and when they were done, there wasn't much left. His father had died when a Cossack ran a sword through him. He had told her that story twenty times. But this was America, not Europe.

"Emil, we should think what to take with us when the soldiers help us. We can put some things in your lap. Blankets, maybe. Some etchings and my plates. You can hold those things. They'll take us both somewhere. I'll need a ride, too."

Emil stared in the thick darkness. "Let it all burn. What are etchings, anyway? Let my reputation burn with it. Who was Emil Wolff? A man without muscles. Why was I born? To die in this fire." He shifted himself in his chair. She could hear it creak. "I can sum up my life— desperation. I had to be clever, and I made good engravings for the magazines. Clever. But I'm no artist. Just clever."

"No, Wolff, you're famous. Anyone in any studio knows who you are."

"Ya! 'Knows who I am!' That says it. Thank you for saying it."

She subsided into silence. She had meant to encourage him, but he was sensitive, looking for the left-handed compliment to denounce.

"Here's what you do. You get out of here. You can walk down to the street. Leave me here with the revolver. When the flames lick the flat, I'll know what to do."

"We will share our fate."

"No. I want you to take one thing away in a box. Your plates. The three of me and the ones you took on Columbus Avenue today. Guard those plates. That's what I'll leave the world: Emil Wolff on Judgment Day, sitting beside a window, the light all from the left. Emil Wolff, old man in a wheelchair whose body trembles and muscles betray him. Clever Wolff, who made his fingers draw lines even when they refused. Take that, and let the etchings go. What good are the etchings? Dead art looked at once and forgotten, yes? But Wolff on the eve of his death, now there is something for the curious. They will see death in my eyes. They will praise you for capturing the death in my face."

"Wolff, stop!"

"I won't. This is what to take from here. Nothing else matters, including me."

She softened at the thought. "I would like to take the plates," she said. "I caught things on Columbus Avenue that deserve to survive the fire. Not for me, but for a record. People fleeing death. Fear in their faces. Not for me, Wolff, but for viewers a century from now."

"For you," he retorted. "You will have a reputation."

She felt too weary to respond. They stared out the windows as if they were seeing a fireworks display. Sometimes it seemed just that, sudden columns of light and sparks blooming in the blackness. The steady thump of the dynamiters, trying to blow down the city faster than the fire could eat it. The winds, bringing smoke and ash with them, and the odor of apocalypse.

She was cold. The sweater wasn't enough. She struggled to her feet, but Emil read her mind and raced toward the bedroom. She slumped back into the chair, cherishing his attentions. Moments later she wrapped a patchwork quilt around her and enjoyed its swift warmth.

"I will take the plates," she said. "Maybe we can sell them for enough to start over." Sometime soon she must force herself up and find the twenty plates and package them carefully.

He laughed cynically.

"Wolff, things go wrong. Maybe no one will come. No policemen, no soldiers. When the fire comes, it will kill us."

"That's a bad death."

"Yes, worse than the pain in my knees. Wolff, make me a promise."

He didn't respond, but she knew he was listening.

"Wolff, when the time comes, shoot me. It will be a mercy."

He didn't reply, but she knew he was accepting it.

"It is better than burning to death, Wolff."

"Maybe I won't be able to. How could I do that?"
"You must. Because you love me."

CHAPTER 22

arl Lubbich watched silently as workmen swarmed over the ruined San Andreas Reservoir line. With the Crystal Springs line so damaged that it would take weeks to repair, and the Pilarcitos line—which had run for miles directly on top of the fault—a total ruin, the best chance of putting water into the burning Market Street and north-side areas for the firemen was to repair one of the forty-four-inch, thirty-seven-inch, or thirty-inch lines draining the reservoir, and splicing into the College Hill system with a temporary line on Valencia Street. The utility had concentrated its emergency efforts there, where the three San Andreas lines had crossed a fault and shattered.

There wasn't much for him to do. The ground under him was soggy. For hours, after the quake, these lines had shot thunderous plumes of water in long trajectories, soaking the whole area and lowering the San Andreas reservoirs, which lay in geologic trenches formed by the fault itself. The water had rivered its way eastward, toward the bay, leaving a broad muddy wake and ruin below.

Now the first of the utility crews were dismantling jagged sections of pipe, while others were wagoning new pipe from the yard, or preparing to splice different diameters of pipe into a temporary line. The city of San Francisco was helping indirectly, supplying support and transportation and engineering resources, which was why Lubbich was there.

Late in the afternoon a khaki-colored touring car pulled up and the pocket general, Frederick Funston himself, got out, silently studied the situation, talked briefly with some of the city's leading lights, and rained instructions on his aides and city officials, jabbing at one thing and another with a swagger stick. Funston was a compact dynamo exuding will, purpose, and command. Lubbich didn't like him.

Lubbich eased into the crowd of onlookers, but then the little general sought him out.

"You're Lubbich, the city engineer?"
"Yes, sir."
"You're the one that oversees the utility?"
"Ah, yes . . ."
"This is a scandal."

"Ah, it was built before my tenure, sir."

"Well? Why didn't you require the utility to fix it?"

"No one foresaw . . . their budget didn't permit it."

"And did you try? Make reports?"

Lubbich saw some light at the end of this tunnel. "Repeatedly, sir. They're in City Hall."

Funston snorted. "Burned. And what sort of reports did you make?"

"Ah, recommendations, sir."

"And what was the result?"

"There were long-term plans to build a saltwater backup system, sir."

"And did your reports say anything about the lines crossing that fault there?" He jabbed the swagger stick toward the broken pipes.

"Ah—"

"Obviously not. That would upset the water company. All Ruef's cronies, no doubt, and none of them willing to spend a spare dime to secure the safety of this city. Your duty as the city engineer was to bring the hazard to the attention of the water utility company and demand remedy. Did you do that?"

"I'd have to check the records, sir."

Funston's swagger stick leapt to within an inch of Lubbich's nose and wavered there like a hovering wasp. "You're the mayor's man. You're Ruef's man. It figures. By God, you've destroyed a great city almost singlehandedly. Four hundred thousand people depended on you and you let every one of them down. Dereliction of your duty! The city's burning. Death and destruction. Hunger and homelessness and disease. The mains are empty. They tell me there'll be no water in San Francisco for another forty-eight hours—if that. And then a trickle from Lake Merced. Lubbich is the name, eh? It'll go down in history. The man who let San Francisco burn. The man who cost his friends and neighbors two or three hundred million dollars. A court of inquiry is going to hear about you."

The swagger stick leapt and wavered and stabbed inches from Lubbich's face, now darting to the crown of his head, then veering toward his chest, then pulsating before his nose, and then slapping smartly against the little general's britches. Around them, people stood listening, blotting up every word.

"I did what I could, sir. No funds were made available—"

Funston snorted. He had a way of dismissing anything he didn't want to hear with a snort. The general wheeled away, climbed into his khaki touring machine and the driver clattered off on the muddy road.

Men furtively peered at Lubbich, their eyes averted. He discovered Homer Book, the water company's president, gazing blandly at him, his eyes opaque and impenetrable. The city engineer understood perfectly. Ruef, Schmitz, Book, and the rest were about to make Carl Lubbich their scapegoat; the city engineer who failed to notify officials or take appropriate measures. The owners, the ones who had raked in the profits, would get off; Carl Lubbich would probably be lynched or spend the rest of his life in San Quentin.

There was no sense standing here on a sunny hillside south of San Francisco; no sense enduring the bitter glares of these self-righteous men. He retreated to his car and found Paisley catnapping.

"It's late. I'm done in," he said. "You can drop me at my home—what's left of it—and then you're free."

Paisley nodded, cranked the machine, which sputtered and caught, and then wheeled along a dirt path leading to San Francisco. Lubbich bounced in the quilted rear seat, too weary to sit upright. This had been the longest and worst day of his life.

He had an odd, desolating thought. His father would never speak to him again.

He had grown up in the family of a fiercely socialist Milwaukee public official, Gerhardt Lubbich, collector of the city's numerous fees and imposts. His father had been as honest as he had been progressive, and it was a family legend that one day when the accounts in his gray buckram ledger were seventy-two dollars short, Gerhardt had dipped into his own pocket, not wanting to be a penny off or be accused of the smallest transgression. That day had cost him most of a month's salary from the city of Milwaukee.

His father handled a lot of money: saloon and tavern fees, restaurant license fees, business fees, water and sewer hookup fees, elevator license fees, delivery wagon fees, fees for duplicate records. Gerhardt Lubbich was a trusted man, an impassioned Progressive, pro-union, ceaseless in his efforts to turn Milwaukee into a blessed haven for working people, impeccable in his conduct of public business. Carl's father had even assailed the Church, demanding that it sell its assets and give everything away to the needy. The Lubbiches were as progressive in religion as in everything else.

Carl had grown up surrounded by reformers and the fierce labor leaders who had crippled Milwaukee's burgeoning industries over and over until the city had won a bitter reputation as the seat of labor warfare. But out of it had come accommodation. Milwaukee was becoming the premier industrial city in the country, and a good place to live.

Carl had earned a degree in engineering, partly on a scholarship. After that he had married Rosemary and worked for the city for seven years as a young engineer. But the wet and mean cold chilled him. Rosemary didn't want to leave; Milwaukee was where her entire close-knit family lived, united in their help of one another, active in the turnverein, which were becoming the social as well as athletic clubs of Milwaukee's Germanic people. But he didn't like the weather, so he applied for a position with the incoming Democratic mayor Schmitz of San Francisco, won it, and they had moved to the city on the bay. Fled to a pleasanter place where he could live in suit coats and shirtsleeves. But he hadn't forgotten his father's admonition: work for the government. The government went on and on, and one would not be laid off with every turn of the vicious capitalist business cycle. Work for the government, not only to have a secure life, but because a man in government had power, levers, ways to make the world better. Government was a place for men of vision, with a clear eye on the evils of the world.

And so they had come to the city on the bay. But it wasn't a bit like Lutheran and Catholic and middle-European Milwaukee. Nothing in San Francisco was strict, and nothing forbidden, and churches didn't dominate each neighborhood, as they did in Milwaukee. At first, Carl Lubbich marveled at the open vices around him, marveled that the city didn't collapse, that its people didn't all sink into depravity. He marveled that the ruthless capitalists went unrebuked in their tawdry monuments to themselves, building ludicrous palaces of just the sort that Thorstein Veblin called conspicuous consumption. He marveled that San Franciscans had devoted themselves to having fun instead of doing their duty. And after he had stopped marveling and started sampling, it was a simple trajectory from the hidebound Carl Lubbich to the present one.

Paisley brought his clattering machine to a halt before the redbrick ruin of Lubbich's home.

"I guess that does it, Paisley. You're a free man."

"And about out of gasoline," Paisley said. "Was I of service?"

"You'll always be remembered."

Carl Lubbich let himself out, and stood wearily before the ruin, haunted by what lay there. Neighbors stood about. One of them, Wallace Willems, approached.

"We got the remains out, Mr. Lubbich. It was a sorry sight. They were taken away."

"My God, where?"

"We don't know. The city—"

"How did they look? My children?"

"The girl was—we got her out and wrapped her in a blanket."

"And my son?"

Willems couldn't speak for a moment. He gathered courage and clapped Lubbich on the shoulder. "Be glad that they died instantly. We saw no chance of suffering."

"Did a doctor examine them?"

"It, ah, wasn't necessary."

"Where's Mrs. Lubbich?"

"She left with the Bierstadts, sir. We've been notified to leave by dusk. The fires are just blocks away. Three of us volunteered to wait for you as long as we could."

"This will burn?"

"Unless the winds change."

"Did they say where—"

Willems shrugged. "City police told us this'd burn about nine or ten unless there's a miracle. So most everyone fled. A few like me stayed to watch over things. You look done in. I would too, losing two little ones."

Lubbich nodded. "Thank you," he mumbled.

"Union Square's gone, whole east side of the city's gone, whole south side. I'm planning to walk up to the panhandle. You want to come along? That's where to go, except some think maybe down the peninsula. There's a big camp going up on San Bruno Road. Some around the cemeteries, too. But the army's setting up relief in Golden Gate Park, so that's where people are going. I'm sure Mrs. Lubbich will be there."

"Was she—composed?"

"It is good to have neighbors like the Bierstadts, Mr. Lubbich. You'll find her, all right. There's something that will help: City Hall's setting up a registry. You can go there and leave word where you are or where you're going. That's how people will find each other."

"Where's City Hall now?"

"Fairmont, I heard, but they're getting out. Nob Hill's burning, or about to."

"Then where?"

"Policeman told me Franklin Hall on Van Ness. Last-ditch place. If that goes, no more San Francisco."

Lubbich sagged. Before him stood the ruins of his house, a death-trap of brick that had been shaken to bits. Soon it would burn. He was glad his little ones wouldn't burn in it. Maybe, somehow, they would receive a proper burial with a prayer or two. Maybe Rosemary would be there. She would know. She would have gotten information.

He felt numb, so drained he could barely stand. Twilight had turned everything gray, but the lurid smoke and flames cast a weird, pearly light over the neighborhood. The day was over. And yet his ordeal wasn't over; it was just beginning. Wearily he wandered around the wreckage, trying to make sense of it, trying to find anything he could use, like a blanket. But he saw nothing. He wished he could grow wings and fly away. He had lost his children; his wife was missing; he lacked food and shelter and water; everything he possessed was gone and he was penniless; and soon the world would be castigating him for everything that befell everyone during these dark hours. That was more of a burden than any mortal could bear.

If he had remained true to what he learned from his strict and virtuous father, he would have a future now.

CHAPTER 23

wo policemen came the next morning. Katharine Steinmetz struggled to her feet, hobbled to the door, and let them in.

"You have to leave," said the larger one. "Fire's four blocks away."

"You'll have to help us," she said.

"We can't. We're checking every building."

"We can't walk. I'm crippled, he's confined to his chair."

The two officers fidgeted, not knowing what to do. "You'll have to make it, lady," said one.

She drew herself up, ignoring her knees. "Then we will stay. That is our choice, not yours." She turned to sit down again.

"You can't stay. We got orders—"

"Then move us."

"You can push him."

She sighed, then brightened. "If you will help us down the hill, then we will try to get away. There will be help down the street."

"Not likely. Area's been cleared out. Nothing but soldiers patrolling for looters, lady."

"Get on with it," growled Emil. "Take us down there or let us alone. We have some dying to do."

The larger officer addressed the other: "You up to it, Clancy?"

"Yup. No choice as I see it."

She had prepared for this. Her twenty plates rested in a compact metal case on Wolff's lap. Two blankets, Wolff's revolver, and a smuggled bottle of beer hidden in the blanket were the rest of the burden. She eyed her Kodet and tripod, yearning to carry the equipment, but it would be all she could do to wheel Emil to safety. Leaving behind her camera was like losing an old friend, losing a hand, losing a piece of herself, but it couldn't be helped.

The policeman wheeled Wolff while she struggled along behind. The other officer abandoned them to examine the flat upstairs. Outside, the fire thundered awesomely, its heat searing her, its own wind whipping by her. The entire sky was beclouded, gray, white, brown, purple, while ash rained over them and earsplitting cacophony assailed her ears. She had never experienced anything so terrible and malign. The officer wheeled them to level ground at the bottom of the block, even closer to the thundering fire, and then retreated upslope. To the east, a massive wall of flame rose as high as they could see. To the south, another wall of fire was roaring north. To the west lay Russian Hill. The route south was more or less level, more so than the route north. She headed south, knowing that she could not for long stay ahead of the fire at her flank.

No one was about. Here was the emptied city awaiting its doom, without a single inhabitant in sight. She pushed the squeaking wheelchair slowly, counting each step in terms of the pain it shot through her. She coughed when acrid fumes swirled past, but kept on through the eerie twilight of life. The heat from the fires blistered her hands and face, and she feared for her photographic plates.

She had gotten only half a block when three hooligans sprang from the shadows, bearing down on them. Wolff stiffened in his wheelchair.

These were misbegotten whelps out of the Barbary Coast or somewhere nearby, wearing black turtleneck shirts and dirty britches. One leered, enjoying prey so helpless. "Whatcha got in that chest?" one said, moving to snatch it from Wolff.

The bark of Wolff's revolver was lost in the thunder of the fire. Katharine saw only a puff from the blanket, and the man staggered backward, astonishment in his face. He landed on the cobblestones, flat on his back. His limbs flailed a moment and then stopped. The others, stunned, stopped dead and stared at Wolff, who swung his revolver toward them.

"Hey, we didn't mean nothing. Just curious," one whimpered.

Katharine felt sick and swallowed the nausea back down her throat. She had never seen a man die. She peered about wildly, needing soldiers, needing police, needing help, but there was none. They were in a no-man's-land. The cordons of soldiers had already cleared this area at bayonet point.

Wolff shot again, spinning another with a bullet in the shoulder. The man howled and staggered away, while the third retreated.

Katharine trembled.

"I must save two for us," Wolff said. He shoved the revolver back into the blankets again. "You want some beer?"

"I will wait until we are farther from the fire, Wolff."

She stopped wheeling, too anguished and nauseated to move.

But they were losing ground. The heat parched her, and her knees refused to function. She had reached the end of her strength. So they would die here instead of in the flat. She wished the policemen had just left them alone to meet their fate.

Then, through the choking haze, she saw an apparition. A youthful man and a woman were walking toward them. He was handsomely dressed in a tweed jacket, had a strong jaw and deep-set eyes, while she was a slim beauty with a tiny waist, an oval face with pouty lips, and a white shirtwaist with a bell-shaped skirt.

He grinned, baring white, even teeth. "Looks like you're in trouble," he said. "Maybe we can help. Not much time left."

"Yes, please," she said, the tears springing to her eyes. "We just—we just . . ."

"We saw it. Lots of ghouls around. Madam, is there any way you could get on that wheelchair?"

"It's too old; it'd collapse."

"Well, let's see. Charmian, would you hold my camera and notepad?"

The lady did.

"Sit in my lap," said Wolff, lifting the case of plates.

Gingerly, Katharine lowered herself into Wolff's lap. The wheelchair did not collapse. Wolff handed her the plates.

"That's the way," said the young man. "We'd better hurry or we'll all buy it."

She felt Wolff shifting under her, the pain of her weight upon his withered legs. But he said nothing. For her, it was heaven to sit. The man wheeled them easily, taking care not to damage the overburdened chair.

She turned to see him, discovering that he was eyeing her just as curiously as she was eyeing him. "I'm doing a bit of journalism," he explained. "Hasty assignment from *Collier's Weekly*. We live about forty miles north of here."

"North? You came here when everyone else was escaping?"

"Oh, that's the way to make a living. Yesterday morning the quake threw us out of bed. We saddled up our horses and rode up the mountain to have a look, and there was San Francisco burning. That looked like a story. We caught a train to Santa Rosa, and another down to Sausalito, and took the ferry across."

His confident strides were taking them south at a good clip, and then he turned west on a level street. She didn't know where they were, but he was outpacing the fires now. She could hardly believe her good fortune.

"You are a reporter, sir?"

"Jack. And this is my bride, Charmian. Yes, I'd call myself a correspondent, actually. I hammer a typewriter for a living. Reporting, war correspondence, short stories, and a few novels, too."

"Novels?"

"A few. What do you do?"

"I am a photographer," she said, and my friend is an engraver and etcher."

"Wolff!" the man said.

Emil turned. "You know me?"

"Who doesn't? Some of your works illustrated my little stories. And you must be Katharine Steinmetz."

She nodded, tears big in her eyes. "Who are you?" she whispered.

"London," he said.

"Jack London?"

"Lucky we ran into each other. Are those photographs?"

"Oh, yes, I took them yesterday. Not of ruins, but of people, refugees, ordinary people with terror in their faces."

"Those pictures must be the crowning achievement of your life."

"The last three are of Wolff, taken with window light. We wanted to leave the world something of him—if the plates could survive. Those are my crowning work."

"Oh, oh," whispered Charmian.

He negotiated the wheelchair up a curb, gently but powerfully carrying them westward on a magic carpet. Now and then Charmian relieved him, laughing as she pushed the chair along, block after block.

"Katharine, are you worried about those plates?" London asked.

"Desperately."

"Would you entrust them to me? We're going to head back shortly."

"Oh, yes!" she cried.

"May I use them to accompany my story? You'd be paid. I'll hold the money at Glen Ellen until you ask for it. I'll have them developed—in fact I'll watch to make sure it's done right—and then I'll hold the plates for you."

Katharine nodded, unable to speak. In ten minutes she had gone from death and loss to life and hope. Tears pooled in her eyes and slid into her bodice.

"What was that dog book of yours?" Emil asked. "I did the etchings, you know."

"*The Call of the Wild*. Yes, you did them, and that's what made that book sell so well. Isn't this a moment? Now I am paying my debt to you."

"You came here?" asked Katharine. "You came here to see the city die?"

"I don't know whether I can write about it. Words are useless. How can I put this to paper? I was telling Charmian I'm not going to do it. I've seen too much. People dying, acts of bravery, whole buildings collapsing, dynamite destroying a city faster than any fire ... people dragging their every possession, soldiers driving people with bayonets."

"Where have you been?" Emil asked hoarsely.

"We watched the city burn from the ferry yesterday afternoon. Spent the night in a doorway on Nob Hill. Then we walked down toward Market, Kearny, Union Square—it's gone, you know. Gone. One hour it was a refugee camp with army tents and food lines; a few hours later it was deserted, and the varnish was bubbling on the St. Francis. Then we watched the fire take the Mark Hopkins house, and then the rest. We started for the Ferry Building to go to Oakland, and it was our good fortune to run into you."

"It's all gone? Market? Mission? Union Square?"

"All gone. Ash and rubble. But they saved the Ferry Building. Some people are filtering over there—around the edges, the shores. Ferries are running like clockwork. Taking people out, bringing relief supplies in. Thousands have gotten out. It's free, you know. The railroads are taking refugees wherever they need to go."

They had reached the crowds again. Soldiers stood about, watching burdened people struggle west.

"I wish we could take you with us," London said. "You'll be all right here. I'll pay someone to wheel you to the Presidio."

"Oh, don't do that!"

"I will. And we'll look after your plates as if they were gold," he said. "We'll know how to reach you if you go to the Presidio."

Katharine Steinmetz rose, hugged the Londons, and knew she had received grace.

CHAPTER 24

he hard wooden floor of the hall and the lack of a pillow defied Ginger Severance's attempts to sleep, so she lay fitfully in a room that reeked of unwashed flesh, crowded by scores of others.

From a dark corner of this place an infant squalled, sobbed, and then gurgled. She peered around, discovering a blanket strung up and movement behind it. A birth. She marveled that new life would emerge in a moment of death and grief, but nature did not abandon its rhythms in the midst of hellfire, and the infant was a holy sign. A child! She wondered what sex and whether that infant would receive a special name, or a special blessing. The newborn child somehow lifted her spirits.

They had brought her here in a horse-drawn wagon, and at least she was warm and had a roof over her. The Presidio hospital, they explained, was the last fully functioning hospital in San Francisco, and was reserved for the worst cases, mostly surgeries. St. Luke's was ash. St. Mary's was in the path of the fire and its patients were being moved to the *Medoc*, a paddle-wheeler in the bay, which was being converted into an emergency hospital riding the safe water of the bay. The Mechanics' Pavilion was gone. There were emergency hospitals set up in tents around the city, some so short of water there wasn't enough for doctors to sterilize their instruments.

She was in some sort of barracks or mess hall or maybe an armory. Her knowledge of the military was so limited she really didn't know. But there were guidons on the walls, a high ceiling, high windows that let in the light of another day, and echoes. Every noise, from snoring to the tread of nurses' shoes, seemed to be amplified by the white plaster walls. Noise and odors, some of them nauseating. She desperately wanted air, just fresh air to fill her lungs. Smoke and ash and cold had taken their toll on her throat and lungs. Was there no clean air anywhere?

They came with a thick soup made of heaven-knows-what, and ladled it out to the patients, using army mess kits. The soup was flavorless but filling, and had beans in it. She felt better in spite of an awful weariness and a sense that the worst was yet to come. She sat up without ill effect, and then stood. She needed to find a latrine and discovered a line, men and women, waiting to use the only one in the building. Rank odors issued from the area.

She waited her turn, and swiftly fled an unbearable cess. A weary-looking young doctor in a rumpled suit and a nurse came an hour or so later; she had lost track of time. He was not the doctor that had found her in the night. This one took her temperature, examined her throat, and smiled.

"Normal," he said. "You just needed liquids and rest and food. We can let you go. In fact, we need to because several hundred others are waiting. You can take your blanket; you'll need it."

"But where'll I go?"

He nodded toward the nurse. "She'll talk to you about that. Things are opening up a bit."

He moved on to the next patient, but the nurse lingered.

"Miss Severance, you can stay at the Presidio for the time being. The army has a breadline, a loaf a day at least, and plenty of drinking water. But not housing. Or you can leave. It's possible now to get to the Ferry Building. It's a hot trip past smoking ruins that are dangerous, but the ferries are taking thousands of people to Oakland. They're free. The Southern Pacific's already operating free refugee trains, and the Union Pacific's cooperating. The coastal trains for San Jose and Los Angeles are leaving from Third and Townsend Streets. You can go anywhere those systems go—even to Omaha. You can go, let's see here, back to Ohio, because the eastern railroads are helping, too. You don't need a cent. At every stop, relief committees are meeting the refugee trains with food. You won't go hungry. People all over the country are helping out. We're getting some clothing in and maybe you'll find a shawl or sweater. And you have the blanket. We're encouraging people to leave, of course. But it's up to you."

"Thank you," Ginger said. The nurse had already turned to the next patient, a bearded man.

That was it. She stood, suddenly aware of being utterly at sea, not knowing what to do. She did not feel very well, but at least she was no longer fevered. And her heart thumped slowly in her chest, not like the previous night when it raced desperately. Her white cotton dress had turned grimy and was stained from grass and dirt. She wished she might be fresh and clean and smell sweet. But the foul odors of the hall permeated everything she wore.

On her own. Just like that.

She made her way out the door into dazzling sunlight. A sea breeze kept the smoke at bay, but off to the east was a gray wall that veiled hellish flame and death and ruin. So the fires still raged. She thought that most of the smoke was farther north this day. Before her, knots of humanity lounged on the Presidio grounds. Some families had made camps, set up makeshift shelters, and were waiting, waiting, waiting—for whatever came. She strolled, wanting to know where the breadlines were, the sanitary trenches, the water, the services. People stirred everywhere; thousands of them, sitting, walking, visiting with one another. People of every shape and description, old and young, infants, nervous children, weary parents.

She felt no connection with them. They were just the flotsam of disaster, as was she. She felt oddly detached from the world. For some, the disaster was a chance to talk, meet people, abandon inhibitions, and compare ordeals and impressions. But not for her. They all looked as if they had come from a different nation, or maybe a different planet. Disaster seemed to strike people differently. She could see friendships blooming around her, and maybe even romances. In times of trouble people opened themselves and shared excitement, pain, sorrow, and hope. She drifted through the crowds, ignoring the occasional glance, shunning the tentative greetings. She greeted none, and hurried away whenever someone spoke. She wondered why she was so afraid. She hadn't the faintest idea.

She knew a major decision was looming; one she couldn't put off. Should she go back to her family in Ohio? All she had to do was walk to the Ferry Building, wait in line, and embark. The Southern Pacific was helping every way it could, perhaps because it had been stung by so much criticism. Once it had been called the Octopus, but that was before Edward Harriman took it over. She wondered what she would do at home. It would be comfortable. She wouldn't have to worry about being supported. She had kind parents, amiable brothers. They would welcome her and listen raptly to her tales of the quake.

But she had come here for a purpose, had given her life to missionary work, and perhaps she should stay on. She might yet harvest many souls. But she felt insecure, and wondered what to do. Nothing seemed right. Was this cataclysm a sign that she should end her present work? She felt torn. She had never before been so pressured by the need to make decisions. Why had God hidden his will from her behind clouds of doubt?

She hiked through pale sun to the brow of a hill where the blue, mysterious Pacific lay before her, the swell of its waves rhythmic and timeless, the horizon lost in white haze. She settled there in the grasses, needing to think things through far from the crowds that jammed the army base. The ocean spoke of monotony and emptiness, and she found no beauty in its flat blue surface reaching toward a hazy blue heaven. Some loved the ocean, but she saw it as a wasteland, devoid of anything that had wrought meaning in her life. But that was what she wanted. If the prophets had discerned God's will in the stark deserts, then she might do the same near the empty sea.

The ocean stretched mysteriously into unfathomable distances. No land stood between her and the heathen Orient. This coast marked the outer extremity of her Western civilization, the rim of Christianity, and European thought and belief. For generations, Americans had migrated west, to this coast, and then were forced to turn inward upon themselves and face their own natures, for there was no more escape, and here, on the shore of the Pacific, the future halted abruptly for hundreds of thousands of people who had run out of land. Including herself. She realized that she, too, had run out of land, both physical and metaphorical. She had run out of West. Surely God existed out upon the waters, existed in Asia, but she could not go there. She would have to turn around and walk east.

She didn't know what to expect, or whether anything would come of her sojourn on the hill, but she waited expectantly, and after a while was not disappointed. A single thought coursed her mind, more and more compelling in its urgency: go back to those crowds and look again. Look at the people. That seemed strange to her; she had wandered through those refugees, observing all that there was to see. And yet something was compelling her to return and look again, this time with a more penetrating gaze. That was all. She waited a while more, and then retreated from the windswept slope, chilled even though she had wrapped herself in her army blanket. San Francisco was never warm enough for her.

She retreated, a solitary young woman walking the remote corners of the Presidio, yet lost for direction. From a low hill she could see the teeming mob of refugees, collected close to the food depots, near water and shelter, thousands upon thousands of them, and beyond, the boiling gray heavens above a city consumed by hellfire like Sodom or Gomorrah. She reached an area where boys were playing baseball, almost oblivious of the tragedy that had engulfed them. What was there to see in that?

But then she saw another youth of ten or so, huddled miserably in a ragged blanket, something desolate in his gaunt face. The stain of tears marked his cheeks.

She approached him.

"Are you hungry?" she asked.

He shook his head. "I don't know where my pa and ma are. They're lost."

"Oh, that's very hard. But you'll find them, I'm sure. Have you told people?"

"How do I do that?"

"There are registries. I hear the city's started some. The army's started some. Big ledgers. You sign your name and say where you are, and say who you're looking for."

"Yeah?"

"You go ask soldiers. Would you like me to help?"

"Naw, I'll ask, lady." He eyed her. "Thanks," he said bashfully.

The youth brightened swiftly. She watched him stride toward the field kitchen. The boy had needed much more than the Word of God.

She drew her blanket tight against the chill of the ocean breeze, and wandered among these homeless people. She discovered an old blind woman who sat on the grass, staring at nothing, deposited there by someone, her face blank with resignation, her task to endure.

"Madam, are you all right?" Ginger asked.

"Huh? I'm a bit deaf."

"Are you all right?" Ginger bellowed.

"It doesn't matter."

"Do you need anything?"

The woman nodded and whispered. "I need to go."

"I will take you, Mother."

"Thank God," the woman said. "There was no one."

She led the ancient woman to the area sheltered by brush where the slit trenches had been dug. The place appalled her, and yet it was the best the army could do.

"There is nothing here but a trench. I'll help you manage," Ginger said.

It took a while, and much arranging of clothes, and then Ginger led her back. "Is anyone looking after you? Food or water? Friends or family?"

"No," said the woman.

"I will. I am Ginger. I'll be back."

The woman nodded.

"Are you missing anyone? I can register you."

"I am all alone in this world, but maybe I will have friends in the next."

"Yes, yes!" Ginger said. "What is your name?"

"Let's see. Perhaps I will be Mary."

"Mary? Is there another?"

"Mary is a beautiful name."

"Then you are Mary, and blessed for it. I'll find friends for you," Ginger said.

A tract would not have helped Mary.

That day she discovered desperate and despairing people at every hand, separated from loved ones, sick, lame, in wheelchairs, devastated by loss of children, parents, brothers, and sisters. Insecure people fearing the future, mad people deranged by a catastrophe, lonely people aching for someone, anyone, to speak to, share with; people who could not speak English and didn't know how to get help; people so paralyzed they couldn't walk to the breadlines, get soup, get some of the used clothing mounded near the field kitchens, people dreading a night in the open in the cold Pacific wind, people too cocky, too angry, too bright; people made obnoxious by calamity.

She saw them not as souls in need of the Word, but as mortals to love and nurture. She saw that she must help them, that memorable day, not because they were fodder to bring to the maw of God, but as desperate people she loved, she ached for, she needed to help because her mission was to love and help and nurture and comfort.

Her mission and her problems no longer mattered. A free trip to Ohio no longer mattered. It would not matter what she wore, when she ate, what corner of the world she slept upon. It would not matter who she was, as long as she sensed she was doing the will of God. The Bible Society didn't matter, theology didn't matter, the pamphlets in her pocket didn't matter. From that moment forward, all that mattered was giving the love that rivered through her soul.

CHAPTER 25

. . . .

Marcia waited for Harrison until she no longer could. A wall of fire swept north toward Pacific Heights, and the soldiers had appeared, routing out people like herself who were holding on. She had heard bad things about them, but these weary men seemed to want to help. They were good-natured in spite of the exhaustion and strain in their faces.

"Time to skedaddle, ma'am," said one who arrived at her door. "Fire's three or four blocks off. We move people out by force when it's a block off, so you have a little time if you need it."

"We're packed," she said. "Where's best to go?"

"That's up to you, ma'am. Golden Gate Park, Presidio, Lafayette Square, but that's mobbed."

"Have you water? My children are desperate."

"Sure, plenty of water. Tanks of it coming in from all over. Navy's shipping it in from Mare Island." He handed her a canteen. She gave it to Harrison Jr. and then Daisy and then lifted it to her mouth and swallowed. It was not a time for niceties.

"Oh, that was good," she said.

"You know, was I fixing to leave, I'd head for the Ferry Building. You can get down Market now, burning still on both sides, but the ferries to Oakland are running I hear. And from there, you can hop a train. They're setting up regular refugee trains. No charge."

"No charge?" She marveled.

She knew, suddenly, where she would go but didn't know how. "It's burning that way," she said. "How . . ."

"Head east, past Nob—that's all ash, and Union Square, all ash. It's hot but people are doing it and the army's not stopping them now that the fire's been through. Or follow the shore. It's clear all the way along the waterfront, but it's an eight-mile walk."

"All right!"

She watched the soldier head for the neighboring houses. Most had long since been abandoned. Pacific Avenue lay silent and desolate, but the fires thundered in the near distance, like the rumble of ten thousand cannons. She knew she would never forget the noise of a city burning; the throaty crack of dynamite, the roar of towers of fire, so loud and frightening that the noise rattled her mind. The noise, even more than the sight or smell, was the thing that would stay with her until her last breath.

She marshaled her solemn children. "We're going to take the boat to Oakland," she said. "We'll walk through some burned-down areas, but we will be all right if we stay in the middle of the street."

"Is Daddy coming?"

"I hope he finds us. But we must leave."

"Can't we go to the park?"

She sighed. This was a fateful issue. "We're going to Cleveland to visit Grandma and Grandpa. Your father will find us there. I'm sure he's very busy."

She wondered if the children caught the acid in her voice.

"I like Grandma. She makes jokes," Daisy said.

Doubt struck Marcia. Was she wrong to be so angry? Wasn't Harrison just trying to provide for them and get ahead? Didn't his conduct express confidence in her strength and ability to cope with crisis? Wasn't he trusting her to nurture the children through all this? Wasn't he seeing the future, the opportunity, the prospect of a beautiful city and a delightful life, just at a time when most people were sunk into despair?

She was being too hard on Harrison, and for the sake of her children if nothing else, she should accept what he was and what he was now doing for them. Her anger at him dissolved with that, and she dared to hope that there might yet be a happy future.

She herded the children through the desolate streets, past soldiers who stared at them, past policemen who eyed her perambulator as if it contained contraband—which it did. She wished she hadn't included the wine. But no one stayed them, and they continued into a burned area, the radiant heat suffocating and frightening and boiling through their shoes, making the children cower and cling to her long skirts. Everywhere lay ruins, charred beams, crumbling brick walls, parlor stoves turned to scrap iron, smoke curling from subterranean fires that still smoldered in cellars or in the middle of the piles of rubble. How little remained of a myriad homes and businesses. She wondered if the burned areas could ever be restored, or whether the city had simply died. How could they find workers enough to clear all this rubble away, and where would they put it?

"Did people die?" asked Daisy.

"Yes, many did."

"Did they hurt?"

"I'm afraid so. There are many things we can't control. But even so, we must always do our best."

"I am thirsty," said Harry.

"There is no water now. But maybe when we get to the Ferry Building we will find some."

"Where did the city go after it died?" Daisy asked.

"People will remember all the good things and forget about the rest."

"Cities don't have souls, so it didn't go anywhere," Harrison Jr. said.

She wondered about that. Something very like a soul had vanished, something larger than the several memories of those who had lived in it. Life was such a mystery, so much of it just beyond human understanding.

She steered them down a steep slope with a buckled cable car slot in it, toward what she thought was Union Square, aware that everything looked the same, and she could not know for sure where Union Square was. Heat scorched her until sometimes she hurried past a malevolent ruin that lay cursing its own death. She did at least reach the square, sickened by the sight. Her only clue was the hulk of the St. Francis. Nothing else offered orientation. She hurried past, as one hurries past an open grave, wheeling her perambulator around rubble, smoking timbers—and a thoroughly cooked body she hoped the children didn't recognize as a body. She shuddered her way past it.

She had come too soon, or anyway, on a route that took her through streets too narrow to shield them from the heat. Once they reached the broad boulevard of Market, things would get better.

"Can we sit?" her daughter asked.

"Not here. Just a little way, two or three blocks."

The remains of Union Square depressed her. She had been all right, buoyed by the goal of reaching the Ferry Building, until she reached the square. But it had shocked her. The Bohemian Club—gone! The great hotel—gone! City of Paris—gone! Tens of millions of dollars—gone! The people—gone! She had not encountered anyone for blocks.

But on Market, she encountered a funereal parade. All sorts of people were quietly walking toward the Ferry Building, some dragging trunks or carrying portmanteaus, others staggering under heavy burdens, a few lucky ones in buggies or wagons that carried whole households. None talked. The ruin of a great city, the smoke still billowing on both sides of them, and sheer weariness silenced them.

Marcia and her children fell into the stream of humanity seeking escape. Some of the refugees rushed ahead, as if it would advantage them. Others plodded so wearily Marcia wondered whether they would make the last blocks, or survive the long wait at the Ferry Building. The human silence was eerie. The destruction they were all witnessing subdued them. The fairest of fair cities had died, and might never be reborn, and they were witnessing a type of death so large and terrible no words could fit the occasion.

The rumble of inferno and dynamite had grown so distant here that it existed only as a faint hum, a reminder that Doom had moved elsewhere, but not far away. The silence itself cast a pall over her, a net of foreboding so gloomy that she struggled with her sliding spirits. The children dragged at her skirts, not wanting to go further. She didn't either. If only she could turn around and go home. But there was none, and in sunny Oakland, just across the shimmering bay, the bright California world would restore her spirits.

They passed towering hulks of what had been the city's proudest buildings, the Call, the Spreckels, the Examiner, the crumbled Palace, and what was left of the Monadnock, one she eyed with special interest. It had defied the army's dynamiting and stood gaunt and skeletal and angry-looking. Ahead loomed the Ferry Building, its clock tower and massive sandstone facade solid and comforting, a beacon for lost souls. But the entire concourse before it was jammed with people like herself, and she had no idea how long she might have to wait, or what food and drink might be available for her fretting children. The silence caught her attention again. Had these people no voice? People whispered, nodded, gestured, but what they had witnessed along the refugee trail on Market had robbed them of tongue.

Where would they all go? How many could cross at a time? How many ferries were running? What would she do in Oakland? She drifted somberly through a somber mob, asking no one, greeting no one because it seemed wrong, like telling jokes at a funeral. She realized that many of these people were loosely organized in a line, five or six wide, leading to the terminal doors and the darkness beyond. Everywhere, she saw ownerless household goods, carriages, crates, a parrot in a cage, abandoned clothing, a seven-day clock, a parasol.

Finally she did discover one group of young men engaged in cheerful conversation, and emboldened herself to ask them a few things.

"Pardon me," she said to a rather dashing fellow, "but how do we get to Oakland?"

"Oh, wait in line half a day or more. It's free but you can take only what you can carry. Not that baby buggy."

"And after that?"

"Refugee trains. The SP will fix you a ticket to anywhere in Harrison's system. One leaves every few hours. Fast as they can get equipment in. Refugee specials. From Oakland you can go down the coast or east. You can also get suburban trains from Oakland now."

"Where does one eat or drink?"

The man shrugged and smiled.

Another dandy volunteered some information. "You got some cash? You can go across on a fishing boat. Lots of boatmen taking thousands across, furniture too, all that, but they're mining the trade for all it's worth."

"Such as?"

"Oh, ten a head. Thirty for you, and no break for the children. The usual is fifty cents."

She didn't have thirty dollars.

"Just follow the wagons and buggies," he continued. "The rich got it figured out. No lines, take what you want—and pay."

"Are they all ten dollars?"

He shrugged. "Only way is to find out."

She felt faint. The long walk through hell had taken its toll. Her children were exhausted and starting to whine. The line before the Ferry Building didn't even move. "Thank you," she whispered.

Nowhere to go; no home to return to, no way to cross the bay, no food or water.

And yet, the boatmen offered hope. She drifted through the silent mob, past old women in babushkas, squalling infants in the arms of exhausted mothers, old men lying on the dirty paving stones, tear-stained children, families huddled in blankets, Chinese women lying in a bundle of rags on the paving stones, and cocky young men. She discovered that the immediate waterfront north of the Ferry Building was not damaged. Anything reachable with seawater seemed to have survived because of the navy's fireboats. The piers stood, the embarkation areas showed no damage. Small sailing and steam craft bobbed on the tides, while their masters dickered.

She headed for the humblest craft she could find, an old fishing boat of some sort that reeked of the sea and salt and dead fish. The master, a gap-toothed, cheerful man in a sea cap and turtleneck, grinned at her.

"What is your price across the bay?" she asked.

"Two a head, ma'am, and I'll take that buggy for fifty cents."

She surveyed the scabrous old tub and the flotsam and jetsam of disaster waiting patiently aboard.

"Have you water or food?"

"Some do. They'll share. And I reckon I could catch a whale if you need one."

His cheer heartened her. She extracted the cash from her small hoard and paid without quibble. Then she herded her whimpering children up a precarious gangway and onto a foul fish-slimed deck where others rested gingerly on hatches and rails, afraid of soiling themselves.

She found a capstan and sat on it, and her children slid to the wooden deck. Then she pulled out a magnum bottle of red wine and corkscrew, and discovered she was being observed with lively interest.

Someone laughed. She laughed. They were all going to have an escape-from-hell party. She needed one.

. . . .

CHAPTER 26

All that burning day, Harrison White wrestled tables and chairs and office supplies in and out of commandeered drays and automobiles, as the seat of government retreated. From the Fairmont it headed for the North End Police Station, only to be driven from there soon after. At two, city government headed for Franklin Hall, a large building on Van Ness and Bush, a mile from fire lines and comfortingly protected by a wide boulevard. Miraculously, by four the Committee of Fifty was back at work, thanks to the astonishing leadership of Eugene Schmitz.

White didn't mind the sweat, or even the smudging of his natty suit and straw boater. The most important men in town needed him and would remember him. He counted it a victory when they began calling him Mr. White, or even Harrison. They were all leaders, but had no armies at their beck and call except for White and a few other volunteers. Swiftly the subcommittees began their work again. No sooner was the food committee resettled than it returned to the business of setting up temporary feeding stations at various precincts, and supplying them with food and utensils.

The city was now dealing with its crisis. Police were conscripting men to dig latrine trenches, organizing breadlines, and commandeering food supplies locked in groceries, which would be paid for later at market prices. Supplies were arriving from Oakland on the ferries, and this trickle of foodstuffs and clothing soon turned into a floodtide that was instantly deployed to the various camps.

Time and again, White watched the mayor assign a task: "Do it; I place you in charge," he said, handing out plenipotentiary authority to act. White pined to be assigned an important responsibility, but these burdens were laid on the prominent men of the committee.

Someone set up a registry bureau, and White immediately saw the value of it. People could record where they were, where they were going, and who they were missing. The bureau was charged with identifying the dead and tracing the missing, and soon had ledger books posted around town, including the Presidio, Golden Gate Park, and the Ferry Building. Lines formed at the ledgers, some people hunting for their families, other people announcing their presence.

That put him in mind of Marcia, Harrison Jr., and Daisy. He wondered how they were faring. Probably just fine. She was no shrinking violet, and had been reared in a family that encouraged each of its members to reach for the stars. He admired her. She would be reaching for the stars now. He heard that Pacific Avenue was being vacated by the army, and that comforted him. As far as possible, they were securing each neighborhood as it succumbed to the advancing walls of flame. Should he go to her? He agonized about it. He might yet reach her and help her move the children to the Presidio. That, not Golden Gate Park, was the place to go. Trust the army. Trust the navy. Between them, they would house and feed everyone on the post.

He agonized over that a while, and then decided that his duty lay here at City Hall. If he were to chase after her now, he would abandon a priceless opportunity to get in on the ground floor in the erection of a new city. This day would transform his life, sear the memory of Harrison White and his abilities into the minds of every important man in the city. It would all pay off for Marcia and the children. They would become part of the elite, the family of Harrison Barnes White.

Still, the decision disturbed him, and he felt a malaise undermine his commitment to the future.

Once City Hall was safely ensconced in Franklin Hall, there was less to do, so White lobbied his plan to redesign the city. He had no problem finding listeners, mostly among those taking brief breaks from their toil. They all were aware that the city was turning into a wasteland. There would be no reason to keep the existing street grid. A new and better plan was needed at once.

"There's really no time," he explained to a merchant. "It has to be done now, before people rebuild. There should be a master plan on the mayor's desk this minute. Otherwise the chance'll be lost. A farsighted administration would freeze rebuilding, adopt a plan, and stick to it."

"But what of the property owners?" asked the skeptic.

"The government has the power of eminent domain," said White.

"We have more important things to do," his auditor said.

That struck White as obtuse. Didn't anyone in the place care about the future?

He discovered, to his great satisfaction, that the food committee had not neglected the government, and that a field kitchen was being set up at Franklin Hall to feed them all. It paid to be among the movers and shakers, he thought.

Then, late in the afternoon, came good news. Schmitz announced to all in the hall that the next morning the water company would be able to supply water from the Lake Honda Reservoir to the Western Addition. The pumps that lifted water from Lake Merced to Lake Honda were functioning, moving three million gallons a day. A cheer arose. That would alleviate one crucial problem, the thirst of the multitudes, though it wouldn't help the firefighters much.

Then, late in the day, James Phelan returned from a tour of the city. Schmitz had assigned his erstwhile opponent the task of keeping an eye on the rampant army, and now the wealthy and powerful Phelan walked to the lectern to deliver his opinion. The hall quieted.

The weary man ran a hand through his hair, trying to form sentences that didn't seem to rise to his mind.

"We have lost civilian control of San Francisco. Without authority, the military has taken over," he said. "General Funston is commanding from Fort Mason, and no longer even consulting with us. Martial law has not been declared and the army has no business being here in violation of the Constitution, at least without our direction.

"But there is a good side to all this. We can thank the army—and increasingly the navy—for its efforts. Naval fireboats have largely saved our waterfront, which is crucial for supplies and transportation. The navy is bringing us thousands of gallons of potable water. The Presidio is the most important relief depot available. The army is distributing every blanket, tent, and ration it can lay hands on, along with its medical supplies, surgeries, field kitchens, and munitions. Company B, Hospital Corps, has set up an emergency hospital under Captain Truby. Lieutenant Colonel Brechemin has secured a circus tent and set it up at the Presidio for hospital use to replace the medical supply depot destroyed by the quake. Medical supply officers in St. Louis are shipping nineteen carloads of supplies, an allowance that will care for sixty thousand people for four months, and the first five cars will be en route in two or three days. Lieutenant Colonel George Torney has been placed in charge of sanitary arrangements and, with utmost skill, has supervised sanitation work throughout the parks and city, no doubt sparing us from epidemics. The army has saved many lives and sheltered many people." He smiled wanly. "At the Presidio several children have come into this world, including an infant who now bears the name Presidio, and a girl called April."

He swiftly interrupted the appreciative laughter. "But there are two problems. One is that many enlisted men are terrorizing and vandalizing the city. They were sent to protect people and property, but I've been hearing numerous reports that they themselves have stolen property, have been drinking spirits, and worse, shooting a number of citizens who were doing nothing more than returning to their own dwellings. Some of the soldiers seem incapable of distinguishing between looters and people seeking to obtain their own property from their own homes.

"There are reports that a significant number of enlisted men are engaged in wholesale pillaging; that valuables have been seen leaving the deserted areas for points unknown. I listened to several women who said they were assaulted at gunpoint; several witnesses who described episodes of wanton shooting of innocent people; and several more witnesses who saw civilians being brutalized and bayoneted by soldiers simply because they lagged, or were annoying to the military. That must stop, and I recommend to Mayor Schmitz an envoy to the general to call a halt to this."

Schmitz nodded.

"The other problem is that army demolition crews are ill-trained and clearly doing more damage than the fire, destroying structures that might be saved. Over and over, they begin a fire line intended to halt one blaze, only to be overwhelmed by other fires coming from one or another flank, their entire effort for nothing. Worse, they know so little about demolition that it is taking them numerous charges to collapse a building, and oftentimes they leave the ruins and neighboring structures ablaze, thus hastening the fire. They are awaiting naval reinforcements trained to use guncotton, but so far it the task of building fire lines has fallen to the army. They need direction; they need experts who can show them how to place charges against load-bearing walls and supports. They need someone with enough judgment to leave some relatively fireproof buildings alone, and the strategic sense to pull back and execute a fire line that will work, and won't be overwhelmed. That issue needs to be addressed with General Funston."

Phelan nodded curtly and left the podium, leaving in his wake a growing thunder of resentment. Whatever good Funston's minions were doing in the refugee centers was more than undone by his amateur sappers and out-of-control troops.

Mayor Schmitz returned to the podium. "Where's that young architect?" he roared.

For a moment, White froze.

"White, that was his name."

White waved a hand.

"You're going to General Funston and volunteer your expertise. Show those sappers where the load-bearing walls are. Are you an engineer?"

"Trained, yes, sir, but not degreed in it."

"Trained is enough. I appoint you to lay this issue before the general, and Mr. Phelan, I would like you to go with this young man and address the issue of his troops. I put you in charge of this. I will give you a pass. Take an automobile. Do not fail."

Stunned, Harrison Barnes White headed for the doors, where a city-commandeered touring car awaited, along with its owner. James Phelan, one of the Committee of Fifty, strode beside him, weariness in his gait. They settled themselves in the open car, instructed the driver, and found themselves traveling down Van Ness to Fort Mason, which lay at its north end.

"Who are you, again?" Phelan asked.

"Harrison White, sir. Architect. Monadnock Building for the Laws. I volunteered."

"You think the United States Army is going to let you advise them?"

White shrugged. "I can show them the load-bearing walls and posts and beams. I know nothing about explosives."

"That's not what I asked."

White realized that Phelan was irascible, worn out, and probably unhappy with his partner on a delicate mission to tell the United States Army that it was running amok.

"Sorry, sir."

"You'd better let me talk to Funston. I've met the man. He's all will, and likely to skewer you with every word from your mouth."

White choked back his own anger. Phelan was dismissing him for a callow youth. "I've been commissioned by the mayor—"

"I know." Phelan sighed and sunk deep into the leather seat, his face a mask. They clattered past the palatial mansions, up a wide and crowded avenue littered with debris from the quake, and finally reached the trim greensward of Fort Mason, which looked like a bastion under seige. A guard directed them to Funston's command.

They left the driver with orders to wait, and approached, through a sea of men in mustard-colored uniforms.

"We're here to see the general," Phelan announced to the adjutant. "I'm James Phelan and this is, ah—"

"Harrison White."

"He's busy."

"We've been delegated by the mayor to discuss certain matters."

"I said he's busy. He has a thousand soldiers patrolling the city every hour, he's running out of munitions and foodstuffs, and he has no time."

"Ask him."

There was something in Phelan's voice that caught the aide's attention. Silently the man retreated to the inner sanctum, from which a high, nasal voice occasionally erupted. And then the aide, a lieutenant, returned.

"He's busy. If you wish to see him before he leaves for dinner with Mrs. Funston, he will give you a minute."

"We wish to see him now," Phelan said. Angrily he pushed past the adjutant, beckoning White to come with him, and entered the lair of the ranking federal officer who, for the moment, owned and operated San Francisco.

CHAPTER 27

General Funston surveyed the two civilians at his door. A captain stood at his side.

"I see," he said. He rose from his desk and nodded them in.

To White, he looked just as a weary general officer of the United States Army should: compact, bristly, his attire wilted and his face red-blotched and showing shadows of fatigue.

"I can spare one minute," Funston said, almost amiably.

"I'm James Phelan, and—"

"Yes, I know."

"—this young man is Harrison White. We've been delegated by the mayor to discuss some things."

"Well?" Funston looked impatient. A city map, streaked with grease pencil lines as if it were a battle plan, lay on his oak desk.

"We'd prefer to address you privately, sir."

"Oh, this is Captain Coleman, who's responsible for our demolition efforts. He'll stay, if you don't mind."

Phelan nodded. "The committee has two concerns, sir. One is that some of your troops are running rampant. We've received numerous reports that soldiers are pillaging property—including relief supplies arriving on Southern Pacific boxcars—drinking the spirits they confiscate. I'm sorry to report that some innocent civilians have been shot. They were doing nothing more than collecting valuables from their own homes. We want these drumhead executions stopped cold."

"And how do you know this?"

"Southern Pacific officials. Neighbors, sir. Witnesses. Several people, in utter shock, have come to us to complain—bitterly, I might add."

Brigadier General Funston, one-hundred-twenty-pound national hero, Medal of Honor winner in the Philippines, and a man not to be trifled with, looked impatient. "First, Mr. Phelan, I doubt that such reports can be trusted. I command disciplined troops and their orders are clear. Second, these reports are always exaggerated, especially by calculating civilians with nefarious plans of their own, and are always used to pressure the army into abandoning its mission. Sorry."

"We have witnesses; we've taken down their reports, sir. We want it stopped. There's no need to take the life of any innocent person. A little checking and caution are all that's needed."

Funston fumed. "This is war, sir. Or very like it. Chaos reigns. I will not call off our men; in fact, I'll tell them to redouble their vigilance.

You've been listening to clever schemers. Looters are to be shot on sight, just as Mayor Schmitz proclaimed. I received confirmation of my initiative from President Roosevelt, through Admiral Goodrich. His flagship's in touch with Mare Island, which has a wire to Oakland. The Pacific Fleet's arrived here, you know. We are delegated to keep order and we shall. Henceforth, by orders of the President, I am in command."

"We would like you to investigate, General."

"What else did you and your committee have in mind, Mr. Phelan?"

"The dynamiting. It's not effective, and it's destroying the city faster than the fires. I've toured the fire fronts and find that the squads set more fires than they put out; destroy relatively fireproof buildings; that they are inexperienced, and require several charges to demolish a building, and don't know how to set a charge to keep flaming debris from landing on other structures. That's what this young man is here for. He's an architect with an engineering background and can assist your men to place charges on load-bearing walls."

Funston glared for an endless moment that ticked along like a bomb fuse. "You are instructing Captain Coleman and the army, sir?" He glanced at White. "Does this young man know the use of munitions?"

"No, sir," White said.

"I see. But you presume to instruct the army. You will tell our sappers what to do. You will instruct the naval demolition squad that's en route. Your committee doesn't feel the army is doing its duty or displaying competence, is that it?"

White chose silence, but Phelan's dander was up. "We know what we see, sir, and it's obvious that you're using crews that lack experience. The defense lines are poorly chosen and overrun by fires every time. And it is taking too many charges to level buildings."

"They're *my* lines, Mr. Phelan." The general turned to the captain. "Captain Coleman?" he said.

"We were just discussing the final solution," the captain said neutrally. "We're going to blow a fifty-yard trench down Van Ness roughly to Mission, out Mission to Dolores, and then down Dolores. Van Ness is a hundred-ten-feet wide, and we'll dig the trench east of it. No fire will leap it. That will save the city."

"A fifty-yard trench! On Dolores too? What'll be left? Does that include the old mission?"

"Whatever it takes to stop the fires, we will do. That's a line we can hold, no matter which way the wind blows, and we have barely time to do it."

Funston added his own comments. "If you don't like it, Mr. Phelan, blame it on the Schmitz administration. It had all the time in the world to strengthen the water system, install a saltwater backup. It's your water supply that collapsed, not the army's. Your lines are broken where they cross the fault. Excellent planning! Blame the utility, or your city engineer, who had reasons not to do a thing." He glared. "Don't blame the army.

"Let me tell you how things are: naval tugboats are bringing us powder from the California Powder Company at Pinole. Mare Island is sending a demolition squad and all the guncotton the navy can find. We're lining up howitzer batteries on Van Ness to blow away structures if we run out of time. You know, you're right in a sense. Our demolitions weren't effective against steel-framed buildings downtown, so we're moving our operations. We can knock down housing and we'll do so. And it doesn't matter whose housing. That's the genius of the captain's plan." He turned to White. "You have any better ideas, young man?"

White shook his head.

Funston continued relentlessly. "Right now, gents, the United States Army is shipping tents for a hundred thousand, blankets for a hundred thousand, bedsocks the same. Your army is collecting every last bit of food, wheat, canned goods, civilian donations, and setting up relief centers all over town. Every dray, every field kitchen, every wagon and ambulance we possess is in service. Our men have suffered injuries. Burns, concussions, exhaustion, disease. Two naval lighters are bringing in drinking water, five thousand gallons a crack so you civilians don't perish. An entire field hospital will be sent from Washington. As of this afternoon, I'm in direct contact with Washington. My Signal Corps has run a line from here to the Ferry Building, which is connected to the Oakland cable terminal. Right down Bay Street, through smoking ruins. Do you know what a feat that was? They made use of every scrap of wire, old telephone lines, electric lighting lines dangling from poles, any old wire lying on the street. But now, because of heroic work by Sergeant Oldham and two linemen, I am in contact with the secretary of war. I have given this city a voice. Is that enough, Mr. Phelan? Perhaps we've missed a trick or two?"

Phelan stood his ground. "We appreciate that. But we would like the looting and acts of violence to be stopped and for your officers to assume more control of your men."

"Thank you. We'll do what is necessary. Good afternoon, gentlemen," Funston said.

Phelan smiled thinly. "General, we're grateful for what you're doing. We'd like to be consulted, however. The committee feels that it is in the dark. We are the civil government, for the time being, appointed by the mayor."

"If you had become the mayor, Mr. Phelan, it might be different," said Funston. "Now if you will excuse us . . ."

Phelan took White by the elbow and steered him out, past an astonishing fire defense perimeter that Funston was throwing up around the old post. Their driver leaped out, cranked his machine to life, and then drove them down Van Ness, past the mansions of many of the Committee of Fifty, and back to Franklin Hall.

"That didn't go well," said White, over the clatter of the machine and the distant roar of fire and dynamite.

"Funston's tired," Phelan said. "He may regret some of his decisions." He turned to White. "Have you been here long?"

"Since the turn of the century, Mr. Phelan."

"And you're an architect. With a family?"

"Yes, Marcia, my wife, and two children."

"And you've seen to their safety."

"I'm going to. I wanted to help out."

"Yes. You're civic-minded. Where are they?"

"On Pacific Avenue."

"That burned this noon."

"Oh, we arranged to meet later."

"Where?"

"At, ah, the Presidio. I suppose your family's been taken care of."

"It has. They're down the peninsula. I suppose that's one of the perquisites of wealth. I was able to hire an automobile and do it."

"I intend to go far, myself, so I can do the same for my family."

"Yes, I can see that. You've made yourself useful to the city's leaders."

"Yes, sir. And I've talked to the mayor about redesigning the city after the fire. So much could be improved, you know. The Burnham master plan doesn't mean much anymore."

"You've talked about that? *Now?* And what did he say?"

"He referred me to his clerk. I left my name there, and said I would be setting up my own firm, and I'd begin drafting some plans. I'd like to run a mall from Union Square down to Market. It's all gone; we can start over, you know."

Phelan nodded.

"City planning's the future, Mr. Phelan. This fire's an opportunity to turn San Francisco into the most beautiful and comfortable and easily negotiated city on earth."

"How's your wife?"

The question surprised White. "Marcia? Why, she's a regular trooper, sir. We met at the Ecole des Beaux Arts."

"How are your children?"

"Oh, they're weathering it."

"They have the necessary things, of course."

"Oh, yes, Marcia has a whole houseful of blankets, food, what have you."

"Do they miss you?"

"No, they're too well behaved for that."

"They must be amazing young people, Mr. White, not to miss their father in a moment of crisis."

"They're understanding, Mr. Phelan. They know I'm helping out here so that we'll have a more secure future. I told them that crisis is opportunity. You know, when things are in flux, that's the chance of a lifetime."

"Yes, things are in flux," Phelan said, settling back into the leather seat. "I am seeing how earthquakes and calamities can change lives, and bring out the essence of people."

"It's certainly changing my life, sir."

"I imagine so, for good or ill. I have no way to reach Mrs. Phelan for the moment, but she's out of harm's way with friends in Burlingame. My home's in the Mission District—or was. I took my family to Golden Gate Park and pitched two tents—and then got an automobile and drove them out of the city. It could be wonderful there, quiet, sunny April days, plenty of food and water, beds to sleep in. My wife at my side, my children around me. I miss her, you know. So much I can't describe it. But meanwhile I have four hundred thousand members of my family to look after because I was called by Mr. Schmitz to do it. It is my duty and I will."

White thought that Phelan was a romantic, calling the whole of the city his family. White knew himself to be more realistic.

They pulled up at Franklin Hall. The motor coughed and died, shaking the automobile for a moment.

"Well, White, what are you going to do next?"

"Volunteer to help Mr. Schmitz, sir. The more he knows what I can do, the better."

"You're a strong young man, White, but I'm a little concerned that your ambitions are trumping your good upbringing."

"I try to keep everything in good order, sir."

"Perhaps your duty is at the Presidio with your family."

"They're getting along. Trust the army. Marcia knows I'm helping out here for the sake of our future."

"Her future, or yours, White?"

The remark puzzled Harrison White.

CHAPTER 28

. . . .

Carl Lubbich stood alone before the ruins of his home, the deathtrap of his children. The fire was coming and he had to leave. It didn't matter where he went; he had no nest. He began trudging north, indescribably weary, the weight of a doomed city on his shoulders. Could he have done things differently? Yes. Could he, as city engineer, had kept this great city from its trial by fire? Probably. A municipal saltwater pumping station, as backup, was all that was needed. Could he, as the regulator of the utility, have required its directors to spend money on a quake-resistant system? No, not so long as Schmitz and Ruef opposed it and protected their cronies.

He was not alone in all this. But it didn't matter now. Hundreds of millions of dollars of property were lost or soon would be unless a miracle saved San Francisco. His carefully orchestrated neglect had yielded death, disease, discomfort, desolation for hundreds of thousands of mortals, people like himself. It was too heavy a burden to bear. He wished the quake had taken him as brutally as it had taken his children.

He passed through streets strewn with rubble, walked by pairs of soldiers who eyed him passively, walked past charred ruins radiating vicious heat; walked north, vaguely knowing where he was going. Not to the Presidio or the park, but to the Fairmont Hotel, City Hall for now, for reasons he couldn't fathom. Better for him to walk south down the peninsula, flee this charnel house, run to the farthest corner of the world. But he couldn't run from himself, not even if he should reach some desert place, or Pitcairn's Island, or Bora Bora, or New Zealand. Nob Hill was a long way from the Mission District and he was exhausted, but still he walked through a dead city.

He reached the grand hotel at dusk. Several automobiles were parked there, ready for city business, some with their carbide headlamps burning. Dull light gleamed through windows above. The work of the Committee of Fifty never ceased. He thought maybe he could curl up somewhere there, maybe in one of the unfinished rooms. It would be shelter of a sort. He smelled food. Maybe the City Hall had its own commissary.

"Lubbich!"

The familiar voice rose from a darkened motoring coach.

Reluctantly Lubbich steered toward the curb.

"I thought you might come. Get in."

Lubbich opened the door and pulled it shut. Glass windows sealed the tonneau from the world, and from the driver.

Abe Ruef shook his hand. "I heard about your children. I am sorry. I hope Rosemary is all right."

"She was stricken. I've lost her in Golden Gate Park somewhere."

"You'll find her. We've all lost many things. I've lost my house and other holdings. But my family's well."

Lubbich sank into the plush seat, glad to be off his feet. His weariness consumed him and he feared he would fall asleep. He struggled to stay alert.

"My friend, you face some difficulties ahead."

Lubbich nodded. He didn't feel like talking.

"Before my house burned, I removed some files. Some of them are here." Ruef waved a languid hand toward pasteboard cartons that lay about his feet. "I have flimsies of almost everything you wrote officially."

Lubbich couldn't even remember what was in them. It didn't surprise him that the gray eminence of San Francisco would have such flimsies. One copy of his reports and letters had gone to Schmitz, and now Ruef was holding those in his hand. Lubbich peered at the darkly handsome Ruef, wondering what would come next.

"There will be investigations. The water mains. Rudolph Spreckels has underwritten an investigation of the Schmitz administration. He's raised a hundred thousand dollars to do it. That's a lot of money. Now they will be looking at you."

Lubbich nodded, too weary to talk.

Ruef waved the folder. "But who's to say there's anything wrong? City Hall is rubble. These are the only surviving copies of your entire correspondence."

"I don't remember what's in them."

"Oh, it doesn't matter. Mostly routine things."

"You're leading toward something, Ruef."

"Well, if you don't remember what's in these papers, I might remind you. Some would interest the Spreckels group."

"It's too late." Lubbich wanted to get out, but the warm seat seemed to pin him in place.

"No, not at all. Many things. Your response to underwriters' criticism of the water system. Your recommendation that certain contractors, who were not low bidders, do work for the city. Your certification that the Pleasant Valley reservoir system was sound. Your rejection of Fire Chief Sullivan's recommendation that a saltwater backup system be undertaken immediately. Your rejection of Sullivan's request for more emergency cisterns. There's more, of course. Years of it."

Lubbich didn't have anything to say, so he sat silently. Neither the Schmitz administration nor the water company had been willing to spend money to bring the system up to standard or deal with a quake that might never happen. And the administration had its favorite contractors, whose work was to be preferred over all other bidders.

"I'm thinking of destroying these files. They are of little value," Ruef said. "But I thought I would hold on to them for a while."

"Why?"

"The failure of the water system will be looked into—and soon. I would hate to see the Schmitz administration blamed for what was really the dereliction of the water company. I'm hoping you'll place the blame where it belongs when you testify."

"That's it?"

"That's it."

"What does it matter?"

"These records will be destroyed—in the great fire, of course. You will not suffer more than a light rebuke."

Lubbich grunted.

"Think about it. Now, if you don't mind, I'll be off. You're no doubt hungry. There's a canteen in the hotel."

Lubbich, with some difficulty, stepped into the whirlwind and clambered up the stairs. He entered a ballroom made eerie by the light of carbide and coal oil lamps which cast cold light and long shadows everywhere. He found the canteen, a table laden with odds and ends of food, and helped himself to some bean soup, bread, and coffee. No one paid attention.

He wandered among the desks in the ballroom, finding the one marked Water Supply. A clerk of some sort was present, working with some sort of schematic of the water system.

"How is it going?" Lubbich asked.

"Who are you?"

"Lubbich, city engineer."

The man scrutinized him. "We have a little water to the Western Addition. Oakland sent over a hundred men, its whole water department. They're plugging up a lot of small leaks. But we won't have water from Lake Merced until tomorrow."

"Tomorrow'll be too late."

The man nodded. "Those lines went right over the faults. Did you know that?"

"Yes," Lubbich said.

"It's a scandal."

"Yes."

"Someone'll end up in San Quentin."

"Yes."

"Have you a schematic? We've drawn one from memory. Utility and city workers helped. But we can't remember where all the gates are. We're supposed to help the utility shut them."

"Burned up in City Hall."

"Where've you been?"

"Out at the reservoirs."

"How can we get hold of you?"

"Is there a place in here I can rest?"

The man shrugged. "Big hotel."

Lubbich found his way to the dais and parted a curtain behind it, discovering a dozen exhausted men curled up on the hardwood floor. He joined them, misery in his every bone. But he was warm enough and had a roof over him. He felt an oppression upon him, a heaviness he couldn't bear, so heavy he could barely breathe.

He had failed four hundred thousand people, so that Schmitz and Ruef could get rich, so that the water company owners would not have to bother with redundant systems that would cope with disaster—and thus get richer. They had paid him well to make sure nothing was done, contracts went to the right companies, and criticism was turned with official reports. Yes, they had made Carl Lubbich comfortable.

He wondered how many had died from fire, or from exposure to the elements. How many were sick from smoke inhalation. How much property had succumbed to dynamiting and flame.

He wondered how many treasures had vanished forever: he knew the Sutro Collection was gone. It had contained an incredible collection of rare books that Adolph Sutro had collected over ten years, all of it stored in the Upham Building and a warehouse. They included four original Shakespeare folios, one of them scorched by the London fire; a nearly complete set of Ben Jonson folios; prayer books and hymnals used by Charles II; early Hebrew scrolls; some Gutenburg printing; thousands of manuscripts from Bavarian monasteries; a vast Mexican archive dealing with early California; original sources dealing with the French Revolution, and much more. All gone. Lubbich had not started the fires, but he had failed to protect these treasures.

The Sutro Collection was only one of the losses. He thought of the Bohemian Club art, the treasures in the mansions on Nob Hill, the ordinary comforts of ordinary people, precious photographs of loved ones, love letters bound in ribbons, a thousand dogs and cats and canaries that had brightened the lives of their owners. All burned. He thought of the goods in the shops, the ready-made clothing, the pottery, the furniture, the furs, the china and silver, the paper money, hardware, dry goods, carriage furniture, confections, lumber, nails, roses, pews, stained glass, sacred vessels . . .

The weight of it became too heavy, suffocating him as he lay in the shadowed corner of the ballroom. He could not bear the weight and squirmed under it. He could not rest. His bones ached. His body and soul lay bruised.

"We've got to clear out," someone was saying. "Nob Hill's going to burn. Franklin Hall's where we're going. Everybody out. Fire's coming."

So the City Hall would decamp once again. He had gotten only one or two hours of rest after the longest, most terrible day of his life.

He arose, sweating, and gathered his courage to walk through the ballroom and into the night. He didn't plan to go to Franklin Hall. Not yet. St. Ignatius, the largest church in the city, lay in ruins, but St. Mary's Cathedral stood. He would go there.

CHAPTER 29

Lubbich struggled down Van Ness, marveling that the street remained jammed in the middle of the night. Pedestrians, horse carts, drays, wagons, and automobiles paraded by ceaselessly. Such was his weariness that he could barely walk. If any of these people passing in the dark knew who he was, and the nature of his dereliction, they might tear him to pieces.

The Gothic cathedral loomed blackly out of the night, but its steps were crowded. He worked through the mass of humanity, through the great doors, and entered a gloomy nave, lit only by the wavering glow of votive candles. But these were light enough. He sensed that people jammed the place, and as his eyes adjusted, he did discover them wedged into every pew and filling the aisles. Some were there to pray. Others had found sanctuary against the chill night. The air was oppressive, the scent of a thousand breaths mixed with the smoke of candle wax, and the acrid smell of a burning city.

Lubbich worked his way forward, only to discover that the silent crowd even occupied the steps of the high altar beyond the communion rail, while above, the redwood Christ rose before him. A faint hum filled the nave, the click of beads, murmured prayer, the coughing and sniffling of the desperate and tearful multitudes. Someone made room for him and he sank onto a step, so close to the altar that he felt he was trespassing.

He slouched miserably, his mind blank, his lips unable to recite the simplest prayer. He grew aware of the desperation and terror of these people, their supplications and hope, their faith and tears. He peered furtively about, seeing the glint of tears in the faces lit by votive candles. Above, the vaulting roof vanished into darkness, and he wondered whether another, final jolt would send it all tumbling down on these anguished thousands.

He wasn't a good Catholic. His family has barely maintained its ties to the Church. In Milwaukee, the real religion had been Progressive politics and then socialism. His father had no mysticism in him and was impatient with the reactionary church, but didn't sever ties, mostly because his mother attended Mass each day, even when the thermometer plunged below zero. Lubbich had often wondered about his name, which he was sure was Jewish. But the various Germanic nations, like the United States many generations later, had been a great melting pot, and at various times a haven for Jews. Lubbich didn't know. He thought his father or grandfather might, but they had put Europe and the past behind them. This was America.

And now the whole weight of America crushed him. He sat miserably. What could he do? Ask forgiveness for destroying San Francisco and its countless treasures? Oh, the earthquake had done much of that, and fires would have destroyed much of the city even if the firemen had water. Nor had he been the only one. If he were to parcel out blame he would include Ruef and Schmitz and their allies, and the greedy owners of the privately held water company. But that didn't help him or assuage his grief.

He couldn't manage a prayer, especially to a God whose very existence he questioned. But as he sat, he felt himself surrender. He had no will left, no courage, no hope, no cheer, and no love. At last, he peered up through the smoke to the redwood Christ above. "Do with me what you will," he muttered. "I have no life left."

That was the ultimate truth. He had no life left.

He stayed there until dawn, oblivious of the shifting crowds, sorrowing for his dead children, conjuring up their images. He blamed himself for their deaths. He could have stayed in Milwaukee. He wished he would weep, wished he could die, wished he could start anew, like an infant. He could not face any of those who had loved him. Not his father or mother or family; not Rosemary. Not his friends or co-workers. Not a priest. He could not face himself.

Dawn crept in slowly through stained glass windows, tinting the nave bloodred and coloring the smoke high above the huddled mass of tearful people. He rose stiffly, knowing what he must do. There was only one thing to do. It would have been better for him to be cast into the sea with a millstone about him than to have been born Carl Lubbich.

He struggled around innumerable people in the aisles, some of them sleeping in that haven of warmth, and emerged into a smoky gray morning, the dawn hidden behind angry black walls of smoke that rose northeast, east, southeast, and south of him. The closest flames would arrive at this cathedral this day unless the wind turned, and this great church, too, would die with the city.

He felt hollow. He discovered he wasn't hungry but needed water. He made his way to Franklin Hall, close by, past somnolent people who trudged silently this way and that, never speaking, weariness in their faces. Few had slept.

There were guards posted at the ornate hall, and they questioned him.

"I'm Lubbich, city engineer."

That got him in. He found the atmosphere within quite the opposite of the weariness outside. Here men worked frenetically, mostly dealing with information: relief supplies from the northern counties had landed at the Hyde Street Pier. Send the drays. Send flour to the Lafayette Square field kitchen. They're out. Find quicklime. Sanitation threatened by decaying bodies and rats. Two carloads of bagged flour trapped on siding at Burlingame. Tell the SP to free them or send wagons.

Almost in a dream state, Lubbich wandered among these tireless people, marveling that some had worked straight through the night, after removing from the Fairmont, in their great-hearted effort to feed and shelter and transport the helpless.

He did not go to the desk where others labored to restore the city water supply. He wandered instead toward the Relief of Famine desks, several of them, looking for young Rudolph Spreckels, whose gargantuan efforts were somehow putting food into the mouths of all who asked for it.

Lubbich stood on one foot and then another, watching this rich man function. Spreckels had gathered a fleet of drays and carts and trucks, which were moving food from depots on the waterfront, and from a SP warehouse, out into the stricken city.

The moment came when Spreckels, dark and blocky and worn, saw Lubbich. "Yes?" he asked sharply.

"Sir, this is not the time . . . but later I would like to speak to you."

"Well, what is it? There is only now."

"I . . . am the city engineer, Carl Lubbich."

"You," said Spreckels. "You. Why are you here?"

"To confess that I have done wrong."

Spreckels seemed nonplussed. "I don't have time for confessions."

"The fires. They are my fault."

"What?"

"You are investigating the mayor, yes?"

Spreckels nodded, suddenly alert.

"I will tell you everything. I was a part of it—for greed, for sin. All this—the fires—are on my soul. I knew the water supply would not survive a quake."

Spreckels stared, turned to a subordinate, whispered something, and then steered Lubbich to the front of the hall, through a fire exit into a hallway, and then into a small office. Several men dozed within.

"Gents, I need this room for a few minutes," Spreckels said in a voice that brooked no resistance. Yawning men slowly plucked themselves up and vanished. Spreckels closed the door.

"Make it fast, Mr. Lubbich."

But Lubbich couldn't speak. "I—I can't."

"You were going to tell me about the water supply."

"I did the bidding of Mr. Ruef, and was paid for it. . . ."

Spreckels listened, intently.

But every thought fled the mind of Carl Lubbich. "Some other time," he mumbled, and retreated toward the door.

"Some other time, then." Spreckels sounded annoyed. "You'll be subpoenaed anyway."

"I burned San Francisco."

"No, Mr. Lubbich, you didn't burn San Francisco. But you helped. You were the city's expert, responsible for making sure the utility could reliably supply water to a large population, even in the midst of disaster. Our fire chief, Dennis Sullivan, got nowhere with his saltwater backup plan because of you. The insurance underwriters got nowhere because of you. A lot of Abe Ruef's cronies got utility company contracts at inflated prices for work on the water system—because of you."

"Yes. That's what I came to tell you. Because of me—" He couldn't finish again. "I will help you any way I can. Then you can send me to jail."

"What was your price?"

"A hundred dollars a week in a brown envelope."

Something softened in Spreckels. "We'll see, Lubbich. Your testimony would be valuable. You're the first person to come to us. That speaks well of you."

"You knew everything."

"A lot. You lived high. Had, or have a mistress. Visited the French restaurants. More than a city engineer could afford. But City Hall's in ruins and we know of no other records—unless Ruef has some."

"He does. He wants me to blame the water company for everything."

"And if you don't?"

"He didn't say. He has flimsies of everything I wrote, every city contract I approved."

"But you came to me."

"Yes, sir, I came to you. The city is dying because of me."

"No, you are too hard on yourself. You didn't engineer this system. It was installed long before Schmitz hired you, flawed before you got here."

"You don't have to defend me."

"I'm not. I'm looking at all the causes. Corruption was only one of many. Stupidity was a factor."

"My life is over. My father is a city official in Milwaukee. He would be ashamed of me. My wife . . ."

"You lost your children."

"Yes, the house caved in."

"Mr. Lubbich, you go comfort your wife. I am sorry about your children."

"They didn't deserve death; but I do."

Spreckels stared at space for a moment. "You know, Mr. Lubbich, a man can acknowledge his failures. You've done that. A man can repent. You've done that. A man can try to undo the damage he's done. You came to me to do that. A broken man can start over. You are doing that."

"Not I, sir. It is too late."

Spreckels sighed. "It may be at that. There's nothing we can do for months, maybe years. Rebuilding the city comes first. But the investigation will reopen some day. You will help us?"

Lubbich nodded.

Spreckels offered a hand. Lubbich stared at it and shook it. The sugar magnate hastened back to his work, and Lubbich drifted through the Thursday morning. He would have to find Rosemary and tell her everything. *Everything.* And help her if he could. She had lost two children and would learn now that her husband wasn't worthy of her. She would have nothing left, but none of it had been her fault.

CHAPTER 30

Willis Hart hurried toward Fifth and Harrison, but was lost. He no longer recognized either street. Nothing was left to guide him. What had been rows of cheap frame houses and flats were now rubble and ash, the area a desolate black wasteland without a landmark to guide him. It stank of smoke, radiated fierce heat, and looked sinister and forbidding.

He was trying to locate his small apartment, one of twelve in a frame building that had burned only an hour after the quake. Perhaps something remained of his possessions, and he wished to find them. In particular, he hoped to recover a pair of photographs of his parents in a glass and metal frame. Maybe he could find that, though the chances weren't much good. Both his parents had died in a typhus epidemic in Carbondale, Illinois, in 1899, and the photos were his only memento of them.

Hart was an insurance adjuster for Waterford Casualty Company, and knew the capriciousness of fire. He had often marveled how fire touched one thing and not another, how fires left treasures behind for people who had imagined everything had been lost. Maybe he could recover a few things, especially since his apartment had burned so early, before the massive plumes had turned into giant chimneys sucking gales of air into their maw while consuming everything in their path. But Fifth and Harrison had vanished. Was he on Sixth or Eighth? Was that Harrison, or was it Folsom or Shipley or Bryant?

It had been a fool's mission. He could not step off the cobbles into that malevolent hot mass of ash and brick and rubble. Nothing made sense. He had come all the way from Golden Gate Park only to shock and depress himself. How could insurance companies ever pay for this? In every direction lay ruin, marked by a few islands, the hulks of brick or stone buildings that hadn't been reduced to ash. He knew some things that others didn't know. The insurers wouldn't pay for quake damage, which was an act of God. And maybe not the fire, either. Most contracts had clauses that ended or reduced coverage on decrepit buildings. While policies covered losses caused by fire, that would not apply to buildings shaken to pieces by the quake. He wondered what the future might be. If the insurance companies paid most or all of the losses, they would collapse. If they didn't pay, San Francisco would never rise again.

He wandered, unable to locate his street. He had come to San Francisco because Carbondale seemed provincial and limited and moralistic, and he wanted the excitement of a great city, lots of girls, good food, culture. He had left behind him a cramped life in southern Illinois, a stiff midwestern culture he despised, and parents he felt ambivalent about; nice, pleasant, strict people but ones who kept too close an eye on a young man eager to test his wings. But he was no libertine. He took life seriously, believed that the virtues were essential to make one's way in the world, and that he had within him the strength to shape his life. He was free, male, good at his profession, and the lord of his destiny. His future was his to shape, for better or worse.

He turned west, only to be waylaid by a pair of soldiers.

"Here's a live one," said a private. "Come along, pal."

"What are you talking about? I'm an insurance adjuster looking at property."

"I said come along."

"Look, if you think I'm a thief, you're mistaken. Here, I'll show you my card. It says Willis Hart, Waterford Casualty Company."

"You coming or do I have to stick you with this rat-killer on the end of my rifle?"

"What is this? I'm a citizen of a free country. You can't do this."

The soldiers laughed. Both of them lowered their rifles until the bayonets pointed wickedly at Hart. His pulse leaped. They were going to kill him!

"Take me to your commander. I'll straighten this out."

"We'll take you to the sarg, all right. You're just what he's looking for."

The private slowly pressed the bayonet into Hart's belly until it pricked through his suit coat. My God! They were going to butcher him. He surrendered in a rush, his stomach churning and his throat hoarse. They marched him eastward toward a collection of men a few blocks distant. What was this, a mass execution?

Then, when he got close enough to see, he was sure of it. A number of young men were feverishly digging a trench while soldiers watched. It became obvious that the civilians were doing it at bayonet point. Something sickening thickened the air, and he recognized the smell of death. But there was something else. Something that smelled like cooked meat. Then Hart knew. They were burying quake and fire victims in a mass grave. And in a moment he would be, too.

"Dig," said a sergeant. He handed a spade to Hart.

"But I'm not fit. I sit at a desk all day. I have a bad stomach."

"Dig."

"I'm hungry; I haven't eaten."

"We'll feed you. Now do you dig or do we run steel through your belly?"

"Yes, yes." Hart felt terror ripple through him. He doffed his suit coat, took the shovel, and stepped into a line. Beside him able-bodied men shoveled, sweated in the cool April morning, cursed, and hacked at the miserable earth. This soil seemed as hard as granite. Hart felt outrage wash through him as he toiled. He was a citizen, with rights, but they were making him do this as if he were a slave. Who let the army come into San Francisco?

He found himself chopping away clay, a bit at a time, and worked out a routine with the bald man next to him: One hacked while the other lifted away the loose chunks.

"Sanitary measures," said the bald man. "Funston and the health authorities want every body under ground. Lot of good it'll do. At the last hole, we barely got the bodies covered over when the rats came. Last I knew they were all over that grave, like flies on meat."

"Where are the bodies?" Hart asked, his stomach roiling.

The bald man nodded. Hart had missed the canvas. Even as he glanced, a gray rat crept toward the canvas.

Gunshot exploded. The rat catapulted. Soldiers laughed. Blood leaked from the pulverized rat.

"You're getting good at that, Casey," one soldier said. "But I'm the bayonet champ."

Hart toiled until he had to rest, his heart hammering, but the moment he paused the sergeant yelled.

"You. Dig."

"My heart—"

"Dig."

The bald man shook his head. "I have high blood pressure but they didn't let me off. Maybe they'll throw me in."

A half hour later the sergeant examined the trench. It was about five feet wide, twenty feet long, but only two or three feet deep.

"Load 'em in," he said.

Suddenly Hart was aware that a new and more sickening task awaited. Two soldiers yanked the tarpaulins off a row of corpses. A dozen rats fled. Soldiers bayoneted a few, enjoying the sport.

There in a row lay the remains, or portions of remains, of about forty mortals, along with assorted dogs and a horse. Hart gaped at something he had never before seen: mortals baked into meat, most of them unidentifiable, their flesh cooked brown or black, their hair and eyes missing. The rats had gnawed away pieces of limbs, ears, chins, feet. Some had been old, but he saw children. Some of what he saw were parts, severed limbs, a head, a leg. He felt his stomach convulse, and then he fell on all fours and threw up what little was in his belly, wave after wave of violent heaving. When he got up, tears impaired his vision and he felt sick.

"All right. Help carry them," the sergeant said, not unkindly. The man's softer tone seemed to recognize that this was a task beyond the endurance of most people.

"Are there gloves?"

"Nope."

He would have to handle this mass of flesh. At every side, rats waited, just beyond catching. He could see them now, tens, hundreds, waiting.

The moment came when he and the bald man had to pick up a body. They chose a relatively unburned one, an old man. Hart lifted feet, feeling the cold, sticky flesh in his hands. The bald man got the shoulders. They carried the corpse and dumped it. Hart fought back tears. His hands felt filthy. They would never be clean again.

"Just a minute," said the sergeant. "Get the ring," he said to a private. The soldier dropped into the trench, yanked at a wedding ring which refused to come off, and finally cut the finger to release the ring.

"See if he has a purse or a wallet," the sergeant said.

The dead man did. The soldier handed the loot to the sergeant, who tucked it into a musette bag. The soldiers grinned. Hart knew none of it would ever reach headquarters.

Little by little, the pressed laborers transferred the bodies to the grave.

"Is there quicklime?" asked one.

"Nope."

"Lot of good this'll do," he muttered.

"You want to join 'em?" asked a soldier, his bayonet lowered.

The man shut up.

They shoveled the lumps of clay over the dead without being asked, until a foot or so covered the bodies.

"We done? Can we go now?" asked one.

The sergeant laughed.

Hart smelled his hands. A foulness exuded from them that he was sure would never wash away, even as the memory of this hour, this day, would generate nightmares the rest of his life.

"All right, we're gonna clean out the next block," the sergeant yelled. "Two crews. One digs, the other gets the bodies."

Swiftly he divided his crew, motioning Hart left, and the bald man right.

"All right. Throw your shovels in that wagon. You, that bunch, you get axes. You're going to pull out the dead. You, this bunch here, follow me. You'll dig."

Hart pulled out an ax and started walking with his group, now under the jurisdiction of a corporal and three privates. No sooner had they left the grave than rats swarmed over it. Hart had never seen so many rats, all of them furiously pawing away the loose soil.

The soldiers laughed.

Hart wondered why anyone bothered. He could not think of a single thing this pressed work crew had done to halt pestilence, stop disease, sanitize San Francisco. He stared at his befouled hands, wondering what fearsome disease would infect and kill him as a result of this frightful labor.

He toiled all that Friday afternoon, faint with hunger because no food wagon arrived. The sergeant did give them ample water, especially after an older man collapsed. At bayonet-point, Hart crawled through rubble, charred beams and posts, the remains of sinks and tubs, shards of glass. Sometimes he found something: the rats were his clue. When he approached a body, rats fled in all directions. He could scarcely believe their numbers. He had never known it, but tens of thousands of the vile animals populated the sewers and tunnels of San Francisco, and now that the quake had broken the sewers open, thrown covers off stubs, the rats were overrunning the city.

The army kept him until dusk, when a mess wagon arrived. They provided a scrub basin, and Hart gratefully scoured his filthy hands and face. But when it came time to eat the steaming stew the army was giving these slaves, Hart knew he could not bring food to his mouth.

They let him go after that. He had lost his suit coat somewhere and felt cold. His clothing stank and he itched to burn it. He brimmed with loathing. He trudged wearily back toward the panhandle, not caring whether he slept warm or cold, ate or didn't eat. What he had witnessed this day had rattled his soul, and then seared away everything that had once been Willis Hart. All pity had been bled out of him. He had dealt with those fried and mangled corpses and body parts only by shutting out of his mind all perception of them as mortals like himself, with dreams and loves and hopes and fears. No one had even tried to identify these bodies. No one in the crew, or among the soldiers, wanted to find a name. A name would turn the dead into mortals, and that was too much to think about. The fate of these dead would never be known to their relatives.

He had learned that he had no rights as a citizen. Learned that Death visited whenever Death chose to visit. Learned that there is no dignity in dying. He had learned that life is cheap and nothing could be insured, especially his own fleeting existence. He had left an innocent and naive Willis Hart behind, and would never see him again.

CHAPTER 31

ella Clapp eyed this John fellow skeptically. She knew what he was: a cad and a bounder. She wasn't quite sure what those were, but she had read lots of romantic love stories, and the authors all called men like this one cads and bounders.

"Well, are you coming?" he asked.

"You have fruit?"

"Oranges, wet and luscious. Grapefruit, sweet and delectable. Gorgeous meaty pineapples. Fat sweet melons. Juicy mangos from Hawaii that remind me of you. Passion fruit."

"Are you sure it's all right to go into this house?"

"They're friends. A port in every storm, so to speak. They happen to be away and missed the shake. But I have the run of the manse. Come along now."

"Don't expect to have your way with me."

"Oh, I'll try. Some more brandy?"

"You want to get me tipsy so you can seduce me. You're a cad and a bounder."

"Why, how did you ever know?"

"I'm very familiar with your sort."

"My dear, I am also a scoundrel and blackguard. One must be precise, you know."

"Well, I'm a good girl." She wasn't going to press that very far, but some things had to be said.

He took an elbow in hand and steered her up the steps toward a handsome brown stucco and wood home that had survived the quake, more or less. She saw some cracked panes, and some cornices had fallen, but the place seemed nearly intact.

"Whose house is this?"

"Never mind. They are patrons of the arts."

He pulled out a key and unlocked the carved oaken door, and she found herself in an extravagantly furnished residence not unlike the one where she had been employed, albeit gloomy because no lamp could be lit without power.

"The fruit, my dear, is in the silver chalice on the table." He pointed toward the dining room that was mostly intact, though shattered figurines from a display case littered the floor. There, indeed, rested a mound of real fruit. Luscious oranges for her parched throat.

She helped herself. Never had an orange tasted better. She peeled one and then another, while he sucked on his brandy flask and eyed her.

"Now let's do some serious drinking," he said.

She didn't want to, but here she was in a big empty house, a roof over her head at a time when tens of thousands had none. Here were blankets for warmth, lots of food, liquids—the oranges had allayed her thirst—and comfort. Why leave? She could be out in the tormented world, hunting for a meal and shelter. If he wanted to have his way with her, she just might. She could think of lots worse things to do. Maybe he would marry her. She thought about the child she was carrying, and her quest for a husband. Yes, she'd drink brandy, get a little tipsy, and then see about this John fellow.

"I've never tasted brandy before," she said.

"Well, you're deprived, child. Our task is to overcome your humble origins." He thrust the flask at her.

She giggled, took it, and let the fiery stuff fry her throat again. He took the flask and tilted it for an awesomely long drink.

"What do you do?" she asked.

He laughed, and she wondered why. "I make fantasies," he said. "I shock the fainthearted, break hearts, evoke tears, woo maidens, practice villainies, insult people, and give as much offense as possible."

"Oh, you're a lawyer."

"We have things in common. It's all theater." He drank the rest of the brandy, sighed, and restored the flask to his breast pocket.

"I'll tell you what I'm going to do. I will write a sensational account of this holocaust. And I will sell it to some newspaper or book publisher, and get rich enough to drink myself to death. I will make you a part of it. The little lady who didn't know my face. I am Barrymore."

She gaped. "Well, how should I know that? You never told me. You're an actor."

"You have heard the name. That will make a nice anecdote. Cataclysms are humbling. They will read it in New York."

After that, he ceased to make conversation, stared out the window, and then slowly settled in his chair and snoozed. She decided he had guzzled altogether too much brandy. What a strange man. She had never met anyone like him.

She spent the rest of the day bored, staring at the crowds on Van Ness, sampling oranges, and fretting. The man continued to doze. She thought he must have had a lot to drink. By dusk she was thoroughly annoyed. If he was going to have his way with her, he was certainly slow about it. She wished he would. She had accepted the idea the moment she realized this grand house was her refuge.

Her mother would approve. She was sure of it. Her mother ran a small hotel in Chico, The Gold Rush, which catered to encyclopedia drummers, hardscrabble miners, lumberjacks, door-to-door salesmen, and farmers. Almost always men. Families hardly ever went there. Her mother had been alone in the world for as long as Nella could remember, and she couldn't remember her mysterious father at all. But her pretty, robust, and playful mother didn't take stuffy ideals very seriously, and that's why she discouraged preachers and horse-and-buggy farm-road Bible sellers from staying at The Gold Rush. Her mother enjoyed men, a trait Nella figured she had inherited, but her mother always seemed to dodge man-trouble. Nella sometimes wished she could talk, just once, to her mother about men, and what to do about them when they were bold. She was pretty sure that if her mother were stuck in an earthquake and could enjoy a big house and food in exchange for some time pleasuring a man, she'd do it. She couldn't think of any reason not to, now that she was pregnant. Especially with Barrymore. That cad. He probably had a thousand women.

She spent the night on a sofa, rejoicing that she had found such a marvelous haven. Maybe he would seduce her in the morning, which was all right with her. She had never been seduced by an actor, and thought it might be exciting. Maybe an actor would do it differently.

She wasn't very experienced in those matters. She thought of going to him in the night, but he was sleeping off all that brandy, so she decided not to.

At dawn she searched the downstairs, but he was nowhere in sight. She was discomfited by the thought that her friend John Barrymore might have wandered off, leaving her in a house whose owners she didn't know. She might be taken for a thief.

She tried again, first the six bedrooms upstairs, which were lavishly decorated, the armoires groaning with clothing; the ornate bathroom with its clawfoot tub and gas-fired hot water heater, the great dining room with high-backed chairs and a long oak table, the chaotic quake-stricken maid's quarters, the washroom, the ruined pantry, the coal cellar. No John. She sat nervously at the parlor window in a Queen Ann wing chair, waiting for her host, while the sky whitened and turned blue and a day began. The whole eastern horizon boiled with fire and smoke, alarming her. Would it never end? The curtains of doom seemed closer, terrible, like dragons, the smoke purling upward as high as she could see, white mixed with black. Surely all of Nob Hill, where she had lived for so long, was ash now.

Finally, midmorning, she could bear it no longer. She would leave, but she would also take an orange. She was reluctant. The house was a haven from weather and wind, from hunger and thirst. But Barrymore had vanished. She suspected he had gone on a quest for more brandy, or maybe he was out collecting material for his article. She thought about taking a shawl, just one little thing to ward off the chill, but decided against it. She wasn't that sort of girl. The lady of the house might not even miss it; she had closets and armoires full of things. But Nella had her principles. And besides, in the novels, the girls who didn't do anything wrong were the ones who came to a happy ending, while the heroines who succumbed to temptation were the ones who were cast into the eternal pits, to be consumed by hellfires.

She left with the orange but not a shawl, carefully closing the door behind her, more annoyed than ever with that perfidious thespian. She certainly would never attend one of his plays. He was all smoke and shadow.

There weren't so many people on Van Ness this dawning day. Mansions lined the broad boulevard as far as she could see. This was almost like Nob Hill, but not so steep. She didn't know where to go, but neither did she have to go anywhere, so she sat on the stone steps leading to the house and watched people awhile. They looked tired, and walked as if they were in shock. What was the matter with them? It was only an earthquake. She had more important things to think about, such as finding a husband as soon as possible, before her belly swelled.

She watched a short, dapper, dark man wander up Van Ness, and knew him to be someone interesting. He had a pointy mustache and bulging eyes and a cocky air. But he eyed the world soulfully, with eyes that radiated pain and vulnerability. He wore a velvet-collared jacket and striped trousers, and a loose-fitting shirt, all of it foreign-looking to her eye. She instantly felt sorry for the poor man. He seemed so lost, so helpless.

"Excuse me, sir, do you want an orange?"

"A what?"

"An orange. You look like you need an orange."

"Bless you, bless you my child. An orange." Tears welled in his eyes. He spoke with an accent she recognized as Italian, and with a rich tenor voice. She gave him the orange, and he bowed. "Bless you, bless you, sweet lady, angel from heaven."

He was carrying something, and on closer examination she discovered it was a portrait of Theodore Roosevelt. He handed it to her while he lustfully peeled the orange, his fingers deftly whirling away rind. "You are a saint," he added, separating the lobes of the orange and wolfing them. "Ah, heaven, paradise, just when I thought I had been condemned to hell. What a terrible city this is. I shall never come here again, no matter if they double my contract."

"It's a nice city. I sure am having fun."

"Fun! Fun!" He stared at her sadly, emotion radiating across his soulful face. "This is worse than Milano, worse than Paris, worse than Madrid, worse than—Roma! They could offer me fifty thousand dollars and I would not come here. This is the inferno."

"Then why are you here?"

"Ah, little wren, that is a long story. But I have lost everything. I cannot even find my manservant or my trunks. I can't find Hertz. Or Scotti? Have you seen Hertz?"

"Who's that?"

"The maestro, who else?" He sounded annoyed. "I cannot live without him, but he has betrayed me. Unspeakable wretch, abandoning me in my hour of darkness. Where was I last night? Safe in Suite Six-twenty-two of the Palace Hotel? No, it was burned. I wandered the streets of this wretched city looking for Hertz, looking for Scotti, or at least my man Martino. But no, they're cowering somewhere. Traitorous devils, miserable curs."

He paused to engulf more orange.

"I carry the weight of the world on my shoulders. I'm ruined. The smoke, the shock, the bad air. Do you have any idea what it means? I'm done for." He pointed at his throat. "The voice. The vocal cords. The magic. It's gone. Smoke! Fumes! It's destroyed. Destroy that and you have destroyed the singer. I am ready for death. Maybe I can get back to Naples—after Vesuvius has stopped erupting, of course—and retire.

Yes, a has-been, a forgotten man, growing old, wandering about in slippers and a robe while the world rushes by, looking at faded pictures of another, greater time in the rush of a miserable life."

"Why don't you wait here? Everyone goes by. They'll come along."

"A good idea. Yes, I shall wait. You are a saint. Sweet maiden, give me your hand."

She did, and he kissed it wetly, with suction. His mustache tickled her wrist. "There. You have been kissed by Caruso."

"Caruso?"

"Yes, it is he, adrift in an uncaring and barbarous city. How does one escape this maze?"

"You're the singer?"

"I'm the tenor."

"Are you sure?"

"My dear lady, I'm no longer sure of anything. But if that picture is signed 'To Enrico Caruso from Theodore Roosevelt,' then I am the very man."

She stared at the presidential portrait. It bore the signature. "Why are you carrying that?"

"It is my passport, dear child. This picture of the President will open doors, put me on trains, put me in parlors, place me at the head of lines, bring me food and drink. I will tell them I am Caruso, and this is the President of the United States, and I will escape this inferno. Are you sure you haven't seen Hertz or Scotti or Martino?"

"I wouldn't know. Don't you want to sit here and wait? Maybe they'll come along."

"No, I must go."

"Where to?"

"Anywhere but here."

"The ferry to Oakland's running, I think. You could get a train in Oakland and go east."

"To New York? Ah! I will do that. The Ferry Building. That's where Hertz must be. And Scotti. And my man Martino. Waiting there for me." He clasped her hand between his. "Thank you, my dear lady."

He drifted back the way he had come, and she watched thoughtfully. He seemed so lost. She suddenly was glad she was just an ordinary person.

CHAPTER 32

Katharine Steinmetz could not remember a more miserable night. She and Emil found themselves among the desperate crowds at the Presidio, without shelter or adequate food as evening settled over them. The army had set up soup lines but it took hours of patient waiting to get through them and she couldn't manage it. She had pushed Emil's wheelchair into line and waited beside him, but starved people surged by, and she did not advance toward the tables where cooks were handing out bread and mess bowls of beans and stew. She endured it as long as she could, until her arthritic knees screamed at her, and then she told Emil to keep their place; she had to lie down.

Some people took pity on them: One lady tore loose a scrap of bread. A youth brought them half a bowl of cold soup, which they shared.

"I guess you need this pretty bad," the boy said.

"Oh, yes, thank you, child," she said, handing it to Emil.

"I'm doing how I was taught," he said. "I gotta return the bowl so I'll wait."

"Your parents taught you well."

"It was the nuns," he said, skipping off.

The little bit would do. Emil was barely eating anyway. She worried about him. He had sunk into a morose silence, shaking his gray mane from time to time. She knew what was troubling him: that morning he had killed a looter and wounded another. The bullet may as well have struck Emil, because it left a hole in his heart. She grieved, too. What a terrible world. Why did a disaster bring out the worst in some people?

They retreated to a place she hoped would be out of the breeze, which eddied relentlessly off the sea, chilling her in spite of the blanket she had brought. She took Emil to a slope in the lee of a barracks and close to some shrubs she hoped would quiet the wind. But the place turned out to be no refuge. The wind wandered the points of the compass, sometimes carrying the acrid fumes of the dying city. The turf was rock-hard. The sanitary trenches were distant and terrible to visit even though the army had hastily built wood-framed canvas shelters over some of them.

There seemed to be no space left. Everywhere, homeless people settled into the hard cold grass for the night. She saw few bonfires because the Presidio offered little fuel. Most people simply endured because enduring was all anyone could do. Endure, wait, dream, hope, starve, and try desperately to find comfort when there was none.

She watched dusk overtake them, watched the somber crowds fall silent with the realization that this night would be spent in the open, without a bed, without the slightest comfort. She sat at first, her blanket tight around her, trying to find warmth in it. She tried to lie on the grass with it wrapped around her, only to ache all the more.

Poor Emil! He chose to sit in his chair, which was more comfortable than the hard ground. She watched him anxiously, wondering whether his frail constitution could long endure such punishment. As darkness settled he wheeled himself toward the trenches, anger in his hands as they jammed his wheelchair forward. He returned exhausted, the glint of tears in his eyes. His stormy silence told her more than words could have.

"I hope London takes care of those portraits," he said to her just after dark. "They're the last of me. All that is left of Emil Wolff."

"Of course he will. But you have many years left, Wolff."

"For what? To rot in a wheelchair? To be helpless when this disease takes away what's left? I should not have left the flat."

"The officers made us."

"I still had a choice," he said darkly.

She thought of the old revolver lying in his lap under the blankets. "Emil, throw that away. We will start over."

"You'll start over. I am sick of this."

"Those will be beautiful portraits, Emil. The light was just right. The smoke diffused the sunlight. It all came in from the window, soft and bright. I saw you in the frame, so I know."

"You see? That was Fate. The portrait of a dead man."

"Don't talk like that, please don't, darling."

"I will talk about death. Long overdue, this death. Stupid of me not to die earlier, while I was almost warm and comfortable." He glared at her. "Make your way. You have life left."

"Please, please, Emil."

"I will talk this way," he retorted roughly. "I give the world lots of good engravings, and a few fine etchings. That is what I bequeath to mankind. No money. Nothing for you. It's all burned away. Not even a good memory. You had to put up with an invalid."

"Emil!"

"Nothing good. Every day you took care of me like a nurse. What good was I. Stupid! I should have shot myself long ago before turning you into my slave."

"Please, please, sleep now. Tomorrow will be better."

"What tomorrow?"

They slipped into silence after that, lost in the night. She didn't even think of sleep. The crowds shifted restlessly, people padded by, children darted, shadows loomed above her and then the stars appeared again. Was there no stopping the parade? No place to hide?

Then she heard a scream and sobbing, angry voices. Shouts. The thud of soldiers' boots and the rattle of metal. She caught fragments of it. An electric torch shot white light onto huddled women. Even here among the refugees, cutpurses and thieves owned the night, probing into blankets and trunks and reticules and carpetbags. The mob settled down again, or seemed to, but Katharine sensed pain everywhere, exhaustion, and the faint sound of weeping did not escape her.

Time had stopped. The clocks all died. Every time she tossed, she hoped she might enjoy a moment of comfort, only to have the cold, dewy grass betray her. Dew collected on her blanket, numbed her hands every time they touched the grass. The moisture caught in her throat and made it ache along with the rest of her.

Could she try some spiritual exercise? She and Emil didn't believe in a divine presence. She had a modern mind and had abandoned folklore. Science would explain everything. Let the mass of people think like dumb brutes, hanging on to superstitions and myths. Too bad for them! She knew what people would grasp in a hundred years: the universe was happenstance, the result of the iron laws of physics and mathematics. It would do no good to pray to some god like a child supplicating a parent, begging for a moment's comfort, a moment's warmth, a moment's peace. But she could draw upon memories. She had those, and good ones. She and Emil hugging and laughing. Yes, that was a good one. Emil opening a letter from *Harper's Monthly* and pulling out a big check. Ah, that was a good one, too. Memories. The time they read that popinjay's review that said her photography lacked imagination and sensitivity and technical skill. They had laughed at that. . . .

When the skies finally grayed, she was aware of spending the longest night of her life. She no longer measured it in pain, but in ticking seconds. Emil slumped in his wheelchair, uncommonly inert. She sat up and touched him, and he gazed at her from a ravaged face, darkened around the eyes. She knew uneasily that he was sick; exposure had weakened him.

"How are you?" she asked.

He didn't reply.

She reached for his forehead, seeking fever, but her hands were so numb she couldn't tell. But she knew he was sick. Fever lit his eyes, smoldering behind the lenses. She was little better off herself. Not feverish, but so drained of life force that she thought she would die of cold.

People still wandered, as they had all night, blanketed shapes clambering around families, single people, couples, sleepless and numb. Even now they were congregating at the sanitary trenches. She eyed the lines and knew her knees couldn't endure the wait. This morning her misfortunes seemed insurmountable. Her courage deserted her, and she buried her head in her skirts and wept. What was the future?

Breakfast lines formed, but she lacked the strength to stand in one, or wheel Emil to one. His breath was raspy, and she suspected he had influenza or catarrh.

A passerby paused. "May I help you?" she asked.

Katharine peered upward at a gaunt, tired woman in a begrimed white dress, who wore a ratty blanket as a shawl.

"Yes. He's sick, and I can't walk anymore."

The woman peered at Emil and apparently agreed. "There's a hospital. But it's full. They have another place for other sick people. I'll take him if you'd like." She turned to Emil. "Maybe I can help a little, if you'd like."

He stared. Katharine was alarmed by that staring.

The woman helped Katharine to her feet. Standing shot new aches through her, but she was determined to walk, and staggered forward.

"I think maybe I should take him in the chair and then come for you."

Katharine shook her head grimly. She would walk. She needed to get to the trench, and lurched forward, one shot of pain at a time. "You are a good woman," she said.

"It's a long way to where they have the sick," the woman said. "Are you sure you can walk that far?"

Katharine didn't respond. The pain was evoking tears.

"I am Ginger Severance. Who are you?"

"Katharine Steinmetz. He's Emil Wolff."

"Friends," the woman said.

"No, lovers."

The gaunt, weary woman in white fell into silence. They reached the trenches and Katharine headed for the line of women. "Go take him. I must wait here."

"No, if you can't stand, you mustn't wait. Let me see what I can do."

Miss Severance left them and walked to the head of the line, and returned a moment later. "Come; I'll help you. People are so kind."

Leaning heavily on Miss Severance's arm, she found herself at the front of the line, and soon had her chance at the noxious trenches. In some odd way, after she had emerged from the canvas shelter, her spirit brightened.

Twenty slow minutes later, Miss Severance wheeled Emil into a long hall of some sort and hunted for help. Emil slumped silently, worrying Katharine. It took a long time, but eventually Miss Severance returned with a nurse, who examined Emil, took his pulse and temperature, and then did the same to Katharine.

"We'll make room," she said to Miss Severance. She turned to Katharine. "Your husband has a fever. You're suffering from exposure. We'll find a corner for you. We have a barracks set aside for the contagious."

"Thank God," said Miss Severance.

Ten minutes later, in an adjoining building, Emil lay in an army cot and Katharine in an adjoining one. A nurse brought them hot broth, but Emil wouldn't swallow it. For Katharine, the hot broth wrought miracles. This was paradise.

"I must go now," said Miss Severance. "My prayers are with you." She clasped a small hand over Katharine's, and then held Emil's limp one.

Katharine wept.

"There is so much to do," Miss Severance said, and slipped away. Through blurred eyes, Katharine watched the angel of mercy walk into the cold sun.

Emil wasn't watching. He lay on the cot, shaking, and Katharine knew, suddenly, that Emil's premonitions were true, and his life was ebbing.

A long time passed before a doctor arrived. He looked as weary as everyone else Katharine had seen since the quake, and as disheveled. He listened to Emil's harsh breathing with his stethoscope, peered into Emil's throat with an electric torch, and frowned.

"Double pneumonia, high fever," he said to her. "What is the nature of his muscle disorder?"

"It is probably Lévy-Roussy Syndrome. It progresses," she said.

"He is having difficulty breathing."

Katharine nodded. He examined her as well, swiftly ascertaining the scope of her arthritis. "We'll need to put you in another place. This is for contagious diseases. You can't manage outside. It may seem mild, but it's too much for you."

"I want to stay here."

"It's dangerous."

"I must be with him."

He sighed and nodded.

That was all. So this was how it would end. All the years, all the joy and pain of a hard, abrasive, and tender relationship. The clock was ticking.

. . . .

CHAPTER 33

Ginger Severance didn't really know what she was doing, or why, or how. She had no goal other than to be helpful to all of God's creatures. She held her weariness at bay, wandered among the miserable crowds, and saw suffering. Nothing impelled her but a hunger to relieve suffering. Wherever she found it, there was her mission. But suffering was universal in the Presidio, where the cold Pacific fog stole the heat from poorly dressed refugees, where not everyone could get to the food lines or sanitary trenches, and where no one had enough to wear, or a sheltered place to sleep.

That day she had wandered willy-nilly, doing what she could. She brought bread to a mother with a newborn infant. She showed numerous people how to sign a register announcing their presence to anyone looking for them. She happened upon a group standing around an old man lying on the ground, and realized he was dead. The long cold night had killed him. She notified the soldiers, and comforted a daughter. She helped half a dozen sick people reach the infirmary, including a gravely ill man in a wheelchair and an exhausted woman too arthritic to walk.

She encountered ignorance everywhere. Old immigrant couples didn't know the army was handing out bread. She saw soldiers erecting large tents, but no one was moving into them. She realized people were waiting for permission, so she brought frail people to the tents and comforted them there. She went through the food lines numerous times, and no one questioned her right to do so. On each occasion she brought bread or stew to someone who could not manage the lines. She discovered a wagonload of donated clothing, much of it rags but all of it priceless to chilled refugees. She found a little coat for a little boy and was gratified to see his shivering stop. She found an ancient paint-stained cardigan for an old man whose body generated little heat.

Some thanked her. Some seemed to regard her as a busybody. It didn't matter. She had abandoned self; who she was didn't matter. All that mattered was that she help wherever she could, and to do it in the name of God, blessing each and every one.

She snatched bits of food for herself, a little bread, some water, and wondered now and then whether her small efforts made any dent at all in the mountain of grief before her eyes. There came a moment of such weariness and ache that she knew she must rest an hour. She had lost track of time, barely realizing that her work had consumed much of that Friday. What good had it been? Her lonely efforts came to nothing compared to the army's field kitchens, the resourceful leaders who were gathering and transporting food, the organizers who sent carloads of used clothing, blankets, tents, shoes—everything needed to survive out of doors.

She had seen too much suffering this day, and needed an hour alone in a "desert place," as some gospel or other put it. So she drifted west, away from the amassed crowds, until she thought she was alone near the Pacific shore. But there, in a windswept hollow, were hundreds, indeed thousands of Chinese, looking just as miserable as the whites closer to the field kitchens. She thought to turn away, leave the heathen to their own devices, but her practiced eye spotted misery here. Maybe much more misery than she had seen closer to the field kitchens. And then she realized she had not seen one Chinese in the food lines. She knew why. No one would permit them to stand in the lines.

Before the earthquake, any Chinaman venturing from Chinatown before or after business hours took his life in his hands. Once they left the district, which stretched from Powell to Kearny, and from California to Broadway, gangs of toughs stoned them, robbed them, beat them, and left them for dead. Now the inflammable structures of Chinatown had been swept by fire, and the teeming residents of that incendiary quarter had fled for their lives, with far less time to gather their possessions than others. Many of them wore little but blue shirts and white pajama-like trousers. Most were barefoot.

She wondered what was sustaining them, and discovered that some had been beach combing, bringing back firewood and anything edible, dead fish, even kelp, that might keep them alive. Some were gathered around pushcarts that had brought vegetables from somewhere. But there were thousands here, and they were starving.

Could she help?

The task was too hard. She would run into walls. Maybe God wished to leave the heathen to their own devices.

They eyed her passively, as she eyed them. Most were young males. Chinatown had been largely male, and what few women lived there were mostly slaves. The men had been imported as laborers, and lived in cramped rooms, often sharing the same bunks in shifts because the outside world would not let them live beyond the confines of their area. They toiled as menials, servants, junk dealers, fish sellers, laundrymen, chrysanthemum and aster farmers, cigar makers, broom makers, gardeners, ragpickers, doing whatever white men scorned.

She knew little about them other than that they were universally scorned, alien heathen, given to opium and every imaginable vice, filthy, and deserving of their fate. She thought to leave them, but something stayed her. They were suffering. She would do what she could. It seemed so hopeless. Chinese filled the entire windy hollow. What could she do? Walk through the breadline and deliver three or four loaves?

Now, as she approached, she saw misery. They stared at her with eyes masking emotion, eyes that may well be hiding rage or despair. She felt a little frightened. She saw no other whites. These people were utter outcasts, scorned as an inferior species. Many Chinamen had returned to China, driven out of the United States by persecution, by ferocious newspaper editorials, by the sheer cussedness of other people.

Her pulse lifted. She hadn't the faintest idea what to expect. She headed directly toward an older man in a Western business suit, gray-haired, pigtailed, somehow radiating authority. He squinted at her from behind a wall of impassivity. She didn't really know what to say, or whether he would understand, but she thought to try. One thing she could do was notify the army.

"Do you speak English?" she asked.

Now others among them gathered around, until she was surrounded by the Chinese. She feared the unknown. Would they sell her into slavery as they did their own women?

No one answered.

She peered at one, then another, and remembered lurid tales about sinister tongs, family clans, protective societies, the Six Companies, the Chinese Benevolent Association, slave girls in cages submitting themselves to white men and dying young, murder, torture, subterranean opium parlors, tunnels, warrens under the streets, and above all, mystery. No one knew what the Chinese did, or cared to know. They lived in an enclave that may as well have been as walled as a prison. Almost without exception, white people wanted one thing: to ship them all back to Canton.

Here she saw no luxury or vice or decadence. No fat people. She saw no silks and satins, no robes embroidered with exotic designs. These shivering people wore the uniforms of laborers, thin cottons that afforded little protection against the sea-winds and April chill.

"If you are hungry I will try to help. I will tell the soldiers you need food and shelter."

The elder Chinese stared at her grimly, his face a wall of granite. But some of the others stirred, seeking the authority of the older man.

She was getting nowhere. "I will go through the food line and bring you what I can," she said.

The older one waved a hand sharply. The Chinese were a gesturing people. "No," he said.

She didn't like him and decided he was flaunting authority instead of helping his own miserable people. "I will do so. Or I can take you to a captain I met and tell him."

"We take care of our own. Go away now, Miss. You make trouble for us. Army come, people come."

Something stubborn in her rose to the fore. "I am going to get help for you," she said. "Who are you?"

The man considered a while. "A merchant. Import and export. China antiques. Come." He motioned her to follow, and walked sedately toward three pushcarts some distance away. At each cart a man was handing out morsels of food to patient people: onions, artichokes, potatoes, lettuce, cabbages, no doubt foraged from truck gardens down the peninsula where many of these people toiled. But there was fish as well, and the carcasses of several sheep.

"Now you see," the man said. "Do not make trouble."

"But this isn't enough—" She stopped protesting. What was being distributed wouldn't feed a hundred a day, much less the throngs here.

"Now go." It was a command.

"You are a proud people. But you need help," she said.

A large crowd had collected around her, all male. She saw women at a distance, bent over cookfires. She saw no young women at all, none of the legendary little slave girls, and wondered what had become of them. Had they died in their cages during the fire? The thought horrified her, and she suspected that some, at least, had not been released and had died in the whirlwind that devoured Chinatown in minutes. Life in Chinatown was cheap, and cheapest of all were the adolescent girls who had been smuggled in from Canada in crates labeled "Freight."

She would make no headway here. Maybe they were right. Bring them to the attention of the army, or take them to the food lines, and she would only double and redouble their misery. She nodded.

"All right. I will go."

The leader's gaze probed her relentlessly, and then he nodded faintly.

She walked away. Her dander was up, though. Maybe that heathen was more interested in lording over everyone than doing his duty.

She trudged wearily back over the military reservation until she spotted the mobs of white people, the long lines, the increasing rows of circular Sibley tents being erected as fast as the army could do so.

She knew she wasn't done with this: the army could help if it would. But finding an officer who would stand still long enough to listen would be a problem.

She headed for the Presidio command building, but was barred by sentries from entering.

"Where can I talk to an officer?" she asked them.

"You can't."

"There are thousands of unfortunate people who aren't being fed."

"Talk to the kitchen detail, lady."

"They are Chinese."

The sentry clammed up.

She could find no one else to talk to, so she stood in the food line, waited a half hour, received the loaf to which she was entitled, asked for more and was refused, and then headed back over the grassy turf. That was how it had been: her every effort would not make a dent in the mountain of misery, but one loaf might sustain one person one day. She felt helpless and useless, but then she remembered the widow's mite, the Lord's story of the poor woman who left her tiny contribution at the altar, and was honored for it above the rich, who had left lavish gifts, because she had given to God everything she had, unlike the rich whose gifts were really the smallest part of their wealth.

Ginger took her loaf, her mite, out to the Chinamen, determined to help as much as she could.

CHAPTER 34

Willis Hart stumbled back to Golden Gate Park in a haze of bitterness. His fouled clothing had become an obsession. He would rather go naked than wear the shirt and trousers that bore the stains of fried human flesh, unknowable juices and slime, a stench of cooked meat or rot or sewage he couldn't bear. He could not live, could not breathe, could not resume his life until he tore that vile cloth from his body.

Washing it wouldn't do. He would not put it on again. He would burn it if he could. He trudged along the panhandle, past a makeshift field hospital in several tents. A row of bodies lay in the shadow of one. Men, women, some bandaged, some not, all dead. He hurried past, afraid soldiers would make him bury them, too. He found a field kitchen, this one run by the city, with long triple-wide lines stretching from it. The smell of food nauseated him. He wondered if he could ever eat again. Never meat. He had seen human meat, human standing rib roast, human steaks, human loin roast, human hamburger.

He had to change. The need howled in him. Was there no used clothing anywhere? Had no relief arrived? Had it all been snapped up? He would not go through the advancing night without changing. There had to be a way. If he still wore his befouled clothing by morning, he would be stark raving mad.

People packed the park. He had never seen so many: families, couples, solitary mortals, lumped and separate. Huge latrine trenches spread noisome odors over the whole area, making him feel even more befouled than he was. He would steal clothing. He would wear any size. He would claw it from someone.

Incredibly, he heard a piano, and followed the dissonant notes to a battered upright surrounded by a dozen youths. One of them, a carrot-haired lad sitting on a cracker box, was hammering out tunes. "Home Ain't Nothing Like This" he sang, and then "Dixie" and "Good Old Summertime." Some of the others, their collars up against the cold, sang harmony.

He spotted a young spectator at this festival sitting beside a formidable black steamer trunk the man had somehow dragged to that place. The man was larger than Willis, both taller and broader. Maybe he would sell something. Willis remembered the gold eagle he kept in a flap of his billfold. Ten dollars.

"Say, I'm looking for clothing. Have you any?"

The fellow peered up from the grass. "No—I'll need this stuff."

"I'll buy it—and I'll give you what I have on. You can wash it. I need a shirt, trousers, underdrawers, and shoes if they fit. A belt if you have it. And I'll give you everything I have. If you have any soap—even a sliver, a little piece—I'll buy that."

"You're smaller than I am, I think. What would I do with it?"

"Wash it and sell it."

"What'll you pay?"

"An eagle. That's all I have. But that would buy me a new suit and shirt and more."

"Yes it would. You sure you want to do that?"

"I can't stand this filth,"

"What were you doing—cleaning out the trenches?"

"Worse."

The man thought about it. "Well, let's see. Maybe I could."

He pawed through his black trunk, extracting a pair of serviceable wool trousers, a wrinkled white shirt, a pair of underdrawers. Then he paused a while. "Aw, for that much I should throw in this, too," he said, pulling out a sweater.

"Soap?"

"Oh, sure. Here, I'll break this in half."

"Belt?"

"No, and mine would be too big for you."

Hart extracted the gold coin from his billfold and handed it to the man. "You want this stuff I'm wearing?"

The man shrugged. "I can't wear it."

The pianist had started on "Bill Bailey."

Joyously, Hart headed toward a brush-rimmed pond a few hundred yards distant, pushing through undergrowth only to stumble over lovers embracing in the dusk, their clothing in disarray. He mumbled his apologies and hastened into the bushes, stripped swiftly, not much caring who among all these mobs of strangers spotted him, peeled away the last of his foul clothing, and retrieved his billfold. He lathered himself with the soap until his arm wearied, scrubbing furiously, his flesh goosebumped. He abraded his flesh until the last of the corruption had been stripped away and his raw skin prickled. Then he dried himself as best he could, donned the clean things, which bagged over him, pulled on the sweater, and tucked the billfold into his new trousers.

The feeling was akin to paradise. He wondered whether to take his stinking clothing to the latrine trench, but decided just to abandon it. He could not stand to pick it up, to let it brush against the clean things.

He almost felt clean.

Around him, people were settling down for a second night in the open air. It would go hard for them. He heard coughing, sneezes, the gurgle of congested sinuses and windpipes. He was ready for food, if he could find his way back over and around countless souls who were spread haphazardly across the great playground of San Francisco. Far to the east, firelight played on orange smoke high in the sky as the city continued its death throes, making the night strange, wobbling, uncertain. He discovered rows of tents, the big circular army ones that could hold ten or fifteen people, rectangular wall-tents, and two-man pup-tents. Some lucky few would escape the worst of the cold Pacific winds this night.

He found the food line and stopped there, wondering whether this time he could down something. He thought he could. The soft clean clothing had made him a human being again. It took a half hour of weary waiting, and then they gave him stew in a tin cup.

"When you're done, throw it in that boiler kettle," a man said.

The stew had no flavor, but tasted just fine, the beans, bits of meat, broth all melting in his mouth. They tore a loaf in half and gave him bread for breakfast.

He needed a place to sleep. Any place, any nest. He was cleansed and fed, drowsy, but chilled. No blanket, no pad or mattress, no pillow. Suddenly he knew he could not stay in Golden Gate Park; the crowds oppressed him, made his heart race. He felt phobic. He had to leave— if they would let him. But where?

Twin Peaks, those great hills to the south, beckoned. He wondered whether he could navigate there in the darkness, or whether his weary body would take him that far. But he knew intuitively that he could be alone there if he struggled high enough up the slopes. He set off through the restless mob, working south, the wobbling orange light of the fires to the east his lantern. He walked through unburnt neighborhoods, fearful of soldiers, walked into foothills, up twisting roads, ever higher, past the last of the frame houses perched on the slopes, up a gulch where the wind failed and the air stood still, higher, stumbling now and then over unseen snares. And then, near the top of the northernmost peak, he found a place. He stopped, utterly winded. Someone had built a gazebo there on a flat overlooking the whole city. It nestled into a cliff that checked the wind. He found a wooden bench. A roof of some sort blotted out the stars. The air was fresh, cedar-scented, clean, with a hint of the sea in it. He settled there, sinking luxuriously into the bench. It was hard, but warmer and dryer than the cold earth of the park. Below him lay the dying city, its death agony eerily like a Fourth of July fireworks display. Now and then great columns of sparks erupted high into the sky, losing themselves in the shadowy smoke. Light prickled and danced below, as one by one by one, the city's buildings fed the columns of flame.

It had been the worst day of his life, and he was desperate for sleep, but sleep eluded him. His mind drifted back to the horrors he had witnessed until his brain was numbed to them. Bodies, fried, baked, broiled, butchered. Grotesque nakedness, clothes nothing more than charred patches on cooked flesh. How fragile was life, and how easily it succumbed to any disruption. Death everywhere. Death hovering about. His own death just beyond the edge of vision. Down below, in that mass of humanity, germs would fell dozens, hundreds more, killing people who were rejoicing because they had escaped quake and fire. Life came and went in an instant! So little time!

He drifted in and out of sleep, but every time he lost track of where he was, specters and dreams disturbed him. He dreamed of cutting himself as a boy, and watching the bright blood well up from his finger, and the sting of it. He dreamed about his father's funeral, the waxen face peering up from the coffin, life gone, his mouth twisted and bloated beyond the cosmetics of a mortician. He dreamed of his father, of his father trying to speak across the mists and veils of eternity, saying something—but what? That he should go back to Carbondale? No. He had written a different story in his Book of Life. He needed a larger, grander world, a larger field in which to test his mettle. He would stay, even if the very city shook under his feet.

He spent the night on the brink of madness. Would he never sleep peacefully? Had the horrors of that day so deranged his soul that he would never know peace? Sometimes he heard the thump of munitions. That would be up on Van Ness, the last resort of the army and the firemen. The army had blown up more of the city than fire had consumed, setting new fires with all their incendiary blasting. And for what? Would insurers pay for a building leveled by dynamite before fire claimed the ruins?

The wooden bench with its backrest was oddly comforting, and he burrowed into it. It beat sleeping on the dewy ground. He did relax, even though sleep eluded him, finding peace and even comfort, and when the sky began to gray in the morning, he knew he had done better than most of the sleep-shocked souls far below.

He arose with a new resolve: he would live the rest of his days and hours and minutes with a fury he had never dreamed of before the earthquake. If life was so fragile, his fate so uncertain, his days on earth so unpredictable, then he would crowd ten years into one year, a day into each hour, and he'd jam joy into each moment.

He stood and stretched.

Let the rest of the city dream of fleeing. He would think of the future and staying. He would start by performing his job: he was an insurance adjuster, so he would begin adjusting. That he lacked so much as a pad of paper and a pencil would not deter him. That the office records had burned and he didn't know what buildings had been insured, or by whom, didn't deter him. The home office could supply all that. He would remember enough of the buildings to get started. With any sort of luck, he would set up shop in a day or two, hang a sign, contact the home office, and begin. Let other insurance adjusters take weeks and months and years to unscramble the mess or pay anyone anything. He intended to deliver his first insurance check before the last of the fires died.

He mapped out a life lived to the hilt: he would marry within a year. He intended to be the regional manager of his company in two years. In five years, he would be an insurance or banking executive. In ten, he would be rich enough to retire if he chose, with all the joys of a family. By age forty, he would achieve what other men spent sixty achieving—if they lived that long. Most didn't, and that was the whole point.

Buoyed with ambition and a fiery need to make every second count, he trotted the long miles down the slope and into the park. He took his place in the food line behind an exquisite young woman who wore no ring, and suddenly his rush to conquer the world veered in a new direction.

CHAPTER 35

 arcia Devereaux White threaded the gloomy confines of the Oakland Terminal, dragging Daisy and Harry through silent crowds. People were too weary and shocked even to talk, and wandered somnambulantly, dazed, alongside the grimy green coaches.

The relief train consisted of venerable coaches and a string of battered boxcars bedded with straw. Some people with possessions were opting for the boxcars, but Marcia could not even imagine such a thing, especially in the April weather of the interior. She hoped to find seating in a coach. But she knew the chances were fleeting. Maybe she would stand all the way to Omaha.

There was something comfortable about solid, stolid Oakland. It had been badly shaken by the quake, and yet stood, its buildings largely intact, its streets and squares harboring hordes of refugees. Its homes and offices basked in the warm California sun, radiating a solidity that San Francisco lacked.

She was as weary as the multitudes around her. She saw their pinched faces, the black circles under their fever-bright eyes, and knew her own smudged face looked no different. But she also saw life and hope in these faces. Every one of these souls had escaped San Francisco, flooding across the bay by ferry or in one of the innumerable little boats that were carrying tens of thousands of mortals out of the doomed city. She had discovered, while crossing the water, that her fishing vessel was one of an armada, and that the water lanes were clogged with such vessels, each with its exhausted and desperate human cargo. Those fleeing the city numbered not in the tens of thousands, but hundreds of thousands, and they were radiating in every direction: south toward Los Angeles, north toward Santa Rosa, east to points across the United States.

The Southern Pacific was making it possible. Edward Harriman's railroads were arranging transportation to any point in the country. The SP was carrying people free in its ferries. It had made arrangements with connecting railroads to carry this cargo of suffering humanity to safety. It had incurred enormous losses to its roadbed, its warehouses and terminals, and yet stepped into the breech. And because it was moving people out of the ruined city, the army was able to feed and shelter those who remained.

But her thoughts were focused on a more immediate problem: finding room in one of the jammed coaches. By the time she reached the coach immediately behind the coal tender, she knew she was out of luck. She lifted the children onto the metal steps and entered that one, worming down an aisle jammed with disheveled, rancid-smelling, dirty people—like herself. Bad breath from a hundred weary passengers cloyed. She would have to stand until she dropped. Only the vision of the comfortable confines of the Devereaux home kept her going.

"Is Daddy on the train?" asked Harry.

"No, dear, he's not coming."

"Why?"

"He's busy."

He needed his father and eyed the crowds fearfully. She had little to offer him except her hand and her presence. But both children were so tired they were past complaint.

The forthcoming trip frightened her. She had virtually no money. It was an act of faith. And yet she was doing what she must. She thought frequently of Harrison and wondered what would become of him—and them. Or when she would see him again—if ever. A certain hard edge built in her when she thought of him. There was portent in this. It wasn't just a trip east to find refuge with her parents. There were more, so many more, things she had to face.

"Are we going now?" asked Daisy, who was clinging desperately to Marcia's skirt.

"Yes, soon. And we'll have to stand. Maybe you'll find a place to sit down after we start."

Then the train did start after another wearing delay, with a great hiss of steam that boiled past the windows, and a gentle tug that rattled the couplers. The train eased out of the darkness of the terminal and the brightness of California sunlight broke through the grimy windows. The train was following the bayshore, and the distant waters glistened and sparkled. For an instant she regretted leaving California, that magical, bountiful paradise she had come to love in happier times.

She steadied herself by hanging on to a seat back. A young mother occupied that seat, cradling two small children. Next to her was an old woman, holding a frail man in her lap. Across the aisle were four men in two seats, looking a little guilty as they watched her standing there. The rush of fresh air drove out the dense, offensive odors that had built in the terminal, and drove back Marcia's deepening headache.

She did not know how she could stand ten more minutes, much less two or three days and nights. She peered down at Daisy, and realized the child was weeping. All this was too much. It was too much for anyone. She knew she couldn't last a half hour, much less to Sacramento, even less to Reno and the whole broad continent beyond. She drew a hand through Daisy's sticky hair, wishing only for a bath and a bed. But there were none.

"Excuse me, madam," said a young man in a seat. "Would you like to sit awhile? I'll trade off. The girl needs a chance to sit, I think."

"Oh, yes, thank you!"

The exchange was effected, and both Daisy and Harrison Jr. found a corner of the coach seat, and fell against her. She had never felt anything so blessed as that cushioned seat.

The young man stood, smiling at her.

"This is the sweetest gift I've ever received," Marcia said. "We just need a few minutes, and then—"

"Take a half hour. We'll just switch now and then."

Marcia found herself crying. The young man reached down and patted Daisy's hair.

"Tell me when the time's up," she said. "You need to sit, too."

He nodded. Almost instantly the rhythms of the coach lured Marcia into a catnap, and when she awakened with a start, it was to the squeal of brakes.

"Sacramento," the trainman announced.

"Oh!" Marcia bolted upright, awakening her children. "I've overslept!"

The young man smiled gamely. He looked as tired as everyone else. Marcia forced herself and her children to stand. "You take it," she said, embarrassed.

"I will, when we get back on."

"Are we getting off?"

"Food stop. Let's see what these good people are giving us."

"Food stop?"

"Every town along the railroad has food and necessary things ready for us. It's a miracle, you know."

"Will we have our seats when we come back?" She reddened. "I mean, will you have yours?"

He grinned. "I'll fight for it."

They emerged into a warm, peaceful afternoon. There, amazingly, stood a row of tables mounded with bread, pastries, ready-made sandwiches, steaming bowls of soup ready to pluck up, oranges, apricots, even pies and cakes, all ready to eat.

And more: here were tables with washbasins and water and soap and towels, a heap of clothing for the taking, thoughtfully provided by a caring world.

Marcia stood before this bonanza and wept. Daisy found a box lunch, but Harry wasn't hungry.

"Is Daddy here?" he asked.

"No, he's in San Francisco."

"Will he come to Grandpa and Grandma's house?"

She paused, pushing back bitterness. She wasn't sure she wanted Harrison to come to Cleveland. "I don't know, Harry," she said gently. "But that's a long time away."

"Why didn't he come?"

She didn't want to say what she thought. "He had things to do," she said. "He's very busy, you know."

Harry eyed her soberly and turned to the food tables, finding a plate full of peanut butter cookies. He glanced at her for permission, and then took one, and another, and two more, like a miser hoarding gold.

Her traveling companion joined them. "It'll be like this right across the country. Americans are pretty nice people," he said.

"Yes! Oh, yes!" she cried.

She headed for the washbasins while the crowd ate, tugging her children. She found one, filled it with lukewarm water from the pitcher, and scrubbed Daisy's face and then Harry's. Then she scrubbed her own. Her face came alive under the soap and water. She tackled her neck and ears and forearms and wished she could wash the rest, especially her grimy hair. But this was paradise. Behind her a line formed, so she hastened through her ablutions and then drifted to the food tables, keeping an eye on her children.

"All aboard in five minutes," the trainman said. "Five minutes."

She commandeered a beef sandwich wrapped in newspaper, and an orange for the children, and sipped some scalding coffee before the brakemen and conductor herded everyone back.

Her young companion had already fallen into his seat and was half asleep. She felt saddened that she had taken his seat for so long. He was just as haggard as she. A few people had gotten off in Sacramento, and the aisle was less jammed. Some were sitting in it now. They could not get any dirtier than they already were. She might do that herself if she couldn't bear to stand.

The overburdened refugee train toiled out of Sacramento, following the broad, sparkling American River across the greening Central Valley. Something had changed. Cheer had stolen into the coach, as if it had been bequeathed to the refugees by the people of Sacramento. Those who had been mute suddenly began conversing with neighbors. She heard snatches of conversation.

All of them, it seemed, had to tell about their experience of the quake. A woman two seats away told about being thrown out of bed and to the brink of the floor. The wall had crumbled away, leaving her poised two floors above the street. A man described his bed as a bucking horse. An elderly man had smelled gas, and feared his flat would blow up. Someone's armoire had tipped over and he couldn't get dressed after the worst of the quake. Another was trying to dress but was thrown about like a rag doll. Another had been in a cable car when it began to career about, throwing passengers out of their seats.

Marcia thought back to her own more humdrum experience, lying in a bed that propelled itself into a wall before it pitched her out of it and heavy things landed on top of her.

Incredibly, some of the men began to boast about how much they had lost. One insisted he saw a hundred fifty thousand dollars vanish in the quake and fire. Another topped that, but most confessed to smaller losses.

A woman described the death of a newborn infant and her weary mother on a tugboat wending its way to Oakland. A man described the shooting of a thief by soldiers. The thief—if that was what he was—had not stopped walking when the soldiers challenged him, and it had cost him his life. A woman tearfully described the death of her own daughter, the result of a gas explosion that burned the child. The little girl had screamed for three hours.

Marcia heard more than she wanted to hear, and wanted to introduce herself to the young man who had so valiantly given her a seat when she was about to collapse, but he nodded and rocked with the swaying coach, oblivious of the world. She intended to get his name and thank him.

A baby started to whimper, and she heard a young mother humming Brahms' lullaby to the little one. In a corner, people were singing. She swore she heard snatches of "Carmen."

Around her, these companions in misery took pity on one another, and began trading off seats.

"Yes, yes, sit right here for a while," said a fat man to an old woman bent almost double. "We'll take turns. We'll all get through if we help each other."

Marcia blinked her eyes. Amen to that.

As the long afternoon progressed, she found people making further arrangements. Some lifted up the divider between seats and lay crosswise on the bench made of two seats. Intimacy didn't matter; rest did. Others dropped their seat backs to the lowest position and dozed, almost reclining. She saw a man share a spare sandwich with a red-haired boy who looked starved. She saw her own Harry cadge a piece of candy from a dimpled girl.

Her traveling companion awakened with a start. "Oh, I overslept. You were supposed to have this," he said.

She smiled wryly. "Now we've both had some rest," she said. "I never had a chance to thank you. I'm Marcia White."

"Mike Jablonski," he said. "Where you going?"

"Cleveland."

"Me, I'm going to Omaha. I think this is a through coach. You can have my seat all the way to Chicago after that. I mean our seat."

They laughed.

He had reclined the seat as far back as it would go. Gratefully she sank into it, pulled the children about her, and rested. Nothing had ever felt better. In a while, she turned the seat back to him, and he perched Daisy in his lap and even made a corner for Harry. They would get through the seconds and minutes and hours, the light and dark, the dawn and dusk. They would share and survive.

As the evening thickened the train slowed to a crawl as it tackled the stern grades that would lift it over the Sierras. They would not see much of the fabled mountains at night, but it didn't seem to matter. At each stop, even in obscure corners to take on water or coal or switch crews, someone greeted them; people sent baskets of sandwiches or bottles of root beer or hot dogs or candies into the coaches, an outpouring that amazed Marcia and filled her soul with peace. It seemed that the whole world had heard of San Francisco's darkest hour, and was pouring its treasure out upon the refugees.

From the moment the quake had torn her home and life apart, people had helped her and the children every way they could. All except one.

CHAPTER 36

Rosemary Zastrow Lubbich found herself ensconced in the Conservatory at Golden Gate Park. Some of its glass had been shattered and no longer kept all the weather out, but her neighbors had shoveled the shards away and made a corner for her. She had become the focus of her neighbors' caring. A dozen of them, shocked by her tragedy, had escorted her to the park and cleaned a haven for her out of the shattered glass.

She had been to this place several times. It had been modeled on the Royal Observatory in Kew Gardens, England, and was one of the joys of the robust city on the bay. They wrapped her in blankets and brought her bread and broth from the city's field kitchens, and stayed with her in a vigil. She had let all this happen and was glad others were making decisions. She tried to think of her dead children, but her mind slithered away from that. The ocean fog eddied through the damaged structure, condensing into a heavy dew, but her friends had chosen well, placing her under a relatively undamaged wing that offered protection. At least a greenhouse surrounded her with plants.

Her poor Gretchen had never known happiness in her brief, painful life. Her cleft palate and harelip had darkened her spirit, even though surgery had rudely mended the defects. But children had made fun of her, her sunny spirits had faded to gloom, and she faced a life as a lonely spinster. Maybe the quake was God's way of sparing the child. But she didn't really believe that. Carl Jr.—they called him Carlos—

broke her heart. That bright child had become a bookworm, reading incessantly, pestering her with questions, showing all the signs of great intellect even at age eleven. Was that death also a gift of God? Angrily she dismissed the whole idea.

"Rosemary, we've sent word to City Hall that you're here," said Walter Eberhardt, her neighbor from across the street. "Carl will get it and find you. Is there anything you need?"

She needed to be alone, but she shook her head. "Thank you," she whispered.

Several of her neighbors were noisily scraping away glass to make nests for themselves. She wished they would stop.

She wasn't very sure she wanted to see her husband, either. Foreboding filled her. This earthquake had shaken apart everything. Nothing was solid anymore, not the solid brick of her home, not the solid bourgeois life she had lived with her children. And now there would be more. The earthquake would shake away the pleasant fraud of their marriage, and the pleasant comforts of an affluent life. She saw intuitively what was going to happen, and recoiled from it.

She hoped he would lie and say nothing; hoped they would resume their lives. She sighed, thinking about him and his two lives. Over many years she had put together tiny fragments, fitting them into an elaborate jigsaw puzzle. And did nothing because her life had been serene and secure, and what could she do anyway?

There had been so much: ticket stubs for two, the smell of perfume, jeweler's invoices for fabulous rings and bracelets and earrings. City business. Monkey business. Affluence, far beyond his city salary. She even knew the woman's name: Helene. There had been several women. Maybe all this came with Carl's Progressive politics, or her father-in-law's socialism. Her own Zastrow family hadn't been devout, but it had been archly traditional. She herself had drifted toward Carl's views, reading the *Nation* regularly.

He didn't show up that day.

Another neighbor, Ellis Wilburforce, said that Carl was doing heroic work repairing the mains.

Her friends fed her and nurtured her and vigiled with her that first night, never letting her sink into loneliness or discomfort. They turned a corner of the shattered Conservatory into a refuge. They were surrounded by exotic plants, shards of glass, and the scent of camellias.

Carl showed up on Friday, while she was sipping coffee that someone had managed to find and heat. He looked disheveled and distraught.

"How have you been?" he asked nervously.

She nodded.

"It's good that our friends have gathered around you. Our neighborhood is like that."

"Yes."

"Have you word of the children—where they were taken?"

"They were buried in a mass grave."

Arlen Baumgartner, who lived two doors down the block, explained: "An army crew came. They said they were under orders from a Colonel Torney, who's chief surgeon of the Department of California, to bury all bodies at once, for sanitary reasons. It . . . wasn't a very proper burial for Carlos and Gretchen, I'm afraid—"

Carl nodded. He seemed agitated. "Would you walk with me, Rosemary?" he asked.

"Whatever you have to say, you can say here in front of friends."

"I must see you privately."

"About what? Helene? Is she alive or dead?"

Carl paled, and glanced nervously about him.

"Helene was his mistress," she said relentlessly to the Bierstadts and the rest. "Carl lived two lives until the earthquake shook them apart."

"For God's sake, Rosemary—"

She was enjoying it. The others gaped. Elsie Baumgartner was all ears.

"Carl is a magician. He knows how to turn one income into three. One for his family and two more for himself," she said.

He looked stricken, which pleased her. Now the rest of the neighbors were listening. She continued, half hysterically, intending to let it all pour out no matter what.

"Carl was watching *Carmen* with his mistress Tuesday night. He forgot to throw away the ticket stubs. Very careless, Carl. You were much more clever when you started. I thought the tabs from the 'French restaurants,' as they're called, were for city business—instead of monkey business. What were you doing at the Poodle Dog night after night? Which floor did you visit? The second, with its private dining chambers, or the ones above? What's the fifth floor like, Carl? Did you sample all the wares? And what about all those nights at Zinkard's and Tate's and Delmonico's?"

Carl stared at her, and the others. "I have done great wrong," he said quietly. "And I will pay for it the rest of my life—maybe in prison."

She almost wanted to like him for that dignified confession. But it was too late.

"That's where you belong." She turned to the others. "Carl Lubbich, San Francisco city engineer, is also Abe Ruef's pet engineer. If the city water system failed, it is because my dear husband shelved all the efforts to fix it—for a price. Am I right, Carl?"

He nodded slowly.

"That's how he got so much cash. How much money did you sell out for, dear? What did they pay you for keeping the underwriters and Dennis Sullivan and people worried about safety off the back of the administration? That was easy, wasn't it, my dear? Just tell everyone that everything was fine; that the city had plenty of water to fight fires. Am I right?"

"How did you know, Rosemary?"

"How could I not know? How many years have I lived alone in my house while you were dealing with crooked contractors, putting kickbacks in the hands of that Abe Ruef, being a talking puppet for Eugene Schmitz? What do you think I am—blind?"

She watched Carl Lubbich wither, and enjoyed it. She hadn't enjoyed anything so much in years.

"Tell them, Carl. As long as you're making confessions, tell them."

Carl stared resolutely at the shards of glass all over the floor. "I am responsible for the death of San Francisco," he mumbled.

She wanted to laugh at his melodrama, but couldn't. In spite of her bitterness, she saw the honest self-indictment of a broken man who had summoned his dignity and aired his secret to his incredulous neighbors.

"I knew of the weaknesses but I did not press the Spring Valley Water Company to remedy them. Mr. Ruef did not want me to. The lines from the Crystal Springs and San Andreas and Pilarcitos Reservoirs run along, or over, faults, and are now demolished or gravely damaged. The Lake Merced line is better and will be repaired soon, when the pumping station is fixed. The city will have some water—a little, anyway. I did nothing about any of this, or require the water company to act. Now I carry the tragedy on my shoulders. It is not my doing alone—the utility and the city administration were at fault—but I was the key man, and the one who sold my soul."

He stood, slumped, his hands clenching and unclenching, a soft, weary sorrow enveloping him.

"It's a little late for remorse," she said sharply. Her own bitterness had been shaken loose, and it was pouring from the broken mains of her soul.

"Carl," said Phil Jessup, who lived across the alley, "I'm sure you're too hard on yourself. Earthquakes are acts of God."

Carl Lubbich slowly shook his head. "No. If I had done my duty there would be backup lines around or over the faults, cross connections, a backup saltwater system, and every cistern under the business district would have been kept full and in good repair."

They gaped at him. He stood resolutely, awaiting his fate.

"I went to Rudolph Spreckels and told him everything," Carl said.

"He said he would welcome my testimony when the time came. I will be punished, but I am relieved that I talked."

All this astonished Rosemary. This was not the Carl she had lived with for so long, the one whose suits sometimes held a long blond filament of hair, whose disappearances on "business" she understood and loathed, whose perfunctory presence on family occasions were shams, and whose betrayals for so many years had stung and then chilled and finally embittered her. She wanted to rake him over more coals in front of them all, but that was the other Carl, not this broken man.

"My life is over," he said. "I am a grafter. I carry a burden on my shoulders and in my heart beyond comprehension. I may be sent to San Quentin. I am not worthy of your friendship. I am unworthy of my father, who is an honorable public official. Or worthy of your love. I have no future. I cannot ever be employed in my profession. I will leave you now. What little remains to me will be spent doing what I can to make amends. I will say good-bye."

He turned to Rosemary. "I am sorry. I will leave you. You have lost children and comfort. Your husband is a crook. I will expect your divorce and will not resist. When this is over, I hope you will go back to Milwaukee and stay with your family. They are good people."

She wrung her hands nervously, his awful public confession trumping anything acidulous she might say. She knew enough not to whisper a word, not one word. She nodded.

She watched Carl Lubbich walk away, shattering the glass under his feet. It snapped and crackled like firing squads. He made his way past strangers, some of whom had witnessed all this, and out the doors. What had his life on earth come to? Through the shattered windows she could follow his movement through the crowds he had betrayed, the multitudes he had bled of their last cent. She thought that they would lynch him if they had any idea of his failure, or how the City of San Francisco succumbed, in the end, to his lecheries and lust.

CHAPTER 37

arrison White spent the night lying in a corner of Franklin Hall and pondering his next moves. He could go hunt for Marcia and the children, but what good would that do? There were, according to reports floating around Franklin Hall, over thirty thousand refugees in the Presidio, with more flooding in by the minute. It would be bootless for him to wander about the army's Pacific base looking for them. Marcia would be quite comfortable there.

He really didn't want to leave the temporary City Hall, where he was privy to everything that was going on. He knew all the scuttlebutt. He knew that Rudolph Spreckels's wife was having her baby a few blocks away on the lawn of their mansion on Van Ness; and that if the fires weren't stopped that mansion would be blown to bits in a last-ditch effort to stop the inferno. Everything east of that broad street was slated to be destroyed, and even now, General Funston was moving the last of his guncotton there, and every artillery piece at hand.

Harrison knew more than almost anyone. He knew more than, say, Captain Dinan of the police; more even than the mayor. He had drifted from desk to desk, listening. He knew much more than the reporters for the combined newspapers, who were hanging around hunting for news. He could tell them a thing or two. The combined newspapers they were printing over in Santa Rosa were nothing but secondhand stuff. Maybe he ought to let 'em know what was *really* afoot.

The navy had arrived. Admiral Goodrich's Pacific Squadron had sailed under full boiler power from San Diego and now the flagship *Chicago* was tied at Pier 24, and the *Marblehead, Boston, Paul Jones,* and *Princeton* were nearby. The *Preble*, sailing from the Mare Island Navy Yard, had offered all available nurses and surgeons to the people of San Francisco, while two navy fireboats, the *Active*, commanded by Midshipman Pond, and the *Leslie*, commanded by Boatswain Moriarty, were pouring streams of water on bay-front buildings. The sailors and marines were already pumping water well inland through fire hoses and defending the waterfront, including the Pacific Mail docks, Folger's Warehouses, and the Sailor's Home.

Lighters from Mare Island were bringing five thousand gallons of potable water at a crack, mostly from Goat Island. And White had heard that the bluecoats were shooting the starving dogs that had gathered in the North Beach area. The dogs were burrowing into ruins and eating human flesh. The Revenue Cutter *Golden Gate* had arrived, as well as the *Slocum*, while the British ship *Henley* had started its evaporators to supply drinking water to the desperate.

All that excited White. The public didn't know much about all this, but the insiders did. He felt he was at the center of the universe, wishing only that he could drop these marvelous tidbits on Marcia, just to watch her eyes glow. Maybe he could feed a few tidbits to reporters. They would remember him later on, and that would be a useful connection whenever he wanted some publicity.

Still, he was restless. He wandered through Franklin Hall, hoping to land some sort of assignment from the Committee of Fifty; disappointed that he had not been given a major task. Still, he firmly believed that crisis was opportunity, and that he could make good use of all this.

It was then that Fate found him.

"Where's that young architect?" asked Mayor Schmitz.

In seconds, White found himself standing before the towering mayor. "You wanted work. Well, here's work. We're moving the Chinamen out of Chinatown. This is one of the few blessings the fire has wrought. I'm negotiating with the Chinese—the merchants, you know—to move the whole lot down to Hunter's Point and take back the best land in the city.

"Go over there. I'll give you a pass that'll get you through police and military lines. Look it over. That hellhole's sitting on the best land in the city. Now it's gone and they're not coming back. I want a plan—streets, a park, water and sewer. I want to know what needs razing and what can be salvaged. I need a plan fast, before resistance builds up. We've been hoping Chinatown would burn up for years, and now it's happened. Report back to me on Monday with a complete plan."

"Monday!"

"Yes, Monday. That's when we start razing what's left of San Francisco, and Chinatown's high priority."

"What of the Chinamen, sir?"

"They're an underclass and they'll do what we require or we won't license their businesses."

"But so fast?"

"We don't want them returning to their lots and camping there. We're moving most of them to a compound up at Fort Mason. The army's setting up tents for them. The rest have fled across the bay to Oakland, or roundabout. But they'll return. We've no time at all. Report first thing Monday morning right here. I want that district to be the choicest area in San Francisco."

"At your service, sir!"

"Now there's one thing more. Before you submit your plan, study Daniel Burnham's master plan for the city. He wanted to remove Chinatown but ended up leaving the area blank. That's your bailiwick. The subcommittee on the restoration of civil government has a copy of the Burnham plan. Take a look. And talk to the Chinese Relief subcommittee. This was their idea." He scribbled something and handed the paper to White. "Here's a pass," he said. It read "Pass bearer through lines, E. E. Schmitz."

White read and reread it. Now he was one of the elite. The big chance had come to Harrison Barnes White. He had ten square blocks to design into the City Beautiful, with parks, fountains, residences, commercial districts, wide macadam boulevards, fine apartments, splendid restaurants, a five-star hotel or two—which he would design; good streetcar connections, a local firehouse and police station; superb new utilities to replace the filthy pits of that hellhole. It would become the prestige locale in the new San Francisco.

White pocketed his pass, feeling that at last he was a man of parts.

After that he examined the master plan that had been completed just before the quake by the greatest American city planner, Daniel Hudson Burnham. He had been invited by the Association for the Improvement and Adornment of San Francisco, and had spent several months working on his master design of the city. Up in Twin Peaks, seven hundred feet above the city, he and his staff set up shop. They had a commanding view of the whole city and the bay, and swiftly familiarized themselves with San Francisco by day and night, sunshine, cloud, and fog.

White had envied Burnham from the first, but lacked the reputation to join Burnham's experienced staff. The master plan included a civic center adjoining a new union railroad station, the whole surrounded by a broad boulevard, with even broader boulevards reaching out to the hills, which were to be turned into parks. Burnham proposed a Greek amphitheater on Twin Peaks, with a statue of San Francisco greeting the Orient. He had included parks and playgrounds reaching clear out to Lake Merced. The plan for Twin Peaks included a men's academy devoted to intellectual and artistic pursuits, while the lower slopes would be devoted to villas. San Francisco was to become a Paris of the West, and he would be the Baron Hausmann of it all.

And in the middle of the Burnham plan was a blank labeled Chinatown. Now, suddenly, that blank belonged to Harrison Barnes White. A wild ecstasy bloomed in him.

He got the rest of the story at the Chinese Relief desk, from a functionary named Brooks.

"The mayor's right. It didn't take much convincing," Brooks said. "Our goal at this desk is to get the Chinamen into camps, feed them, and move them out of the city. We've been talking to their merchant princes—if that's the word for them. Sing Fat, the merchant. Wing Chong Wo, the flour dealer. Sun Kam Wah, the yellow millionaire. They'll get the money out of China to rebuild down the peninsula. They're looking for land right now."

"What about titles? Some of the Chinamen owned their lots."

Brooks shrugged. "What's it worth to them now? The important thing is to get rid of that pesthole by whatever means. We'll do it properly, of course. Some are American citizens. But there've been twenty- to twenty-five-thousand yellow men jammed into ten square blocks, sometimes fifteen to a room. And we're going to end it."

"What a blessing!"

"Let me tell you in all sincerity," Brooks said, "that this is the answer to a lot of prayers. These are the lowest-class Chinese, you know. Not the Mandarins. I don't wish them harm, but they've been a blot on San Francisco, a vice-ridden quarter in the heart of the city—and now's our chance!"

"How did you persuade their leaders?"

Brooks shrugged. "They didn't need any. The Chinamen're stacked fifteen to a room, sleeping on their filthy pads in shifts, miserable because they're all jammed in. We'll move them out of sight, and they'll like it better. They'll have more room. No one will bother them. White people won't have to walk pass that cesspool of vice, knowing that a few yards away are hundreds of slave girls in cages, knowing that one can go there and smoke opium or gamble or engage in any evil known to mankind. How do you think our women felt, knowing they were so close to entire hotels devoted to vice? Of course! Terrible!"

The whole idea caught fire in White's mind. The quake was changing San Francisco, and he would be a part of the change. He knew then and there that the city would be a better place if the Chinamen were removed.

"Thanks, Mr. Brooks. I'm on my way over there."

He commandeered a pad of newsprint and a pencil and headed east, running into a Citizen Police patrol almost at once.

"You can't go in there," a tough fellow said.

"I'm on city duty."

"Scram, fella, or we'll shoot you for a looter."

"I'm on city business, damn you," White snapped. "Here!" He shoved the mayor's pass at them.

"I don't care who signed this. You're not going in there," said one.

"By God," bellowed White, "I'll go back to City Hall and get some reinforcements."

"Let's see that pass," said the other, a skinny young man toting a rifle.

White thrust it at him.

"Signed by Schmitz," the skinny one said to the other.

"That don't mean nothing. Lots of fake paper around. This guy just wants to cut rings off dead fingers."

White sighed. "The fact is, the mayor wants me to look over Chinatown and come up with a plan. He's moving the Chinamen out and he needs a plan fast—parks, circles, boulevards, water and sewer."

"Yeah? Moving out the Chinamen and the slave girls? I thought he was getting a cut. Him and Ruef get a cut. Everyone knows that."

White took his pass back. "I'll get reinforcements. I'm going to talk to the mayor." He wheeled to leave.

"Hey, you. Go on in. I don't want no trouble," said the skinny man.

"There will be if you don't honor this pass right now."

They let him through. White boiled and fumed, but no one molested him the rest of the long walk to Chinatown. He saw pairs of soldiers, but they didn't stop him. He dreaded the soldiers less than Schmitz's hastily commissioned militia. White thought highly of the army, and General Funston, and their disciplined minions.

The whole burned-over area still leaked acrid smoke and fumes and radiated heat. Down in basements, and underneath heaps of rubble, fires still smoldered. In some places, where the structures had been wood, the city had been leveled to black ash, dotted by pits that had once been basements. In places where brick and stone had been employed, ruined walls stood, some of them dangerous and murderous, teetering and ready to tumble. He became aware of swift darting movement, and realized this whole wasteland was populated by rats; thousands upon thousands of them, up out of the sewers and cellars, eating flesh—human, dog, cat, bird, and decaying butcher meats, as well as anything else. This foul spectacle shocked him. Where had they come from? Had San Francisco been laid over a whole rat-field?

The idea came to him that these were Chinatown rats; that they could not possibly have lived under the rest of the city. He had heard about the maze of secret tunnels, makeshift cesses, stinking holes, used by the Chinamen, and now he had proof. The rats hardened his resolve to scrape every last shred of Chinatown away and turn it into a modern white men's city, with sanitary conditions, gardens, parks, squares, fountains, and every amenity of European civilization. It wasn't a dream; it was a mission.

CHAPTER 38

Harrison White peered into the smoking ruins on DuPont Street, looking for the fabled tunnels that ran under Chinatown. Everyone knew about the tunnels, a labyrinth below grade-level, where the Chinamen engaged in unspeakable Oriental vices, kept slave girls, smoked opium, and most significantly, murdered one another in vast, vicious tong wars conducted by the Six Companies.

But there weren't any tunnels. Puzzled, he walked from one ruin to another, peering into the shallow pits, where debris still smoked. Maybe they were simply buried under the rubble, so he poked and probed carefully, even clambering into one hot hole for a closer look. No tunnels. What he did discover was countless rats, and they were eating human remains. The sight nauseated him and he hastily retreated to street level. The crude sewers of Chinatown had broken open, and every subterranean rodent was freed. He tried to map the sewer system, and realized it was beyond mapping. The city would have to start over, running lines down streets.

But no tunnels. Were the stories all nonsense? He knew men who had descended into them, led by Chinamen who were taking them to opium dens. Was it all a mirage, deliberately concocted to give white men a sense of danger and mystery when they visited the hellholes of Chinatown? It would certainly seem that way.

He made notes and then drifted north, toward Waverly Place. Something was happening there, and he wished to see just what. He spotted twenty or so Chinamen, plus some soldiers and a policeman. The Chinamen had knelt in the ashes, or prostrated themselves in the ruins of what had been Chinatown's most prominent Joss house, the Temple of Shaie Tai. White recognized the burned place—but just barely, and only because the Chinamen were holding some sort of ceremony there.

"What is this?" he asked the copper.

"Chinamen come over from Oakland, had to get permission, so they could propitiate their gods, I guess. See that burned thing? That's it, what's left of Shaie Tai. That's what they're here for, to pay the charred devil his due."

"And they were let in?"

"Yeah, it's important to 'em, so they wangled it after getting turned back a few times. They spent the night at the Ferry Building. Finally got permission and I was assigned to run 'em over here."

White listened to the priest's plaintive chanting to the fallen Joss, while others spread the offerings of food and incense, or prayed silently. The prayers were surely heartfelt, and no doubt intended for all the thousands of Chinamen made homeless by the quake and fire. But it all seemed strange and heathenish to White. All the more reason to move the whole lot down to Hunter's Point, he thought. What a spectacle to describe to Marcia! She would be so envious of him!

He watched the supplicants for half an hour and then drifted away, wandering the streets, much preoccupied with the plaintive prayers, the chants done in unison, the rites, the fragrances, the fervent pleading of these Orientals to their fallen and charred deity.

While thus engaged, he heard the soft chatter of a motor car, and discovered a massive one, lacquered ebony, working its way patiently south on DuPont. The street was impassable, littered with brick and stone, scorched beams, and rubble. But whenever the long, low-slung touring machine was stymied, several agile Chinamen hopped out and cleared the way, sometimes removing smoldering timbers.

Some tong leader, some Oriental lord of all the vices, had come to examine the devastation. White waited, uncertain about what to do. The machine halted half a block away, and its occupants emerged. The one who caught White's eye was wearing a gray business suit, white shirt and cravat. He was stocky, heavy, with straight jet hair graying at the temples of a massive, square face. The touring car had halted before the ruins of what had been one of the great Oriental trading companies in San Francisco, Sing Fat & Co., at 614 DuPont. The man and his minions peered into the pathetic ruins of what had been a goodly mercantile chocked full of treasures, ranging from Ming vases to bamboo furniture and silks. The inferno had consumed it all.

Smoke eddied up from the rubble, most of which had fallen into a stonemasonry-lined basement. White watched from a distance, not wanting contact with those he would be dispossessing, especially the Chinaman who was probably Sing Fat.

But he had not gone unnoticed, and the Chinaman walked directly to White, surveying him curiously, especially the pad of newsprint in White's hands.

"It is a tragedy, yes?" the man asked, offering a hand.

White took it gingerly. "Yes, sir."

"I have lost everything. But I will rebuild and start over. May I introduce myself? I am Sing Fat, whose misfortune you see before you."

"I, ah, am Harrison White."

"I see that you are not a looter. I feared there would be many, and that the Chinese would have little recourse. But you carry paper in hand and it is filled with notes."

"No, I'm just curious. There are no tunnels."

The flesh about Sing Fat's eyes crinkled slightly, as close to a smile as he would come. "No tunnels except for a few frauds. The Chinese make money, however they can, with what is left to us by your restrictions. Some of us pick rags, work as houseboys, do laundry, garden, pick up trash, sew for pennies an hour. Others make silly tunnels with many corners for those white men looking for danger." He paused. "And what brings such a one as you here, while heat still pours from these ruins?"

"The mayor sent me, to, ah, inventory things."

"I see. And has this anything to do with removing my people to Hunter's Point?"

"Well, sort of."

"Ah, it is plain. Would you be in the employ of the city designer Burnham?"

"No, sir. I'm an architect and city planner, but not connected with him."

"But you have come to fill in the hole."

"Fill in?"

"The blank place in Burnham's master plan. I have seen it. You are here even before the heat dies away, so the mayor can begin his work."

"Well, the mayor just thought to take advantage of the opportunity to see what exists here, what needs doing."

This time Sing Fat smiled. "The gentleman before you is a citizen of this great nation, and has designs upon his own deeded property. While it is true that the people of this city may not wish Sing Fat and Company to exist in this place, and while it is also true that the honorable mayor and the courts may bend the laws to effect change, and trample ever so gently upon the state and federal constitutions all in the name of good order and high principle, it also remains true that I am vested with certain inalienable rights. Would you not agree, Mr White?"

"Well, of course, this would all be voluntary—"

"Ah, an amazing word, *voluntary*. We could voluntarily move to Hunter's Point and render ourselves invisible, while still conducting a rich import and export trade that would benefit the city, is that not so? It would take so little. A loss of a city business license. A condemnation of a district for sanitary reasons—substandard sewers, for instance. A quarantine against disease. A little encouragement for a voluntary move. And would the city purchase title to my lot? Or would it be a voluntary surrender of my ownership? Ah, Mr. White, you are a just and good man to listen to Sing Fat."

"I'm sure you would be compensated."

"Oh, yes. And how much? They will say this lot is worth so little because it lacks proper sewer connections, or whatever." He nodded slightly. "Thank you, Mr. White, for hearing me. Now we must begin cleaning the foundations. We intend to rebuild within the week. By tomorrow, this pit will be cleared of rubble. By the time you submit your plan to Mayor Schmitz, we expect to be putting up walls. Possession, Mr. White, is nine-tenths of the law. Tell your friend the mayor that Sing Fat has started to rebuild."

"I'll do that, sir."

The merchant swiveled away. White watched him direct his crew into the pit. They were wasting not a moment. Even as White stared, transfixed, the gloved Chinamen were lifting hot bricks and stones, one by one, and piling the rubble outside of the basement.

That appalled him. How could he develop his master plan if the treacherous Chinamen were going to rebuild before anyone knew what was happening? He would have to hurry; submit a plan so compelling that it would be unstoppable. His whole career hung in balance.

He retreated from that site, his mind seething, his spirit unsettled. He cut over to Stockton, needing distance from the merchant. On Stockton he paused at an above-ground heap of rubble that seemed alive with rats. He could see scores, maybe hundreds, crawling everywhere through a maze of charred timbers, wire mesh, brick and stone. A powerful stench nauseated him. The rats swarmed one area and he approached it gingerly, afraid of what he would see. There, in a collapsed room half full of rubble, the rats were devouring several human bodies. They were Chinamen or -women, but that's about all he could tell. The straight black hair was his only clue. The rest was mostly bones and red-stained remains, ribs and femurs, skulls and tibias and fingers. Revolted, he retreated from the whole appalling scene, and ached for a handkerchief to turn away the frightful stench.

He ran, helter-skelter, up Stockton until a shot rang out and he heard a yell. Behind him stood two soldiers, their Krag-Jorgensen rifles leveled.

"Stop where you are, looter!" bellowed one.

White's pulse soared. He hardly dared reach into his breast pocket for his papers.

"We caught ya red-handed," one said. He was relishing the moment. "Ya know what we do with looters? Shoot 'em. Orders from General Funston himself." The soldier was grinning.

"For God's sake I can explain."

"They all can," said the other. "Dandy fella like you, out looting."

"I'm with the city. I've got papers."

"You're with the city, are ya? We're with the army."

"Look, let me get my papers. In my breast pocket. I'm a city planner. The mayor sent me."

"Sure, and you was running the moment you saw us."

"No, for God's sake I was running from all those rats eating the Chinamen."

"That's a likely story. You saw us and was running."

"Look. Search me. If I'm a looter then I should have loot. I don't."

"I see a big fat ring on your finger, pal."

"That's my class ring. I'm Harrison White. Just let me show you my papers. Ask the mayor. He wanted me to draw up some plans for Chinatown. We're moving them out. He wants it done before they swarm in here and rebuild."

"And you was runnin' your little heart out to get away from us."

"Please listen! Look at my pass."

One of them smirked. "Okay, maybe we'll take a gander. If you ain't what you say, it's curtains, pal."

White stared at the leveled rifles, their bayonets gleaming wickedly in the sun. He could die! He'd heard several reports of people who were simply returning to their homes or flats to get things they'd forgotten, being shot. And now it was happening to him. His heart tripped.

"I'm going to reach into my breast pocket. I'm not armed. I'm just getting a paper from the mayor. Read it and then check me out. I'll prove it. I'll prove everything."

The smiling soldier nodded. With trembling hand, White reached into his breast pocket, half afraid the pass wouldn't be there. But it was. He pulled it out slowly, opened it and started to walk toward the smiling one.

"Stop," said the other one. "Lay it on the ground and step back."

White did.

One of them kept his rifle leveled. The other picked it up and read it, his lips forming words. The man was barely literate.

"I don't see nothing about anything," he said.

"Let me read it to you," White begged. "It's a pass from the mayor that says I'm on city business and should be shown every courtesy. In fact you can help me. I need to examine this whole district. See this notepad? That's what it's for. If I were a looter, what would I be doing with notes?"

He found himself babbling, talking, thinking about running, barely able to keep himself in place.

The soldier studied it and turned to the other. "See what you think. I think this lobster's a looter." He backed away, lifted his rifle, and then handed the pass to the other, who read it.

"It's a pass all right, 'less he stole it. Maybe he stole the thing off someone. He was running from us." He eyed White. "All right. Take off that coat and toss it here. I want to see them pockets inside out."

White managed to pull off his suit coat and toss it. And managed to unload his pants pockets, which contained little. He carried his billfold in his breast pocket, and there would be little in that, either.

One soldier continued to hold White at gunpoint, while the other ransacked his suit coat.

"Why were you running?" he asked. "That's what I want to know. I still think you're a looter."

Somehow, White sensed he would live. This was just talk now.

"Take me to Franklin Hall and talk to him. Take me to General Funston."

The one guarding him put up his rifle. "Well, I sure would like to shoot you," he said.

Sweating and half-crazed, White collected his grimy suit coat, the pass, and his billfold, and restored himself.

"I still think you're guilty as hell," said the soldier.

illis Hart studied the young woman just ahead, determining first off whether she wore a wedding ring. She didn't. A good sign. He wished to get to know her. Life was too short to fiddle around.

"Good morning," he said.

She turned, her gaze taking him in. She was prettier than he had thought, and her eyes were warm and her face inviting.

"I guess it is," she said, and laughed.

"Did you sleep in the park?"

"Where else? Some fellows invited me to stay in their tent."

"You stayed in a tent with strangers?"

The cheer drained from her face. "You're pretty quick with your notions," she said.

"Just envy," he replied.

She laughed. He liked the laugh, which dissolved all the world's troubles in its music.

"I'm Willis Hart, and I'm an insurance adjuster."

"Nella Clapp," she said, turning to shake his hand.

"You're holding up the line," said someone. He hastened forward with her.

"And what do you do?"

"Domestic service, I guess. I just was discharged. Since then I've been talking to people. I talked to Caruso. I talked to John Barrymore, but I didn't know that at first. They're just like us."

"I doubt it."

Her face wrinkled into a grin. "You certainly are contrary."

"I just doubt that those two are anything like me. I'm a practical man." He wondered if she were one of those hopelessly romantic young women who got crushes on notable people.

The line edged forward. Breakfast this morning would be bread and coffee. Not bad, he thought. He could use a gallon of coffee. His body ached.

"Well, I liked them. Especially Barrymore. He gave me fruit. He was staying in a home on Van Ness. I don't suppose it exists anymore, the way they're blowing everything up. I like him because he's a cad. I never met a cad before. He's going to write a book about the earthquake and he said it would all be an invention." She laughed merrily. "Actors. The real world just gets in their way."

"Please join me for breakfast. I have something I want to talk to you about," he said.

That piqued her. "You do? We don't even know each other."

"Maybe that's best."

"Are you going to offer me a position?"

"Oh, just talk."

They each received a loaf of bread and a tin mess cup full of coffee, and he steered her toward a knoll where they could sit in the early sun. The distant fires seemed subdued. The breezes swept out of the west, driving the conflagration back upon itself.

She tore into her bread, breaking off chunks as if she hadn't eaten in days. He watched, eating more daintily himself. She had magnificent complexion, smooth-fleshed, peachy and warm. She had gusto, and innate good humor. All that he read into her with a few glances. She caught him gazing at her and pursed her lips.

"Am I interesting?"

"You're beautiful."

"I've sure heard that fifty times."

That disconcerted him a little. He had expected a demure "thank you."

"I guess I am," she continued. "But I don't like my chin and my neck's too thick. All the heroines in romances have swan necks."

"I guess you're stuck with it," he said.

She laughed. "You're not supposed to say that. You're supposed to say that I'm just imagining things and my neck is as graceful as a swan's. That's what men do in the novels I read."

"And then what happens?"

"You can guess."

"Why were you discharged?"

"Oh, ah—well I didn't steal anything if that's what you're thinking."

"I wasn't thinking anything. I was just curious."

"And nosy. I was in service to the Argentine consul on Nob Hill and his son discharged me. They're in Monterey, I guess. That's all I'm going to tell you."

"How old is the son?"

"Old enough to be trouble."

Hart grinned. He didn't mind this lady at all. "What are you going to do now?"

"I've got to do something," she said.

"Get a new position?"

"Ha!"

He wondered what that meant. "Who are you—I mean, where did you come from?"

"You sure are nosy."

"Well, I have something in mind. I need to find out about you."

"I get it. You're an insurance adjuster and they sent you to see if I took something."

"Nothing could be further from the truth." He felt reckless, and he decided to be reckless. "I will tell you what happened to me, and my purpose, and see what happens."

She ate lustily, but she was obviously all ears.

"Yesterday morning I returned to my neighborhood south of the Slot, and an army burial detail collared me. I couldn't escape. They had bayonets ready to stab anyone running off. I spent the entire day doing things too terrible to describe. It was so repulsive that I want to forget it. But I can't. I finally wangled some clothing—this doesn't fit but it's all I have—and I still didn't feel clean. I spent the night up in Twin Peaks in a gazebo there where I could see the whole city die.

"Well, yesterday changed my life. I hadn't thought much about disease or accident or death—I've always been healthy. Here I am, an insurance adjuster, and I hadn't really thought about it. But suddenly I was burying pieces of the dead, people like me, whose dreams and lives ended abruptly. And I wondered, Why them? Why not me? Well, to shorten this a little, I decided to speed up my life. I'm not going to wait for anything, because tomorrow, or ten minutes from now, maybe it'll be my turn."

She nodded. She had stopped eating and was listening intently now.

"Well, I decided to live every second as if there's not going to be another. I will find my happiness wherever I can. I'm going to start up the insurance office immediately and start helping our customers. I'm going to do what I want and get what I want, and not be patient. Then I saw you."

He let that sink in. He could see she was getting an inkling of what this was about. Her face glowed. Maybe this was a scene she had read in a romance.

"I'm courting you," he said. "If you like me, and I like you, we can make the rest of it work fine. I don't think I need to know a whole lot about you. Just a few things. If you're happy or sour, if you're nice or not. Nothing else matters much. I want you to find out as much about me. And if you like me, then let's get married. Right now."

"Married?" She marveled.

"Yup, hitched."

"But I don't know—" She paused, giggled, and took his hand. "You're reckless," she said.

"You are, too," he replied.

"Don't you think we should talk?"

"Sure. What do you want to know?"

"Lots of things. Would you be mean to me?"

"Never."

"Would I have some freedom?"

"All you want."

"Can you support me?"

"I was doing pretty well. Now I'm going to do very well."

"Do you like children?"

"Very much. In time. There's so much to do first."

Her face fell. "I can't," she said.

"Why not? I like children."

"I just can't."

"You were interested. You didn't just say no. Then something happened and now you're saying no."

"Don't be nosy. Maybe you're not my type. Maybe I'm not as reckless as you."

"But you are. You're a daring woman, Nella. I can tell."

"Maybe that's the trouble," she said darkly.

She sank into silence and he sat beside her, puzzled.

"You want love and a long courtship and romance."

"No, none of that. I'd marry the right person right now, today, if I could. The earthquake changed things for me, too. I hardly know what to do."

"Then why not me?"

"Well, why you? There's lots of fish in the sea."

He felt her drifting away. Maybe that was good. Maybe she wasn't the right one. But he thought he would keep on talking.

"I guess people think there's a Miss Right or Mr. Right, and sometimes there is. But most people are strangers when they marry. I watched my older sisters when they were being courted. You know what? They barely knew the men they were marrying. The gents would come to call. They'd sit in the parlor and take tea and make talk. They courted a long time—two years for one sister, one year for the other. But it was just as risky for them as for us. They did have one advantage: they were from the same town and they could always check up on things. But both my sisters are quite happy now. It's not risky. People just become comfortable and then they're friends. Maybe that's not like the passion in those novels you read, but it's what the real world is about."

She nodded gravely. She was listening, and he could see she was looking him over, blotting up everything she could about him. That was good. She seemed to glow. Here she was, just as fresh as if she'd come from a bath, but she had been living helter-skelter for days, like everyone else. He decided her joyous spirit had something to do with it.

"Don't misunderstand me. I'm not against love. I hope it comes. I'm not even suggesting that we should love each other now. All we can be is new friends."

"But you don't want children."

He sensed that this was what was troubling her.

"I would be a good father," he said. "My parents raised me carefully. You would like our children's grandmother. She's in pretty good health."

"But you want to wait."

"Only for a while. We have a burning city before us. Doesn't that say something to you?"

She smiled suddenly. "This is crazy," she said.

"It's unusual. Look at that smoke. Look at the ruins. On Tuesday, who would have imagined that by the next morning there would be refugees in a ruined city—without food or clothes or water or shelter? And that San Francisco would burn to the ground? And that nothing meant anything anymore."

"Things mean a lot to me," she said. "I like babies."

There it was again.

"I do, too," he said.

She stirred restlessly, took his tin mess cup and carried it back to the boiler and dropped it in. He wondered if she would just walk away. So fragile was this encounter that he expected her to. But she didn't. She turned back, and settled herself beside him. The chill breeze from the ocean cut through his clothing and the sun wasn't helping.

"Let's see if we can get some loaves. Then let's walk up to that place I found on Twin Peaks. We can see the whole world, almost. We can see across the bay. We can see across the Golden Gate. We can see way down the peninsula. It's a bench with a back, too. We can sit on it instead of on the grass. And it has a roof."

She nodded. There was something in her nod that seemed tender. But her face had a tragic cast, as if she bore secrets, as if she could never bring herself to marry. She puzzled him, but maybe if they talked, heart-to-heart, it would all come clear. Sometimes she was all smiles and cheer; other moments, she turned distant and looked at him like a doe ready to bolt.

"I'll get my blanket," she said. "They gave me one."

Minutes later the pair left Golden Gate Park, and he resolutely led her up long foothills, past unscathed villas and homes, around thickets of manzanita brush and cedars, until the city lay below them.

"Oh!" she exclaimed, when they rounded a bend and she beheld the gazebo. "Is this where you slept last night?"

"Not sleep, exactly. But my thoughts changed my life. Like it?"

She turned to him. "Yes. It's a dream compared to the park. But I'm not in the mood for romance. You understand?"

"Yes."

"Then I'll sit and talk, and after a while—before dark—we can go back down to the panhandle."

"Why go back? This is better."

She smiled. "You're a cad and a bounder. But I don't mind. I'm tired of all those people. I'm tired of waiting in lines for everything, and having no place to go. Okay, you and me'll talk if you like. You first, and then my turn."

That seemed promising. Willis liked the place, too. It was a haven from soldiers, desperados, crowds, and even rain because of the roof. And it was also, he realized, the perfect place for a man to court a woman. He and Nella were alone.

CHAPTER 40

mil Wolff died that evening. He never spoke another word to Katharine. She lay in her cot beside him, listening to his rasping breath, which came in gusts between long and frightful pauses. At first he looked at her now and then, but later he closed his eyes and did not open them.

She knew he was glad to go. Life had become too hard, and this brutal end was more than he could endure.

She knew he was gone but didn't want to summon the nurse. She just wanted to lie there in the cot beside his, get through the night. She feared they would put her out if she told them. If they put her outside, she would die, too.

But they found out in the middle of the evening. A new nurse checked. She tried to find a pulse. She pushed an eyelid back, but Emil was seeing nothing. She retreated, and then returned with a new doctor, who did his own swift examination. Then he wrote something in a folder.

"You are his wife?" he said, turning to her.

"Yes."

"He's gone. I'm sorry. Pneumonia with complications."

"I know."

"We'll have to take him away now, Mrs. Wolff."

She didn't correct him.

"Where?"

He paused, choosing words. "There is no mortuary. The dead are being taken to a place outside. They'll be buried as fast as possible for sanitary reasons. If you want a service—"

She shook her head.

"We need these cots. It says here you're suffering from exhaustion, exposure, and arthritis, but not contagious disease. Would you like me to check?"

She nodded.

He took her temperature, listened to her heart and lungs, examined her eyes and throat, and stood up.

"Unless you've caught something that hasn't presented itself to me, you're getting along. I have to make room. We have a dozen serious cases without cots."

She was afraid of that. Her few hours in paradise had come to an end. So she would get up and walk into the night. Emil was gone. She shed no tears. She had been steeling herself for this ever since the woman in white had wheeled them here.

"Mrs. Wolff—you're listed as Katharine Steinmetz, is that right?"

She nodded.

"You aren't well enough to go outside. We need the cot, but we'll make a place for you on a pad in the building. There's a room next to this. You'll have your wheelchair. I'm sorry. This is the best we can do."

"It's paradise," she said, thinking of the endless, cold, desperate night she and Emil had endured. She watched two orderlies, both soldiers, lift Emil into a khaki canvas stretcher and take him away. That was her last glimpse of him. She would weep later. In a week, or a month, if she lived.

Then they lifted her into Emil's chair and wheeled her to a gloomy storeroom, where they made a place on a cotton-stuffed pad on a wooden floor, and gave her two blankets. She was not alone. This corner was filled with the suffering.

She lay on the pad, almost comfortable, and warm enough at last. No one knew her; no one loved or cared. And yet she had met with all sorts of kindness these past days. But as she lay there she wished she had gone, too. What would she do? Where would she go? How could she survive? She no longer had the Kodet, or the darkroom, or a few dollars for films and chemicals. No longer a home. No clothes, shelter, food, comfort—or hope.

She dozed that night, in spite of the endless stir, the people, the nurses coming and going. She didn't think of anything. Not of Emil, not their friends in the galleries and Bohemian saloons, not her immigrant family or early life. She realized she was too tired to think of anything, including her future. Ever since the quake, she had lived in the present, as if the future had ceased to be. That was all too true. Her future had ceased to be, and she wondered why they were keeping her alive. She would surely perish in a week or two or three.

Still other nurses and a doctor checked her the next day, and said she was better. They brought her breakfast, a bowl of oatmeal without sugar or salt or cream. It sufficed to sustain life.

"We have a place for you," said a nurse, this one young and fresh and rested. "The army's put up new tents, and there's one for single women. Sixteen to a tent. We'll wheel you there. You can keep the pad and you have your own blanket."

So they took her there, through a sharp April morning, the sun blinding her on this the first day of her widowhood. The orderlies announced themselves politely outside the circular walled tent, and then wheeled her in. A dozen women lay about within, amid a turmoil of clothing and bedding, valises and trunks.

"This is Katharine Steinmetz, ladies," said one of the soldiers. "She'll be staying with you."

Katharine could not imagine where. The place seemed to bulge with things. But then a middle-aged woman rose, pushed and pulled, and made a slot for Katharine's pad, all the while eyeing her, even as Katharine glanced at all of these women whose lives had suddenly become enmeshed with her own. Then, suddenly, the orderlies vanished and she felt the gazes of these tentmates. They studied her, studied the wheelchair.

"I fear you're overcrowded and I—"

"Oh, the more the merrier," said one.

There were introductions: Beth, Marcy, Drusilla, Mrs. Williams, Annette, Evelyn, Helen, Phaedra . . . Katherine couldn't get them all straight. She discovered one infant and one little girl among them, but most were older women like herself.

"You're the photographer," said one, Evelyn, she thought.

"Yes."

"I saw your exhibits. You showed with that engraver."

"Emil Wolff. He died last night."

"I'm so sorry—"

"It's all right. Every one of us here must be dealing with loss."

That proved to be true. Husbands and children and parents missing and presumed dead. Women separated from loved ones, and without news.

The sun beat through the tent, bathing the interior with amber light. The musky smell of canvas mixed with those of the barely washed women, and the heaped clothing. It wasn't unpleasant. An earthquake had catapulted her out of her flat, taken her lover, destroyed her possessions and means, sickened her, and now deposited her with a dozen strangers. But she was alive, with a roof of sorts over her, and help when she needed to go to the latrine trenches or eat. Things could have been worse.

"What happened to you?" asked one of them. "Everybody's told her story."

Katharine told hers. It turned out to be not exceptional.

She needed to be alone, but that wasn't possible, so she retreated to her pad. "I'm going to take a siesta," she said.

"Can we use your wheelchair?" asked one.

Katharine nodded. That chair was pure gold. Even before she had settled herself on her pad, the women were allotting themselves ten minutes each in the seat.

She dozed, frequently interrupted by the endless stir within the tent. Sometimes she listened quietly. Hers wasn't the only tragedy. One of them had watched a falling cornice from a Kearny Street building kill her husband beside her. Another, a young woman in tears, worried about her missing fiancé. Another's daughter had died in the fires. All of their homes and possessions had been destroyed, and they faced the world with empty hands and purses.

They talked of escape, of finding lost relatives, of wondering what happened to a husband or parent, of what tomorrow might bring, of renewed quakes, or unquenchable fires, or failure of the tenuous food supply.

They came and went, and when she finally did sit up early in the evening, she found not twelve but sixteen jammed into the darkened tent. She peered about her, hungry and thirsty, not refreshed but at least she had kept exhaustion at bay. And there was something else here. Sisterhood. Fate had tossed them together but now they were looking after one another, sharing, sympathizing, comforting the bereaved.

"You're awake," said one, addressing Katharine.

"Yes. I'm better now."

"You lost your husband. That must be desolating."

"He thought it was a blessing to die."

"Oh . . . but you're alone."

"I've been alone ever since I left my family. I've made my own way. I've survived arthritis, poverty, earthquake, and fire. I've earned my living, and helped Emil—my man, too. I'm strong. I hope you all think of this as a test of your strength. I ask myself, Why am I upon the earth, but it is the wrong question. The right question is, What is to be done?"

Katharine sat up. One of the women instantly vacated the wheel-chair, and Katharine took it. This was not a bad place. It was comfort-able. Sixteen women in a circular tent, their beds laid out like spokes, warmed the air without a fire. Laundered clothing hung from every pole. Some of the women had washed their hair, and now sat comb-ing it.

"We've been talking about notifying families, Mrs. Steinmetz," said one. "We could help you. The post office is accepting mail without stamps. And they have the telegraph working again. You can send a wire anywhere in the country without paying. The Army Signal Corps has been stringing wires. And have you heard about the registries? You can sign one, tell people where you are and who you're looking for."

Katharine sighed. She had not been in contact with her family for many years. The trouble had begun when she plunged into the Bo-hemian life and politics of lower Manhattan and deepened when she took up Progressive causes. They had retreated in pained silence. The rift worsened when she and Emil lived together.

"I am not in touch with my family, thank you. I'm quite alone," she said.

"What are you going to do? Do you have a place to go?"

Katharine smiled. "I'll deal with that one day at a time. But with good people like you around me, I'll be all right."

Someone laughed.

"I'm not very good at names, but I hope before we separate, I'll know you all and someday we'll be exchanging postcards. It just hap-pens I'm ready for sisterhood just now."

"Oh, we don't know what we'd do without everyone," said the girl, the one whose fiancé had vanished during the fires.

That evening, with help so abundant and instantly offered, she was able to eat, drink, attend to her needs, and settle comfortably on her stuffed pad, a tiny haven against the world.

She had lost Emil that very morning, yet these women had swiftly filled the void. And for once, she was being waited on, rather than serv-ing. The thought made her feel guilty. But for the first time in days, she felt secure, and the discovery of such goodness and grace in others brought her close to tears.

But that evening, as she lay quietly, listening to the scattered con-versation, she felt strong. Perhaps she had nothing, but she had herself. And within her was the power and strength to shape a splendid new life. She had skill and an artistic sensibility. She knew where she would begin: with a letter to the Londons.

CHAPTER 41

. . . .

Carl Lubbich stood outside the makeshift tent hospital in Golden Gate Park watching army orderlies carry a body, a young woman apparently, toward a place where other bodies lay in a row. He counted seventeen bodies waiting to be taken somewhere and buried.

He could see into the tents, where surgeons were operating on bloody tables made of doors yanked off their hinges, and sawhorses, with no light save for whatever sun leaked in, and whatever the hanging coal oil lamps could provide. Outside of one tent a steaming kettle over a fire sterilized instruments. Another nearby tent did not muffle the groaning and weeping of the wounded and burned, many of whom were lying on the cold ground wrapped in blankets.

There were other makeshift hospitals functioning all over San Francisco, and St. Mary's had moved itself into the paddlewheeler *Merced* out in the bay.

The doctors, most of them in grimy street clothes, looked worn. The nurses, in blood-smeared and stain-soaked clothing, looked even more exhausted. Many had been on duty almost continuously since the quake, snatching only bare moments of rest. They were heroines and heros.

Things were getting better, people said. Crews had patched or plugged the mains on the west side, and Lake Merced was supplying water to some of the city. No one would die of thirst, and the exhausted fire companies had something to fight with. The Spring Valley Water Company and city maintenance crews, aided by help from Oakland, had pulled things together.

The quake had killed a lot of people—no one knew how many—straight off, and injured hundreds, maybe thousands, more, and some of those were dying now. That was an act of God. The fires had burned and killed many hundreds more. Exposure, evacuation of frail people, lack of medical attention because the hospitals were ablaze, had taken lives, left others desperately ill, and would continue to kill in the weeks ahead. Some, not all, of that could be laid at the feet of City Engineer Carl Lubbich.

To be sure, others were culpable. He could name a roll of honor, starting with Abe Ruef and Mayor Schmitz, and including those gentlemen whose water company had failed the city. But all in all, Lubbich supposed he was responsible for the death of a thousand or two thousand mortals—he found himself thinking in terms of thousands of deaths as if the numbers were an accounting problem—and responsible as well for the destruction of unfathomable amounts of property.

He wondered why he had been born.

As he stared at the hurrying nurses and doctors, darting in and out of tents, he beheld a pile of stuff—he could give it no other name—taken from or abandoned by patients, the sick and dead. Ruined suit coats, dresses, bloody shoes, various purses and bags, a few pocket knives, what appeared to be a Phi Beta Kappa key on a tether, homburgs, battered fedoras, a crutch, bloodstained newspapers, a cane, a shirt cut to shreds, a birdcage with a dead canary in it, and a revolver. It simply lay there, half buried under the debris.

He took it.

It was loaded.

He stuffed it into his breast pocket, where it weighted down his lumpy suit coat. No one saw him, but if they had, it didn't matter. Nothing mattered. Carl Lubbich was a man without a future.

Losing two children was bad. Losing his wife was bad. Losing his home and job was bad. Losing his reputation was bad. Losing his self-esteem was bad. Losing hope, dignity, and faith were bad. But losing all reason to exist wasn't so bad.

He retreated from the hospital, from the moaning, the sobs, the shrieks, the groans, the weary voices of doctors and nurses, the shouts and wails. He wandered ponderously through mute crowds that were fashioning shacks out of crates, blankets, boughs, sheets, and brush. He wandered eastward along the panhandle, past tens of thousands of refugees from the ruins. They did not see the devil in their midst, and let him pass.

He wished to see what he had wrought, and where better than Union Square, in the heart of the burned city? Getting there would be easy: a parade of refugees was headed for the Ferry Building, and Market Street had become a passable thoroughfare through the smoking ruins. Throughout the rest of the city, Funston's troops, along with city police, and the mayor's trigger-happy volunteer auxiliary police, patrolled. That didn't bother Lubbich.

He trudged past rubble and ruin. But people before him had opened passage, pulled aside fallen timbers, bridged enormous cracks opened by the quake, pushed away brick and stone in their haste to reach the ferries. An odd demonic heat radiated from the wreckage, and acrid odors filled his nostrils. Around him, people carrying their entire possessions toiled toward the ferries.

His victims.

He turned off on Powell, immediately entering an eerie no-man's-land, and hastened to the square. Soldiers watched, but did not stop him. The blackened hulk of the St. Francis lorded over the ruins. Everything was different. Were it not for the hotel, he doubted he could orient himself. He wound through debris left by all the campers who thought the square would be a refuge, and parked himself on an iron bench with partly burned seats. This was as good a place as any. He settled on the bench, knowing that the charred wood would stain jail bars across his suit.

Around him stretched his handiwork, block after block of macabre skeletons of buildings, tumbled walls, fire-blackened metal, a devastation so complete that nothing could be rebuilt—except maybe the St. Francis itself, which stood grinning and gap-toothed and laughing at the ghosts. Across the square, only charred beams and ash remained of the Bohemian Club, once the cultural center of San Francisco.

He had thought that maybe coming here would help him pull the trigger. Here was guilt, a thousand guilts, a million fingers pointing at his corrupted soul. He sat quietly, absorbing sights too awful to put into words. Not all his doing, but enough of it was.

What was he worth?

To Rudolph Spreckels and his reformers, he was a pawn.

To Eugene Schmitz and Abe Ruef, he was a pawn.

To Rosemary, nothing.

To himself, nothing.

To his parents and family, shame.

To all the people he had betrayed as corrupt city engineer, a debtor.

To God, if He existed, he was worth something. No person was beyond redemption or grace . . . if he chose to believe all that.

What would it take to pay back everyone who suffered loss because of his neglect of the water supply? Or even just a share of it, if the guilt were to be allocated among, say, a dozen people? He couldn't say. Maybe he owed others fifty million dollars. But what of the burned things that couldn't be replaced? The rare books in the Sutro Collection, the illuminated medieval texts from German monasteries, the Gutenberg Bibles, the complete Shakespeare portfolios and rare Hebrew manuscripts, the mementos, the burned art? There was no price.

Was there any exonerating circumstance? Yes, the quake had set more fires than the fire department could handle with all the water it could use. Much would have burned, even with faultless mains and backup systems.

Did that change anything? No.

If perchance he was rich as Croesus and paid everyone full value, would that make him less a debtor? Not very much, because his debts extended to burns, suffering, exposure, illness, death, homelessness, and madness. Walking through Golden Gate Park one thing had struck him: the catastrophe had driven many people mad. They bawled and blubbered or sat in mute desolation. One had been manacled to a hitching post.

He sat mutely, surrounded by blackness that matched what was in his heart. All he had to do was pull that revolver from his pocket and shoot himself. Around him he saw ten thousand ghosts, each of them urging him on, laughing, mocking him.

He thought of Rosemary, who had loved him, married him in all innocence and anticipation of a sweet life and the joy of motherhood. Long before the quake and fire, he had betrayed her. Helene had been—delicious.

But that was the past. His mind lingered in the past because the future had become a blank. He could start a new life somewhere. No one held him. He was free to walk away from San Francisco. He could go to Australia or Canada or Hong Kong and start over, bit by bit. He had a valuable profession: engineering. The world needed engineers. He was relatively young, years of life left to enjoy. He could get a free trip out, courtesy of the capitalist Harriman's railroads. He could sail on any of the foreign and domestic ships in the harbor, all of them currently detained by the navy if the need should arise for them to lend assistance. As soon as they were released, he could head for foreign shores, leave a failed life behind him, and venture into the large and marvelous world. Nothing stopped him. It would be years before he was even missed, before some prosecutor began hunting for Carl Lubbich. He might even wangle some resources out of his old friends, especially some cash from Ruef, who was eager to control what Lubbich would say before a grand jury.

There was no need to take his life. Why do anything so terrible, so final, so drastic?

Walk away. The great majority of men would do just that. He had observed little conscience in the sporting crowd at the French restaurants. Most of those gents would do whatever they felt like, without the slightest compunction. They were worldly men who took whatever they wanted from life. Did the lowlifes and ship's masters who shanghaied men from the Barbary Coast ever feel remorse because some poor devil's life and hopes and dreams were demolished? They had no conscience. Most men didn't. But Carl Lubbich did, much to his own astonishment. He knew for an absolute fact, as he sat there on that charred bench, that he could not run away from himself, could not be happy in Bora-Bora or Turkistan, could not long evade the madness and despair that would overtake him if he ran and ran and ran. He was one of the few whose soul would howl.

He couldn't walk away from his innermost self, where the catechists had done their work and his father's sense of justice and fairness had planted themselves. He might walk away from prosecutors, from this arena of disaster, from family and friends and country. He might change his name, become someone else in exile. But he couldn't walk away from himself. He might become Hauser in Argentina, Grolier in New Zealand, but it wouldn't help him any, or wipe clean his soul, or erase the memories, or lift the burden on his heart.

But suppose, just suppose, he spent whatever time was left repaying what he could? If he repaid ten thousand dollars against an incalculable debt, he might at least like himself a little, just for trying. Ah, that was something. It boiled down to this: shoot himself or give the rest of his life to his city, at least until they put him in prison.

He furtively slipped the revolver from his breast pocket and examined it. It was nickel-plated, with ivory grips, short-barreled, deadly.

He slipped it under the bench and walked away.

CHAPTER 42

ergeant Major Jack Deal knew he should be standing at attention and being smart about it. But he couldn't bring himself to do that. The Old Man damned well knew who ran the army, and Deal's posture served to remind him of that reality. So he lounged, not quite insolently but certainly not at attention, before the Presidio's Commanding Officer, artillery Colonel Charles Morris.

The CO observed Deal's posture, grimaced, and said nothing. In the midst of crisis, he had larger matters to worry about. Deal understood that, too.

"Sergeant, I've received numerous complaints about the conduct of enlisted men. Several civilians swear they've seen our men looting. Some of the civilians we've put to work in the burial details have come to me with reports that valuables taken off bodies have been pocketed by our men. Not one item taken from the dead has been brought to us."

He glared at Deal.

"That must stop. You go out and stop it. I could bring in the provost marshal and all that, but we're in the midst of disaster, and you're in the best position to stop it cold. We'll bust any man we catch. And I mean bust. Guardhouse, hard time, pull the stripes—you name it. I want results. Report to the OD when you're done."

"Count on me, sir," Deal said, relieved. He saluted smartly, wheeled out, and figured it would be a lark. For a moment there he thought maybe he was in trouble.

He commandeered a staff automobile usually reserved for officers, corralled two artillery corporals he knew, opened a locker that contained manacles and foot irons, selected an assortment, issued revolvers to the corporals, and then instructed them.

"The Old Man wants to stop petty thievery in the burial details. So you and I are a three-man police outfit. We're going to get results. The man wants results. Got that?"

Corporal Clute nodded. Corporal Binn grinned.

"We'll start with that detail in the Mission District," Deal said, climbing into the backseat. He pointed at Clute. "Drive."

"I can't."

He pointed at Binn, who slid behind the wheel, pulled the choke, flipped the ignition, retarded the spark, put the olive drab machine in neutral, and nodded to Clute, who gave the crank a hell of a yank. The engine erupted to life with a noisy clatter, and Binn pushed back the choke and advanced the spark until the engine settled into a bellicose hum. He undid the wing nuts and pushed the hinged windshield forward to let air pass through, and eased the clutch back. The staff car staggered forward by leaps and lurches, and then Binn steered it south, dodging rubble.

They located the sanitary detail at a pair of vacant lots on Dolores Street, near an ice and coal dealership.

"Just sit and watch," Deal said. An infantry squad commanded by a corporal was lounging around while about thirty civilian males yanked off the streets hacked through clay. Four-man civilian stretcher crews, each commanded by a pair of armed soldiers, carried remains to the site and rolled the fried, crushed, broken bodies and body parts, dogs and cats included, into a heap. The corporal and a private wandered through this deathpile, poking at bodies, flipping them over with bayonets, chopping off ringed fingers, pulling pants pockets out while the hapless civilians gagged and dug and eyed the soldiers.

The loot was going into a haversack. Deal saw a silver watch, a ring, and some gold coins disappear.

"You want us to round 'em up?" said Clute.

Deal shook his head. "They'll say they're just collecting valuables to turn over to the Old Man."

"How we gonna prove anything, then?"

"We aren't," said Deal.

Binn pulled out a handkerchief and pressed it to his nose. Deal figured it wouldn't cut the stench one little bit.

"What time is it?" Deal asked.

"Almost four."

"That's perfect. We'll wait for the relief."

The corporal commanding the squad noticed the automobile and came over.

"You want something, Sergeant Major?" he asked.

"Just looking," Deal said.

"We're going off duty. Got to let these men go now."

"Sure," said Deal. The relief squad would round up another lot of gravediggers. "You and that private there, get your stuff and get in. You stink. Don't get too close to me."

"Thanks, Sarg. A drive to the barracks after a detail like this, that's living."

It took another five minutes, and then the corporal and the private, toting the haversack plus a pair of begrimed rifles, boarded the auto and Binn steered through the barely passable streets and lanes.

"We're in the F Company barracks," the corporal said.

"Sure," Deal replied. "We got to stop first at the Officer of the Day."

It went easily. Binn parked at the command. Deal reported to the OD, a shavetail, who came out to the machine with a service pistol in hand, marched the corporal and private into the post, collected the haversack, recorded its contents, recorded what Deal, Binn, and Clute had to say, sent a detail over to F Company barracks with instructions to bring back the footlockers of everyone in that sanitary detail, scooped up thousands of dollars of valuables, threw the lot into the guardhouse, and commended Deal and his worthies.

Jack Deal grinned.

The thieving corporal glared at Deal but then crumbled under the weight of the charges he would face. The private quietly cursed Deal in cracker language Deal admired. He winked. The boy was out of the Georgia swamps and knew a good measure about cussing. Deal thought he would befriend the man after the poor devil got out of the stockade. The private was twice as much man as the corporal.

"We knew there would be some looting, Sergeant," said the OD. "You handled it well. I'm adding a commendation to your files."

Deal smiled. "It had to be done, sir."

It had been a good afternoon's work. That sanitary squad would be pounding rock for a few months. The corporal would lose some stripes and pound rock an extra month. The officers would have some loot— probably keep half and make a show of the rest by finding some owners. Sergeant Major Deal had come through. He always did. The CO would give him a warm smile and tell him he had the makings of an officer.

Word would get around. Henceforth the loot taken from the stiffs would trickle into headquarters—most of it. The sanitary squads would pay more attention to what they were doing in front of civilian eyes. Within an hour or two, every noncom commanding a burial detail would see the light. The officers would consider the trouble ended. They could tell Colonel Morris everything was fine, and Morris could tell Fearless Freddie Funston everything was shipshape.

Which was all the better for Lucky Deal. It hadn't been easy to keep his own operation out of trouble. For one thing the Presidio was awash with civilians, and getting to that abandoned bunker behind the bushes was dicey. But he solved that the army way. He collected a squad of reliable men, established a cordon that kept civilians a hundred yards from the bunker, where they couldn't see anything, ran a wagon in there, moved the loot in and some ancient six-pound artillery shells out—that scared him because ammunition that old was unstable—and pushed the loot back to the rear of the stonemasonry bunker, the contents of those new crates unknown to the detail moving out that old stuff.

His bunch had collected a mountain of loot. His cut was a third; the rest would split two-thirds. No one would get a penny for six months. He wasn't going to fence so much as a wedding ring for that long, and anything with initials on it would be melted down or pitched into the sea. They had grumbled about all that, but he didn't think it would be bright for a bunch of noncoms to wander around with fat purses right after the quake and fire. They weren't dumb. They'd get their share if they were patient; if they weren't, he would deal with them hard and in ways they never dreamed of, like Philippines duty. Or Panama duty. Live in the jungle and drain swamps to keep the mosquitoes from breeding.

Six months. Let the dust settle. Then he could do what he always wanted to do, help his sister and mother. Life hadn't been kind to the Deals. His father, a farm implement salesman, had died when the combine he was demonstrating fell over on him on a hillside. His sister, Rusty, had been bitten in the face by a water moccasin and the bite had so tormented the flesh that her whole left cheek was permanently twisted into a grotesque leer. And now she spent a miserable old-maid life taking care of their frail mother in a frame shack in Birthright, Texas, hopeless and poverty-stricken. They survived on what Deal could send them, plus a little sewing, and whatever they could raise on four-and-a-half weed-choked acres.

Jack Deal was going to remedy that. His sister would get some cash, some security. Nothing he could give her would compensate for the rotten luck, the spinsterhood, the face that caused people to avert their eyes. And his ma, too. She hadn't seen a luxury for years; hadn't even had a good cup of coffee because coffee wasn't something she could raise on her acres. She ate chickens, hogs, okra, stuff like that, but nothing else. She was going to get a new wardrobe, and get to see a doctor, and take a little holiday down to Lake O' The Pines.

He was gonna do that with some of it. And next year he wouldn't re-up. He was gonna get out, go down to San Diego where the weather was nice all the time, and start a saloon and club called Sergeant's, and the deal was that any sergeant could get a free drink and meal there, and he'd keep some bunks upstairs, too, and it would be a sort of non-com club, mostly for bachelors but he had nothing against married men. Maybe he'd let in the navy, but he would have to think about that. Sergeant's was going to be the place, and he was going to own and run it. And he could think of nothing better than that. From Maine to Florida to Seattle to San Diego, every sergeant in the army would know about Sergeant's, and they would all drop in. He'd be ready, with a mug of beer and a meal ticket, and after that the brotherhood he had always enjoyed. He outranked almost all, and when he had his own club, he'd be the chief rooster. His outfit would be a force in the military, too—he wasn't done with the army and never would be, and Sergeant's would be the place to come when there was pension trouble or something needed fixing in the service. A place where an officer could get help on the q.t. if Deal felt like helping.

He had busted a greedy dumb corporal today, and maybe he would bust a couple more and a mess of privates and keep the Old Man happy. But that was only a diversion. The whole burned city lay ripe for the picking.

CHAPTER 43

O ne loaf. Ginger Severance carried it out the long reaches of coastal land to the Chinese, wondering why on earth she bothered. Some acts were just dumb, without merit.

When she crested the brow of the hill, she found the Chinese better organized and sheltered. These industrious people had foraged for tenting, and now some of their sickest and weakest were protected from the sharp ocean wind. These toilers in the truck gardens of the whole area had been scavenging and gleaning, and she spotted food lines.

They saw her coming and the men hastened to meet her. They gathered around, their queues dancing to the wind, but their almond eyes steady upon her, and their bronze faces a mask.

She stood, waiting, not wishing to be intrusive.

"I have brought you this," she said, when they approached. They stared at the loaf, at her, and did nothing.

"Take it. I walked a mile each way to bring it to you."

A man new to her nodded and accepted the loaf. Then he bowed, surely a mark of respect. She bowed in return.

"I will bring more if I can get it," she said, not knowing whether these Chinamen understood.

Then the powerful man she had dealt with earlier appeared, listened to his compatriots, and came to her.

"You have blessed us," he said.

"I will find a way to do more."

"This is enough. How are you called?"

"Ginger Severance."

"It will be remembered."

"What do you need most? I will try to get it."

He paused, absorbed. "Our very old and young are cold."

Most of them had fled Chinatown wearing very little. The quake had started one of the first blazes in that volatile district. She saw not a blanket or wrap among them.

"I will see what I can do," she said.

He hesitated, and finally bowed slightly. "We will feed this bread to many," he said.

They strolled away. She stood on the hillside watching them, sensing their suffering and pride and courage, witnessing their industry. Then she started back, yet another mile to the kitchens and crowds, filled with a sense of futility.

She faced walls of indifference and worse. There would be those who would just as soon see the Chinamen leave or die.

She had tried to talk to the army command, without success. Maybe she could talk to the mayor or his Committee of Fifty. But Franklin Hall was a long walk from the Presidio. Fort Mason was nearer, and that had become General Funston's command post.

She felt weary, and paused close to a clamorous crowd of children, just to rest. They darted like a school of fish, playing some game, oblivious of the disaster that shadowed their very existence. They were all lucky: no one questioned their right to food and drink and shelter, or their right to their land and homes.

Then she walked to Fort Mason, so exhausted that she no longer cared about pain. She climbed hills and descended them, the downslopes harder on her calves than the climb. The Chinamen needed help, and that was all that mattered.

She reached the fort at the north end of Van Ness late in the day, found it entrenched and heavily guarded, its perimeter bristling with armed soldiers as if those within feared an invasion. She approached what appeared to be a sentry post at the long walkway.

"I wish to see General Funston about an urgent matter," she said to the uniformed man. She wasn't quite sure of his rank.

"Ma'am, the gen'ral's not seeing people. He's a busy man."

"Of course he is. But if there are thousands who are not even receiving food because no one knows about them?"

"Not even getting chow?"

"Yes, the Chinamen."

He looked long at her. "Tell you what. Gen'ral's got someone handling civilian complaints. I'll just send you on in there. Ask for Lieutenant Boswell."

That was progress. At least Funston was listening. That was more than anyone at the Presidio was doing. Maybe that trait was why Funston had been made a brigadier. She made her way into the dreary building and was directed to a man at a desk right in the hallway. He looked worn, but his uniform was crisp. She found herself peering into a square face under close-cropped brown hair. The man wore oval, wire-rimmed spectacles. His gaze took in the grubby rag and blanket that covered her, and she suddenly wished she had fresh clothing of any sort, something warm and soft and sweet-smelling.

"Are you Lieutenant Boswell?"

He nodded. "Madam?"

"And you listen to people?"

He smiled. "You could say that." He tapped the desk with a chewed-on pencil. "Everyone should have a Boswell."

He seemed open enough, so she braved his indifference. "Does the army know there are thousands of Chinamen in the Presidio, near the ocean, and no one is feeding them? They're not welcome in the breadlines. People crowd them aside."

Boswell tapped the pencil on the desk, staccato. "We hear there's a lot of Celestials out there." He squinted at her. "How do you know this?"

"I found them and talked with one. They're desperate."

He sighed. "There's about two hundred thousand desperate people around here, ma'am."

"But they're being fed."

He nodded. "Yes, one way or another. Tell me everything you know."

She did, describing what she saw, the chilly ocean wind, the lack of shelter, women hugging themselves because their teeth were chattering, scavengers plucking up anything edible from the seaside cliffs. The two or three windblown fires fed with driftwood that warmed no one.

She told of her gift of a loaf of bread, the mysterious cultural walls she had run into.

He listened. She marveled at that. He was doing much more than listening. She grew aware that he was taking her in, his attention divided between her message and his examination of her. She wondered why.

"We're supposed to be feeding everyone," he said. "That's the mission. Help everyone without favor. That came down from Teddy Roosevelt, like an Eleventh Commandment. I guess those are our marching orders. We had other plans, but I'll see what I can do."

"You will?"

He looked annoyed. "The general won't be happy, but I'll risk that. Thank you for telling us. What do you suppose they eat? Dragons? Pandas? Carp, I imagine."

"They need shelter, too," she said.

"Madam, we're building a camp for them right outside the door here. Tents coming in tomorrow from Fort Lewis. We've set aside the whole flat just west of Van Ness. The mayor's committee's going to get the word out tomorrow. A lot of the Chinamen went to Oakland, you know. There's a swanky Chinatown there. And some went out to the farms where they work. But we still got a lot of 'em to feed."

"I didn't know," she said, feeling useless. Powerful men were dealing with the multiple crises as best they could, and she had achieved exactly nothing. She was wasting his time.

"You're the first person who has listened. God bless you," she said.

He reddened, nodded, and shuffled papers. "You're welcome," he said. "If there's any more trouble, Miss Severance, ask for me." His gaze caught hers and held.

She retreated, wondering if the long walk had accomplished anything at all. Her legs hurt so much she didn't know whether she could make it back to the Presidio. When she stepped outside, she knew she couldn't. She needed rest, but if she stopped walking, she would not be able to get up and continue.

Sure enough, in the flat next to the fort, soldiers were digging latrine trenches. Soon it would be full of tents and Chinamen. But tomorrow or the next day was a long way away for cold and starving Chinamen.

She toiled her way toward the Presidio, one step at a time, wishing she could find a haven where she could collapse, and had gotten a few hundred yards when a motorcycle pulled to a halt beside her. "You going back to the Presidio, ma'am?"

She recognized Boswell behind the goggles, and nodded.

"Hop on if you want a lift."

She stared, half paralyzed at the thought of such intimacy, but her exhaustion decided the case for her. She clambered over the long seat behind him, hiked and adjusted her frightfully dirty skirts, and waited.

"You better put your arms around me and hang on, lady. This is the Winged Chariot, comin' for to carry you home."

She did, primly and with pursed lips.

Then he accelerated the cycle. She felt the acceleration tug her back, and was sure she would die in a wreck. But minutes later he pulled up before the Presidio field kitchens and she dropped off.

"Stick around, madam, and see what you've started," he said.

She sank to the ground, too weary to walk, and watched cooks boiling massive amounts of food in kettles, making stew of whatever was at hand. Lieutenant Boswell was conferring with the staff. A commissary sergeant barked some orders, and men began loading copper kettles into a dusty drab truck, one after another, and a load of mess gear.

Some soldiers carrying field jackets appeared, and she watched them unload the jackets into the truck. They added a stack of blankets.

Boswell approached her. "Long as you know where the Chinamen are, why don't you go out there? Have yourself a hot meal. You look done in, ma'am. Or is it miss? Sorry, I've neglected to ask."

"Miss Severance."

"Well, Miss Severance, you just navigate these men out there. They're instructed to feed the whole lot. If there isn't enough, they're to come back for another issue. That suit you?" Boswell grinned.

She stood suddenly, her pain forgotten. Some searing sweetness passed between them.

Ginger Severance did something she had never done before in her brief life. She wrapped her arms around Lieutenant Boswell, kissed him mightily and on the lips, too, and then just hung on, unable to pry herself loose.

He wasn't shy about hugging back, but then he gently pulled free.

"Got to get back to work," he said. "These men are enjoying this exhibition."

"I'm Ginger."

"I'm Paul. Hope to see you again."

She nodded. He kicked his motorcycle to life, waved, and roared away.

"Do enlisted men get a kiss, lady?" asked the driver.

"Yes," she said. "Every one of you." And then she wept.

They laughed and swung open the creaking windowless door. A couple of hard cranks brought the engine to life, and she settled into a stern and unyielding seat between two men.

"There's no roads out there," she said.

"Well this is equipment that don't need roads," the driver replied.

They rattled off through waning silver light, the driver impatiently squeezing the horn bulb to move sluggish people aside.

She directed them past the last of the rude tents and shelters, over fields dotted with fewer and fewer people, and finally over a ridge that required gearing down to double low. And there, before them, huddled the dark mass of outcast Chinamen, huddling about a few miserable fires robbed of heat by the wind, and very little tenting or clothing between the knife-edged wind and their bodies.

"They haven't got brains enough to get to good shelter," said the soldier to her right.

She started to rebuke him, and then settled into silence. She could not change the world.

The truck chattered and screeched down the slope, and stopped, at last, at the edge of the throng, which stood silently, awaiting whatever the gods brought. The light had grown tricky, pearl-colored, and she didn't recognize any of them. They looked so alike, thin and wiry men with long queues, many standing with arms folded before them to stay warm.

"Guess we'd better dish it out," said the private. "This ain't exactly like sitting around a stove."

The two soldiers in the cab, and half a dozen others in the back, set up a serving operation off the bed of the truck, a corporal running the show, barking commands. The Chinamen swiftly realized that succor had come and formed a line, but making room for some very old people and some small stoic children. One of the soldiers handed the field jackets to the old, and sometimes to a child. A little boy sucked in his breath, popped into the jacket, wrapped his small arms about himself, and bowed almost to the ground.

She watched from the cab, too weary to get out.

It was a good thing to see.

Then, in the dusky light, the blocky one, the leader with the white hair, approached the cab and peered in. He handed her his bowl of stew. She started to shake her head, but then accepted it and ate it swiftly as he watched. It tasted marvelous, its warmth settling in her stomach.

"I thought so. You will be remembered," he said. He tugged from his finger a ring set with an oval jade stone and handed it to her. She shook her head, not wanting payment, but then realized he wished to thank her in this fashion, and accepted.

"You are most kind," she said. The green stone glowed in the pearly light. She would give it to the Bible Society, and it would buy many tracts.

"K'ung-Fu-tzu's ambition was 'to bring comfort to the old, to have trust in friends, and to cherish the young'. This have you done."

She smiled, uncertainly. "I guess I don't know that person," she said.

"He is called in the West, Confucius. And you have followed his footsteps."

CHAPTER 44

B y the time Marcia White and her children reached Cleveland, she doubted that she could endure another half hour of travel. But her parents met her at the station, and she collapsed into their landau and fell asleep en route to Shaker Heights.

The last lap had been hard. The Southern Pacific and Union Pacific had been generous and taken her and Daisy and Harry as far as they wished to go on their route, which was Omaha. But the central and eastern railroads had been another matter. The farther from the epicenter of the quake, the less people cared. Only a collect telegram to her father, Drake Devereaux, kept them from being stranded and penniless in the Windy City.

But that was over.

Her parents took one look at her, at the black circles under her eyes, and the grimy clothes, at the white-faced and worn children, and hustled them off to her childhood home. She had been too tired even to bathe, and fell silently into the clean, comfortable bed after barely washing. Her parents were busting to hear the whole story, but contained their curiosity until their desperate daughter could speak coherently.

They had asked only one thing: Where was Harrison?

"I don't know," she had replied.

"Was he hurt? Is he in trouble?"

"No, he has things to do," she'd mumbled.

"I can imagine," her mother had said. "There's nothing like a good quake to make Harrison Barnes White happy."

When Marcia awakened fourteen hours later in the middle of a new morning, she discovered some ready-mades in her bedroom, a fawn skirt, puff-sleeved white blouse, and underthings. She didn't feel like getting up. Shy lay in the four-poster, watching motes of dust dance in the sunlight, feeling the quietness and stability of the bedrock undergirding this place, knowing this place wouldn't shake apart. She wondered how Harry and Daisy had survived, and whether they had caught anything, colds or catarrh or fevers, from their ordeal.

She didn't want to get out of bed. Beds were treasures, unspeakably sweet places. She had not known what a bed could mean until she had gone a week without one. She grew conscious of her own greasy hair, an aching body that hadn't been scrubbed for a long time, teeth that had not been brushed, fingernails that had not been trimmed, and gardens of the mind that had not been cultivated.

She would bathe, dress, see about the children, and then decide what to tell her parents about Harrison and a marriage that had been shaken apart along its fault lines. She wished she could say nothing. She didn't want any of her burdens known to anyone just then.

She forced herself out of bed, and rejoiced because the earth didn't heave under her. The house seemed silent and she supposed her father was at Western Reserve, lecturing. And her mother probably had taken the children on a shopping binge, no doubt worming much of the story from them.

She didn't hurry through her ablutions, luxuriating in things she had never thought twice about before her life had been shaken to pieces. She washed her hair, pleased when the strands turned silky and no longer stuck together. The skirt and blouse fit. Her mother must have gotten the measurements from the travel clothing—which was nowhere in sight—and gone shopping.

She was hungry. At many places along the tracks, people had gathered to feed the refugees, but the farther east she had traveled, the less help the refugees had received, and from Chicago onward she and poor Daisy and Harry hadn't had more than a few apples.

When she reached the kitchen, she found a note on the white enameled countertop. Her mother said she was buying clothing for the children, and that the *Plain-Dealer* wished to interview her about her experience. She didn't wish to be interviewed. She didn't wish to relive a nightmare. Her mother had set out some Quaker Oats, and Marcia thought that was a good idea. She also found a blue-speckled coffee-pot on the gas stove, ready to percolate.

Her weariness had not left her, and she thought that she would return to bed after eating. Being alone was a blessing. For once she had the luxury of not having to shepherd the children. She prepared her simple meal, sipped coffee, wondered what to tell her parents about Harrison, about her intent to dissolve the marriage—and confess that she had utterly no idea how she would support herself and the children after that. Something crabbed at her, told her to be quiet about all that, at least for now. With a few more days of rest, she could deal with it.

Late that morning her mother returned with two scrubbed grandchildren in tow. Harry wore brown corduroy knickers, argyle stockings, and a tweed coat, and looked almost civilized except for his cowlick. Daisy had been done up in an embroidered sky blue summer cotton dotted with white blossoms and looked as fresh and flowery as her name.

"Oh, my darlings," she said.

"Look at this, Ma! Knickers!" Harry said.

"I have a blue dress full of daisies," said Daisy, not to be outdone. "I like earthquakes."

"You're up," her mother said, surveying her. "But you still have black circles under your eyes."

"I could sleep a week."

"Did you contact that reporter?"

"I'm too tired to deal with that."

"Are you well?"

Marcia stared into space a moment. "I will never be the same. The earthquake shook my life apart. I have nothing now . . ."

"You have a new skirt and blouse. Like them?"

"Oh, yes."

"I threw out your travel clothing. There was no hope for them."

"I know. We put on what we could find and not long after that we had no home."

"Your turn this afternoon," her mother said. "We'll buy you a change or two. Lou will look after the children."

Marcia didn't resist. She was grateful to come from a family in comfortable circumstances. She had seen nothing but desperation, ruin, and death for days, and now found self-indulgence to be the tonic she needed. But a trip to the department stores would be all she could manage.

"We'll have lunch," her mother continued.

"I'm not up to it."

"Tea, then. I know a little parlor."

They ventured out, Marcia in a borrowed shawl against the brisk April breeze, but all she wanted was to retreat to that soft bed and down pillows. She had always loved her parents' home, spacious, sunny, chocked with art—her mother painted bright and cheerful canvases distinctly Impressionist in style—and her father's tumbling towers of books, of which he had read only a handful. He just liked to be surrounded by them, draw sustenance from them, and conjure himself as a literary light, though he scarcely wrote anything. He was too active, too much a man to bounce on the balls of his feet, ever to settle into the solitary labor or penning page after page of organized thoughts onto a pad of foolscap. But he did occasionally read when cornered.

Not long after, Marcia found herself in a bamboo-furnished tea parlor on Euclid, not far from Western Reserve, sipping Oolong and nibbling raspberry tarts with her mother. She braced herself. Her mother wasn't a woman to resist her curiosity.

"Now, where's Harrison?" her mother asked after an indecent interval.

"I wouldn't know."

Her mother lifted an eyebrow. Her mother's lifted eyebrow was famous in Shaker Heights. It conveyed more than a Van Gogh canvas.

"I knew it wouldn't work out," her mother said.

Marcia stared. That was a reckless gambit on her mother's part. And yet the same intuition that inspired Mona Lisa smiles in her mother's portraits drove her to fathom unspoken things.

"Architects seem to be needed just now," Marcia replied.

"I thought so. He's busy doing everything but being with his children."

Her mother's hazel-eyed gaze settled serenely upon Marcia, and there was triumph in it. A daughter's secrets had never been very secret to her mother.

"He'll know where to find us," Marcia said, stubbornly.

"Ah! He lost you."

This interrogation was not about to disappear into the tea leaves.

"You don't understand. No one knows where anyone is. People fled their homes and ended up in safe places—the Presidio, the parks. Some got to Oakland or went down the peninsula or crossed the Golden Gate to Marin County."

"But he was architecting and planning and . . . ambitioning."

"That's a way to put it, Mother."

"Harrison has the soul of a fish."

That angered Marcia, but her mother had a knack for angering people, at least momentarily. It was all part of what made her mother a social phenomenon in Shaker Heights. Her mother's tongue guaranteed the success of any dinner party.

"Mother—"

"I knew it when he first began sniffing about. For the sake of the children, you must abandon him."

"Mother, children need a father. And besides, I don't know that divorce is a good idea. And I don't have grounds."

"We'll find some grounds. I'll invent grounds. I'll cover the court record with grounds. Just as soon as this earthquake business is over, we'll drag Harrison through the mud."

"Mother! He's the children's father. We mustn't—"

"Well, I should hope so. He's competent at something, anyway." She laughed and sipped Oolong. "I'll enlist Drake. He's good at this, and has lots of lawyers for friends, though I don't know why. Now tell me about Harrison."

All this and her mother had yet to wait for a story. Marcia dimpled up, amused. "Harrison is more in love with himself and his career than his wife and children," she said.

"Well, I knew it. I don't know why they let architects into the Ecole des Beaux Arts. It's just another trade, but the French have notions. You must return to your art."

"I have two children to take care of. And if I leave him, I'll need to make a living somehow."

"Oh, fiddle. Live here."

It was tempting, but one of the reasons Marcia had leaped to marry Harrison was to escape her overbearing mother. "Not here," she said.

"Certainly not California? Why the rock under it is all jelly."

Marcia laughed. "You have strange notions of what California's like. It's warm and alive and—different. People come from all over."

"Tell me. Did Harrison take care of you after the quake? Did he gather you together, comfort the little dears, get blankets and things, lead you to a safe place?"

"No. And he used up the last of the water shaving."

"That's Harrison. I am the perfect, classic, original mother-in-law, with mother-in-law instincts and claws. I knew there'd be bad blood. He won't even look me in the face. I spotted it. He comes from a good family, but he's a weed in the garden. Now, tell me the rest. You were on the brink even before the earthquake, right?"

That intuition again. Marcia nodded.

"I knew it! Mothers see things that daughters miss. When Daisy's your age, you'll see what an ass she married."

"Daisy will do better than I did. She's old enough to know what's missing."

"Well, let your father and me deal with this. You just stay right here. If you can't get a divorce or separation in California, we'll just bend the law right here. That's why Drake traffics with all those lawyers."

"But I'm deserting him!"

"Ha! He deserted you about ten minutes after he slid that gold ring over your finger. Did he woo you that night? I'd guess he had a sketchpad and was designing boudoirs."

Marcia laughed. She hadn't had such fun since she had half a dozen beaux and was going to every cotillion in Shaker Heights.

"Yes, Harrison wooed me," she replied. "Once in a while he does that."

"Once a year?"

"Once every two or three," she replied, and meant it.

CHAPTER 45

. . . .

Nella Clapp wasn't going to let this fish get away if she could help it. She needed to get married, but she figured this insurance adjuster knew how to count to nine. Or anyway, seven. And she didn't have the faintest idea how to tell him.

So she grilled Willis Hart instead. The gazebo atop Twin Peaks was just the place. Before she was done, she'd wring him out and hang him up to dry.

"Do you snore?" she asked.

"Why do you ask that?"

"Well, if we're going to talk about marriage, I guess we'd better know everything. I'll tell you everything—almost. You have to tell me everything."

"I don't know. You'd have to find out."

"Do you help clear the table?"

"I've taken my meals out, or eaten in a boardinghouse."

"That's not an answer. You should promise to help clear the table if you're serious."

"Yes, I'll clear the table."

"And change diapers?"

"Ah, no, that's something for mothers to do."

"Well, will you earn enough so I can have a scrubwoman wash them?"

"That I intend to do. But you certainly have babies on the mind."

"Well, you would too if you were a woman."

He laughed. She liked his laugh.

She wondered what tack to take next. Below them, the moribund city lay in smoky haze. The columns of fire had largely vanished this Saturday, but every pile of rubble still smoldered.

"Did you go to college?" she asked.

"No, but I took a correspondence course in accounting an actuarial science."

"What's that?"

"I know how to calculate insurance risks, things like that."

"Are you pretty smart?"

"Well, Nella, I don't know, but the earthquake made me smarter. I'm not going to waste my life. It's too short."

"Do you like your mother?"

He peered at her. "Why shouldn't I?"

"Because I think men who don't like them won't be good husbands."

"I see. Maybe I should ask you the same question: Do you like your father?"

"No, I never met him."

He laughed.

Then she didn't know what to ask him. She thought she should find out about a thousand things. She should know whether he picked up his clothing, whether he drank too much, but none of that seemed to matter. She sensed that people just grew comfortable with each other, and marriage went on.

"What religion are you?" she asked suspiciously. If he was one of those papists, she would start down the hill. She had just been employed by some of those.

"My religion is to succeed in business."

"No, I mean religious religion."

"I guess I'll know when I'm an old man. I figure it takes that long to find out."

"No, I mean what denomination?"

"My parents are strict Unitarians."

"What's that?"

"They believe that God is one, not three. Just God, that's all."

"I never heard of those. Are you one?"

"I'm debating what I am. Science is finding answers to everything. Like how the world was made. It wasn't made in seven days. How could there be days and nights anyway if those are caused by sun and shadow on the globe? It took a long time, which we can read in the geology."

Suddenly she was into realms that she knew little about. But at least he wasn't one of those Holy Rollers or something like that. And not a Catholic. She had feather-dusted gaudy plaster saints, fascinated by them. The only ones she liked were those of the Virgin. Those were beautiful and always made her sentimental, especially now that she was pregnant. She and the Virgin shared something.

"I like the Virgin Mary because she was a mother," she said.

"There you go again," he said. "You have motherhood on the brain."

She didn't know what to do or say after that. Her curiosity and courage had deserted her. She had supposed she could just grill him and decide. Instead, she was becoming confused.

"Now it's your turn. What is your denomination?"

"I don't know," she said. "I guess maybe we should go back to the park. You're not interested in me. If you want a wife, I'd like to be courted, not questioned."

"I was thinking of saving time, but all I've done is make a hash of things. Nella, let's forget all that. I like you. I hope you like me. I would like to proceed on trust. If we are utterly truthful with each other, we won't have any trouble."

"I think I'll go down the hill. It's a long walk."

"Is that a rejection?"

"It wasn't a very good idea. You shouldn't just marry some stranger."

He looked puzzled. "What have I said that troubles you?"

"You're always worrying about children."

"I what?"

"Never mind." She rose, not really wanting to go. Willis would be a good husband, and she needed one. But she couldn't tell him the whole truth.

He caught her arm and gently drew her back to her seat. "Nella, something's between us I don't understand. I'm willing to listen and find solutions."

She started to weep. She couldn't help it. Being with child, and alone, and in the middle of an earthquake, and out of work, and hopeless, all conspired to demolish her. She sat miserably, her tears welling hotly from her eyes, while he held her hand.

"What is it?" he asked.

She knew she should tell him but she couldn't. She was so alone. She squeezed his hand. It was good to hold his hand, even if he would yank it away if she told him. She didn't want this moment to end, but it would.

"This isn't much of a courtship," he said. "The city's dying. It's like there's no future, but there is. We just can't see it now, in all this mess. I couldn't buy you candy or roses even if I wanted to. I thought we could just talk it out, but I was wrong. But I can say this, Nella. If there's something you're not ready to talk about, that's all right. One thing I've discovered is that everyone has problems and hurts and fears. I'm afraid, too."

She wiped away a tear and just sat mutely, staring into the smoky ruins below. The whole world had changed. He didn't press her anymore, just sat beside her and held her hand while they watched the city die.

"I'm going to have a baby," she said. "Now let's go back to the park."

"Nella!"

"The son of the family I worked for had his way with me. But that's not the whole truth. I invited him to. He was an exciting Argentine boy. Full of Latin charm and courtesy. I thought maybe he would marry me. I was also—curious." She rose. "Let's go now, Willis."

But he stayed her. "I don't want to go back now. You can if you want, but I hope you'll just sit down. I would like you to."

"You would? But why?"

"I want to hear your story."

"I don't have any story. I just read too many romantic novels about servant girls who marry well and live happily ever after."

He laughed suddenly. "Fiction is mostly nonsense. But important nonsense because it feeds upon our hopes and dreams. Your dream was a fine husband, higher station in life. What's so bad about that?"

"I encouraged him! That's what's so bad."

"Maybe he seduced you."

"I don't know. I'm confused. Let's go, Willis."

"Maybe he had his own designs."

"Maybe he did. But I'm going to have a baby."

"When?"

"Seven months."

He plunged into a long silence, and she knew she had lost him, but he didn't take his hand away. Finally he turned to her, gravely.

"Well, Nella, I wanted to speed everything along. I told myself that we don't know from moment to moment if we'll live or whether our world'll fall apart. Now I'm getting my wish. A fast baby who will do the rhumba before he's two."

"Willis! What are you saying?"

"Well, you could call it a proposal. Will you and your little tangerine care to bond yourselves to a temporarily unemployed insurance adjuster and live semi-happily ever after?"

Something danced in his eyes. He seemed on the brink of whooping laughter, the gaiety irrepressible.

A rush of joy swept Nella, so she hugged Willis and wept upon his shoulder. She had a home. She had a lover and soon a husband. Her child would have a father.

"Forever, Willis," she whispered in his ear.

"Do I get to name the baby?"

"What?"

"The baby. It will need a name. Like Frederico or Ricardo or Juanita, or Conchita."

"Oh . . . I haven't gotten that far."

In fact, she hadn't yet thought of that tiny creature as a person. It had been only a problem. But now Willis was swiftly turning her thoughts to the little person within her. She kissed him on the cheek, and then the lips.

"Yes, name the baby," she said.

"I will. Let's go get married." Something husky in his voice told her that his thoughts were of her.

"Now?"

"Why not?"

"The city's burning. Where'll we find a minister?"

"There were ministers leading prayer services in the park. I must have seen three or four."

"But a license. We have to have one, don't we? And how are we going to pay for it, or for a wedding?"

Willis hugged her. "When people want something badly enough, they find a way. Let's go see. We can still make it to Franklin Hall this afternoon and see if the city'll issue one."

"If they can't—who cares?" she whispered, aware of the undertow that engulfed them. "We can get married and come back here. We'll honeymoon right here."

"I was thinking maybe we should try to get across the bay. Then we could have a real honeymoon."

"With no money?"

"That's a problem," he acknowledged.

Reluctantly, she released him and they tripped down the long path to the city, hand-in-hand. It would be two hours before they reached Van Ness and the temporary City Hall. But she didn't mind. She could walk on clouds.

CHAPTER 46

Harrison White fled Chinatown, his legs barely supporting him, his composure ruined, and his mind so disturbed by his brush with death that he couldn't think.

He had never in his young life faced menace so profound, stupid menace, wrongheaded menace, brutal wasteful idiotic menace from two ignorant brutes who could barely read but had a license to murder innocent civilians. He would march into Funston's lair and rail at the idiot general for unloosing such killers on the people. He hated the army. What right had they to march into a city and murder its citizens? What kind of untrained army was it that unleashed animals, brutes, killers on the American people?

By God, he was going to make this known from one end of the country to the other. He was going to write Teddy Roosevelt and tell him a thing or two about the idiots who were loose in the city of San Francisco. He raced toward Franklin Hall, driven by sheer frothing energy, but then it quickly deserted him and he sat down suddenly, his body rattling and quivering uncontrollably. He leaned into a pile of rubble, unable to move, his last strength drained away by the terror he had experienced.

When he stood up ten minutes later, his fright had turned into hate. He would spend the rest of his life exposing the army as a den of thieves and barbarians. He walked wearily toward the temporary City Hall on Van Ness, his mind preoccupied with the vices of the army. Now it all came to him: Fearless Freddie Funston had blown up the city. It might have survived the fires but for the fact that his artillery men and dynamiters kept setting new blazes every time they reduced some proud building to rubble all in the name of stopping the blazes. Earthquake, yes. Fires, yes. But the army and its henchmen in the navy had blown San Francisco to bits and inflicted the worst damage.

He was going to howl to Mayor Schmitz, spill it all to Phelan, orate the episode to anyone in the temporary City Hall who would listen. But when he finally got there, dragging himself through the battered doors, he found the place half deserted. Everything had changed. It seemed quiet. Gone was the pervasive throb of desperate energy that had permeated the place. Men still manned each of the desks in the steady light of coal oil lamps, but they weren't busy. A certain exhaustion had replaced the frenzy.

The city lay in a sullen shambles that Saturday evening. The conflagrations were out at last, or sullenly burning up the last of their fuel, and most of the firemen were sleeping after three straight days and nights of desperate toil. The relief operations had smoothed out, and the frantic efforts to get food and shelter and medicine to desperate thousands was functioning almost of its own momentum, the supply lines from the wharfs working, the railroads bringing up boxcars over repaired and circuitous roadbed to the southern reaches of the city, the tent hospitals receiving all who needed them, the field kitchens serving everyone and staying just ahead of hunger. Bakeries had even been opened, and were manufacturing bread around-the-clock.

"Where's the mayor?" he asked a city clerk slouched at a desk on the dais.

"Asleep in one of the offices upstairs. Leave him alone. He said not to wake him for anything short of another earthquake."

"I have to talk to him. It's urgent."

"No, it's not that urgent—unless it's fire or plague. Let the man sleep."

White turned away. He would be a fool to wake up the exhausted mayor. He had been crazy even to think of it. He was as tired as the mayor, maybe more so. He had become filthy, like everyone else, a two-day stubble on his face, his suit caked with dirt, his underclothes foul, his body crying for rest and warmth and soap.

Tomorrow would be another day. He eyed the men curled in blankets, trying to sleep on hardwood flooring. The field kitchen offered loaves, broth, some canned items, oranges brought in from Southern California, and coffee, but he felt too numb to eat. The afternoon had rattled him.

He curled up in a slot on the hardwood floor between two other men, and lay uncomfortably on the unyielding surface, without so much as a pillow to comfort him. He found his spirits spiraling down and down until he was once again facing two brute soldiers, the bayonets and muzzles of their Krags aimed directly at his belly, disbelief and mockery in their faces, and more: a heightened expectation of blood and death seeping from their eyes, bloodlust, the kill alive in them. He had come that close. He had never before looked Death in the eyes, seen that fire flickering in another mortal. His own death in cold blood—for nothing. He had seen Death, the smallest twitch of a finger from him. He had seen those bayonets, just one easy thrust from his soft belly. He shuddered. The floor tormented him. He writhed on it, unable to drive that murderous moment out of his skull.

He forced himself to think of other things, but wasn't successful. Always, his mind returned to the murderous moment, to those two faces—fellow citizens, men who spoke his tongue. Men who could barely read and weren't interested in his story. But as the desperate Saturday wore into Sunday, he drifted into a haunted oblivion, his mind never far from the gallows.

When he awakened in the murky gray of Sunday, it was raining. His first thought was that it would at last extinguish the remaining smoldering fires cached deep in the bowels of the city. Rain streaked the tall windows of Franklin Hall, entering the several that had shattered in the quake. He sat up with a start, fighting off the weariness of his body, and a nascent headache. He felt rotten.

Was Marcia out in that rain? Surely not. She and Daisy and Harry would be safe in a tent. The army would have seen to it—women and children safe under canvas. But he didn't know. He suddenly was wild with need to find them. They could be anywhere. But as the water slid down the windows, and sometimes hissed when a gust slapped water against the windows, he realized he had no way to get to the Presidio without getting soaked, catching catarrh, and endangering his health. Marcia would be well cared for. The army had received acres of canvas from every depot in the West, and now, he supposed, all those refugees at the Presidio, and in the parks and squares and the empty meadows south of town, would be snug.

But he didn't really believe that. He no longer trusted the United States Army to do anything right. He could go look, but what good would it do? He couldn't bring them to City Hall. Other men hadn't brought their wives or children here. The mayor's volunteer police were challenging those who crowded in simply to escape the elements.

He stood stiffly, dreading even to head for the sanitary trench chopped into the alley behind the building. Maybe he could use his influence to reach his family; find a hack that would take them somewhere. Maybe even take them to the Ferry Building. That was one place he knew had a roof.

Around him the committee men and their aides talked glumly about the rain: White listened, growing aware that the army's tents didn't protect but a small fraction of the homeless, and that even within the tents life would be miserable if the rainwater soaked mattresses, blankets, bed socks, spare clothing.

"The next wave into the hospitals will be pneumonia," said one man.

That alarmed White. He thought of his boy, Harry, dangerously ill, or Daisy, the apple of his eye, sick and in mortal peril. Why hadn't Marcia contacted him? She knew he was working with the mayor's committee. This was her fault, actually. She could have gotten word to him. He had made himself known around Franklin Hall. She had certainly changed in recent years; it was as if she didn't care anymore. Perhaps he should speak to her about it. A little heart-to-heart talk, maybe an evening alone to address the strains in their marriage. He had a list of complaints, and it was about time to give it to her. Yes, he would arrange it after he had drawn up his plan for Chinatown and won its approval. Burnham might be known as the great planner of San Francisco, but Harrison Barnes White would be remembered as the man who had transformed Chinatown into a garden and the choicest quarter in the metropolis, the man who had taken Burnham's blank space and filled it with grace and beauty.

He wished Marcia could see him now, employed by the mayor himself. He sighed, knowing he would have to put up with her idiosyncrasies. If she wouldn't search for him, he would have to search for her. Maybe he could find an umbrella and walk over to the Presidio. He would have a look. If the rain cleared by afternoon, as it usually did, he would check the registries in Golden Gate Park. She would be at one or the other. He couldn't imagine that she would stay at Lafayette Square or some other out-of-the-way place not suitable for a woman of her circumstances.

But she was annoying him. She should have sent word.

Then again, maybe she had. He had not examined the growing registry right there at City Hall. She might have come and gone while he was out on the mayor's business.

He turned to the great ledger, which rested on a desk beside inkpots, nib pens, and blotters. The ledger had been divided into alphabetical segments, but he soon realized that many signers hadn't realized that and he would need to canvas the entire list.

Some of the entries simply announced a presence while others sought a loved one:

"L.G. Newton, wife, at GGPark."

"Carl Behm, Laf. Sq. Looking for dtr Maybell."

"Styles, Erma, missing hsb. Walter. Dear, I'm at N. Beach, Hyde St. Pier, in boat."

"For Garnet March. Leaving for parents. Bessy."

"Missing. Albert Quist, son of B.J. Quist. Quist Fam in Oakland at C.C. Quist."

"C.V. Pritchett. I'm at Bill's. FT."

White began a systematic survey, running a finger swiftly down the columns, line after line, page upon page. People gathered behind him, patiently awaiting their turn. He tried the *W* files first, and then the *H* for Harrison and *M* for Marcia, but came up with nothing. It was a chaotic system, but at least there was a record, and no doubt the ledgers had wrought their own miracles and tearful reunions, and in time they would help materially to sort out the lost and abandoned and separated.

But no sign of his family. Where was Marcia? She had to be somewhere. He hogged the ledger as long as he dared, and then unhappily clapped the covers shut. The drizzle hadn't let up. Moodily he peered out the window into the rain, watching the pooling water collect ash and river it away. The rain would cleanse the city—and make life miserable for the hundred thousand people trapped in it. Tomorrow he might walk the streets without suffering the acrid smell of ash.

He spotted someone he knew, one of the committee's assistants named Boyle, who laid a wet umbrella behind his table to dry. Maybe there was a chance.

"Is there any chance I could borrow that for the afternoon?" he asked.

"It's the only umbrella in San Francisco. I was offered twenty-five dollars for it on the street."

"I need to go to the Presidio. My wife and children—"

Boyle stared through the window at the steady rain, then nodded. "I'm leaving at six. Can you have it back by five-thirty?"

"I promise."

"Go find your wife if you can. I hope she's not drowned."

White took the umbrella and stepped into a cold, wet world.

CHAPTER 47

. . . .

It rained on Sunday, deviling Katharine Steinmetz and the other women in the army tent. Cold water dripped through the canvas and pooled around the base of the tent, seeping in and soaking bedrolls and blankets. One could not escape the occasional icy drip oozing through the canvas. The women hadn't so much as a teaspoon among them with which to trench the tent and draw water away, and so it rivered in, icy pools of misery that forced the women to stand on wet feet rather than sit in icewater.

Katharine's wheelchair was the only refuge, and not even it protected the women from the dripping canvas or from soaked shoes. Katharine insisted that they take turns in the chair. She needed to stand, even on her inflamed knees. Reluctantly, then gratefully, the various women did sit for short periods. Some stayed long in the chair; others guiltily relinquished it after a few moments. It all served to remind Katharine how helpless she was now, how little stood between her and death, and how utterly impoverished she was.

And yet the women were a small army devoted to benefitting one another. Katharine had never witnessed mortals so ready to set aside their own troubles to help others within that jammed, airless tent. They brought her food and even hot coffee, so she didn't have to stand in line or be wheeled through it. They took her to the sanitary trenches. They jointly scrubbed and wrung out clothing and hung it to dry any way they could. But best of all, they supported one another with companionship and caring.

They even established quiet times, so those who needed rest could have it. But for the most part they talked—too much talk for Katharine, who could never get used to it—and sewed and speculated, and shared triumphs and losses. Mostly they shared losses. One's husband had died. Two of the women had lost track of loved ones and feared for them. One haunted the registries, searching for her mother. Katharine listened, aware that she had no circle of friends; she and Emil had lived largely isolated lives, in part because of his disability, in part because they chose to.

Late that miserable cold Sunday, two poncho-clad soldiers appeared with shovels and dug a shallow trench around the tent with a carry-off ditch at what they supposed was the low point. But it wasn't the lowest, and that led to flooding of one corner of the circle. One of the women volunteered to find the soldiers, or maybe a shovel, or even a knife—anything that might cut another trench to drain away the wa-

232

ter. But she returned soaked and empty-handed, her body shaking even though they threw blankets around her.

Katharine settled miserably on a soaked and icy pad, knowing that the only recourse was to endure this, as she had endured that endless and terrible night with Emil. That Sunday night her spirits plunged again. The false gaiety of her tentmates didn't conceal their desperation. Most were bereft. The army might supply food and shelter for a time—but what then? How could she get a living? What would the new widow, Elsie, do? Who would care for the young mother? What would happen when the nation's generosity faded away, and the donated wheat and spuds and tins of food trickled to a stop?

That night seemed as long and cold and mean as the first one at the Presidio with Emil. She writhed on the icy pad, found no comfort in the wet blanket, counted seconds and minutes in misery until the long-lost dawn came, and with it, blue skies. Monday, the sixth after the quake, brought the promise of sunshine, and some weak warmth, and a chance for the breezes to dry out the bedding. She took no joy in it, and wished she had died with Emil. He had gone at the right moment, when nothing was left for him. Her own bitter lot was penury and pain.

Yet, as the morning progressed, the sun wrought uninvited cheer in her. The sun was kindness, the warmth coming from some incalculable distance, an eternal fire of mysterious origin that never burned itself out and cast its energies out upon a universe, even into the chilled flesh of Katharine Steinmetz. She marveled at this commonplace miracle that escaped the attentions of the world.

Apart from the precious wheelchair, she did have one asset. Maybe she could turn it into something. With luck, it might even finance a new camera and darkroom to sustain her.

"Is it true the post office is accepting mail without a stamp on it?" she asked one of the women—she could never keep all their names straight.

"Yes, that's what I've heard. For a while anyway, so people can let the world know they're safe, I guess."

"It's the first good thing the government has ever done," Katharine said.

She hunted down some stationery and a pencil, since no one had a nib pen and ink, and began composing an urgent letter:

Dear Mr. and Mrs. London—

Too formal. She started over.

Dear Jack and Charmian,
    I am grateful for the help you gave Emil and me. We were transported safely to the Presidio that day, but I regret to

inform you that Emil died of pneumonia; the exposure that night was too much for his frail constitution. So the illustrator of your books, and my beloved mate, is gone to wherever restless souls go.

And I am alone, with memories of him, of your kind help, and of Emil's magnificent work, very little of which will have survived this.

My sole assets, apart from the wheelchair, are the plates we placed in your hands. Upon those plates rest all my hopes for the future, including new photographic equipment. I am unable to do anything to market those photographs from the Presidio, where I am ensconced in a tent with other women, and will burden you with one more request. Could you market those photographs for me? There surely will be demand. I imagine the various magazines and newspapers across the country, if not the world, will be eager to purchase just such material.

If you would do me that great favor, I would gladly pay you a commission—whatever you ask. Just hold the receipts there until such a time as I can resettle. I remember well just what photos I took, and in the next mail or two, I will send along captions that you can match to the photos. If you could do this for me, you would give me a new lease on life.

Your grateful acquaintance,
Katharine Steinmetz

She sighed. Why should the Londons do that? But somehow she knew they would, more for Emil's sake than hers. Maybe she could give them a print, one of Emil at the end of his life, as a way of thanking them. She had no envelope, but folded the sheet into thirds and hoped that would do. She thought maybe the post office would, for once, exercise tender care for all the San Francisco–franked desperate messages from desperate people.

She paused, not knowing the Londons' address. But she knew where they lived and hoped that would do: Mr. and Mrs. Jack London, Glen Ellen, California. Surely the letter would find its way there.

"How do I mail this?" she asked.

"I'll find out," said the young one, the mother. Trying to remember names made Katharine dizzy. "Do you want me to take it?"

"Yes, but mail it only if you know for sure it is the right way to do that."

The woman vanished into the sunlight with Katharine's dreams in her soft hand.

Katharine waited patiently in the early light, yearning for more sun, heat, warmth, anything to drive the bone-cold chill from her old body. Her tentmates were busily hauling soaked bedding outside, wringing it out, stretching it over the sunny side of the tent. Others were wrestling with cold mud, muck, clothing streaked with new stains. Would the nightmare never end?

The young mother returned and sought out Katharine. "That was easy," she said. "The soldiers have a mail basket. They take it to the post office twice a day. They say they are glad to do so because it is helping people get away and into better circumstances. At least that's what the officer told me."

That was good. If it was in the army's interest to deliver the mail carefully, that's what the army would do. She was glad the army was good for something.

No, that wasn't fair, she thought. The United States Army had probably prevented an epidemic by acting promptly. Its knowledge of field sanitation had, so far, halted disease in its tracks. No dysentery, no typhus, no cholera haunted the refugee camps in the stricken area, and that was because those military men had dug trenches, buried the dead, cremated or buried dead pets and drays and stray animals, supplied fresh or boiled drinking water, isolated the fevered, all with the same hard discipline with which it had fought yellow fever in Panama, tropical illness in the Philippines, and malaria in its own southern posts. She had the army to thank for her very life.

The thought that her letter would soon be speeding away from San Francisco cheered her a great deal, and drove away those morbid thoughts that she had entertained through an icy night. A word from Jack London would sell those photos anywhere. She wished she had said something about rights: she would like to sell them again and again, eking the most from her sole assets. But she hadn't. But Jack London, of all people, would know about rights and would protect her—she hoped.

Since there was no more she could do, she put the matter out of mind and tried to help with the sodden mess. But the others shooed her off. She alone among them was disabled. Her knees had all but stopped functioning ever since she had abused them after the quake.

She sat in the sun, letting its tender early light bathe her. Everything was all right. The whole world was coming to the rescue. With every gaze about her, she saw people being fed, people clothed with donated castoffs, people sheltered by rows of tents, most of them the army's but plenty of others, too. She saw people being treated for illnesses by doctors and nurses who had rushed in from Los Angeles and other distant places.

The papers said that Congress had appropriated two and a half million dollars of relief. She knew that President Roosevelt had ordered the army to deploy its entire West Coast resources. She knew that the railroads and ferry boats were carrying people away from the disaster free. The Southern Pacific was doing everything it could.

Nor did it stop there. The city's richest capitalists had donated huge sums, in spite of their own losses. She heard that one of the Spreckels had pledged a hundred thousand dollars even though some of their sugar refineries had been shaken to bits. Even those who lacked funds were contributing time and energy. A whole crew of engineers from Oakland was repairing the San Francisco water mains, and some were now functioning. Amazingly, some of the rival newspapers had combined and were printing editions out of town and distributing them free. The first, published by the *Call-Chronicle-Examiner* appeared the day after the quake. And now each paper was publishing its own sensational editions on out-of-town presses, and they all brimmed with valuable information that made life infinitely easier for the dispossessed. She read all of these, intently.

Incredibly, Chicago had sent a platoon of detectives who were experts on looting. The foreign ships in the bay had offered food, water, cabins, and medical attention, all without charge, especially Captain Sanderson, of the ship *Hartfield*, out of Liverpool, who turned his vessel into a haven for women and children, and the Master, O. B. Musson, of the steamship *Henley*, who started his distillers and provided the only drinking water on the waterfront for a day and a half. Governor Pardee had put every resource commanded by the state of California to the relief of San Francisco. The American National Red Cross, in the person of Dr. Edward T. Devine, was taking over the relief operation at the behest of President Roosevelt, and flooding supplies and funds to the stricken city. The navy's fireboats had doused the whole waterfront with water. General Funston's men had worked night and day until they virtually dropped in their tracks.

What did all this mean? The hazy sunlight, that chill Monday morning, was shining down upon a miracle of caring. The world might have let her die. The world might have shrugged. She thought of all this, the miracle, the sacrifice, the dedication, the swift and loving response from all over the globe, and didn't know whether to weep or sing.

But she chose song. For the rest of that day she hummed old songs, happy songs, words forgotten but the notes sweet. And before that day ended, all the women in that dried-out tent were singing, and by eventide, the camp was singing, and by dusk, the soldiers were singing, and before dark, they were singing hymns, and she wondered how her small cracked voice had started such a thing.

CHAPTER 48

Desire consumed Willis Hart. He gazed at Nella, mad with rapture. Her face was the sort to break a thousand hearts, yet she had chosen him. Nella smiled back, and he read the eagerness in her lips.

They raced pell-mell toward Franklin Hall, hand-in-hand, smiling, laughing, squeezing each other's fingers. How odd it seemed, this gaiety in the midst of ruin. And yet it all made perfect sense. Life was precarious. They would gather their rosebuds while they could.

They reached Van Ness, and Franklin Hall, well into the evening and Willis feared the time was wrong; it would be business as usual, come back in the morning. He knew he couldn't endure bachelorhood until morning, and gazed hotly at Nella, whose eyes spilled promises.

They pattered up steps and into the cavernous building, hunting for a clerk.

"Is it possible to get a marriage license?" he asked a man lounging at a desk.

The man pointed toward a dais where some desks stood. "Try that one," he said, and surveyed them shrewdly. "Looks like you're in a hurry." He smiled enviously. Willis enjoyed being envied, and glanced at his sweetheart, aware that she would turn heads wherever she went, especially now with that look on her face.

One desk bore a crude hand-drawn label that announced the city clerk.

"Sir, how do we get a marriage license?"

The bald clerk looked them over, up and down and sideways it seemed to Willis, and then smiled. "It happens we rescued the records from City Hall. Now, if you'll just answer a few questions—"

"We haven't any money. Will we need a fee?" Willis asked.

"They all ask that. We've had sixty-one couples here since the quake wanting marriage licenses. Amazing. Who can explain it?" He eyed them. "I guess it explains itself," he said. "Normally, there's a small fee, but under the circumstances we're waiving it. Nobody has cash. Now, then. Name, address, age—"

"We don't have addresses anymore."

The clerk looked annoyed. "No one does, but everyone did. I trust you lived somewhere, and not in a boxcar? And you're of legal age? And in sound mind?"

Taking his own sweet time, the minion of the city of San Francisco penned in the necessary information in duplicate because he had no carbon, blotted his handiwork, and handed Willis a copy. "When you tie the knot, you'll have a clergyman or judge add his name and date, and have a witness sign it also, all right?"

Willis nodded.

"Lucky devil," said the clerk under his breath. "Where are you staying?"

"Ah, Golden Gate Park."

"Ah! Thought so. Woman-hunter's paradise. If I could bail out of here I'd go proposing, too. They'd line up and plead for me to marry 'em."

Willis swallowed a sharp response. What did he care about randy clerks and their fantasies?

"They'd have to be pretty desperate," Nella retorted.

The clerk grinned and picked at his incisors with a penknife.

"Is there a judge around?" asked Willis.

"Nope, but I hear there's ministers all over the park, holding prayer services. Prayer's so thick over there you'll just about have to interrupt it to get yourself in double harness. Just head for one and don't look quite so eager, and he'll oblige."

Willis glared at him coldly, but the clerk smirked.

"Let's go, Willis," Nella said. She had pursed those bee-stung lips into a pout.

Gaily, Willis and Nella tripped down the steps and raced toward the park. Finding a marriage-man at ten at night would be a challenge, but the quake had nullified time and place and order. People were singing minstrel songs at two in the morning, sleeping at noon, eating salted beef at midnight, and holding prayer services at all hours. This Saturday night they would all be up. Nobody had slept since the quake, anyway.

It was all madness, and he felt almost light-headed with the sheer joy of it. He wondered where they might honeymoon. Privacy would be a real problem. There was the gazebo, of course, but he wanted something much better, some sheltered place and not just a bench on a mountaintop. Down the peninsula? Maybe. Oakland? Too crowded with refugees. Marin County? He liked that. Somewhere across the bay they would find a honeymoon haven . . . if he could talk a boatman into taking them across for nothing. It was all madness, ricocheting around the Bay Area without a dime—but what did it matter?

This Saturday evening the whole panhandle of the park was alive. It had become a tent city, magically organized into some semblance of life. In addition to the shelters, the field hospital and kitchens, entertainments had sprung up: Amateur theatricals and variety shows, lit by a few coal oil lamps, had drawn hundreds. In other hollows, clergymen were holding prayer services. Elsewhere young people with guitars were conducting sing-alongs. Golden Gate Park was no longer a desperate place.

He paused at one such place, where the congregation was just breaking up for the night. In the dim light he beheld a man with a Roman collar.

He turned to Nella. "What are you?"

"What am I? A woman."

"I mean, what denomination?"

"Oh. Mother was a strict skeptic. My daddy was a strict Lutheran." She laughed. "So I'm half Lutheran, half skeptic."

"Well, let's try this one. He might turn us down, but we'll find others."

He steered Nella toward the clergyman, who was dismantling his makeshift altar.

"Sir? We have a request."

The cleric paused.

"Would you marry us?"

He eyed Willis and Nella and smiled faintly. "I presume you mean Monday. We might arrange something, given the circumstances."

"No, right now. And I have to tell you, sir, we don't have a cent."

"Well, this is rather sudden indeed. Are you Episcopalians?"

"Uh, no."

"Are you sincere and committed Christians?"

"Me, I'm going to be," Nella said.

"I was raised as a Unitarian. If you call that Christian, then I am," Willis said.

"And baptized?"

They nodded.

"And has this union been planned some while? You know each other, are willing to make a sacred lifelong commitment, in love and holiness?"

"We haven't known each other long, sir. But we are certain about our feelings and commitment."

"How long?"

"Since the quake, sir." Willis felt the chance slipping away as the clergyman eyed them. "Yes, sir, it's sudden. But this crisis, this event that has torn lives apart, has thrown us together and we carefully explored our feelings and our commitment, and, sir, we believe we are ready and willing to be together the rest of our lives. Yes, the earthquake hastened things, but maybe that was all for the good."

The clergyman quietly returned a small crucifix and Bible and Book of Common Prayer to the flat rock serving as an altar.

"You have no one to stand up for you, I suppose," he said.

"No one. We can't locate our friends."

"Will I marry you? Yes. I do God's work. I am Father Barstow. Who are you, and have you a license?"

"Yes, sir, we do. This is Nella Clapp, my fiancée, and I am Willis Hart."

"All right then. We shall proceed, this Saturday night in the middle of Golden Gate Park." He smiled. "And I'll enjoy it. There's nothing like a little quake to evoke matrimony, or reasonable facsimile thereof."

He laughed, and pulled a stole about his neck. "Would you care to dragoon a spectator as a witness while I make a few preparations?"

That was easy. Two of the priest's middle-aged parishioners lingered, and Willis asked the couple whether they would kindly witness the nuptials. They agreed at once.

"Good," said Father Barstow. "We'll attract a crowd, you know. What better to do on a Saturday night?" He paused, something gentle and quiet filling his face. "This hour may be unusual, but it is nonetheless a sacrament sacred to all Christians. We will proceed accordingly."

The father donned rimless spectacles, lifted the Book of Common Prayer to the lamplight, and beckoned Nella and Willis closer.

"Dearly beloved," he began, "we are gathered together here in the sight of God, and in the face of this company, to join together this man and this woman in holy matrimony, which is an honorable estate instituted of God in the time of man's innocency . . ."

Willis peered into Nella's face, which had become serene and radiant in the warm light of the lamps.

"I require and charge you both, as ye will answer at the dreadful Day of Judgment when the secrets of all hearts shall be disclosed, that if either of you know of any impediment, why ye may not be lawfully joined together in matrimony, ye do now confess it . . ."

Willis wondered if there was anything. Nella remained silent.

"Willis, wilt thou have this woman to thy wedded wife, to live together after God's ordinance in the holy estate of matrimony? Wilt thou love her, comfort her, honor and keep her in sickness and in health, and forsaking all others, keep thee only unto her, so long as ye both shall live?"

"I will," Willis said.

"Nella, wilt thou have this man to thy wedded husband, to live together after God's ordinance . . . ?"

Nella was listening with a Mona Lisa smile, transfixing Willis with love.

"I will," she said.

The priest leaned forward. "Take her hand now, Willis, and repeat after me. . . ."

Willis took Nella's hand. A quiet crowd was collecting about them. Sea breezes swept moistly through the park. It was growing chill.

"I, Willis, take thee, Nella, to my wedded wife, to have and to hold from this day forward, for better for worse, for richer for poorer, in sickness and in health, to love and to cherish till death us do part, according to God's holy ordinance, and thereto I plight thee my troth."

Willis repeated it quietly. Nella stood listening, and in turn repeated her vow: "I, Nella, take thee, Willis, to my wedded husband, to have and to hold from this day forward, for better for worse, for richer for poorer, in sickness and in health, to love, cherish, and to obey, till death us do part . . ."

"Have you a ring?" whispered the father.

Willis shook his head. Nella had none either.

And then, out among the observers, a man spoke up. "I do. Take it." The man approached, handing a plain gold band to Willis. "Take it. I am a widower."

"But—"

"We will use it and return it," said Father Barstow.

"No, it's yours. I'm glad some good came of the quake."

The priest nodded. He took the ring and handed it to Willis.

"Repeat after me: With this ring I thee wed, and with all my worldly goods I thee endow. In the name of the Father, and of the Son, and of the Holy Ghost, amen."

Nella wept. The ring, much too large, rested over her finger.

Father Barstow led them in prayer, and then concluded:

"Forasmuch as Willis and Nella have consented together in holy wedlock, and have witnessed the same before God and this company . . . I pronounce that they are man and wife, in the name of the Father, and of the Son, and of the Holy Ghost, amen."

That was it. Willis discovered a joy in Nella that equaled his own. In the space of hours he had won his heart's desire.

CHAPTER 49

. . . .

The crowd melted away, leaving Willis and Nella alone in the night. Alone, just married, and with no place to go. The iron scent of rain lay upon the breeze, and Willis feared that he and his bride would be drenched.

"Willis?" she said gently. "I can't walk another step."

He was expecting that. He doubted that he could either. That hectic day they had hiked up and down a small mountain, trekked over to Van Ness for a license, and then returned to Golden Gate Park to hunt for a clergyman.

His fancy of somehow making it to Marin County could only be a fancy. The wharfs were several miles away, and who would take them across the treacherous waters of the bay at that hour, and for nothing?

"I can't either. But it's going to rain, I think."

"Oh, Willis."

The despair in her voice told him she had run out of energy and hope. It wasn't going to be much of a wedding night. He felt the first mists in the air, and knew that soon it would become icy droplets and then probably a drizzle. They had no shelter. Most of the people around them had none either, not the kind to turn out rain at any rate. A few had strung up blankets and sheets against the cold, but almost no one had a waterproof haven. It was going to be a miserable night for two hundred thousand refugees.

Fog enveloped the park, snuffing the dim light of lanterns and campfires. One moment he could see a light; the next, it vanished. Icy drops needled his face.

"What are we going to do?" she cried.

"It's our boudoir," he said, trying to find something comic in it. "Now we have privacy."

She laughed. "I know how to stay warm," she replied. He liked that. Nella possessed something ebullient, something that would serve her and their union well during its bleakest moments. He hugged her. Her cheeks were wet.

"It looks like we're not going anywhere," he said. The fog had stolen all the light. They could be a few yards from a lantern and not know it.

He took her hand and walked, one step at a time, not knowing where he was going but hoping to blunder into some sheltering trees. He stumbled over something, and she giggled. Tiny droplets of rain bit at him, chilled his face. He found no trees, but several minutes later he did find a sharp rise, a place where they might sit with their backs to the wet grass.

Melancholy took hold of him. He and his bride would spend their first night together in utter misery.

"I don't know what to do. Sit, I guess," he said. "It's going to be a bad night."

He helped her down and sat beside her, and then clasped her to him and kissed her. She kissed back enthusiastically. He kissed her eyes, and her wet cheeks, and caressed her.

She responded with equal ardor, but when he went further she stopped him.

"There could be someone ten feet away," she whispered.

"There is," said a male voice.

Nella laughed, ripples of desperate delight pouring from her, and then Willis laughed, too.

"I don't know what's so funny," said the voice.

"It's our wedding night," Nella said.

That was greeted with a long silence. Then, "You stuck in the rain with nothing?"

"We have each other for warmth," Nella said, and Willis winced.

"I think we should have a shivaree," said the voice.

"A what?" asked Nella.

"Supposing I light a lamp. It'll take a minute to find the goldarned thing," said the voice. "We got to see the bride and groom."

Water dripped down Willis's nose. He noticed that Nella was shaking. He was getting cold. Bravado and gaiety might take them far, but not through this desperate night.

A blinding light startled him. Actually, someone had simply scratched a match to life. He glimpsed a hand, a face, and a tent about ten yards distant. And then the steady light of a kerosene lantern. It wasn't really a tent. It was a half-shelter some lucky people had rigged from blue-striped awning, and under it were half a dozen people, jammed together: the lamp-holder, a man of uncertain age, a woman beside him, and several near-adult children as far as Willis could gather.

"You look like some pretty wet hens," said the man. "We can make room. I guess we'll have to celebrate a little. You the people that hitched over in the Episcopalian hollow?"

"Uh, yes."

"Well, if you're too dumb to come out of the rain, not much that Elsie and I can do."

Willis didn't need another invitation. He and Nella raced to shelter. It wasn't much of one, and the awning wasn't perfectly tight, but suddenly the icy drops no longer stung Willis's face. Somehow the family made room.

"You sure are shaking like a leaf, lady," said the woman. "Here, this is the only blanket I got but I'll share with George."

Nella drew Willis close and then pulled the blanket over their shoulders. It felt marvelous.

"Well, now, I guess we'd better know who we're shivareeing," George said. "I'm Harding G. Wilson, and this is Elsie, my one and only; and these are Davis, Melanie, and Slocum Wilson, lately of the Potrero District, and now of the world."

"I'm Willis Hart, and this is Nella Clapp—ah, Mrs. Hart. Nella Hart. First time I've said that."

"Well, we're sorry to interrupt your honeymoon."

Nella laughed. Willis felt her laugh until her body shook, almost in convulsions. And she was crying, too. Under the blessed blanket, Willis squeezed her hand.

They laughed with her.

"We're some misplaced rubes from Jefferson, Missouri, come to the big city a few years ago to sell patent medicines, which we manufactured until last Tuesday. Now I reckon what you both need is a picker-upper tonic. Elsie?"

"We don't have any spoons," Elsie said. "But you just swallow one good slug of this, and you'll warm right up."

"We were pretty warm," Nella said.

Slocum, who was about eighteen, cackled.

Mrs. Wilson popped a cork from a rectangular brown bottle. "This is Dr. Grosvenor's Salvation Oil, good for catarrh and lung congestion," she said, handing the slender bottle to Willis. "Now, take a good one. Two tablespoons are the recommended dose."

Willis swallowed fiery stuff, coughed, sputtered, and felt liquid heat tunnel down his esophagus and warm his belly. "Holy smokes," he said, wheezing, and handed the bottle to Nella. She whomped down a load of it, wheezing cheerfully.

"It's liquid heat!" she announced, and swallowed another dose.

"Pretty well cures a fella," Wilson said.

Willis permitted himself another dose, relishing the well-being that stole out from his belly into his numb limbs, and then handed it back to Mrs. Wilson.

"Now how about some Balsam and Wild Cherry?"

"Ah, I think the Salvation Oil did the trick," Willis said. He suspected it was about a hundred proof, with maybe a tincture of opium in it.

"I'll try some," said Nella.

"My favorite," said Wilson. "I have me a nightcap of Wild Cherry. Lucky for us, we rescued our samples when fire chased us out."

"I, ah, think the rest of your stock might have fueled the fire," Willis said.

Nella whooped.

Wilson laughed. "We use it when we can't get the parlor stove going," he said. "One tablespoon starts anything. Well, now, let's just serenade the lucky couple. We've got to keep their mind off more serious matters."

Nella giggled. "This is the second-best wedding night we could have."

They laughed. Willis heard someone in a neighboring tent laugh. He felt a stealthy warmth invade his toes as well as his tonsils and earlobes.

Harding Wilson began humming "The Blue Tail Fly" in a pleasant baritone, and pretty soon the rest chimed in.

> *"When I was young I used to wait*
> *on Master and serve him his plate.*
> *And pass the bottle when he got dry,*
> *And brush away the Blue-tail fly*
> *Jimmy crack corn and I don't care,*
> *Jimmy crack corn and I don't care,*
> *Jimmy crack corn and I don't care,*
> *My master's gone away . . ."*

That was fun in an odd way, something earthy in the ruin of urbane San Francisco. The Wilsons had sung together, and now formed cheerful harmonies.

Wilson started in on "Careless Love," and soon had the whole camp singing:

> *"Love, oh, careless love.*
> *Love, oh, love, oh careless love,*
> *You see what love has done to me . . ."*

"Buffalo Gals" came next:

> *"As I was walking down the street,*
> *Down the street, down the street,*
> *A pretty little girl I chanced to meet,*
> *And we danced by the light of the moon.*
> *Buffalo gals, won't you come out tonight, come out tonight,*
> *Come out tonight,*
> *Buffalo gals won't you come out tonight,*
> *And dance by the light of the moon."*

That was fun. The Wilsons kept right on, one ballad after another, joined by a chorus that spread through the fog and darkness heaven-knows-how distant. These miserable bone-cold refugees were singing through a mean night, celebrating a marriage with all the good humor in the American soul.

The Salvation Oil made its rounds, followed by other concoctions that turned Willis's cold body into a furnace, and caused Nella to snuggle hotly against him within their shared blanket. He sensed something sweet and good in all this. People made light of their miseries. Even as rain and fog bit into them, chilled them to the marrow, there they were, warming themselves with melody.

"Now that I'm properly warmed up with Salvation Oil," said Harding Wilson, "I shall digress into profound rhetoric."

He paused, gathering attention. "A little praise and honor are in order," he said. "We have here a brave man and woman who tied the knot in the middle of a disaster. The world caved in on us, and they looked into the future and said to themselves that they would like to rebuild it together. And it didn't matter that they were going to start with only the clothes on their backs, and with no shelter on a rainy night. They said their vows, and now they're double-hitched for life. A cheer for them, I say, to all you out in the dark."

And the wet world cheered Willis and Nella, and then waited for the rain to go away.

CHAPTER 50

Carl Lubbich drifted through Franklin Hall, wanting to give himself to anyone who could use his skills. No one perceived him as a disgraced man; that would come later. The Committee of Fifty treated the city engineer affably, even commending him for repairing the broken mains swiftly—as if he had much to do with it. Utility and city maintenance workers, fortified by crews from Oakland, had done it. He did not see Rudolph Spreckels, who was no doubt looking after his wife and newborn infant, who arrived on the lawn of the Spreckels mansion just hours before it was blown to bits during the last stand on Van Ness.

Spreckels was lucky. He had a new child.

Lubbich perused the lists of known dead, and found his two children recorded there. He could only guess at their fate. They had probably been buried in a mass grave by an army sanitary detail, maybe doused with quicklime to hold disease at bay, and probably eaten by rats. That was their ultimate fate. Most of the listed dead were unknown; a sketchy physical description sufficed for the record. Sadness filtered through him.

Eugene Schmitz knew Lubbich was about, but did not call on the city engineer. Things were humming smoothly now, the sixth day after the quake. The city was recruiting laborers to clean the streets so that private contractors could begin clearing the mountains of rubble. Streetcar and railroad tracks were being repaired on a priority basis so that gondola cars could be drawn into the heart of the city and loaded with rubble.

At other desks, relief efforts continued unabated. Transportation had become the key to the future: getting people out of San Francisco and resettled elsewhere was crucial. It would be a long time before the city could welcome people to its bosom again. Mountains of food, clothing, bedding, tenting, lumber, and medical supplies were arriving on the wharfs and being distributed as needed. Lumber and canvas were turning parks into tent cities, where life was returning to an odd normalcy. Even classrooms were operating at full tilt in Golden Gate Park.

He wrestled for a while with the idea of tracking down Helene, and consulted the formidable registry there at Franklin Hall. But he found no listing, and felt oddly relieved. Helene was a closed chapter. So were the French restaurants with their curtained upstairs alcoves. He was a different man now.

No blueprint of the city's sewer system had survived, and Lubbich thought that one small contribution might be to draw one up from memory. But to think it was to know that it was fantasy. He was a structural engineer with a degree from Rensselaer Polytechnic Institute, happiest with bridges and trestles. He had turned over the hydraulic engineering to his assistant, Alvin Camden, who had not been seen since the quake. If he had to, Lubbich could manage hydraulic pressure, velocity, volume, grade, the construction of a drainage system suited to the peak volume, and all the rest, but his soul delighted in a good bridge or a fine wharf.

The maintenance crews would have a better idea than he, anyway. But there was something he might do: Chinatown had been almost a blank in the city's schemata. A major sewer bisected Chinatown. It drained the eastern portions of Nob Hill and the area north of Union Square. But no one knew where Chinatown's drains connected with that artery, or even what Chinatown's sewers had been constructed of. Masonry, probably, but everything from cast iron to hollowed logs had been found under the city.

For years he had eyed that blank on the diagrams with idle curiosity. He had never, during his tenure as city engineer, even tried to find out what lay under that quarter. Nor had he attempted to discover how the water mains ran in the district. The Chinamen had discouraged city inspectors, or misled them, or paid Schmitz to call them off. Now, suddenly, all that could be rectified. It wasn't much, but it might pay back some small portion of the debt that crushed him.

It would require investigation. He could to that much: map the system under Chinatown, see what was salvagable and what needed redoing, and lay the information on the mayor's desk. It would not be difficult. That Monday he armed himself with a notepad he found among the stores at Franklin Hall. He needed a measuring tape and could find none, but a ball of twine, which he marked off with ink every foot, would suffice. He would map what existed, determine if the diameters were adequate for population densities, and make a report. What else could a man do who owed the world scores of millions of dollars?

He felt oddly good about it. He was going to do something valid, something redemptive, even if it counted for nothing against the tragedy his corrupt negligence had caused. He took the precaution of obtaining a pass from the city clerk. Armed patrols, some of them Schmitz's trigger-happy volunteer police, roamed wolfishly through the dead city looking for targets. Some prominent citizens had died as a result.

A great silence had descended over moribund San Francisco. Few people penetrated the burned area because the word had reached them of the murderous patrols, including those of the army, the regular police, and the undisciplined vigilantes. Sea breezes swept the rank odors away, and pleasant April weather smiled benignly upon the ruins.

An army patrol stopped him, and he showed them his pass and described his purpose, and they left him alone.

He reached Chinatown by the middle of Monday morning, and barely recognized the place. Nothing stood. The wooden buildings had all been consumed. Along DuPont, shallow hollows, each once a basement, lined both sides of the street. He peered into them, one by one, and in many instances his presence sent varicolored rats sulking away with sudden darting movement where none was expected. He had never seen so many and they fascinated him. He should have loathed them, but they were performing a public service of sorts, consuming all the putrefying flesh that still lay under the rubble. Let them perform their work.

He had heard around Franklin Hall that there were no tunnels honeycombing the area, much to everyone's surprise. He confirmed that as he studied the basements one by one. It had all been white men's nonsense. A crevice where the street had buckled during the quake gave him a glimpse of the septic sewer draining Chinatown's main street. He guessed it might be a foot in diameter, grossly inadequate in a district jammed with humanity. But he could not clamber down the crevice to measure.

Near the corner of Stockton and Sacramento, he discovered a basement that straddled the primary sewer. The rough masonry artery was intended to carry storm water as well as sewage away from Nob Hill and the Union Square area. It would be something to measure and investigate. He eased his way into the basement, using rubble for steps. Rats scattered. Whatever they had been gnawing lay about, malodorous and blackened. They did serve to steer him toward a breech in the artery, where the quake had twisted it apart. Lubbich knew he was looking at the one drain that did appear on the city diagrams. All he had to do was determine how the Chinamen had plugged into it, and with what. He wished he had a handkerchief, anything to filter the noxious odor. He stumbled over rubble, climbed a small mountain of it, and descended down to the crudely mortared drain. It had been torn asunder from top to bottom, leaving a gap wide enough for Lubbich to pass through if he crouched. This one was rectangular, with a traditional vaulted roof, built of crudely laid masonry that employed anything at hand, from brick to rock, and probably had been constructed from torn-down buildings. Foul water, most of it from Sunday's rains, ebbed slowly, but only an inch or so deep. He could walk in it. His shoes would be soaked, but what did it matter? What did Carl Lubbich matter? He squeezed in, felt the water tug at his shoes, and found himself in a rat kingdom. Everywhere the crude masonry provided perches or niches for the rodents, and his sudden presence sent a shrieking chatter through them. The dripping walls seemed to twitch and come alive.

They did not retreat, and he suddenly felt the need to escape, and fast, sensing that they might attack. He edged back toward the sunlight and began the awkward clamber out of the hole when several landed on him from above. He convulsed violently, shaking them off, appalled by their ferocity. One bit him in the neck, another landed on his scalp and scratched it. He burst free, into the basement, and the rats fell off him, writhed on rubble, and raced into the sewer.

He clapped a hand to his neck and found blood. More blood covered his hair. Shaking, he wiped himself with pages of the notepad he was using to record his discoveries. He wondered how he had been so foolish as to crawl into a vile hole. He needed desperately to cleanse himself; to scrub away the blood, scour his flesh. But in earthquake-stricken San Francisco, that could be only a dream. If one thing demarked the surviving population of the city, it was body odor. Everyone stank.

He swallowed, retreated from the basement, clambered up to grade and stood in the sunlight, shaken and afraid. Curbing rats had been his responsibility. A city's health depended on good sanitary measures. How many rats were there? A hundred thousand? Four hundred thousand? More rats than humans? He felt the accusatory finger pointing at him once again. There would be hearings, and rats would be one of the topics. Why had the Schmitz administration done nothing, endangering citizens with its neglect? What would he reply? That he was too busy patronizing the French restaurants to worry about all that?

He walked, trembling, back to Franklin Hall, feeling so dispirited that he wondered why he had ever been born. The malaise continued the rest of the day and through the evening. He sat about in the temporary City Hall, doing nothing, feeling some dread infect his mind, his fingers touching the blood-crusted wounds. He began to feel desolate. He walked restlessly about the place. A great tiredness afflicted him, and he ascribed it to a chastening of his soul.

He found a corner where he might lie down. Franklin Hall beat sleeping outside, even if the hall hummed with action all night long. The canteen didn't interest him. He had never felt less hungry, though he welcomed some cold coffee.

Lying on the hardwood floor, his mind turned to the most terrible of all the Schmitz administration's vices. Lubbich and only a handful of others knew about it. The rats under Chinatown had been infested with parasites brought from China: worms, flukes, and bubonic plague. In March of 1900 plague cropped up in Chinatown, no doubt carried there by those escaping plague in Canton, which killed 180,000 people, and another 12,000 in Hong Kong, and then clawed the populations of Africa, Russia, and the rest of China. And America.

The Schmitz administration had ferociously denied the existence of plague in the city, going so far as to delete reference to it in Board of Health reports. The administration tried to remove four members of the Board of Health who persisted in warning the public about the menace. The city even arrested a federal health officer for trying to do his duty, and it arranged to have the state discharge its bacteriologist, one Ryfkogel, who had found plague germs in the city. Schmitz had feared a national quarantine of the city, and had been determined to stamp out all evidence of plague, especially because eliminating the rats meant tearing up Chinatown, letting in sunlight and air into basements, removing garbage, filling in holes and cesspools, tearing down shacks—all of which Chinatown's leaders resisted.

The issue had not gone away. Even during the deliberations of the Committee of Fifty, during the fire, it rose. Lubbich had heard all about it. Dr. Marcus Herstein, one of the Fifty, warned that the sewers had been opened by the quake and the rat population had been loosed upon the whole city.

"Gentlemen, there will be quarantine. People will be afraid to rebuild in case they come into contact with that plague."

"There is no plague," Schmitz had replied.

"There will be—unless the rats are controlled," Dr. Herstein retorted, and warned that the ruins would be a rats' paradise.

The doctor's concerns had been pushed aside. Plague was considered an Oriental disease, and besides, the first business of the committee was to put out the fires.

All this City Engineer Carl Lubbich knew. He tried to set aside what he knew, but couldn't. He told himself that if plague did exist, it was so rare, so isolated, that his chances were excellent. But he had been bitten. And so he spent that Monday night waiting, waiting, waiting.

CHAPTER 51

day off. Lieutenant Paul Boswell could scarcely believe it. The Old Man had worked every officer in the command twenty hours a day, not sparing himself either. But now, a week after the quake, military discipline had been imposed on chaos. General Funston had divided the city into six districts, each with its own command, with each district connected to the others by Signal Corps lines. The field kitchens supplied food. The army engineers had even reconstructed the bakeries around the city, and flour was being turned into bread as fast as it could be baked. Tent cities were springing up. Things had started to hum, to settle down into routine.

Boswell had worked himself ragged. Each long day, he had tried to help desperate people, and usually couldn't, which he regarded as true Sisyphean labor. One of his most desolating tasks was to tell relatives of the dead, or the missing, that no, the army had little record of who was buried in the mass graves around the city. They would likely never know.

It had been painful, depressing, exhausting work for which a bookish man was not well suited.

Fearless Freddie, as he was called behind his back, had called him in that evening: "Take a day, Lieutenant. Sleep, that's what I'd do."

"I'd welcome that, sir."

"Report at six on Thursday."

"Yes, sir."

"Mrs. Funston wishes to thank the command. And retrieve me for domestic duty for a few hours. She outranks me."

That was the Funston version of humor. Boswell smiled, and departed with a smart salute.

Boswell left Fort Mason well into the evening, and noted that the Chinamen's camp was swiftly filling. They were minding their p's and q's, he thought jovially. The engineers had laid it out with military precision, tents in severe rows, not an inch out of formation. Boswell had wondered all the while why the Chinese were being relocated right there, under the brooding brow of Fort Mason and the command. He could think of several reasons, none of them just, but it was not his to reason why. He had risked the Old Man's wrath to feed them days before their resettlement, and didn't regret it.

He cranked his motorcycle, which proved to be a balky Pegasus that night, but finally coughed to life, and then he made his way through the rubble-strewn streets to the Presidio. He had officer's quarters there, albeit the lowliest of them, a small and plain room, reflecting his low rank and lack of seniority. But he had what the remaining two hundred thousand San Franciscans pined for: a bed, a roof, ample food, a hot shower, and laundry facilities, courtesy of the army.

He would welcome his slim iron bed like a lover, but intended first to shower, to lather soap over his lean frame, let the stinging heat of the water wash him clean, and then surrender under those army-issue brown blankets to the arms of Morpheus. He would slumber until he awakened. The need was primordial. But then, tomorrow, he would turn Turk, find the red-haired lady, Miss Severance, and kidnap her—if he could. He wondered about that. There were thousands of people all over the Presidio, but he would seek only one.

There hadn't been many bright moments during the week, but one of them turned out to be Miss Severance. Whenever he thought of her, which was frequently, he remembered a worn but spirited young woman seeking nothing for herself, but sustenance for the city's outcasts. For a change, there had been something he could do about her request, and he did it on his own authority. He remembered several things: the look on her face, that memorable not-so-prim kiss and hug, and something else—a grace of soul that lay behind those chiseled features. Miss Ginger Severance had awakened something in Second Lieutenant Paul Boswell, who knew and understood exactly what was happening to him, and didn't mind it a bit.

He didn't awaken until mid-morning on Wednesday, and then lay quietly, luxuriating in comfort and at last, rest. His thoughts were upon gifts. What might Miss Severance wish for the most? Need the most? What she probably wanted more than anything just then was a bath and fresh clothing. None of which he could readily supply without getting into a jam. But then again . . . soap was easy to come by. And relief committees across the country were sending everything they could think of, including women's attire. Some of it was heaped in quartermaster depots.

But he lacked her size. He struggled to remember how she looked, not at night out at the field kitchen, but when she barged into Fort Mason. She had been slim, medium-tall, a little thinner than was fashionable, though not lacking female curves under that grimy white dress. But she had seemed larger, as if her slender body couldn't contain the fiery torch within; the pleading for the Celestials larger than the person from whom it issued. It didn't surprise him that he had registered so much about her as she described the plight of the Chinamen. There had been something about her. . . .

Maybe, if he gathered his courage, he could simply lead her to the warehouses and let her choose. It would take a little doing, but he knew and trusted the quartermaster sergeants who had been assigned to relief duties.

He smiled at that.

He bathed, shaved, and dressed, then hooked his wire spectacles over his ears, breakfasted on oatmeal, with ample steaming java, and ventured into a bright morning. How might one find, among twenty-odd thousand refugees, one bedraggled mademoiselle?

A reconnaissance from a knoll confirmed that he could waste his entire day hunting for her in that sea of tents and rude shelters that harbored tens of thousands. There was a better way.

He collected *Heart of Darkness* from his quarters and repaired to the field kitchens, there to study the several lines that waited patiently day and night for food. She would sooner or later appear in one.

Luck was with him. She stood near the rear of one of the lines, looking small and unwell. With luck, he would not crack the great Conrad novel this day, though he considered the options about equally attractive.

He halted before her. "Miss Severance," he said.

"Oh, Lieutenant Boswell."

"I've been looking for you. We have some business to attend."

"We do? Is it the Chinamen?"

"No, us."

She surveyed him coolly. "Lieutenant, just because I gave you a token of my gratitude doesn't mean that . . ." She paused, reddening.

"It's called a kiss, and it was delightful. Come along with me."

"But I'll lose my place—"

"Then lose it. I will provide."

People stared. He commandeered her elbow and steered her away. "I shouldn't let you do this. I have important things to do. . . ."

"Where did you sleep last night?"

"I just dozed somewhere."

"How long have you been out-of-doors?"

"Since the earthquake."

"How long have you been without a change of clothing or a bath?"

"You're very presumptuous, Lieutenant."

He was leading her through rope barriers into an area the army reserved for itself.

"Where are we going, may I ask?"

"Clean clothing and a bath. Quartermaster depot first, for your pick of relief supplies, and then I will prevail upon my friend, Elizabeth Langley, wife of Captain Langley, to spare you her lavatory."

"But—others need things much more than I do."

"Miss Severance, the look in your eyes tells me my instincts are quite correct. I cannot and would not invite you to bachelor officers' quarters, but you will be my guest at the officers' mess, and I am pleased to invite you."

She surrendered with a small sweet smile. "This is a dream," she said.

"Once you change, I can arrange for the post laundry to clean whatever you wish."

She glanced at her rags. "I think I will turn them over to the laundry for washing, but I never want to see them again. Give them away."

At the depot they found her a stern gray woolen dress that would do, and he wandered away while she plucked up other more intimate items. Then he presented her with a bar of soap, which she held in hand as if it were a twenty-dollar gold piece. An hour later she emerged from Elizabeth Langley's lavatory all aglow, her hair shining, her face scrubbed, and lights playing deep in the bottoms of her eyes. He had known she was beautiful, even when her hair had been matted to her head with grime, even when she wore grimy and forlorn clothing. But now, scrubbed and vibrant, he knew he beheld a stunning woman. She was setting him afire.

She rewarded him with a small, gentle kiss on the cheek.

"I had forgotten how it feels to be clean," she said. "You have given me such a gift. That bath—this soap . . ."

"It's dinnertime. I'll take you to our officers' mess."

"But then I must go. There are so many who need help."

"Yes, Miss Severance, and you would help them all if you could."

"Yes, I would. That is what I want, with all my heart."

"You have magnificent instincts and I wish to hear much more about them."

But that was not to be. At the mess, every bachelor officer in the place found reason to stop at their table and banter. Miss Severance didn't banter back, and plainly wasn't enjoying it.

"We'll escape these scarecrows and go hide somewhere, Ginger," he said.

"Yes, call me that—Paul. But after we finish, I really must . . ."

She seemed so afraid, and he wondered why. "I ask only that you spare me an hour or so. I would like to know more about you."

"I would not be comfortable. But if you wish me to explain my faith, my vocation, the things I learned from the Bible Society, I would be most happy to. Are you a religious man?"

"You could make me one," he said, just a little slyly. "My temptation is books."

"I hope you don't read bad ones."

"Very, very bad ones," he said. "I am reading *Heart of Darkness*. What could be worse? It's all in the title."

"If it's ungodly, you shouldn't read it."

"It's about a man who discovers his own evil."

She eyed him, the faintest humor lifting the corners of her lovely lips. "They used to try that when I was preaching on my street-corner near the Barbary Coast. They would say they were beyond redemption and ask me to try to reform them—in their rooms." Her eyes lit merrily. "I would give them a tract. Do you want a tract?"

"I'm a voracious reader."

She sighed. "I don't have any left."

He spotted Major Willard Plunkett, the very paradigm of a stuffy old bore, and decided it was time to retreat.

"Ah, Boswell. What have we here?" Plunkett loomed in.

"A woman, Major. This is a female."

Plunkett extended a soft and horny paw in her direction. "I am an artillery captain and half deaf. What was your name?"

"Miss Severance—"

Boswell stood. "Just leaving, Major. Just taking Miss Severance back to the Palace Hotel."

"Ah? Ah? How can you do that? The hotel's—"

"I am a prestidigitator."

"Haw! You bookworms."

He steered Ginger away. He chose to stroll the grounds, and offered her his arm, which she took reluctantly, like a doe poised to flee. A sea breeze cut through their clothing, and he marveled at the courage and endurance of all those homeless thousands in the Presidio.

He decided simply to say what he wished to say: These were uncertain times. She might vanish. Life might tear them apart.

"Ginger, the moment I saw you, I saw something I treasured. I have never known a more loving woman, with a heart as big as the whole world. You are everything I ever dreamed of. There's no way to say this except to say it; I wish to court you, and let it lead wherever it may. These are difficult times, and unless I tell you plainly what my intentions are, I might lose you forever. I don't know what might become of all this, or whether you'd accept my suit. But I hope you may let me take this as far as it might go."

"No, Paul," she said.

CHAPTER 52

· ·

Harrison White could not locate Marcia and the children. Sunday afternoon he checked the Presidio registries and did not find her there. That evening, after the rain had passed, he tried the registries in Golden Gate Park. And Monday he took time off to examine registries elsewhere, from Lafayette Square to the Ferry Building. But his wife and son and daughter had vanished.

At first he feared for their safety. But then the fear dissolved into anger. She knew where he could be found: he had been helping the city administration. She could have sent word, but she didn't. That was inexcusable.

He worked desultorily on his Chinatown plans, sketching in a modified street grid, with culs-de-sac and intimate parks, and only one arterial, so that the area would become a choice, quiet residential backwater. He put his artistic skills to work, penciling trees and playgrounds, circles with fountains in them, an equestrian statue in a square surrounded by Parisian-style cafés without outdoor seating. He had been tempted to draw in some Oriental buildings, some pagodas, as a cultural memory of what the area had been before the quake, but rejected the idea. The Chinamen should be out of sight and mind, and San Francisco should be the premiere city on the rim of Western civilization. If anyone wanted to celebrate the city's brisk trade with the Orient, let it be done in a waterfront park where it would mean something, and not in the heart of a white man's city.

But in between his desultory sketching, he fretted about Marcia, and his fretting turned more and more sour as another day slid by without word. By now he was certain she had fled the area. He had asked Police Chief Dinan to keep an eye out for her, and the chief had nodded unenthusiastically. The chief no doubt had thousands of similar requests to deal with.

Finally, on Tuesday, almost a week after the quake, Harrison decided it was time to notify her parents in Cleveland that she and the children were missing. Western Union and the Postal Telegraph-Cable Company were still sending messages from the stricken city for free. He penned a terse message: AM WELL WORKING FOR CITY MARCIA AND CHILDREN SEPARATED BUT BELIEVED SAFE CONTACT CITY HALL SF HARRISON.

He gave it to a youth hanging around Franklin Hall's front steps.

"Take this to the telegraph station at Fort Mason. This is important, kid. I'm a city planner."

"There's a long line waiting to send stuff."

Harrison knew the kid was angling for a tip, but he hadn't a dime. "How about a sandwich? I'll bring one out. Some ham and bread in there."

"Yeah? Okay."

Harrison assembled a sandwich, handed it to the skinny kid, and the boy raced away, the paper flapping in his hand.

"Report to me when you get back. I want to know it was sent," he yelled at the retreating figure.

The Signal Corps had established several telegraph stations in the stricken city, stringing thousands of yards of wire through ruins to connect the military posts and precincts of the city to the terminals at the Ferry Building, which were connected by cable to Oakland and the rest of the country.

White returned to his efforts to fill the blank space in the city's master plan but found himself severely hamstrung by lack of equipment and information. He didn't know the size of the city blocks in Chinatown, had no access to surveys or topographic maps, or water utility and sewer schemata. He had no knowledge of the soil or rock underlying the area, easements, titles, or anything else a planner needed to know. Neither did he have so much as a drawing board or T square or compass. But all that would be remedied. What counted just now was what he could achieve with his sketches, his notes, and the ideas he would place before Mayor Schmitz in a few days—before the refugee Chinamen sneaked back in and ruined his chances.

He toiled in various corners of Franklin Hall, feeding at the canteen, an unkempt, unshaven, odoriferous man, not unlike everyone else. No one other than a privileged handful had soap, razor, hot water, or a change of clothing. He had slept for so long on hardwood floors he had finally gotten used to the brutal discomfort, and wondered whether he would ever enjoy a soft mattress again.

Then, on Thursday, a messenger brought him a wire.

HB WHITE CITY HALL SF AM IN CLEVELAND WITH CHILDREN YOU COMING? M

The wire irked him. Why hadn't she let him know? Why had she done this without consulting? She was being inconsiderate. Why did she want him to come? What good could he do in Cleveland? Here he was working for their future and she didn't even grasp that crucial fact.

He set aside the telegram, brimming with sharp retorts. He'd sort them out and fire off another, just as soon as he honed the words down.

But he couldn't work. He penned another telegram.

CANT COME BUILDING OUR FUTURE WHY DIDNT YOU TELL ME?

He corralled another boy, bribed him with a sandwich, and went back to work. He would hear in the morning. The whole thing had suddenly chafed into a blister in his plans. Maybe it was good she was there. They were all safe, fed, and warm. But marriage was supposed to be a partnership, and she had gone off and left him, and that got under his skin like a splinter. Now he had to resolve the matter. Go to Shaker Heights, insist she return . . . Put aside all his hard work and desire to support her in style, and lounge in the East. No, he was damned if he would do that. He had a commission from the mayor himself and he would follow through, and he intended to make sure that his plan was so admirable that Harrison Barnes White would be one of the preeminent men in the West.

And so he toiled, sketched in his pad, threw away designs, revamped his ideas, walked twice more through Chinatown, more and more alarmed as the Celestials began cleaning up debris. It would be a race: submit the plan within days, even hours, or see the busy yellow men wreck everything. The only good thing about those hikes over there was that the army and volunteer police had relaxed. They could no longer keep citizens away from their own dwellings, and after several violent and vocal encounters with people sifting through rubble for their own possessions, the soldiers retreated.

The city was rife with horror stories, though: crushed, rat-eaten bodies, decaying corpses with bullet holes through the skulls, fingers chopped off, rats the size of poodles, murderous gang wars between stray cats and rats, bank vaults too hot to approach, much less open, iron cages full of baked girls in Chinatown, large diamonds that had been incinerated by the fire, leaving empty sockets in gold rings.

Nor was the army done with forced labor. It was worth a young man's liberty to walk alone through the ruins, because he was likely to be conscripted at bayonet-point for street clearing. Funston's iron claw hadn't pulled its talons out of San Francisco, and the people were seething.

Then one afternoon White discovered Sing Fat's Chinamen laying up new foundations, using the very rubble tumbled by the earthquake plus some mortar they had brought in. And there was the fat gray merchant, calmly watching his swarm of coolies.

This time, White didn't tarry to talk with the Chinaman, but retreated pell-mell to Franklin Hall, and thundered up on the podium.

"I want to talk with the mayor," he snapped in a tone that brooked no objection.

The clerk shrugged.

White pushed past busy clerks to the mayor's corner, and waited impatiently while Schmitz dealt with a railroad official who wanted protection for boxcars that were being vandalized by mobs of angry, shouting, fist-waving people determined to distribute the contents of each car.

"It's the young architect," he said at last, fishing for a name.

"Harrison Barnes White, sir. Yes. I'm almost done with my plans for Chinatown. Rough, of course—I haven't access to a single topographical map or survey or anything else. But even so, what I'm almost ready to show you will be a transformation from a sink of iniquity and vice and peril to grace and beauty and the finest design of European man."

"I'm busy, Mr. White. Have you a specific request?"

"Yes! The Chinamen are rebuilding. They're weeks ahead of everyone. Sing Fat, the merchant, already has his foundation going up—rubble and mortar. You must stop it, keep them out."

Schmitz smiled and shrugged. "You know, my young friend, it's their property—most of it, anyway."

"What? What?"

"A citizen has property rights, you know."

"But they aren't citizens! They're aliens. They're a blot on the city."

"Who am I to stop a man from rebuilding on his own lot?"

"But you can't do this to me."

"Mr. White, it wasn't a very good idea to begin with. Now that the city's rebuilding, we must do what is practical and right. Thank you for your efforts."

Resentment washed through White. The smiling, bland, damned mayor was selling out, letting the Yellow Peril back into the heart of San Francisco. Suddenly, coldly, White knew what all this was about. Money. If Chinatown were turned into a prime business and apartment area, there would be no money for Ruef and Schmitz.

White stared icily, seeing everything with terrible clarity. The most corrupt mayor in the city's history was doing business as usual.

"I suppose you don't even want to see my plans," he said.

Schmitz shrugged. "Anytime they're ready, I'll have a look. But I won't be able to get back to you for a while, maybe a few months."

White felt something deflate within him.

"So, that's how it is. Sing Fat's paid you. So have the rest. And now you'll line your pockets with Chinatown loot."

Schmitz, a towering man, suddenly loomed over White, his eyes glittering, but he said nothing. Instead, he waved at a uniformed policeman.

"Take his pass. Don't let him in again," Schmitz said.

"Now I know," snarled White. "Now I've seen it."

Schmitz gestured. The cop started to haul White away, but White furiously stalked ahead of the copper and out the door of that stinking, corrupt den of iniquity, and down the steps and onto Van Ness Street. He scarcely knew where to go. He didn't even have his Chinatown sketches with him. He stood there, shocked at the sudden turn of his fortune. All the work he had done for the city had been for nothing!

Where was Spreckels? By God, he'd find the financier and describe the whole thing, and when those hearings resumed, he would testify that Schmitz was grafting even before the city's ruins had cooled down.

He stared at the sunny street, feeling like a hobo.

The problem was, he had no place to lay his head. The corners and hallways of Franklin Hall had sheltered him for a week; the canteen for the Committee of Fifty had fed him. Within the hall he had availed himself of cold water and soap to keep his face and hands clean, and his attire reasonably respectable. But now he'd gone from somebody to nobody.

He took stock of himself: he stank. His legs and belly chafed from foul underdrawers, his face was covered with a week's stubble. His clothing was vile, his hair greasy, and his temper volcanic. Now he would have to become one of the peons, the nonentities in the park or the Presidio.

CHAPTER 5 3

C arl Lubbich awakened in a dark corner of Franklin Hall, anxiously registering everything about his body. Apart from the aches he associated with sleeping on the floor, he seemed much the same. But something had changed. Some black dread threaded through him, like a condemned man staring at the guillotine that would separate him from his head in a few moments.

He was sweating a little, and queasy. But he did not discover fever, rapid pulse, or anything else that might suggest doomsday. He arose uncomfortably, knowing himself to be restless, irritable, edgy—and afraid. He would probably get something or other from the rat bite. There was little reason to suppose it would be the black plague. The denizens of the sewers carried so many vile diseases he could die of anything. He thought bitterly of the days when he had blithely brushed off such concerns. Rats under Chinatown were no concern for the city engineer, or the Schmitz administration.

He nibbled at whatever lay about for the benefit of the bureaucrats. Bread, some surprising cheese, the first sweet roll he had eaten in days. Coffee. He wasn't really hungry.

One thing consumed him that morning: He needed to know who he was. Yesterday his passion had been repayment, if even a few dollars of labor against an impossible obligation. That had vanished in the restless night, and now he needed something else: an identity. He didn't know why he wanted to be able to call himself something; maybe it would help him put off the horror of disease lurking just beyond his horizon, the fanged demon crouched and waited.

He wandered the echoing confines of Franklin Hall, aware for the first time of how everything within reverberated from the hard walls and high ceilings, the building as hollow as the souls within it, amplifying everything from sneezes to footsteps. There was no desk for the city engineer. He thought to take a walk, refresh himself in the April sun, but he didn't feel like it.

He had something to resolve, and the need grew urgent. Who was Carl Lubbich? The Milwaukee-born Progressive, the rational socialist who believed in powerful city administrations? Was Carl Lubbich a Catholic? Was he descended, as he suspected, from a Jewish family that had converted in the misty past, probably to escape some middle-European prince's persecution? Was Carl Lubbich nothing, having abandoned every one of those ideals, as well as his patrimony?

He rephrased his question. What had he betrayed? His father's firm Progressive rectitude? Yes. His father had been a man to account for every penny, and if even one was missing, to make it up from his own pocket. Yes, if the new secular socialism was to take hold of men's souls and give birth to a just and kind world, he had betrayed it. And there could be no redemption. Socialism did not redeem its fallen.

A Catholic, maybe. But not in his heart. His bare, pro forma connection had been mostly to please Rosemary, and before that, to please his mother. Altar boy. Carl Lubbich, altar boy, spending his recent years in the arms of Helene, and enjoying fast company. But what of that? Did he *believe?* The whole thing? The Trinity? The divinity of Jesus? The Holy Ghost? The Catholic belief that the Church spoke without theological error in its most sacred declarations and articles of faith? That it alone was the true and faithful church of Jesus Christ? Did he believe that, and the writings of the Church Fathers, and the Nicene Creed and Marian Doctrine? And redemption for any faithful and believing person, no matter what the sin, if the sinner truly repented?

Could a repentant man, shrived by a priest, see God? If there was a God and heaven. The thought stirred through him, probing restlessly into his consciousness. He knew why. It came down to one thing: hope. There was only hope for a lost man with no future.

He didn't know, but the idea stirred within, moved around like a fetus in a womb. He was not comforted. Quite the opposite, he experienced agony. What he needed seemed to lie just beyond consciousness, something unfathomable over the horizon of his soul, something that tormented him as he paced the busy hall.

He gave up: His seeking wasn't leading him anywhere.

He spent that day doing nothing, a restless observer.

The work of the Committee of Fifty had shifted dramatically. It was still concerned with relief: food, clothing, shelter, medical assistance, sanitation. But now it was just as concerned with transportation. Almost every man in the room—there were no women—toiled at one thing: the urgent need to move as many people out of the stricken area as possible. That was why Schmitz was consulting with Southern Pacific officials. Repair the roadbed, move 'em out. Relief camps in Southern California. Send 'em to Los Angeles. Every departing soul was one less mouth to feed, body to shelter.

Lubbich listened inertly. The price-gouging railroad, the very SP that farmers and passengers and orchardists had railed against, was shipping relief supplies in and people out for nothing—at a dead loss. What sort of heartless capitalism was this? The news unsettled his beliefs. Maybe Edward Harriman was not a ruthless Jay Gould or a Morgan or a Vanderbilt.

And so the day passed, crawling on beetle feet toward its conclusion. Then at dusk, Carl Lubbich felt chilled. His hands and feet turned cold and sweaty. The chill passed, only to return again, and Lubbich felt that not even a pile of blankets could warm him.

He felt a rush of fear. If these were the premonitory symptoms of plague—or anything else—then now, in ruined San Francisco, in April of 1906, Carl Lubbich would surely depart from the living into the eternal nothingness. He lay quietly, fighting back the trembling. Maybe all this would pass. He had no future but did not want to die.

The chill passed, and Lubbich lay quietly, in a dark corner of the temporary City Hall, ignored by busy men through the whole evening. He dared to think maybe that was the end. The hall darkened and quieted except for those warders whose lit lamps signified an unsleeping effort to preserve what was left of San Francisco and sustain the lives of the desperate. Sometime in the night, Lubbich felt another chill that robbed him of heat and set him to clenching his teeth. He would see a doctor in the morning if this continued. But he began to hope that he would survive whatever this might be. Had he not weathered several such chills, and had they not subsided?

But in that dark corner, fear took him again. Would he even see the sun rise? Life would flow on, but what if he wasn't present? Would anyone know or care? Then a wave of sorrow engulfed him and he wept. He felt tears ooze from his eyes and wet his face. He had never known such helplessness. What could doctors do to stay the plague—if that was what had stirred the coldness in his limbs? Nothing. They were as helpless to heal the plague as they always had been throughout history. Only sanitation, only relentless war on rats, had held the awful Black Death at bay.

A long ghost-ridden night slipped by. When he arose to relieve himself his wariness shocked him. He felt worn down to nothing, as if a great grinder had slowly rubbed away all his substance. He grasped sometime in the small hours—having lost track of time—that he would soon die, though the full animal viciousness of the disease had not yet pounced. He was heading for the third day, and wondered how long it took for the Black Death to incubate. Not as long as usual, he thought, thinking of the rat bite in his neck which had bled copiously. Not long. He wept, but tears wouldn't come, and he realized he was desperately dehydrated.

With dawn came fever, aching heat, mad heat, his soul burning as fast as his flesh. He moaned and thrashed, and that was when they found him. They gathered over him, staring down, mumbling, and he heard his name.

"Water," he said.

They gave him some. It went down like acid and did not console his body. Then a stranger knelt over him, taking his pulse, peering into his mouth, inserting a thermometer and then withdrawing it.

"Can you talk, Mr. Lubbich?" he asked.

"Yes."

"I'm Dr. Benet. Tell me what happened if you can."

"Bit by a rat, Chinatown, looking at sanitation for the city . . ."

The man frowned. "A rat? Where?"

Lubbich pointed to his neck below his right ear. And at his scalp.

"You have a high fever. One-oh-three. Do you have a headache?"

"Yes."

"Pain all over?"

"Yes."

"You can hear me all right?"

Lubbich nodded.

The doctor's fingers pressed against lymph nodes in the neck. "These are swollen," he said. "I'm going to unbutton your shirt."

A crowd had gathered. Lubbich peered up at solemn faces. Dying had become a public event.

The doctor palpated various organs. "Your spleen is enlarged," he said.

Then he studied Lubbich's hot, dry flesh, running the beam of an electric torch over Lubbich's torso. He frowned. "Petechiae," he said, swiftly peering at the onlookers. He did not explain.

"Mr. Lubbich, how long ago were you bitten by the rats?"

"This is the third day coming up."

"Do you know what day this is?"

Lubbich shook his head. He couldn't remember much.

"We're going to take you from here. To a hospital," he said.

Lubbich trembled. He felt awful. "Is it the plague?" he whispered.

"I wasn't sure until I saw the black patches—petechiae."

"The Black Death . . ."

Suddenly the onlookers bolted. He heard shouting and mayhem. Then he heard Mayor Schmitz's commanding shout: "Say nothing. I forbid you to say anything. One word and the whole relief effort is doomed. One word, and San Francisco's doomed!"

Lubbich heard the sound of escape and then silence. Franklin Hall had largely emptied. He was afraid. A great blind sob racked him.

Time passed. Lubbich felt himself being rolled onto a stretcher and carried to an army conveyance by army corpsmen. Benet accompanied him. They took him somewhere—he didn't know where—and put him in a room entirely alone, except for the nurses and doctors who peered into the door and then vanished. But Benet stayed with him, watching, watching.

"How much time, doctor?"

Benet shrugged. "A day or two. This is the first case I've seen. It's a textbook case, except it's coming faster than usual. That bite in the neck . . ."

"Will my death save the city?"

Some sort of tenderness filled the doctor's face. "Let us hope so. No matter what the mayor says, I will insist upon a public airing." He smiled gently. "Yes, let us say so. Your death will not be in vain. I will promise you that. No matter what the abominable mayor says, I will tell the world. Now the city will destroy its rats."

Tears rose in Carl Lubbich's eyes.

"We live for a purpose," Benet said. "Maybe this is yours, painful as it may seem to you."

Lubbich hurt so much he felt half mad. "A priest," he said.

"Roman?"

"Yes."

"All right. But now we are going to give you as much water as you can drink. And try to bring down your fever with compresses."

Lubbich shook his head.

He drifted, his body hot and nauseous. They tried to cool him with cold wet towels. They bade him to suck on a straw, but little did he care.

Then a man in a Roman collar appeared, and the others vanished.

"Mr. Lubbich?"

"Shrive me . . ."

"I will."

"Forgive me father for I have sinned . . ."

Lubbich couldn't remember why he was there or who he was. So he said he had done evil and was sorry, and then drifted into a whirling desolation. He tried to make order out of chaos. He mumbled and the priest bent over him to hear.

He heard the Latin absolution. He heard the priest pray. He felt the holy oil.

He felt comforted. There would be life after death.

CHAPTER 54

There was nothing to do but wait, so Katharine Steinmetz did. The days rolled by, one by one, and no news came. Nights on the hard ground were bad, but the daylight wasn't unpleasant; everyone waited on her. That was a novelty and she was enjoying it. She had waited on Emil for years, and now it was her turn.

She yearned for a book, something to fill the time. But no one had any. She managed short walks in the glowing sun, limbering her painful knees after their abuse during the quake and fire. One day she got a block or so away from the tent before heat and pain in her knees drove her back.

Often she sat on a rock twenty yards from her tent and watched the children. She was glad she had none, and knew she lacked the slightest maternal instinct. But for that very reason, she could enjoy the half-grown, who darted about like schools of fish, playing one made-up game after another when they weren't being taught in open-air class-rooms. She let the afternoon sun soak her flesh, warm her against the chill nights, and watched outlandishly dressed girls and boys—wearing the world's castoffs now—play Red Rover, or some sort of baseball, or hide-and-seek.

Then a thick manila packet came to the Presidio. It had been addressed to her at the Presidio, and had found its way to her. It was postmarked Glen Ellen. Her heartbeat lifted. She tore open the heavy envelope and discovered a letter and a set of contact proofs. She unfolded the letter, and found that it was written in a dark, angular script. Jack London's hand.

She was much more nervous than she had expected to be when this moment arrived.

Charmian and I are glad to know how to find you. We had your plates developed at once. Proofs are enclosed. We sent some out, and described others to newspaper and magazine editors, by mail and once or twice by wire. So far we have sold only one, the picture of the boy in knickers staring straight at the camera while black smoke fills the entire sky behind him. That will net you five dollars.

I'm afraid we are encountering some difficulty with these. The editors want cuts of fire, rubble, ruin, upended streets and rails, gaping clefts where the earth divided—things of that sort. I have so far been unable to interest them in the human element. We think these capture human terror and desperation and are more newsworthy than a half-standing wall of brick, or a column of smoke, but the editors don't agree. Collier's would take none with my story because they were on deadline and couldn't wait for shipment.

We will redouble our efforts. Some day they will have enough of twisted streetcar rails and want something more, and then we will sell the lot. Be patient; you will sell all of these.

Emil Wolff's death grieves us deeply. You will see from the contacts that you took three handsome portraits of him, capturing him in his last hours. We will buy one of those from you, and want you to tell us the price.

Now, one last thing. We are sending you Charmian's roll film camera. It will take some doing to get it there, but we are entrusting it to a Tiburon boatman who makes the run across the bay, and he will make sure it reaches you. We are sending five rolls of Eastman's dry film, and hope you can do something with that. We think the photos you took of the refugees fleeing the fires have put you on the right course. Your campground is filled with the same sort of subjects. When you are ready, send them to us and we will have them processed and try to sell them.

She read it again, her spirits plummeting. Five dollars. That would not pay the Londons for processing, postage, time, and effort. It would not start her toward a livelihood. She stared into a sunlit bower, wondering how she would feed and house herself.

Only then did she examine the proofs, and those lifted her spirits. They were strong, contrasty, stark, brimming with feeling and desperation. And the portraits of Emil—my God, what the Kodet caught in his face. If only she had seen what the lens saw, Emil erect and dignified, the side lighting casting shadows, his eyes beseeching the viewer to note a dying man's worth. He had known he would die!

She sat quietly, not wanting to look at her proofs again, not wanting to think about the five dollars and the unsold ones. She would just sit in the sun and absorb it and think nothing. But her benefactors came to mind. Her only link to them was through Emil, and yet they had done everything they could for a virtual stranger. She would thank them in her next letter.

That very afternoon a bearded man with salt-and-pepper hair was directed to her by her tentmates.

"Miss Steinmetz, this is from the Londons," he said. "They said to tell you to send the rolls back with me. I'm Thompson Newton, and I often dock in the basin east of Fort Mason. Or look around the Hyde Street Pier."

She thanked him and stared at the pasteboard carton that contained a camera. Then she untied the string and beheld a rectangular black box camera, a simple device intended for people who didn't know much about photography and didn't wish to involve themselves with darkrooms, processing, printing, and all the rest. She lifted it, eyed the lens and shutter, and noticed the brand. It was one of Eastman's new Brownies. An earlier version required sending the entire camera back to New York, where the forty-exposure roll of dry film was removed and replaced, and the camera returned with the photographs. This version had removable rolls.

She eyed it, disturbed and pleased. This one had its limitations, and yet if she were careful, she might take good photographs with it. She would need to stay within its fixed focal range and watch the light carefully. She no longer had her Watkins exposure meter, but if she worked during bright periods and avoided overcast, she would be all right. She fondled it, pleased, hefting and pointing, getting a feel for it. Could this modest contrivance be her future? Could she hold her old hands steady enough to keep from blurring the photograph? And what would she do for a darkroom, for an enlarger, for papers that would increase contrast if she wished, or improve gray tones? All that was gone. The challenge delighted her. This limited camera would test her every skill, and she intended to triumph.

This treasure from Charmian London might yet lead to a future for her. Certainly it inspired daydreams. Here in this refugee camp she had unlimited and powerful material to capture. Let the others click their shutters upon ruins; she would capture desperate and courageous refugees, just as she had before, during the holocaust.

Her tentmates crowded about, and she showed her prize to them.

"Take my picture," said one.

"Take us all," cried another, and almost without consulting they lined up before their tent.

Katharine didn't like to take such posed shots, but there were things one did in life because life required that they be done. So her first two shots were of her tentmates, seated and standing, formed in a

RICHARD S. WHEELER

slight concave arch because she asked them to and because she thought the arch might overcome the Brownie's focal limitations.

Then she was left alone with her Brownie and her dreams. Slowly, she wandered through the strange tent city at the Presidio, resting frequently because her knees howled at her. This slow film and small-lens camera would require that she pose her subjects and keep them utterly rigid for a tenth of a second. That would undermine the sort of photo essay she had in mind.

Clothing would be one thing. People were wearing whatever the world provided. Men's stubble would be another thing. Most of the males in the Presidio hadn't seen a razor since the quake. The field kitchens and food lines would be another. They all queued up to eat. The soldiers would be another. They were providers and policemen here.

She resolved to photograph anything out of the ordinary. It came down to that. She had seen no photographers at work among the refugees, though no doubt some were prowling the various camps. Still, she suspected their minds were on the ruins, not the flotsam and jetsam of a place like this.

Slowly, ever conscious of pain, she labored down the rude streets of the tent city, pausing now and then. She asked a woman who was hand-wringing clothing and draping it over a line to pause, and she caught the labor. She halted at an impromptu classroom and asked the young woman who was teaching, as well as the children, to pause. The click of her shutter released them, and they laughed.

She discovered boys playing baseball. They had a ball, but only a stick for a bat. She waited patiently for a swing, knowing it would be nothing but a blur, but that was what she wanted that time. They laughed at her.

She discovered a tent convalescent center, twenty or so people lying on cots, the walls of the tent rolled up to air the place. Sun poured through one corner, illumining several bunks. She gathered her courage, approached the cots, and asked those who lay there whether she might photograph them. One turned away. Two smiled. She examined the tableau carefully in her viewfinder: cots on grass, a pillow slip full of possessions perched on lawn, drooping canvas, a man whose shoulder was immobilized in a plaster cast. Another with a haunted look and black circles under his eyes. She took shots there, carefully winding the roll film forward.

Then, not far from there, she found a woman who stared vacantly at the world, and instantly sensed tragedy. This one's eyes seemed to see nothing, as if the exterior world had vanished from her mind, and only memories remained.

"May I take your picture?" she asked.

The woman didn't respond.

Katharine asked again, and this time the woman slowly focused on Katharine, but still didn't respond.

"Would you tell me what happened?" Katharine asked.

"I saw him die," she said.

"Would you like to tell me what happened?"

The woman waited so long Katharine feared she had gone back into her own world.

"The soldier shot him."

Fear roiled through Katharine. And bitterness.

"We saw them stealing. We ran, but they shot him."

Katharine scarcely knew what to say. "I'm sorry. The army—"

The woman closed her eyes. Katharine decided to leave the woman alone, and started to retreat.

"Aren't you going to take my picture?" the woman asked.

Katharine took several, capturing a haunted face, a frail woman beyond tears, a woman with hurt in her brown eyes.

"The eyes are the windows of the soul," the woman said. "Now you have photographed all the pain that is in me."

Katharine returned to her tent because her knees—and spirit—could endure no more.

Maybe, some day, some editor would want photographs of ruined people instead of ruined buildings.

CHAPTER 55

Time dragged. Nella waited impatiently for the drizzle to abate, but the rain fell steadily through Sunday morning, sometimes working through the Wilson's makeshift shelter. She and Willis stared silently at each other, both of them aching to escape, even though the Wilsons made life pleasant with occasional banter and good cheer.

But Nella was a woman newly bound, and she had just one thought in her head: Go somewhere private with Willis, be alone with this new husband, hug him and kiss him and curl up in his arms, and begin the marriage with joy. But it was not to be. The Wilsons themselves grew restless. They were all trapped in a tiny shelter of awning, so jammed together they could barely even stretch, much less limber their muscles.

The songs had died away in the night, and they all lay huddled, chilled by every wet breeze eddying in from the Pacific. And the sun never rose. Sunday was ushered in by curtains of gray.

Then, at last, the clouds drifted away and they discovered patches of blue, and finally sunlight turning every drop of water on every leaf into a prism.

Willis stood. "I guess we'll be off," he said. "Sure want to thank you. Guess we'll be buying your tonics when you get going again."

"Glad to celebrate a little old marriage," said the family patriarch. "We're going to give you a wedding gift. Now here's half a bottle of the Balsam elixir to start your life right. Not that you'll need it tonight." The Wilsons laughed merrily.

Nella thought her feelings must be pretty obvious.

Willis thanked them, and borrowed a few matches and some scraps of paper.

"You know where you're going? If you run into troubles, you just hightail it back here," Wilson added.

"I guess we know," Willis said.

The gazebo. A roof and a bench. And Willis intended to start a bonfire if the surrounding brush wasn't too wet. Privacy and paradise! Visions of a wedding night danced in Nella's mind. The gazebo, a roof and a bench and a warm fire. Oh, that would be paradise.

They went through the food line, got bread, and then hiked through chill air southward toward Twin Peaks, getting little comfort from the pallid sun. She felt the wet grasses and brush soak her skirt, but what did it matter? They were going to be alone, and she and Willis could hug each other all night.

Willis seemed somber, and spoke little, which made her insecure.

"Are you happy?" she asked.

"Nella, you're the light of my life. How could I not be happy?"

"I just thought maybe you're having doubts."

"Tell me truly, do you have doubts?"

"No," she said, knowing it was a lie.

"Well, I'll confess to some," he said.

"Don't you love me?"

"That's not it at all. It's that we plunged in, and I can't help but wonder how it will be." He held her hand. "I'll tell you how it will be. We will make it good because we want it to be. And because I love you, with love that's as high as the sky."

He was more honest than she was, she thought. She peered at the virtual stranger she would take into her arms and her life, and wondered how it would be in a month or a year or after the baby came.

"I don't have any doubts," she said.

He didn't reply, but concentrated on the steep slope, made slippery and treacherous by the rain.

"I hope you can start a fire," she said, feeling the chill air once they reached an elevation above the city.

"Who needs a fire?" he replied.

She didn't laugh. Living out-of-doors, even in mild San Francisco, had proven to be a hard, uncomfortable experience.

An hour later they rounded a ridge and beheld the gazebo—and a crowd of people under it. Her heart sank.

Willis sighed. "I guess other people figured out how to get out of the rain, too," he said. He squeezed her hand, but she withdrew it, somehow wanting to blame Willis for this new disappointment. She was feeling worse and worse.

A dozen or so people, mostly men but with two or three women, crowded under the shelter and seven or eight occupied every inch of the bench. They had a fire going. It smoked heavily, apparently from the wet wood on it, and radiated no heat at all.

"Pretty crowded here," said one young man as Willis and Nella approached.

"We have no place to go."

"Rain stopped."

"It's dry under the roof; everything else is soaked."

"Aw, Barry, let 'em join us," said another young man.

Nella stared glumly at the crowd. So much for a honeymoon night, she thought. She eyed Willis uncertainly, wanting him to make the decisions.

"You want to try somewhere else?" he asked her.

"I don't know. You do what you want," she snapped.

"Nella . . ."

The way he said that melted her. She was half crazy with this earthquake, this fire, losing her job, hardly knowing where her next meal would come from, and nothing but the clothing she wore to keep her warm. She wondered if she could stand one more minute. One more miserable night. One more breadline. One more trip to the foul sanitary trenches. One more hour of not knowing where she would be the next day or the day after. She wanted to rage, or weep, or howl. And there he was, as helpless as she. There they were, without a dime between them.

"Oh, Willis," she said, unable to stem the tears welling into her eyes. He hugged her, neither of them caring about their audience.

"We can keep warm if we walk," he said.

He turned to the assemblage. "I guess we'll look somewhere else."

He held her hand and led her down slope.

"I think we'll do better if we get out of the city," he said. "You have that ring the man gave you. It would get us over to Marin County, I think." He paused. "I'll buy you a ring the moment I can, before anything else. One that's engraved with our initials and a date and everything. One that comes from me."

She smiled. She hadn't even thought about the ring and what it might do for them.

"It's a long walk to the wharves on the north side. Miles and miles. Are you up to it? It'll be dark and we might be out of luck when we get there, But I hear there's all sorts of people camping along the waterfront, from Fort Mason east. And a city breadline there. Maybe we could stay overnight in a fishing boat or something."

She nodded. She was up to anything that would take her and Willis somewhere safe and warm.

They hiked an hour and she felt her strength waning. Days of sleeplessness, catch-as-catch-can food, fear, anxiety, had taken their toll. And pregnancy.

"I can't make it, Willis. I just can't."

Dusk was thickening. "We'll go a bit at a time, Nella. We'll think about the future. Someday soon, we'll be past this and laughing about it. I'll be earning a good living—I promise you that. We'll have the baby, and another and more if you'd like. I'm a good earner, and you'll have a laundress for all those diapers."

He was heartening her and she liked that. She was beginning to admire Willis. Maybe there would be more to this than she thought when she was looking for a father for her baby.

"Just think. The whole city'll rise up again. And we'll rise with it. Everyone'll want fire insurance. My company'll have more business than a two-man office can handle. And you, my very own, will enjoy everything this beautiful city can offer. . . ."

He stopped every few minutes, whenever there seemed to be a good place to sit. They reached Van Ness, and then started north through an incredible devastation, at least on the east side of the street where the army had shelled or dynamited every structure. It was very dark, and she supposed they were out after the military curfew, but they had no place to go. She felt doomed to forty years in the wilderness.

Whenever she faltered, he stopped and buoyed her spirits by painting a dream: a fine California home with sea views; a big warm bed. Nursery for the children. A maid, a nanny, a laundress. Watching John Barrymore tread the boards.

She laughed at that. John Barrymore couldn't stand upright last she saw of him.

"There are bad patches in all lives, and we learn how to be strong when they happen. If life is too smooth, then it hasn't been well lived. We take risks. We could have been comfortable in that gazebo, but we walked. We are *going* somewhere, and that is what life is—going somewhere."

She loved him for making sense of her random worries and fears.

The footpads struck on a black corner.

One moment they were trudging along; the next moment she heard a soft noise and saw Willis fall down, groaning. Someone clamped arms around her. She screamed, but a hand caught her mouth and clamped it shut viciously. She writhed, unable to break free. Willis rolled on the ground, moaning. They had hit him! Someone loomed over him, poking and probing. Someone else was poking and probing her, without the slightest care about her virtue. She boiled and tried to bite that hand, but the man in the dark just laughed while his hands explored her ruthlessly, finally discovering her ring.

"Ah!" he said, and yanked it off her finger, breaking open her clenched fist.

"You swine!" she yelled when his hand slipped off her face.

He laughed.

A violent shove toppled her over Willis, who squirmed on the ground holding his head.

She heard steps in the dark, faint laughter, and then nothing. The hooligans were racing into the ruins on the east side of the great artery.

Where was the army? That's what she wanted to know. This was one of the busiest streets in town!

She felt herself tremble, and heard Willis groan, and struggled to help him sit up. He slowly ran a shaky hand through his hair. She did too, discovering a bloody lump. They had hit him with a sap or a blackjack.

"Nella!" he whispered. "You all right?"

"They took our ring."

He sighed, unable to sit up, his hand combing the bloodshot hair on his bruised head. "Did they hurt you?" he asked.

"No. We have to get help," she said.

He nodded, but when he tried to get up, he couldn't. It was all beyond bearing, and she wept.

CHAPTER 56

Harrison Barnes White, architect and city planner, knew he needed a connection. That was how the world worked. Talent counted, and he had an abundance of that, but just as important was knowing the right people. That was the real way to get ahead. He believed devoutly in the American dream, and believed the earthquake was the opportunity he had waited for during years of apprenticing.

There, in the middle of Van Ness, he took stock. He stank. His stubble bristled. Grime permeated his suit. A week of living like a tramp had done it to him and everyone else. He knew at once what he had to do: refurbish himself. Once he had scraped off the stubble and filth and cleaned his clothing, he would make an impressive figure once again, call the shots, be taken for the upcoming personage he was. The old adage, clothes make the man, was certainly true. A man with a natty exterior was always perceived as a man of great interior quality. Clean him and put him in fresh clothing, especially a suit and cravat, and he would command the world, even this ruined world.

He could go on out to the Presidio and maybe wangle something to wear and sleep on the ground like a hobo. Or if he were smart—which he knew himself to be—he could come up with better options. What did he want? A snug bunk, a chance to clean up, and shelter. And where would he find such rare commodities? He knew at once. Not on land, where over two hundred thousand refugees wandered, jamming into every shack. But at sea. Ah, yes, a ship's master would understand. White would give the man a chit, payable as fast as the banks reopened and he could get to his accounts. Ah, there was the solution.

He began hiking up Van Ness, with visions of a clean bunk in a trim cabin in his mind. The navy had compelled all merchant ships to lay to and stand-by to render assistance, and now there were dozens in the bay, some at wharfs, others anchored out a way. If he could not find a bunk, at least he could find a shave and bath and maybe some clean clothing. He would simply sign an IOU and in time the ship's master would be that much richer.

Heartened, he strolled north under a benign heaven. All was well with the world. Nothing could ever sink Harrison Barnes White. When he reached Fort Mason he turned east, intending to examine the merchant ships berthed at various wharves. During the fire, not a one of them lay beside a wharf, but now, with the danger past, there were dozens. He had always loved the sea, and had enjoyed his two Atlantic crossings that had taken him to and from Paris and the Ecole des Beaux Arts. He knew ships and would be discerning in his choice.

But such ships as he encountered were not very promising. Some were rotting old sailing vessels, relics in the age of steam. Some were coasters probably up from Southern California or down from Portland. One hybrid steamship, with two masts and two stacks, was a bucket of rust. Most seemed idle. He found few signs of activity aboard any of them. Not a one suited his needs. He walked a mile and another, clear to Telegraph Hill and down the Embarcadero, without finding what he wanted.

Well, he could compromise if he had to. He had passed a clean freighter, another old hybrid with masts and stacks. This one had fresh paint, trim lines, gleaming wood, and best of all, a bearded master in a black turtleneck sweater who was overseeing a work crew that was loading some steam engines sitting on the wharf. The master was obviously putting his enforced idleness to good use.

This vessel was called the *Manitou.*

Good enough.

A man in a sea cap and long-sleeved shirt lounged at the steep gangway, which reached from the wharf up to the deck. Harrison was a little vague about merchant seamen's titles, but thought this must be a bosun or mate or something.

"Say, mate, may I talk with the captain?"

The man eyed him, faintly amused. "He's busy, friend."

"Well, I have a proposition. I'm in need of a shave and wash and clothing. The quake left me with nothing. I'm an architect here, and I thought I might give him a draft, payable as soon as my bank reopens, for some services and a bunk if he has one. I'll have funds the very day the banks reopen."

"An architect, eh? You don't look like one."

"Yes, and city planner. The Monadnock Building, which I designed, withstood the quake."

The man smiled. "You're in pretty rough shape, eh?"

"All I need is some sleep and a chance to clean up. If I could rent a bunk for two nights I could wash my clothing and dry it. How about it?"

The man shrugged. He rubbed his jaw, squinted, and then climbed the steep incline to the deck and vanished from sight. But a few moments later, the master peered down upon him from the rail above.

"You want something?"

"Yes, sir, I was explaining to the gentleman that I'd like a bunk and a chance to clean up for a couple of nights. I can pay. I'd give you a draft you could cash when my bank reopens."

"How old are you?"

"Twenty-eight. Why do you ask?"

"Oh, I like to know, that's all. What's your name?"

"Harrison Barnes White."

"A three-piece name! I don't see many of those."

"Well, is it a deal?"

The master grinned suddenly. "Larson, show this man to quarters. Give him some seaman's duds so he can wash his stuff. Find him a razor and shaving mug and soap and towel." He turned to White. "Would seven dollars suffice?"

"If you throw in meals twice a day."

The master nodded.

"I knew the *Manitou* would come to the rescue, sir," White said.

But the master had already returned to his task.

Larson led him past an array of cargo booms and capstans to a block of white cabins aft, each with a porthole. The seaman stepped through a riveted bulkhead door and opened an interior door. Harrison found himself in a tiny cabin with two bunks, each with a clean gray blanket on it and a hard pillow. He saw no washstand. Larson bustled about, digging up a razor, brush and mug, soap and towels, and even a comb.

"Head's down the way, there. I'll rustle up some gear. You're about medium, eh?"

"A little taller than medium."

"Medium," Larson said, and vanished. "I'll leave the stuff on your bunk. When you're dressed, I'll have you write that chit. The master's name is Stern."

Paradise! White congratulated himself for having the savvy to cope with the world. He stripped, ran some water into the metal basin—it was tepid but what did it matter?—and began working up some lather in the shaving mug, expertly whipping the brush into the soap. Then he brushed the lather over his stubble and began scraping. The tug of the blade and the smoothness of his shaven cheeks were almost sensuous to him and he rejoiced. This would be something to tell Marcia! The whole city was full of idiots who didn't know how to get what they wanted, but he had had no trouble because he was resourceful.

He heaped his foul clothing on the floor and stepped into the cramped shower down the hall. Tepid water again, but he could bear that. He washed his hair and scrubbed himself, rejoicing to be clean at last. He had become so rank he could not bear it, but now, now, now . . . he was a man again. Larson had even provided a toothbrush, and White completed his toilet by scrubbing his teeth. He could hardly believe his good fortune.

Just as promised, a change of clothing lay on the bunk, and White donned some blue trousers, a pullover blue shirt and a coarse-knot navy sweater. It all fit fine. He returned to the head and set to work on his filthy clothing, the underwear and stockings first, then the grimy shirt, and finally—with some hesitation, he soaked his wool worsted suit. It would be ruined and shapeless, but it would be clean and that was what he needed for the duration of this ordeal. He soaped and scrubbed and rinsed, and then wrung the water out. He wondered where to hang the stuff, and decided it would have to be outside somewhere.

He ended up laying the clothes out on the curved copper roof of the cabins, which radiated the sun's heat. He would have to watch, to make sure no breeze came up and blew away the duds. That done, he felt like a new man, and wandered along the well-scoured deck toward the master, who was standing close to the prow. The stem, he reminded himself. He would try to learn a few naval terms during his sojourn.

"Mr. Stern?"

The master turned, eyeing White. He seemed a hard, hawkish, formidable man, an assessing man who was always taking the measure of anyone who caught his attention with glistening yellow eyes. White instantly felt respectful, and even a bit like a boy in the presence of this man who radiated willfulness.

"If you'd provide me with pen and paper, I'll draw up a note for seven dollars."

"Oh, that. I'll get to it," Stern said. "You satisfied?"

"Feel like a new man."

The master nodded.

"Where's the *Manitou* bound?"

"We're a tramp."

"What did you bring in?"

"We stopped to pick up redwood. It burned. But we're picking up some steam engines for Asian mines."

"And so you're off again—as soon as they let you go."

Stern smiled. White had never seen a smile like that, dangerous and devoid of warmth.

"Well, I'm done in. This is the first bunk I've seen in a week. I'll rest until dinner."

"Dinner," Stern said, as if amused.

"I've no watch."

"Six bells."

White luxuriated in the narrow bunk, but held off sleep until he could eat. A hot meal at a table; what a luxury.

He missed the bells, but Larson knocked at his cabin door, and soon White was savoring beef and gravy, with plenty of coffee to wash it down. The crew ate silently, eyeing him now and then. He didn't have much in common with them, and Stern ate elsewhere, so he simply downed his food and retreated. He remembered to collect his clothing—which remained damp—and then closeted himself for the night. He felt a thousandfold better, cleaned, shaved, fed, with fresh clothing covering him, than he had not long before. He lounged in his bunk, trying to decide what to do next.

It actually wasn't a bad thing that Marcia had gone east, he decided. He wouldn't have to worry about her. Now he could focus on his architecture. The first task would be to start his own firm. Print business cards. Operate from Oakland for a while. A whole city awaited rebuilding. It was an architect's paradise. He had better start in by designing some standard San Francisco–style frame houses he could modify to suit each customer. Within a year he'd be rich, with all the business at hand. There weren't enough architects in the country to fill San Francisco's need during the next months and years. Finding an office would be tough, but he thought he could share a room with someone. Of course he would have to let his firm known that he was resigning. But there was no rush. He didn't owe Wolper and Demaris anything except two-week notice.

He pulled that clean blanket over him and drifted into well-earned sleep.

He slept like the dead until dawn, when a bell awakened him. He stretched, clambered out of his marvelous bunk, felt the freighter rock gently, peered out his porthole, and discovered he was at sea.

CHAPTER 57

ergeant Major Jack Deal didn't like what he was hearing. The Presidio's commanding officer, Colonel Morris, was instructing him to accompany an ordnance colonel from Fort Lewis who, with his staff, was inventorying munitions on the West Coast.

"Right now, sergeant, the United States is almost defenseless against an assault on its Pacific rim. We've used most of our guncotton, cordite, and a good share of our howitzer ammunition putting out the fires. The thirteen-inch guns protecting this harbor are off their carriages and useless. Colonel Irwyn and his staff will inventory everything we have in our bunkers, and resupply us. Your duty is to take them to the bunkers, open them, assist in any way, and supply enlisted men to them if needed."

"Yes, sir."

"I'm giving them a diagram of the post. It shows the location of each bunker. I'll supply an inventory list of what is supposed to be in each, though no one quite knows what's there now."

"Can I see that diagram, sir?"

Morris handed it to the sergeant. One glance told Deal that the abandoned bunker, located some distance from the rest, had been included.

"No need for a map, sir. I'll be on hand to steer them."

"It's a courtesy, Sergeant. They should have a complete diagram of the post and an inventory."

"When are they due, sir?"

"Here now. Came in last night. You can start right in. I'll introduce you."

Jack Deal didn't like that one bit. He hadn't gotten wind of this one. He had no time to get the goods out of that bunker. A fortune was sitting in there, wrapped in oilcloth and concealed in a few old crates. His operation had collected a glittering pile of rings, gold jewelry, watches, silver service, diamonds and other gems, coins, and whatever else his men were able to scoop up. None of them had the faintest idea of the value of all that stuff.

Deal had made it plain that no one was going to touch that loot for six months. And then it would be shipped in small lots to places like Los Angeles and Seattle and fenced far away from the Presidio. Anyone who squealed or grumbled would end up in the bottom of the Pacific Ocean. Some had grumbled anyway, not wanting to wait six months. Deal was adamant. That stuff wasn't going to show up in jewelry shops weeks after the earthquake and fire. There was going to be nothing to trace. If they didn't like that, they could give up their share.

They liked it. At least they said they liked it. Jack Deal was making sure they damned well liked it.

But now Sergeant Major Deal had a little problem. Nothing he couldn't handle, but he would have to be careful. He grimaced, straightened his tie, and marched dutifully, a step or two behind the Old Man, over to the officers' mess.

A bird colonel and two lieutenants were waiting.

Morris made the introductions.

"Gentlemen, this is our esteemed sergeant major, Jack Deal. He knows every nook and cranny of this post. When I need something, I call on Deal because he's a magician. He conjures up matériel in some occult fashion. He's instructed to accompany you, unlock the bunkers, and provide any service or manpower you request." He turned to Deal. "Sergeant, this is Colonel Irwyn, Lieutenant Gregg, and Lieutenant Tobin."

He saluted and welcomed them.

"Now, Colonel, here's a portfolio. It has a diagram of the post, a munitions inventory—hopelessly out of date because of the fire—and copies of shipping orders going back to nineteen hundred."

"Well, sergeant, we're in good hands," Irwyn said. "Let's see how quickly we can wrap this up."

They left the commanding officer, and Deal steered them across greensward through an area unoccupied by refugees because the army didn't want them in the vicinity of munitions bunkers. That hadn't stopped boys from playing baseball, though. Deal frowned at the little devils, but decided to ignore them—for now.

"May I see that diagram, sir?" he asked.

"Surely, Sergeant."

Deal swiftly examined it as they walked. "This is out of date. Pretty old, sir. Probably drawn about eighteen ninety-five, ninety-six. Before the Spanish war. It won't be good for much. New things added since this was drafted."

"We'll just use it to make sure we've not overlooked anything, Sergeant."

Deal smiled. "One or two I doubt we could find. Never knew they existed." He handed the diagram back.

"All the more reason to find them," Irwyn said.

Deal didn't like that. Maybe he could wear them out, making the whole process as slow as possible. That was it. By nightfall these gents would be weary of the whole thing. In the night he and Nils or somebody could move stuff out of that bunker and into one that had been examined.

He chose a vector that would put the abandoned bunker last on the list. He started with one of the newer ones, this one lined with thick concrete and set under a mound of earth. The painted iron door was recessed, and the arrangement was intended to channel an explosion forward.

"You have electric torches?"

They did.

"All right. This is a recent one, concrete. Some of the early ones were masonry. They tended to get wet." He hunted for the key to Bunker 12 on his ring, inserted it into the iron door, and opened it.

The gloomy bunker, dimly lit by light from outside, contained nothing. But Deal intended to drag this out. "This was a light artillery bunker," he said. "Those wooden slats on the floor keep the stuff off the pavement. Now, your inventory may show some shells here, but the howitzer batteries made off with them during the fire."

"I hear the artillery shelled half of San Francisco," Irwyn said, looking amused.

"Van Ness Street, sir. No dynamite, cordite, or guncotton left, so the artillerymen leveled those big places along there with howitzers. Quite a sight, sir. Mansions flying apart. They leveled those barrels and blew those houses to bits. But it stopped the fires."

"Well, shall we move on? Gregg, have you noted that this one's empty? What was supposed to be in it?"

"Hard to say, sir. This material doesn't really say."

"We can go check the records, sir. There'll be some sort of records," Deal said.

"No, no, Sergeant. We're more concerned about what to ship and what's left. We understand that the munitions were put to use as fast as possible, full-scale emergency. We're thinking of the future, not the past."

"Yes, sir. The next bunker's modeled like this one, sir, and it holds munitions for the shore guns. Big stuff. We didn't use any of it for the fires. It should all be there. The quake destroyed the emplacements at Fort Point and Lime Point across the Golden Gate, and those guns are useless."

"Yes, the next three should be coastal munitions, the big thirteen-inch guns, and the next two small-arms munitions."

The next bunker did contain crate after crate of artillery projectiles of various types, canister, incendiary shot, but no powder. Deal asked questions, slowed things down by bringing up irrelevant details, and cost the quartermaster officers the better part of an hour. That was good.

And so the morning passed. The munitions were in shambles. Irwyn was clucking and shaking his head.

"Sergeant, we'll request that your ordnance staff put all this in order. Remove empty crates, stack everything, oldest munitions closest to the door, to be used first. And supply us with an inventory when they're done."

"Yes, sir. City was burning and they came and got what they needed, sir."

Deal locked the door behind them and stepped into the warm sun. The bunkers had been icy.

They broke for lunch, and Deal debated whether to send Walt and Wayne over to clean out that hot bunker. The loot filled six crates. It would have to be done in broad daylight, and possibly within sight of the inventory party or others. He decided not to chance it. But there still was something he could do. He skipped lunch, raced over to the bunker, entered, layered some of that outdated brass over the loot in the cartons, and made it back to the officers' mess just in time, hoping the patches of sweat under his armpits wouldn't be noticed.

He stalled away the afternoon, but the light colonel was on to him and began speeding things along. One by one, they penetrated the bunkers, inventoried the munitions, ascertained the age of the loads, and locked up. Deal began to sweat in earnest. It was only midafternoon and they were getting closer and closer to the hot one.

"You must prefer cool weather, Sergeant," Irwyn said. "I find San Francisco chilly, myself."

Deal's usual starchy uniform had dissolved in his own sweat. He was growing angry and anxious. Why didn't this bird colonel just quit for the damned day? Why the hell didn't Sergeant Major Deal hear about this little visit beforehand? What would happen if these lobsters found the stuff? The thought started a rage in him. His cut might be ten thousand dollars—ten grand!—maybe more. That was guesswork, but they had cleaned out the whole northern tier of San Franciso's burned area. Was he going to lose it now, because his usual access to the scuttlebutt had failed him? And what if the bird colonel figured it out? And wondered why Deal had been delaying all day long?

Then they were down to two bunkers, the last one in regular use, and the abandoned one eighty yards off, bordering on a brushy area.

"One more, sir," he said. "Then we can call it a day."

"Diagram says two more."

"Two more? Where?"

Irwyn's manicured fingernail pressed against a number on the diagram.

"I think this is mistaken, sir."

"We'll find out."

"We could finish up this one, and call it a day, sir. I'll hunt for another and let you know in the morning. It wouldn't affect your numbers, even if we found something."

"Sergeant, we'll find it if it exists. We will do this as thoroughly and completely as we can. We'll do it the army way. Before we're done, we're going to have an exact count of every piece of ordnance in the Presidio, including stuff that's old and dangerous. There is no other proper way."

"Yes, sir."

"Have you a key for it?"

Deal felt pinioned by the question. "Well, let's see," he muttered. Why hadn't he thought of that? Why the hell hadn't he ditched the damned key while he could? Without a key they might have quit, or at least decided to bust in the next morning.

He fumbled through the keys on the ring. "Don't see one here, sir."

"Try that one." Irwyn's polished fingernail touched the brass key that Deal had artfully slid past his fingers.

"Looks like it might be, sir."

"We'll go take a look. Come back to this other bunker later. You've awakened my curiosity, Sergeant. I love a mystery."

Deal nodded. The sweat soaked farther down his shirt.

He let Irwyn do the scouting, and hung back. The officers beat him to the area and saw immediately what was there to be seen.

"Lot of traffic here, sergeant. Grass is beat down. Some wagon and tire impressions in this clay. I'd say this has seen some recent use. Open it up."

"Yes, sir."

Deal unlocked the ancient metal door, and pushed it open.

. . . .

CHAPTER 58

Ginger Severance wasn't really torn. She was fond of Paul Boswell, who had been her Galahad when she needed one. But she had her mission, her life work, before her. She dreaded his advances, and didn't quite know why. She knew only that whenever he steered their meetings toward a certain level of intimacy, she could barely sit still, grew distracted, and sometimes wanted to flee pell-mell, as if from the Devil himself.

Nothing prevented a romance, of course. She could continue her life work married as well as single. She was not a nun who wore a ring on her finger symbolizing her spiritual marriage to Christ. But her reasoning was much the same: Anything that distracted her from her life-commitment, including a husband, would weaken her efforts. There was a whole world in need. She repeated that idea over and over, a litany that ran through her mind day and night.

Meanwhile, Lieutenant Boswell was a gift from God. She wore warm, clean clothing. Twice a week she bathed at the quarters of Boswell's friends. What a luxury that was. And he eagerly sought her company for lunch, for dinner, even for breakfast at the officers' mess. What more could a lady in earthquake-ruined San Francisco ask for?

And besides that, she liked him. He was bookish, and that appealed to her. She had never imagined a soldier would read books. And she liked the attention, though she took pains to discourage him because she didn't wish to lead him on, or let him think for even an instant that he might change her course. She particularly dreaded his probing into the future. He had a way of becoming frightfully persuasive.

One day he gently approached the subject of marriage, and she in panic deflected his probing. It was all she could do to sit still.

"Is it because I'm a soldier?" he asked.

"Yes, Paul."

He cocked an eyebrow. "Who's Cornelius?"

"I don't know any Cornelius. Oh! You mean the Roman centurion? The first Gentile to become a Christian?"

"And what's a centurion?"

She smiled, reddening. "I believe it was the Roman equivalent of a sergeant, a man in command of a company of a hundred."

"So God chose a Roman sergeant to be the first Gentile convert, but Peter wasn't happy about it. He sent Peter to Cornelius to see for himself. Am I right?"

She nodded. The officers' mess had conjured up a delicious lunch, given the shortage of so many foods and condiments. She was eating a delicately flavored lamb stew. How could any woman living among the ruins be so lucky?

"So God has nothing against soldiers. The peacekeepers and protectors of the vulnerable."

She laughed. She couldn't help it. She suspected that this scholarly Paul Boswell was more than her match on anything biblical, and far outstripped her in his knowledge of literature. She liked the way the corners of his mouth sneakily lifted when he was full of humor. Why was she so afraid?

"So if soldiers are just fine with God, what's your objection—abstractly speaking of course?"

She felt flustered. This was going further and faster than she wished. Maybe she was a little torn after all.

"Paul . . . ," she said, hardly knowing what to say. This warm-eyed man gazing so fondly at her would have been her dream—once. And that only made all this more painful. "I've made a promise. A vow, I guess. I gave my life to Jesus Christ. He is my only Lord."

She waited for the frown, the disapproval, but it didn't come. He smiled gently. "Well, that's Boswell's luck. I meet the lady of my dreams—and she's taken by the commanding officer."

Her heart ached for him. She didn't want to cause pain, but she was causing copious amounts of it. She could see it in the slow weariness and defeat settling in his face.

"That is very beautiful," he said gently. "The world needs ten thousand more Gingers. This small corner of the world"—he pointed at his heart—"needs only one."

"We scarcely know each other, Paul."

"I knew you from the moment you walked into Fort Mason. I knew you when you were watching the Chinamen line up at our field kitchen. Perhaps you think that just because my world is books, I have no God. I do. This morning I asked him for a small favor—a very large favor—"

"Don't say it."

"In this world of disaster and homelessness and heartache and insecurity, I think I will say it. The earthquake foreshortens everything, the way war does. You know what happens on the eve of a war? Marriages. If a man and a woman join together and have only a week remaining to them, nothing, not even a deadly war, can steal those sweet memories. We live in the midst of a disaster. We could be torn apart in a trice. If ever your heart sings a melody that has Paul Boswell in it, you will know how to find me. I have no plans to leave the service. My address is the United States Army."

She blinked back tears.

"May we continue just as we are? Lunch each day, here at noon, unless the Old Man ties me up?"

"Yes, Paul."

"If I can't count on Cupid's dart, maybe I'll get an assist from ordinary familiarity, best known as friendship. This is all rushed. I see the lady of my dreams, the next thing you know, I'm proposing."

"Yes, let us be friends."

That wry uplift of the corners of his lips delighted her.

"Maybe that's best. I've been a bit headlong. Maybe you are saving me from a mistake. Act in haste, repent at leisure, as it goes."

"I enjoyed the haste," she said, and wished she hadn't. Why did she blurt out things like that?

That evoked another of his wry smiles. "One thing you should know about me: I may have no hold on your heart, but I like to think of myself as a good and true friend. I have a few, and they go back a long way. Maybe that is how I'll come to know you—the friend I can never touch."

Just then she wanted to touch him, stand right up in that dining hall and hug him. But that evoked the fear again. She had been much more torn than she wanted to admit to herself.

He did not bring up the question again, not that lunch or the several thereafter. She found herself full of girlish shyness around him, tongue-tied, wanting to ask about him but not daring to; wanting him to ask about her, but not inviting him to. But it didn't matter. What did count was that she had a friend, and he was helping her in the midst of this darkness that had enshrouded the fallen city, and that somehow, she was nurturing something in him. They would meet, he usually arrived haggard and crestfallen, and by the end of the lunch he was glowing.

But even that troubled her. She didn't want Paul Boswell to depend on her company for happiness.

She spent her days trying to relieve misery, but as the quake and fire receded, so did the need for her comforting. By some magical process, city life had reorganized itself. Separated people were finding their loved ones. Newspapers were fountains of information, and running columns of missing-persons ads. The hospitalized were healing. The destitute found food and clothing and a blanket, and canvas over their heads. The bereaved held services and began to pull their lives together. The lost and bewildered were making decisions, or being helped. The city's clergy were everywhere, consoling and comforting and doing much the same thing as Ginger, person by person, case by case.

People were leaving, taking advantage of the free rides to havens elsewhere, so the populations of the tent cities declined. The Chinamen had been largely gathered at Fort Mason, and were being cared for by the army. The days were growing warmer. Not exactly warm—when was San Francisco ever warm?—but pleasant and sunny.

The massive relief funds appropriated by Congress were already being employed to help the city recover. Paid workers were removing rubble, restoring gas and water mains, stringing electric and telephone lines, running temporary railroad tracks down city streets, cleaning out damaged buildings. The banks were opening, and one of them, the Bank of Italy, was making modest loans to people who needed cash to recover. A. P. Giannini, its owner, had set up shop in his brother's house on Van Ness, and was making small loans while all the other banking houses in the city were locked tight and intending to stay locked for months. Cash! The little bank didn't have much cash, but somehow it was lending something to almost all who asked, and that had suddenly lifted the enervated city out of its torpor and put it to work. Cash! People were marveling at that. And who was this Italian fellow and why was he succeeding and making loans when some of the great banks run by the city's elite hadn't yet opened their fire-seared vaults?

There was always need, but its nature had changed as the disaster ebbed. Now, when she wandered the Presidio seeking to be of service, she found herself baby-sitting, or wheeling an invalid, or rescuing a doll, or sitting beside utterly deaf oldsters, patting them on the shoulder and being friendly.

The world didn't need her so much. And as disaster ebbed, so did her certitude about her mission. She still slept wherever the end of each day took her, and tiredness still dogged her, but something had imperceptibly shifted. She knew she should be making plans. She was a ward of the army, like most everyone else there. And, in a way, a ward of Lieutenant Boswell, whose endless courtesies enabled her to bathe, clean her clothes, and enjoy the strange luxury of sitting in a real chair at a real table to eat a real meal.

Paul brought it up one evening, while they strolled.

"The worst is over. Now what are you going to do?"

"There are people in need. I'll continue."

"For how long, Ginger?"

"People are hungry for things other than bread, Paul. Man does not live by bread alone. They're desperate, still don't know what tomorrow will bring, and it's up to me to help them in new ways. I have none of my Bible tracts, but it doesn't matter. Maybe I can do more just listening than I did when I was scrounging clothes or medicines or a meal or blankets."

"But what of yourself, Ginger?"

"My faith has been challenged. I had to learn that God will provide. And not to worry about tomorrow."

"God and the army and Congress and the people of the United States, and all those hard-hearted businesses and railroads we loved to hate."

She eyed him. "That's what I mean. The hand of God, if you will."

They walked a while more, drifting toward the Pacific through a smoky dusk.

"I love you," he said. "Odd, but I've never said it. Everything was backwards because of the crisis."

"I love you, too, Paul."

"But as a sister loves."

"Yes."

"I love you as a man loves a woman," he said. "And always."

She felt the agony and pushed it deep down, and then started running.

CHAPTER 59

It could not be! Harrison White stared, transfixed, at the surly seas and empty horizon. A trick of light. Or maybe the ship was riding an anchor chain in the bay. Yes, surely, that was it. He tugged clothing over himself, half mad with fear, and plunged out the gangway onto the deck. Blinding sunlight and salt-scented air enveloped him. A balmy breeze filtered by. The blue-green ocean rose and fell under him, restless and serene. The California coast stretched distantly, a blue blur to the east, under the rising sun. The benign swells of the Pacific Ocean shouldered the vessel, lifting and lowering it. They had forgotten him!

His heart hammered. He had to find Stern, tell him to turn about, let him off. Where would he be? He discovered the crew in the rigging, setting sails. He realized he no longer heard the throb of the steam engine down in the belly of the ship.

Where was Stern? Where was the helmsman, the—bridge? Was that the name of the place? Yes, over there, atop that structure amidships. Running, his shoes skidding on the slippery deck, White raced to the place, bounded three steps, barged into the bridge, a glass-walled command post. A helmsman stood at a wheel on a wooden pillar. Stern stared at the sea.

"You've forgotten me! Take me back!"

Stern gazed at White, cold amusement in his yellow eyes.

"No," he said.

"But you must. You can't take me with you."

Stern's eyes glinted dangerously.

"Where are you going? Maybe just down the coast, yes? I'll get off there."

"Singapore, Manila, who knows?"

Stark terror flooded through White. "But you can't. You can't just kidnap me. It's my life, my life!"

"Yes, your life," Stern said.

"I'm an American citizen. I'm a free man. Slavery's illegal. Now come to your senses and turn around."

"Needed more crew. Still one or two short," Stern said.

"Crew! You've kidnapped me."

"Shanghaied. We'll teach you the language."

"Shanghaied!" He knew the term. That's what they did sometimes to men around the Barbary Coast—or what used to be the Barbary Coast, a bed of ashes now. "Mr. Stern, I am not some ordinary seaman. I'm a well-known architect. You'll find yourself in serious trouble when they find out. I have connections right up to Mayor Schmitz and the wealthiest men in town. You'll never dock in the United States again. Do you realize what you're doing? Have you no sense of maritime law?"

"I'm sure you'll find a lawyer right around the corner," Stern said. "Let me know if I'm to be sued."

"Who are you? Are you an American?"

Stern stared at the horizon. "My nation is the sea. I am a citizen of the saltwaters. My mother was the tides and my father was the typhoon."

"You're an American. You speak it."

"I was."

The man was maddening. He wasn't even responsive, and stood there amused, toying with White, his yellow cat's eyes cruel and disdainful.

"I have a wife and children and family. What will they think? Who will support them? Why do you suppose you can tear another human being's life apart, turn me into your slave?"

"Needed a man or two."

"There are hundreds of men who'd sign on. It means a wage and a bed and food, all the things they can't find now in a dead city. They'd leap at the chance. Why didn't you inquire or advertise?"

"You were convenient."

White stared, so rattled and distraught he couldn't even think. "If you'll lower one of those lifeboats, I'll row it. I can reach the coast."

Stern laughed, and stared at the sea. The ship's engines stopped entirely, and White felt the ship heel in the wind as its sails filled.

"How long to—where?—Singapore?"

"We're a tramp. Who knows? I have cargo for Manila and Brunei."

"The South Seas? My God! I appeal to you as a civilized man, a man of honor and conscience, a man with your own family, no doubt, loved ones, friends—let me off. The Golden Rule. Treat others as you wish to be treated."

"White, this is the sea, and this is my ship. And I am the only law there is. Consider me God."

White was close to tears. Only the cruelty of this man kept him from sobbing. If he wept, this monster would just smile. "You're perfectly willing to destroy a life. I trained for years. I know engineering, design, art, aesthetics. I schooled myself as a preparation for the life I chose. I've worked hard. And now you, casually, without a care for the will of others, are tearing this from me. Have you no thought of evil?"

"Maybe I'm the Devil, eh?"

Maybe he was. "What can I do to change your mind? I know something! Money. Yes. Turn around, let me off, and I'll give you a note for a thousand. A thousand dollars for a small delay, an hour or two. And if you give me another hour or two when we get there, I'll find all the men you need! You don't even have to go through Golden Gate. Just go back, lower one of those boats near the Presidio and row me to land. Just to land. A thousand dollars in your account—for an hour or two's delay."

Stern sighed. "Eat or not, as you choose, and then report to Larson. He'll start showing you the ropes."

"I won't work! I'm not your slave. It's bad enough being an enforced passenger on a trip I didn't ask for. But I won't work."

Stern shrugged. "Then you won't eat."

"Won't eat! You would do that?"

"Every man earns his keep here."

"Or what?"

"Every man is free to leave. One small jump."

The chill in Stern's face appalled White. This man was a monster, a robber of life, a tyrant.

"Put me in your brig, then. I'll sit in your brig until we reach land."

Stern laughed again, that cold, almost silent mirth that struck horror in White. "A brig," he said. "We have no brig. This is an old freighter. Eat or not, and be quick about it. Larson's waiting."

This time White couldn't hold back tears. "You—I've never met such evil," he said. "A slave. You won't pay me."

"Yes, I pay wages."

"But why? Why bother?"

"I sometimes ask myself the same question. One hates to shanghai a new crew in every port. And train them. A good experienced seaman is worth much."

"How much?"

"Fifty American a month."

"And what'll you pay me?"

"Enough for you to repay me for the clothing and sea gear I'm giving you."

White laughed, hysteria bubbling crazily in him. "And when can I put foot on shore?"

Stern's eyes glittered again. "It will be amusing to see what happens. I'll tell you one thing. The harder you work, and the more responsive you are to everything I require, the more inclined I'll be to let you go. You see, I'll hold your freedom over you as a weapon. Wages? They offer me no leverage with the likes of you. Freedom? Ah, there's the hold I have on your throat. A hopeless man does me no good. There's always the lash, and I've used it from time to time. But I prefer to use it for insubordination. For mutineers. But the lash can put a man in his hammock for a week, and I lose labor. Those are my weapons: starvation, the lash, and hope. Work hard, work until you drop, and maybe I'll let you go."

White gaped at this man, whose life-and-death grip upon him he was only just beginning to grasp. Then he retreated into quietness and resignation under the calm gaze of the master, stumbled back to his cabin, his bunk—only to discover it wasn't his anymore. Nothing of his remained in it. He should have guessed that, too. They'd put him in a seaman's hammock along with a dozen sweating, odorous men.

He found his way to the galley, found a kettle of gruel and bowls, helped himself, and ate, delaying as long as possible the moment when he had to face Larson. That mate was in on it! Larson, that devil lounging on the wharf, must have known! What a fool, what a sucker he'd been to trust that seaman who made it so easy to step aboard, step into a trap!

The oatmeal was tasteless, with the consistency of India rubber, and the sole fare available to him. Was this what he would survive upon for days and weeks and months? Was this how he would live, he, an architect?

At least the hot, bitter coffee offered some sort of comfort, and he swallowed one mug and then another. The java was as bitter as his soul.

Then he beheld Larson at the door.

"You ready?"

"No, I'm not. I'm an architect, not a seaman."

"Now you're a seaman. We'll start you cleaning the heads."

"What?"

"Gives a man some perspective, I say. Start him at the crapper end of it, and he'll get the idea."

"Then what?"

"Lots to scrub. Stern runs a tidy ship."

"How long is my day?"

"We have two watches. You'll be on half a day, off half a day. We're already two hours into your watch. You're lucky."

"Then what?"

"You're an architect, eh? Engineer. Well, Mr. Pencil Pusher, you'd be useless in the rigging, but you'll do just fine down below. Fireman, maybe. Shovel that coal. You know mechanics, iron and steel, pressures. Engineer. Oil that engine. Mechanic. Fix a valve, patch a pipe."

"Is that it?"

"You got any better ideas?"

White thought of the rigging, of climbing up there, setting or riffing sails or whatever they did, hanging on in a typhoon, the mast swaying wildly in a stormy seas. The thought made his palms sweat.

"No," he said. "Take me down to hell."

CHAPTER 60

No word. Marcia waited day after day. Sometimes she thought that Harrison would step off the train and summon the Devereaux family to pick him up. Other times she thought he would wire her another dozen excuses for ignoring her and the children—White roses, she called them. Neither happened. She was mystified at first, then fretful, then angry. But not alarmed. She had come to understand that for Ambition Barnes White, a wife was an afterthought, and children barely existed.

In a way, that suited her fine. The quake had done her a favor, shattering what had not held together very well beforehand. It was as if the quake had been along the fault lines of her marriage instead of the fault underlying San Francisco. The only annoying thing about his silence was a lack of closure. She wished to get on with her life.

Sometimes she felt guilty about her current annoyance with Harrison, and wondered whether she should try to reconcile when he did check in from somewhere. But why should she? The only reason she could think of was the children, but he had been a cipher to them all those years, so why should she worry about that? And anyway, she thought she just might find a new father who'd do much better in that department than the natural one.

For a while her mother's acid-edged wit had fueled her feelings. Sally Devereaux was enjoying her role as mother-in-law, finding funny things to say about Harrison. But after a while that didn't sit well with Marcia. Even Harrison, lost in his world of architecture and getting ahead, had goodness in him. She had found it and enjoyed it and married him. Her mother kept forgetting that: There had been reasons to say yes when Harrison proposed.

Days slipped by. She wrote him, care of the Presidio, care of Golden Gate Park, care of the Ferry Building, general delivery, Oakland general delivery, care of Franklin Hall. No letter was returned, and Harrison did not reply. What seemed at first like his usual casual negligence had turned darker. And more mysterious. Why was life such a riddle?

Harrison had vanished. Maybe disastrously. Shot by the soldiers? Killed by roving bands of hooligans? Dead of disease from exposure or bad food or contamination or anything else that was taking lives in the funereal city?

"I told you so," said her mother one day. "The man is in love with rivets and Corinthian arches. You're too pretty. Now if you had a cantilevered bosom or Doric legs, or a fireproof vault . . ." She whooped. Marcia smiled. Her mother's wit usually had a target, and these days it was Harrison.

"Something's happened to him," Marcia said. "He always wandered in, sooner or later. I always knew more or less where he was and what he was doing. Something's wrong."

"The quake brought out the best in him," her mother retorted. "Now we're getting the true, honest Harrison."

Marcia laughed, not wanting to. She had loved him dearly once. Even now, if he should appear at their door, she would do her utmost to rebuild a marriage. She would nurture him, help him recover from the earthquake, draw the circle of love around him and her children. She had given herself to him for better and for worse, and she had meant every word, every syllable, of the marriage vow. Even now, when the marriage seemed shattered, her heart cried out to heal it, not discard it. Her mother wasn't helping any, but that was Sally Devereaux. There was less malice to her sharp tongue than people realized, and she did it to scintillate—those were her own words, when Marcia had once assailed her.

Harry and Daisy, thank heaven, had not missed Harrison very much. She had put Harry in a private school where he could catch up, while Daisy stayed at home and received abundant attention. Harry spoke of his father, sometimes solemnly, sometimes with yearning, although Daisy seemed not to care much. But Marcia wondered how deep the hurts went, and suspected each child was feeling rejected by that negligent man.

Marcia's future was blank. And filled with painful choices. She should not linger for long in her parents' capacious home, as amiable as that was. She had almost no social life, other than to resurrect a few old friendships with school chums who were busy matrons now. She really wanted a divorce, and if the law prevented it, then a separation, and money enough from Harrison to live on and raise their children. The little ones needed plenty of loving, not only because they had scarcely known two parents, but because the quake had torn their lives asunder.

She thought to pursue her art, if the children didn't gobble all her time, or making a living imposed its burdens. She knew how lucky she was: Most women in her circumstances would be destitute, homeless, and without any future at all, while her dilemma was kinder. Which of her many options would be best?

Marcia tarried through another week, uneasily waiting, and now deeply alarmed. Something awful had happened out there in all that chaos. Had he been killed, or left for dead? Was he desperately ill? Each day she hounded the mail, pouncing on the postman the moment he arrived.

Nothing. Harrison had dropped off the edge of the world.

Then one evening she cornered her father in his study, where he pretended to read books, but mostly snorted and bellowed at Theodore Roosevelt's posturing.

"Ha! That squeaky-voiced poseur thinks he's a man. Did you see his get-up leading those barbarous Rough Riders up that hill? Shameless. He makes Cody look like a shrinking violet. They ought not to let anyone who's been west of the Mississippi run for office. It ruins them!" he had bawled at the dinner table the previous night.

"I believe they were shooting at him, dear," said her mother. "Primarily bullets."

"That doesn't mean a thing."

"Would you ride up that hill under fire?"

"Not wearing that flamboyant get-up, I wouldn't."

That had silenced the conversation. Devereaux dinner exchanges had become famous in Shaker Heights, which is why some sniffy people didn't invite them.

Marcia found her father holding his *Plain-Dealer* and fulminating again.

"I want to talk to you," she said, closing the door behind her.

"Harrison."

"Yes. I can't bear this wait. What can be done?"

"Put the bloodhounds on. Pinkerton's could look."

"And what if they don't find him?"

"Desertion."

That was how he was. His mind leaped nimbly ahead of conversation, leapfrogging a dozen rungs on the conversational ladder.

"Give the peckerhead another week, Marcia, and then I'll go roust out the lawyers. We'll run him out of the family."

"Daddy, he's my husband. Not a very good one, but he's the children's father."

"Well, if he isn't, then he should run you out of *his* family."

She laughed. Life was never very serious in Shaker Heights. The avant-garde Devereaux family was cherished in some circles, and anathematized elsewhere.

The week ticked by as slowly as a seven-day clock, and not a word drifted in from San Francisco. Marcia was sliding into melancholy.

"Cheer up, dear," said her mother. "Silence is golden, especially from him."

But her mother's wit didn't seem right. Something awful had befallen Harrison.

"He's in trouble, Mother, and I intend to help if I can."

For once her mother was silent.

"All right, Marcia," Drake Devereaux announced in the middle of a summer's day. "We're off to Lewis, Crutchfield, and Moulton. Get your female paraphernalia and we'll crank up the touring car. We're going to hire Attila the Hun, or at any rate, some high-priced Mongols."

They arrived eventually at a seedy brick edifice in downtown Cleveland, and Drake Devereaux marched his daughter up three flights of marble stairs to a pebbled glass door, and then steered her into a stark waiting room, devoid of art, rug, or anything to read. A frosted glass window opened, a male clerk peered out, nodded, and closed the window. Marcia lowered herself into a back-busting wooden seat, and her father settled beside her, groaning cheerfully. Marcia focused on a slight smudge on the gray plaster wall, in lieu of anything else to do. Ten minutes later the clerk, a bent blond bookworm, ushered Marcia and her father into the office of Melvin Moulton.

Marcia noted that the office was as barren and utilitarian as the reception room. Its possessor stood behind a shiny table and motioned them to sit in the hard wooden seats before the table. The attorney looked like a porcupine with thick gold-rimmed glasses, squat and dangerous.

"Ah, Drake, it's terrible to see you," he said, in a voice as warty as a toad's flesh. "Anyone who walks into a law office deserves a kinder fate."

"Yes, Melvin, you look worse than ever," Drake said. "I did not think it was possible, but it is. I want you to meet the victim."

Marcia marveled. She peered about, seeing none of the accou-
trements of a law office.

Moulton noticed. "We believe in winning," he said, somehow supposing that his cryptic observation would explain the parsimony. "Now,
tell me about this alleged husband."

Drake chuckled. Marcia debated whether to feel offended. But
then she told her story, while the porcupine's bristly eyebrows rose
and fell.

"You haven't heard from White since the exchange of telegrams?"

"Not a word."

"Did you leave word for him in those registries?"

"No. He would know where we would go if we could."

"Why was he turning himself into an errand boy for the mayor's
committee?"

She shrugged. "Ask him."

"And how long has it been since you've heard?"

"It was still April."

Moulton blinked. Marcia had never seen so much deliberation go
into a blink. His lids drooped, settled slowly, eventually cutting off light
and vision, and then slowly opened like shutters. "This is routine. We'll
nail him on desertion. He's alive, having survived quake and fire and
pestilence; he's floating about, gorgeously important and ignoring you.
We'll advertise for him, Missing Persons, six weeks, maybe two months,
all the papers in California. They've started up the papers out there
again, you know. And if Wandering White doesn't respond, we'll go to
court and put his neck on the block. A regular guillotine of a case." He
smiled. "Be of good cheer. We'll either reel him in and drop him in the
creel, or free you to paint or sing in the opera or pluck the harpsichord
or whatever." He turned to Drake. "What does she do? All the Devereaux do something."

"She's very good at conception," Drake said.

CHAPTER 61

illis Hart huddled on the sidewalk, too nauseous to stand.
The blow to his skull had almost killed him. Wave after
wave of vicious pain washed through his head, neck, and
entire body. He buried his head in his hands, wanting
the pain to go away. He was aware that Nella was weeping, her hands

gently caressing, but even that feathery touch shot blinding pain through him.

"We've got to get help, Willis," she whispered.

"I can't. Not now," he said. It hurt to talk.

"Are you hurt bad?"

He didn't respond. His hair was caked with blood. He couldn't see much, and wondered whether he had lost his vision, or whether it was just because night had fallen.

"I'll help you. We've got to get help."

He tried to stand, and slumped back to the ground as blinding pain racked his entire body. "Can't," he mumbled.

All he could do was sit there, rest his head on his arms, and wait.

"Willis, Willis," she cried. "What are we going to do?"

He felt so nauseous he couldn't respond.

Time passed, though he couldn't say how much. Not long.

"Someone's coming," she said, and then stood up.

"Help!" she cried. "Help us."

Two men loomed out of the darkness. Both carried rifles. He could see that much.

"We've been attacked. We need a doctor," Nella cried.

"We'll see about that," a man's voice said. "What are you doing out? It's after curfew."

"Who are you?"

"Auxiliary police. And what are you doing out? Mugging innocent people?"

Willis absorbed that, slowly focused on the two men looming over him. "We were on our way to the waterfront because we wanted to find a boatman who'd take us across."

"Likely story. You can be shot on sight for wandering around this time of night."

"For God's sake, help me. Someone hit me with a sap."

A blinding light from a torch shot pain through Willis's head. The beam stayed on Willis, and then examined Nella minutely, up and down, this way and that.

"How do we know you weren't trying to mug someone and got caught?" The truculent voice bore down on him. Willis was able to separate the two voices now.

Willis sighed. "Back of my head," he mumbled. "I was hit from behind."

"That doesn't mean a thing. Get up."

"If I could, I would have left here long ago to get help."

"Get up, damn it."

Willis felt the prod of a rifle barrel. He tried to stand, felt another wave of nausea sweep him, and found himself tumbling. He fell to the ground, got up on all fours, and vomited, the convulsions frightful. Tears filled his eyes.

"Maybe you're drunk. Spirits are illegal."

Nella snarled at the man. "He needs help! He's not drunk. We were attacked! Help get him to a doctor."

Willis felt a rough hand poking about, and lifting the Wilsons' tonic bottle from his breast pocket.

"Look at this," said one to the other.

"Probably hunnert proof. Balsam, eh? Take a whiff."

"It was given to us as a wedding present," Nella said.

"A wedding present! Now I know you're a pair of crooks."

"My ring was stolen! Get help!"

Willis had heard about these amateur cops that Mayor Schmitz had prowling the streets. They had killed innocent citizens.

"Do what you want, but get me to a doctor," he mumbled.

"You the bridegroom? What's your name?"

"Willis Hart." He remembered the paper in his pocket and fumbled for it. "Here's the license."

One of the amateur cops took it and studied it.

"It's a license, all right. You got married, all right, less you stole this, too."

"What is the matter with you!" Nella snapped. "He's hurt!"

One of the cops sighed. "We'll check you out," he said, sounding disappointed. He plainly wanted to catch and maybe execute a pair of prowlers.

Willis retreated into his pain. He was beyond caring.

"If we help, can you walk?" asked one.

"Not far."

"I'll get someone," the bigger cop said to the other. "You guard these two."

"Give me the marriage license," Nella said.

"No, we're keeping it."

"But it's ours!"

"It's evidence."

Willis had had more than he could stand. "I've been seriously injured and robbed by a pair of cutpurses. My wife was pawed over by one. My head is broken. We've just gotten married. We were going to try to get out of here for a honeymoon. Now help us or leave us alone."

The auxiliary cop handed the license back. One left to get help. Willis curled up and waited, feeling Nella's loving hands gently cloak him. A long time passed, metered out in throbs of pain, but eventually a horse-drawn cabriolet pulled up, and the auxiliary police loaded him in, and helped Nella in beside him.

"Take him over to the Presidio General Hospital," the temporary officer said to the driver. "We'll go write this up."

Willis sighed. Somehow, they had escaped the clutches of Schmitz's vigilantes.

He felt the hack lurch, and closed his eyes against the new assault of pain that flooded through him with every movement of the buggy. The Presidio hospital had handled the most serious cases since the quake. It meant he would be getting excellent care.

Pain marked the passage, but eventually he was borne into the hospital on a stretcher, and two doctors swiftly examined his head wound. Nella stood silently by. He pitied her. Not much of a way to start a marriage.

After checking his vital signs, the doctors examined his vision, asking whether he saw double, and just what he did see. All he could say was that light was painful, and seemed much too bright. They also tested his motor functions. Everything worked.

Finally one of them, the one with a walrus mustache, announced his verdict.

"I'm Dr. Borden, Mr. Hart. This is a concussion, more likely mild than severe, but bad enough to keep you quiet for a while. It's dangerous. Concussions can cause trouble down the line. Not much we can do for your nausea or pain. It'll weather away. You're going to need a quiet place and some care."

"Have none," he mumbled. "Just got married."

The doctor turned and examined Nella, who stood solemnly just out of the lamplight. San Francisco, including the Presidio, still had no electricity.

"Just married? Congratulations, you two. But not much of a honeymoon, eh?"

"Married in Golden Gate Park Saturday evening, and haven't found a place to go to," Willis said. "We were going to try to get across the bay, Santa Rosa or someplace."

"That's out. You can't endure a trip like that. That water's choppy and it'd just about kill you to try that."

"Where can we go?" Nella asked. "We haven't got a thing. The thugs took the only thing we had, my ring."

The doctor sighed, helplessly. "We've some temporary wards, some in Presidio halls and storerooms, some in tents. We'll find room."

They did find room. Willis dozed on the examining table, glad to be in a warm, quiet place. Nella held his hand and squeezed it now and then.

Then two army orderlies lifted him onto a stretcher and carried

him to a large tent facility, a hastily erected ward crammed with the injured and sick. They gently lowered him onto a canvas cot and tucked a
blanket over him, under the watchful eye of a young nurse.

"Sorry we don't have room for the missus," said one orderly.

"Where can I go?" Nella asked.

The nurse sighed and shook her head. "I don't know, Mrs. Hart. I
wish I could help."

"Could I just sit on the edge of his cot?"

"It'd collapse. I'm afraid not."

"Could I sit on the grass here?"

"No, we need to get through. I'm sorry. We're so swamped."

Willis felt utterly miserable about her fate. Everything had gone to
pieces, not just once, but over and over since the quake. "We could go
outside. We want to be together," he mumbled.

"No, Mr. Hart, we will be watching you closely."

"Willis, I'll find something. I'll stay nearby," Nella said, but there
was a quiver in her voice.

"Not much of a honeymoon," he muttered.

"You two just married?" the nurse asked.

"Yes."

"Really? Just married?"

"Saturday evening. We're trying to find someplace . . ."

The nurse held up her lantern. "Let me take a look at you, Mrs.
Hart." She held the lamp close, examining Nella, who stood patiently.
Nella was still disheveled from the assault.

"You look pretty sick to me," the nurse said. "Let me check your
pulse." She clamped a hand over Nella's wrist and held it. "Yes, defi-
nitely sick. I'm admitting you. Gonna shift a few cots around. Honeymoon, eh? Well, you have matrimony fever. That's what I'll put down."

"Is that the same as morning sickness?" Nella asked.

Willis wheezed, trying to stop the laughter that tortured his head
with every convulsion.

The nurse smiled. "Maybe I shouldn't put you side by side," she
said, but she obviously didn't mean it.

CHAPTER 62

· ·

Katharine Steinmetz's life settled into waiting. Others came and went. The Presidio steadily emptied of refugees, as people found shelter and transportation and means. The children, in particular, had fled somewhere like the birds of autumn, and she wondered whether parents were placing them with grandparents and other relatives, and seeing to their schooling.

At the height of disaster, the Presidio had been almost merry. Social barriers were down, and people easily visited with strangers, made friends, shared the terrible ordeals they had been through. But that was changing now, and day by day people drew into themselves. The remaining denizens of the tent cities were utterly sick of camping, and that revulsion was driving them away. Anything was better than eternal camping, sleeping on hard ground, vulnerable to every shower and breeze, and the lack of laundry and bathing facilities.

Katharine's tentmates had evolved as well. The young mother had left and been replaced with two sisters. A half dozen of the women had found somewhere to go and departed. The newcomers were less interested in befriending the rest. With every day, the quake and fire slipped deeper into the past, and the bonds forged in those desperate hours had withered.

These strangers bickered, failed to help one another, and offered Katharine no assistance when she went to the food lines or the miserable sanitary trenches. One day someone stole Emil's wheelchair, a blow so terrible that she wondered how she would survive. That chair, the chance to sit, the chance to roll slowly wherever she needed to go, had been her life preserver. Now it was gone. So she had made her slow way, using a stick for a cane, and endured new pain.

She was sinking. Each night she spent on the cold earth drove the arthritis deeper into every joint of her body, until she ached so much that not even the warm afternoon sun of early June baked the pain out of her. The tent had become a pit of bickering now, and all the courtesy and helpfulness that she had found there in the days of crisis had vanished, along with the original women. She alone remained, helpless to put any sort of new life together.

Her work with the Brownie disappointed her. The little snapshots so lacked contrast and brilliance that she despaired. At least the subjects were absorbing. She had, willy-nilly, caught the desperate masses in their moment of agony. Even the inadequate little Brownie could not conceal the depths of despair, the faces lit with courage, the improvised living, the poignant scenes everywhere around her, from little boys crying to lovers holding hands.

The boatman regularly picked up her exposed rolls and delivered the snapshots, and sometimes a note from Charmian London. They had sold no more of her photos, not even the fine ones taken with the Kodet. But they were going to keep on trying, because at bottom, she wrote, the quake and fire afflicted mortals, not just real estate.

Katharine sighed. The Londons had gone out of their way to help her, but they would weary of that now, weeks after the disaster. Katharine had about two hundred little snapshots, no darkroom, no enlarger or chemicals or paper, no way to solicit editors or galleries, no living. Each day, conditions got worse, no matter what cheer she mustered within. She stared at the mysterious and empty heavens, wondering where Emil had gone, if anywhere, and wishing she might go there, too. It wasn't that she wanted to die or didn't relish life, but that she had been overwhelmed, and had no resources. When life reached a certain level of impossibility, could death be so bad?

Then one sunny afternoon she decided that she would take what life had to offer, even if it meant pain, poverty, and long nights worrying about where her next meal would come from. That proved to be a milestone, almost as if Fate was waiting for her to come to that.

She received a brown envelope with some bills in it—twenty-one dollars—from the Londons. Some of Emil's etchings had sold. The money had come from a New York gallery, which had deducted 30 percent of the thirty-dollar sale. So Emil had blessed her from beyond the grave. She had a lot of money, or anyway it seemed that way. She wondered how to spend it.

That evening five of the wretched women in her tent began to bicker. First it was about odors, then about dirt, then about snoring, then about getting up in the night and stepping carelessly, then about coughing, then about whiny criticism. It was three against two, and then four against one, while the rest of the women maintained an embarrassed silence.

"We must be patient," Katharine said during a lull. "These are very difficult times. You are all fine and gracious women."

They turned on her, savagely complaining that she snored, she was privileged because the boatman came and went, bringing her things. They hastened to inform her that she should mind her own business, and if she didn't like it there, she could get out.

"You're the queen bee," snapped the one who whined constantly. "That's what you think. I think you're no better than the rest of us."

Shocked, Katharine absorbed all that, and decided it was time to leave. She had twenty-one dollars, a packet of snapshots, some rags to wear, and a stick to lean on. Anything would be better than this tent full of bitter and increasingly uncivil women.

She had lost track of the days, but knew it was early June. And it was a fine, balmy morning. And she had enough to hire a hack, if such things existed. And with luck, she might get that boatman to take her across the Golden Gate, and with more luck she might reach Sonoma. She had been once to the old mission town with its great square and crumbling adobes and redolent history, and she thought there might be a corner in one of those old places for a destitute woman, who could perhaps, sell tourist trinkets.

If she had to sleep on the ground, at least Sonoma would be warmer than chill San Francisco, But thinking it was one thing, and doing it another. Here, she would not go hungry, and she could get immediate medical attention, and she had a canvas roof over her head. Would she have the courage to abandon that modicum of security?

She sat on the ground, her old bones aching, the women restless and unhappy and looking for another fight. She clambered to her feet and drifted into the sun, and knew. Life was risk. She could not hope for a good life without daring it to happen.

She returned to the tent and began collecting her few things. She would have to carry them the way a bindle stiff would, in a bundle on a stick. She would use a spare skirt for that. One by one she placed her small possessions within—the Brownie, some rolls of film, some underthings, the packet of snapshots and proofs.

"What are you doing?" asked the whiny one.

Katharine thought it best not to answer, but continued to collect her things.

"You're leaving! That's the dumbest thing I ever heard of. Where'll you go? You'll starve to death."

"That's possible," Katharine said. "You could help me by getting a loaf from the breadline before I go."

"You can't go. You can hardly walk."

"It would be kind of you to help me, then."

"Why should I help you? You've made everyone miserable here."

"Then you should welcome my departure, and help me off."

"Listen to her! Still the queen bee around here."

"I cannot walk but a little, and would be most grateful if you would write in the register that I am going to Sonoma."

Oddly, no one objected. One mousy woman, Katharine thought her name was Phlox, said she would do it.

"Thank you," Katharine said. "You are very helpful."

Katharine stood in the sun, wondering how she could even manage the first step. But she took it. She walked slowly toward the Presidio's administration building. She took her time, not wishing to inflame the arthritis. But twenty minutes later she stood there, amid a welter of motor and horse-drawn vehicles.

"I need a ride to Fort Mason," she said to a soldier.

He gestured. "Try him."

The next vehicle over was a khaki-colored touring car. She asked the driver, who was wearing goggles.

"Can't take civilians," he said.

"I can barely walk and I need a ride. I'd give you a dollar."

"Yeah?"

The driver opened the door, and then yelled to his neighbors. "Tell 'im I'll be back in five minutes."

She got her ride, enjoying the wind in her face as she sat in the open machine. "Actually, I want to go beyond Fort Mason, to that boat place—the Hyde Street Pier."

He grinned. His goggles hid the rest of his young face.

Minutes later he deposited her at the wharf used by so many boatmen, She gave him his dollar. He saluted and clattered off, the engine stuttering protests.

Now, truly, she was on her own. A world beckoned, but it would be a world without means. But wasn't that the very situation confronting so many leaving the bosom of their family for the first time? Just as she had once done? Wasn't that the very act of becoming an adult? Was this earthquake a way, at bottom, for her to achieve her independence once again?

She missed Emil, and thought of him as she lumbered slowly toward the waterfront and all the boats nuzzled into the pier like piglets at the teat. She wished this journey could have been both of theirs, that she was wheeling him along this wharf. But Emil was gone. She sighed, feeling fondness for the wasted man with whom she had shared so much life and hope.

The familiar boatman, Thompson Newton, wasn't there. Or if he was, his boat hid him from the world. She discovered a bench, something precious and rare, and sat upon it, smelling the water, feeling the pier absorb the waves, creak, and blot up sun, watching the seagulls wheel.

Katharine thought she would ask, but she wasn't in a hurry. She would watch and wait. Living in a tent for weeks had taught her to watch and wait and make herself as comfortable as she could when there were no comforts. She had no idea what his boat might look like; indeed, boats were coming and going all the time, doing busy traffic across Golden Gate. So she sunned herself, enjoyed the faint tang of fish in the air, and studied the steady parade of people on the wharf.

But then she discovered she didn't need the boatman. The Southern Pacific ferry to Belvedere and Tiburon was running. She watched it dock, discharge passengers, and begin to load, so she boarded it. She thought it was like sailing for Pitcairn Island.

CHAPTER 63

Ginger knew it was time to leave San Francisco. She had watched the refugees stream away, and the opportunities to help people, be of service, were fewer and fewer. She had no home, and there were no street corners left where she might pass out tracts or preach or admonish. She didn't have any tracts anyway. She had always defined her mission as spreading the Word of God. Charity was a blessed labor, too, but not the one she had devoted herself to. When people had the biblical keys to a holy life, everything else followed naturally. That was what she had always believed, and now, having gone through the quake, she believed it more than ever.

She had no home, either. Various people had opened their tents to her at night; she slept beside elderly couples, or in the midst of families, only to depart at dawn, seeking to give love and hope and comfort to the needy. But she believed that even the most selfless of God's laborers needed a nest. And she needed one.

She had thought about attaching herself to one of the Protestant churches still standing in the unburned areas, but swiftly discovered they didn't want her ministry. They probably disagreed with her about theology, or maybe it was just a case of status. There was something bottom-rung socially about anyone, like herself, who would stand on a street corner and hand out Bible tracts. She had always understood that. She had stationed herself in the most vicious area on earth, a place where heartless men enslaved women for immoral purposes, where half the men on the streets had stolen or ravaged or betrayed or murdered or assaulted the innocent. She had done it because those were the people who needed the Gospel, the Good News, the most. She had taken her message to the brink of hell, and plucked a few from perdition.

She had placed herself in harm's way every day, ceaselessly until the earthquake, and passed through unscathed because God intended that she should. She was ministering to the dregs of the earth, the ones routinely ignored by all the well-meaning, respectable, upright clergymen in the teeming city. No evil had touched her. Not even the saloon men who tried to drive her off with baseball bats had touched her. None of the pimps who threatened her for driving away business had touched her. None of the crooks and yeggs who had paused to stare at her had touched her or stolen from her. None of the dozen threats a day ever amounted to anything. That was why, in her soul, in her heart and mind, she knew herself to be an instrument of God.

She sounded out some ministers she came across in the Presidio, and swiftly discovered the averted eye, and noncommittal answer. Very well, then. She would serve humbler precincts and be a humbler worker herself in the vineyards of the Lord.

She had prayed about it, wanting foremost to do God's will, and her every instinct was to leave. Start somewhere else. Visit the Bible Society and talk to its elders and receive from them a new mission in a place where people might pause to listen, a place where people had homes and employment. Not in a wasteland, which is what this city would be for years to come. Yes, she would do that. The Southern Pacific and Union Pacific were still carrying the destitute away for nothing, although they now asked payment from those who could pay. She remained penniless, and that meant a free ride as far as Omaha. But they would help her get to Chicago, which was where she needed to go. She would find her way to the Bible Society offices on La Salle Street, and see what fate awaited her. She would wire them. The telegraph was available to refugees, as before, and various stations had sprung up throughout the precincts of San Francisco to help people contact the outside world.

Yes, she would do that. Wire the society for instructions and funds; wire her parents in Ohio—she would love to visit her family there—and begin over. She didn't know where she would end up, or where she would find the means, but it was time to trust in God's providence and in the mysterious workings of his will. Yes, that was it. With faith, she would face the future without knowing what it might hold.

One bright May morning, when the browning fields of the Presidio baked in the sweet ascending sun, she went to the telegraph station open to the public and sent messages. To L. B. Carlton, president of the society, she explained that her work could no longer proceed and she needed a new mission and funds for a trip. Then she wired her parents to say she was safe and hoped to see them soon and if she could borrow a few dollars she would welcome the money. Later that day, she would see what the responses might be.

She told herself that all this was just fine.

There remained only the painful task of telling Paul, which she would do at lunch that day. She dreaded that. He had been such a kind and patient friend, and even now she depended on him for the few amenities she had. The refugees could now obtain lukewarm showers, and could launder their clothing using army equipment, but life remained hard and uncomfortable for most. She had been luckier.

She decided the best way to ease Paul through all this would be to tell him there was no hope. She did not wish to encourage him with professions of future friendship, promises to write, or anything of the sort. She was going to vanish from his life forever, and the best and only honorable way to do that was to say it and close all doors.

She wondered why she should do that—what reason she had to sever even friendship—and couldn't very well say. But lurking in her soul was an answer that wouldn't go away: She would sever her connection to him for her own sake, as well as his. Paul's love was drawing her away from her mission, her passion, her sacred dedication to her Lord. But there was something more: It frightened her.

Oh, why did intimacy trouble her so? Why was she so afraid?

She spent the rest of that May morning making arrangements. The SP had set up information offices around town, and the eastern railroads had set up an office in the Ferry Building. Telephones now connected the various offices. She waited in line until a harried clerk was able to help her.

"It's free if you can't pay. But what we're doing is issuing through tickets on a loan basis—cut-price fare but you reimburse us when you can. That all right?"

"Yes, I'll repay every penny if I can. I want to."

"Most do," he said. "Thing is, hardly anyone wants charity. Most just want a loan to start over, help to get going, but something they can repay. Now, the eastbounds to Omaha are here on this schedule, Oakland Terminal, and you pick one and the date. And we'll put you through to Chicago. Pay when you can."

She hesitated, anguish upon her. "Eastbound Thirty-one? Day after tomorrow?" she asked. That would allow time to get some responses to her telegrams.

"Sure enough, Mrs.—Miss Severance."

"Thank you."

"Now, you're reserved but you'll need to pick up your tickets in Oakland, ground floor, Union Ferry Building at the Oakland pier. Just present this. And you can complete your travel arrangements at the Ferry Building."

He gave her a form with a dismissing smile. She smiled back.

This was a miracle. These giant companies were still whisking people out of the stricken city, even now, and losing money on virtually every passenger.

It was time to head for the officers' mess—and Paul.

She walked slowly, making her feet move forward toward an appointment that would be painful. She prayed for strength. Surely God would help her.

Paul was waiting at the door, and quietly led her to a table, where he surveyed her.

"All right, Ginger, what is it?"

"I didn't know I could be so easily found out."

"I have learned to read your face and your moods. I don't really mean to—it's just that I love you and I am alive to whatever lies in the soul of my beloved."

She enjoyed the graciousness of his approach, even as the tendrils of pain clamped her heart. "I've come to realize that my work in San Francisco is done, at least for now," she said.

"And what was that, Ginger?"

"Bringing the Word of God to people."

A waiter brought two luncheon plates. Not even in this privileged place was it possible for anyone to select a meal, and that was how it would be until food supplies and warehouses and transportation were reestablished. She beheld sliced ham and scalloped potatoes and lima beans garnished with brown sugar.

"I sense that I'm competing with God, which is not a contest at all. I wish not to compete."

He wasn't helping her.

"Oh, Paul." She reached across the table and touched his hand. "Neither of us can change what must be."

He smiled gently. "You're preparing me for something, I guess. I await my fate."

"Paul—I'm taking the train east the day after tomorrow. I've wired the Bible Society in Chicago that I'm coming. I can't continue my mission here."

Paul sawed on the ham a moment, and set down his knife and fork. "So it's good-bye."

"Yes."

"You're a beautiful woman. I am stirred by your courage and dedication. I wish you every success, and the fullness of heart that comes from a victorious life. Ginger . . . I'll always remember you. You're my every dream. You are one small person changing the whole world, as if you had a hand on Archimedes' lever and could pry up a civilization and set it down again on a better foundation. Would you do me one small favor?"

She nodded, touched by his grace.

"When you reach wherever you're going, would you have a portrait taken and send me a print? I would like to remember you, the lady of my dreams, with some small photograph that I can tuck into my favorite book and pull out when I wish, in the lonely night, in the bright sun."

"No, Paul. A picture would give you wrong ideas."

He nodded, a wry smile on his face.

She ate desultorily, having lost her appetite. He ate quietly, neither saying anything at all. She needed to ease his pain.

"You're an officer, with rank and privilege. You know what I am? A girl of the streets. You know where I used to give away tracts? A block from the Barbary Coast. I gave them to humble people, some would say the dregs. Outcasts, easy women, rum-soaked men, tramps and madmen, people who mumbled, people missing limbs and eyes, people with hooks for hands, and peg legs, people with nothing to live for because they didn't count for anything. That is still my mission—to bring the most precious of all gifts to each desperate person. I was an introduction service. 'Here, sir, meet God. He will help you.' 'Here, lady, you don't have to live in fear, your body bruised, your soul imprisoned, your dreams smashed.' I helped only a few. But those few escaped. I will continue to do that. You see, Paul, you need someone different."

"And you? Who do you need?"

"I have my work."

"Ginger, you're very forthright about most things but not that. Try again, please."

"Right after the quake, I didn't want to go outside. I wanted to stay in my bed. I didn't want to comfort people or bring them the gifts of God. But I did. I made myself do it."

"Yes, you make yourself do it," he said.

CHAPTER 64

Paul Boswell watched the woman of his dreams slip away. He had joined her every moment he could spare and she had permitted during the weeks following the city's mortal crisis. They had walked and lunched. At the end of an evening stroll she had permitted a chaste kiss on her cheek, but that was as far as their relationship had progressed—or would go, apparently.

She remained a mystery to him, having withheld a large part of herself. He wanted especially to know what had driven—or inspired—her missionary endeavors. Was she so deeply religious? Were there reasons other than the blindingly beautiful vision of her Lord and God? A family problem? And why the Bible Society, handing out tracts on street corners?

Some intuition told him that she loved him, as much as he loved her. Why, then, her terrible fear? Or was it fear at all? Maybe the barrier really was her sacred commitment, just as she claimed. But that didn't explain Ginger Severance. She poured out her love upon others, sensitively helping those in trouble—and yet seemed alone and friendless. He found out she had lived in a tiny warren near Telegraph Hill, largely subsisting on donations placed in a small box on the street when she passed out her Bible tracts. Her beauty alone had garnered coins. She had been isolated and alone, and yet didn't seem to mind. He ought to be wary of such a woman, but he really wasn't. Nothing at all in her conduct suggested she was disturbed or mad or without social graces or even eccentric.

And yet that wasn't the whole story, either. She shied from love as if it terrified her. She had never had a beau. He had discovered that in their strolls. What was so alarming about men? He knew he had awakened fear and anguish as well as yearning in her, and that he had unintentionally shattered her serenity. And he knew also that her impending trip east was flight—from him as well as the dead city.

He had asked her, during that fateful lunch, whether he might be with her through her last day in San Francisco, and she had agreed. He knew he could get a day off; the general himself had suggested it. They were to meet at noon and spend the afternoon together. She had nothing to pack, nothing to prepare, and didn't lack time. So he had that final afternoon to plead his case, or let go, discover where his own feelings lay, and probably say good-bye. He knew his chances were slim.

Sometimes, that quiet, sunny May morning, he rationalized everything: They scarcely knew each other. They had been thrown together by crisis. He had never met her family. They had not been together during normal times, meeting friends, doing ordinary things. They did not share the same values or beliefs or ideals. His military career stood in the path. Her Bible Society pamphleteering stood in the path. He really didn't want a wife standing on a tenderloin corner, proselytizing the vicious. His own sense of God, wrought from a broad education, was less literalistic. He thought the biblical texts were inspired, but not necessarily without confusion, and not always applicable to all times and places. Indeed, there had been errors of translation from the Greek that had altered meanings. How could two souls with such diverse beliefs ever join?

That was what his mind said. But it was trumped by his heart. He could not even say what it was about her he adored so much: her spirited nature, bright eyes, carrot hair, chiseled face, wry smile, erect posture, grace under pressure, sheer generosity of soul, sensitivity to the plight of others, or the husky timbre of her voice that suggested a ruthlessly repressed sensuality she would be shocked to discover within herself. All that, and something more. He was simply drawn to her, and had been ever since she had ferociously pushed her way into Fort Mason to inform the callous army about the suffering Chinamen.

He smiled at the recollection. She had been hell-bent to remedy the problem, and heaven help any poor soldier who resisted.

She appeared at noon that last day, freshly scrubbed, her hair gleaming, her face all clouds and sunshine at once, her hand-me-down clothing worn with amazing grace. She was the sort who could make rags look elegant on her. It pleased him that she had gone to great lengths to make herself attractive on this, their last meeting. That was the paradox: She was unavailable; she was romancing him. In some women, it would have been teasing. In her, it was only innocence, and something that lay unresolved in her heart—perhaps fear.

"Ginger," he said. "You're beautiful."

"Skin deep," she replied.

Already she was deflecting his compliments, and he knew she would deflect anything more serious that day. But why had she done herself up? She had even borrowed lilac cologne, and now it caught in her hair and trailed in her wake.

He led her into the officers' mess, drawing the usual stares from his envious colleagues, and sometimes from their wives as well. This day, the bachelors left them alone. Most days, they patrolled his table.

"Well, have you heard?" he asked, once they were seated.

"Yes. They have no money to help me, and think it is not a good idea for me to go east."

His heart lifted. "And—?"

She made a small moue. "I'm going anyway. My work here is finished."

"Why do you say that?"

She faltered briefly. "I have nothing to do now."

"What about your family?"

"I didn't hear from them."

"Maybe the time isn't right. 'To everything there is a season, and a time to every purpose under the heaven . . .' "

She laughed.

That lunch did not go easily. Paul waited for her to finish eating—she was only toying with her food anyway—to say things on his mind.

He took coffee; she didn't. She never touched it and said it stimulated the body, which was wrong.

"Ginger, I'm going to talk about myself a little. I've been a commissioned officer for six years, and am still a second lieutenant, and there is little hope of advancement in a peacetime army starved for funds. I worked long and hard to get where I am. Some people think all officers come from West Point, but that's not the case. I'm not one of the elite. Actually, I'm a scholar, and I love military history. I was heading in that direction, waiting for a chance to work within the War Department in a scholarly field.

"But now I'm not sure. I'm tugged in another direction. I've thought often about becoming an army chaplain. Resign active duty, go to a seminary, and then see about returning."

"You? Why, Paul?"

He grinned. "Because ministering to men who make war is the thorniest of all religious professions. You and I both like a challenge."

"I never considered what I do a challenge."

"Well, that's what I admire in you. An army chaplaincy is a challenge. What do you say to men who seek God's protection before marching into war? What do you say to men who are about to kill other men who believe God is protecting *them*? And what if you—or those you minister to—believe that they are about to fight an unjust war? And what do you say to men who dread wounds, pain, disease, and death—which are inherent in their vocation? Or whose duty requires them to kill, maybe even kill noncombatants and inflict wounds and hardship and pain on others? And how is all that reconciled with the will of God? See what I mean? Thorny."

"You would do well at it, Paul."

"I'm not so sure. What would you say to soldiers?"

"That their fate is not in their hands, I guess."

"And thus not responsible for their own murderous acts?"

"I'm in over my head," she said.

He sipped coffee, curious about her. He knew he could never have her, and was slowly reconciling himself to that.

"More questions," he said. "You lived through this quake and all that followed, and you've watched human nature at work, the good and bad, firsthand. What did this do to people?"

"It brought out their natures, I think. Some people rushed to help others. Others were ruthless or cruel or selfish. It just exposed everyone's most private self. Some people weren't even aware of their natures until this happened. I think a lot of people will be aware now of how mean they really were—and are. They did receive vision."

"And was all this the work of God?"

"Do I think God caused the earthquake? No."

"The papers have been full of the opposite view. There are plenty of people in the country who think that this disaster was God's punishment on San Francisco for its wickedness."

"I saw innocent people die, Paul. Children."

"That didn't stop a lot of clergymen from saying it was God's punishment of this city. Especially across the South. They were dancing on San Francisco's grave. Some ministers rejoiced and praised God for his punishment of the wicked city. They celebrated!"

"Why are you asking me this?"

"Because you're leaving, and I'm curious, and I won't have the chance to ask you again."

She stared at the sunlit window. "When it happened, that Wednesday morning, my first thought was that this was God's punishment, his rod of iron. But almost the first person I came across in the street was a tearful woman whose little girl had died when a dresser landed on her. Then I stopped thinking the way I had—that here was the vengeance of an angry God, flaying a wicked city, destroying all its proud works, shaking it to its foundations, ruining its best citizens, consuming it in a pillar of fire."

"Like Sodom?"

"Worse! I thought maybe this time God was really scorching away evil. Four hundred fifty thousand people in a giant funeral pyre! But then I wandered among the suffering, and knew they were just ordinary people, people like me. I remembered the story of Sodom and Gomorrah. It's all there, in Genesis, you know. God promised Abraham He would spare the innocent. Angels led the innocent—Lot and his family—out of Sodom before destroying it. Only the wicked were punished. That's when I knew for sure that God did not cause the earthquake."

"Ginger, if that story weren't in the Bible, would you think the earthquake was God's punishment of San Francisco?"

"I don't know." She looked uncomfortable.

"I don't either," he said, "but I'm not inclined to worship a mean or petty God." The mystery, the will of God, the chastenings of God, the uses of adversity, the visions of justice and goodness given in moments of grief—all this was truly beyond his fathoming, no matter how much his orderly mind wrestled with the ultimate questions.

He wondered what it all meant—or whether an earthquake had any metaphysical meaning at all. It was beyond reckoning.

He sensed that she didn't want to pursue such things any further and he didn't either. He was experiencing an odd paradox: The more he conversed with her this final meeting, the more of a stranger she became to him. Why wasn't it the other way around? He had loved a chimera. They talked a while more, long after the luncheon crowd had vanished and the hall had turned quiet. And then the conversation died.

She excused herself. "I think I should prepare for my trip," she said. "So much to do."

He smiled. She had nothing left to do. "Yes, surely, Ginger."

"Thank you for everything, Paul. I will remember."

He nodded. She rose and he followed her slowly through the silent room and into the sun. He clasped her hands between his, and sought to kiss her, but she averted her head.

CHAPTER 65

Sergeant Major Jack Deal watched the massive door of the munitions bunker creak open, and sunlight extend itself along the damp cement floor. He forced himself to stand quietly, but in fact he was dripping sweat and had started to stink. Colonel Irwyn walked in, followed by Gregg and Tobin, their electric torches playing over barren floor, stonemasonry walls, and thick overhead beams. Deal had a wild impulse to slam the door shut and lock it and let them croak. No one would hear them.

It was a stupid idea.

But he stayed outside. He didn't want to go anywhere near those wooden munitions crates.

"Not much here," said one of the lieutenants.

"Some brass," Irwyn said. He picked up a shell case from one of the crates and examined it. "Been here a decade, I imagine."

"If there was anything in here, it's gone now," Tobin said. "We'll mark it empty. Gunners must've come looking, with all those tracks outside."

"I guess that does it," Irwyn said. "I just was curious."

"Lookit this," Gregg said. His torch threw a circle of light around a gold ring on the concrete. He picked it up. "Someone's wedding ring. Some initials. I can't make them out. We'll give it to Colonel Morris. Some poor gunner lost it."

He handed it to Irwyn who looked it over.

Deal stood outside, in agony. And then triumph. They had it all figured out.

"That's a small ring. Look, it doesn't even fit over my little finger," the bird colonel said. "A woman's ring." He walked out the door and into sunlight.

"I wonder," said Lieutenant Tobin. "Wait a bit."

Deal watched the damned shavetail swing back in, his light playing around those crates. Then the lieutenant lifted the empty brass from one of the crates, one layer, two, and then stopped.

"Colonel!"

Deal sighed. There it all went. Because he had left that key on his ring.

The three officers stared. Gregg began tearing empty brass out of the other crates. One, then another, then the rest.

"I'll be damned," one muttered.

Deal resisted a wild impulse to run, run and never turn around. "Something wrong, sirs?" he asked.

"Come in here, Sergeant."

Deal reluctantly entered, smelling his own armpits in that close air.

"Who has access to this bunker?" Irwyn asked.

"No one, sir."

"You do. The key's on your ring."

"Didn't know it was there, sir."

The colonel stared. "Give me that key ring, sergeant."

Unhappily, Deal turned it over. "Lots of keys, sir. Base commanding officer has a complete set, and so do all the Coast Artillery officers and the quartermaster officers."

"But you told us this bunker was abandoned."

"I don't think anyone's been in here for a decade or two."

"Or anyway, since the fires."

"I'd say seven, eight years, sir. Probably not since the Spanish war."

Tobin was pawing through the crates, pulling apart the oilcloth wrappings. He whistled. "Colonel, there's jewelry, silver service, some altar items, including a gold crucifix and silver chalices, some miniature art, some silver pocket watches. This is all loot. It's from all sorts of places, including churches, homes, jewelry stores, galleries . . . Look at this; a tiara with rubies, sapphires, and diamonds. My God!"

The officers huddled over the loot, lifting it, studying it, poking into each crate.

"I'll get a truck and an armed escort, sir. We'll need to inventory this," Tobin said. "There must be a fortune, all of it from quake victims."

"Yes, go on back to Colonel Morris on the double."

Lieutenant Tobin raced off.

"Well," said Irwyn, "if this is loot, someone's going to pound rocks in the stockade the rest of his life. We'll find out who had access to these bunkers. That'll narrow the suspects down to a handful. I'm afraid Colonel Morris and General Funston won't like to hear about this. Civilians have been howling for weeks about looting, but General Funston's dismissed all the complaints. If anyone was looting, it was the California National Guard or those auxiliary police running around the city." He sighed. "But they don't operate from the Presidio. This is Regular Army." He turned to Deal. "We'll lock this for the moment and wait for help."

"I can post guards. That's my responsibility. I'll call up some non-coms and post 'em here."

"No, Sergeant, that won't do," Irwyn said. His piercing gaze raked Deal. The corners of the colonel's lips tightened into hard lines.

The wait became an eternity. They stood outside the brush-choked bunker while afternoon sun and playful breezes toyed with their hair, and then the truck drew up. A squad of armed men dropped off the rear, and under Irwyn's direction began loading the crates of loot.

A few minutes later the crates rested on a conference table in Colonel Charles Morris's headquarters. Deal stood silently while Irwyn reported the discovery.

Morris turned to his adjutant. "Round up every set of keys for those bunkers. That will tell the tale," he said. The adjutant trotted off.

"Sergeant Deal, what do you know about this?" the commanding officer asked.

"Nothing, sir."

"Colonel Irwyn says you were reluctant to explore that bunker and argued that it was out of use."

"Of course, sir. A waste of time."

"Yes, a waste of time."

Deal felt eyes upon him. Half the officers on duty were present, eyeing him, eyeing Deal's own key ring, now in the CO's hand. He was sweating again, rank wetness under his armpits, on his brow. He'd get out of this. They didn't have a shred of evidence. He cursed himself for not ditching the key. That's all he had to do. Ditch that key.

"Do any enlisted men or noncoms have access to the bunkers, Sergeant?"

"None that I know of, unless one stole a key and had it duplicated. I think that's what happened, sir."

"Who would you suspect?"

"No one, sir."

"A noncom, wouldn't you say?"

The colonel had a point and there was no use denying it.

"I think a noncom was involved, sir. I would check the California National Guard, too."

"We will check everyone, Sergeant. This had to be the work of many men. A ring. A systematic pillaging of property after civilians had been driven out and before fire destroyed it all. A perfect time to loot. But this"—he waved at the awesome wealth lying on the table, chairs, and floor—"this was the work of many. I hope they weren't men in my command. If it was, I will prosecute them relentlessly."

The adjutant returned with seven key rings, each in a manila envelope, and set them on the CO's desk.

"Colonel Irwyn, show us which key opened that abandoned bunker, if you would."

The colonel swiftly fingered the key.

"All right, we will see whether there's a match."

It took awhile. Deal's key was carefully compared to each key in each ring. Each ring was different. Coast Artillery officers had keys only for the bunkers they used. Field Artillery officers held keys only for howitzer ammunition. Jack Deal watched his fortunes diminish as one by one, key rings were eliminated.

It ended up as Deal knew it would. His ring was the only one that contained all the keys. Not even the post command's ring included a key to the abandoned bunker.

All the eyes in the room studied Sergeant Major Deal.

"Do you have an explanation, Sergeant?" Morris asked.

"Yes, sir. During the fires, I lent this ring to various artillerymen several times. They needed munitions; their officers weren't in sight. There was no time. Any one of them could have made use of the key."

"You will provide us with a complete list of those you say you lent the keys to. We will check every one. Please name them."

This was getting tough. Deal's gut roiled. "Hard to remember, sir. It was an emergency."

"It would be advisable for you to remember."

"I'll put together a list this evening, sir."

"Did you lend the keys to infantry- or artillerymen?"

"Artillerymen, sir. I don't know them by name. Seen them around."

"Bull. Your ring. Who was in it?"

"Ring, sir?"

"Deal, it might go easier on you if you spill it all out. We'll find out anyway. We'll learn who your cronies are, and we'll start with them. If you cooperate, I'll consider recommending a reduced sentence. But, by God, we'll find out. We have our ways and we'll use them. We'll break someone."

It would be Nils. He never took pain well, and whined a lot. Deal sighed, weighing his options.

"You're confined to quarters, Sergeant Deal. When you're ready to talk, we'll listen. We'll be doing an inventory nonstop all evening. No matter how long it takes, we'll list every item in a ledger before a one of us retires. Maybe we can return some of these things to their owners. Damn you, Deal. Stealing from churches. Stealing off corpses. Stealing from homes and stores. Right here, under my nose, in my command, in my United States Army!"

Confined to quarters! That was good news. By dawn they'd be looking for Jack Deal, but he would be en route to China or Timbuktu, or someplace.

"Adjutant, take the sergeant to his quarters. Process him. Empty his pockets. No . . . on second thought, lock him up. Lock him and throw away the key."

The someplace would be the stockade.

CHAPTER 66

Willis Hart managed to get a few things done during his stay at General Hospital, even though his head throbbed. He had Nella wire Waterford Insurance, report his whereabouts and injury, and seek instructions. A response came swiftly. The company was setting up temporary offices in Oakland. Hart was to report there as soon as he was able, and then return to work as an adjuster. His colleague, Orval Yerkes, who had managed the former office, was already in Oakland dealing with claims that even then were starting to flood in. As soon as officials allowed people back in the city—they were turning away anyone who did not have urgent reasons to enter San Francisco—Hart was to commute by ferry to San Francisco each day, examine insured properties, and report. A full list of such properties was en route to Oakland because all San Francisco records had been destroyed.

When Willis received that word, he sighed. He and Nella had not had a minute together. And now the company wanted him back on the job the moment he was able. But there was good in all this. He had a paycheck coming soon, a source of cash. He even had some back pay due. Suddenly the great crisis was over and things were returning to normal. For days they had lived on the edge, by their wits, never knowing what would happen, every moment a challenge—and suddenly the horizon promised only the humdrum. He found himself facing the prosaic with less relish than he had faced disaster.

The next day, Nella bravely sailed across the bay, explained matters to Yerkes, and returned with twenty dollars in cash. "He wasn't very happy about it," she said. "And he didn't trust me. But he gave it to me anyway."

General Hospital discharged him the following day, telling him to stay quiet if possible. Suddenly he and Nella were homeless again. As long as he didn't exert himself, his head was all right; mostly a background pain that didn't bother him except late in the day. But he was weak and nauseous.

Some honeymoon.

They could stay in the Presidio. The steady outflow of people, plus the influx of new tents and supplies, meant that shelter was available but in tents still jammed with refugees. The company didn't expect him back until he was well, and not until he could commute into the ruined city. He and Nella could be stuck there for days, maybe weeks.

"Nella," he said. "I can't stand this place another hour. Let's go. We need a place."

"But where, Willis?"

"Camping. Just you and me."

"But you're so sick."

"I'll make it." He wasn't so sure. His head was tightly bandaged, he couldn't walk more than a few yards, and nausea dogged him.

"The Southern Pacific ferries to Sausalito and Tiberon are running, Nella. And they're still free for refugees. Let's go."

"Oh, Willis. I can't stand this place. I'll help you. We'll go."

"We have to get to the Hyde Street Pier. And the only way to do it is walk," he said. "But I'm game."

So they walked. At first he doubted that he could make it, but he kept on. He wanted so badly to escape from San Francisco that his need impelled him. Nella half supported him when he faltered. She carried a flour sack with some clothing; he carried two blankets.

They reached the pier, boarded a ferry, and got off at Belvedere Terminal. The area was crowded with refugees, but something was palpably different. This was not the stricken city. Buildings stood, though some had been damaged and various windows were broken. Commerce flourished. Hacks waited for customers. Groceries purveyed goods. Telegraphs and telephones were available. Electric lights shown in buildings. It seemed miraculous. A few miles away, a death-pall hung over an empty city. Here . . .

"Oh, Willis," she said. "I'm so glad we came."

He felt so worn that he slumped onto the nearest stretch of grass, and let his dizziness pass, while Nella scouted. He knew what he wanted—if the twenty dollars would cover. He wanted a honeymoon, sacred and private, in a redwood grove. Would the twenty dollars buy a honeymoon?

That was exactly what Nella was ascertaining. He left it to her. She had been uncomplaining, but subdued. Whatever misgivings she had about marriage, him, the future, she had buried within herself. In fact, she had become something of a mystery to him, and she seemed more a stranger than when they met. He wondered whether their impulsive marriage would last.

But he intended to try. He adored her and he would give her the best life he could. He was uncertain what she wanted, what she dreamed of beyond a father for her child. Maybe, if they could find a grove in the redwoods, and achieved their first intimacy of soul and body there, she would confide in him.

He felt old. It was as if the earthquake, the fire, the forced labor in a burial detail, the days and hours and minutes of uncertainty, hunger, thirst, cold, fear, dread, had stolen his youth from him. He had read of men whose hair had turned white after an ordeal. He didn't think that would happen to him; it was his soul that had aged. Not his body.

He rested quietly, his eyes closed because seeing evoked pain in his skull. Then he felt her hand on his.

"Willis, I want you to meet this man," she said.

He found himself staring up at an ancient and toothless old gent, the last wisps of his hair hanging to his collar.

"McAvoy," he said. "Lady tells me you're needful. I'm making a small income helping refugees."

Willis struggled to his feet and beheld a man radiating innocence from rheumy blue eyes. Willis wondered how he had arrived at that notion. How could anyone exude innocence? Maybe it was a con man's ploy.

"My wife and I are just off the ferry. We wish to camp for a few days, alone, in the redwoods. Our means are limited."

"Oh, ho! You've come to the right bloke! I've a wagon, and some canvas for a shelter, and ye can load up hither"—he waved a languid blue-veined hand at a grocery—"and I know just the place. Fact is, I know lots of places. Groves are crawling with refugees, but I'll find ye a spot."

"We're honeymooning," said Nella.

"I knew it! I spotted it. You wear it like a war medal. Well, you leave it to McAvoy."

"Ah, what is this going to cost us?"

"Three dollars each way, and I'll just throw in the canvas and some gear. Ax, skillet, stuff like that. Need a two-dollar deposit on all that. You got yourself hurt in the quake, eh? Now who'm I dealing with?"

Willis remembered his manners, and introduced Nella and himself.

An hour later Willis and Nella found themselves jolting along in a springless dray, through a late-afternoon peace. McAvoy's route took him south of the eastern peak of Mount Tamalpais, which rose gloomily, lit by the dying sun. The jolting troubled Willis's head, but it didn't matter. What counted was that he and his bride were out of the stricken city, piercing deeper into a silent, spice-scented wild, the majestic redwoods about them, ancient sentinels of well-being and peace, trees that had endured for centuries, surviving fire and storm and pests, their height so great that the hilly land under them seemed like an open park.

They passed several campsites, each the haven of refugees, but McAvoy kept on until he reached an empty glen with a tiny spring at its head.

"This do?" he asked.

It would do. The aching peace touched Willis. The last of the sun filtered through the crests of the noble trees high above. Below, where the wagon halted, blue night-shadow swiftly conquered the remaining light.

"I'll unload ye, then I'll skedaddle. Need a little daylight for the first mile, and after that it don't matter."

McAvoy gallantly unloaded everything, and even strung up a stout half-shelter on a pole lashed between a pair of saplings. Ample dry firewood littered the grassy ground. Nella gathered it while Willis cleared the ground under the half-shelter, filled a jar with spring water, unrolled blankets, and organized the camp.

"See you in a week, then, early in the morning," McAvoy said, and turned the dray home. Willis and Nella watched him go, and then the silence enveloped them, along with the high pungent scents of the coastal pines, and the eddies of night air mixing with the day's warmth, and the spongy carpet of brown needles under their feet. This was real; San Francisco had been a mirage.

He turned to Nella and drew her to him. She responded eagerly in the silence of the lavender twilight, clasping him to her gently, as if he were porcelain and she was afraid he would break. They were alone, amid a natural world that nurtured them, and Willis rejoiced. He drew strength from her embrace, from her gentle hands as she caressed his neck, ran a hand lightly over his bandaged head, discovered his shoulders and arms, and kissed his lips.

Desire welled through him, so powerful it could not be denied, and yet there was something else, small, sweet, unbidden, and soulful.

"Nella," he whispered. "This is deliverance. We have been lifted out of chaos and ruin, and placed here like Adam and Eve, alone with each other."

"I know," she whispered. "This is the first moment of peace and joy I've had for—ever since the earthquake."

He held her gently, prolonging the moment. The feelings that were flooding him now needed voice.

"Nella, my beloved, let me tell you first that I love you. I'm the luckiest man on earth. You came to me in the midst of disaster, your needs as large as mine. But this wasn't only a bargain—it was so much more. We haven't had a moment together, even though we've been married for days, so I just want to say it again: You are my wife, to have and to hold, and I will always cherish you."

Her response was a hug, so warm and surrendering that she melted into him and turned him to wax. He had never known such a hug, not even in his dreams. It was more than an embrace. It was a giving, a surrender, an entrusting, and a commingling of breath and heart and soul. Now he understood the sweet mystery of marriage, and the idea that within it, two would be made one. As he held her, and she held him, the utter beauty of that embrace, and her freely given love, and the bright promises of sweet tomorrows, and the end of loneliness, lifted his spirits until they soared above him, through the towering redwoods that guarded their bower.

"I will be the best wife I know how, and the best lover I know how, and the best friend I know how," she said. Then she laughed softly. "Willis, I'm going to have a baby and I sure needed a husband in a hurry. I guess you needed a wife in a hurry. Aren't you glad there was an earthquake?"

He laughed softly, and she laughed, and then they forgot about everything.

CHAPTER 67

The days stumbled by. Harrison White scrubbed toilets, washed dishes, scoured floors, boiled laundry, an unending stream of menial chores from six each morning to six each night. After each watch he dropped into his hammock, too dispirited to do anything but sleep. He ignored the camaraderie of his bunkmates in the forecastle, and supposed he had nothing in common with them anyway. His whole universe had shrunk to the confines of a miserable iron freighter plowing the Pacific.

For days, self-pity engulfed him. His life, his genius, his career had been brutally ended. Sometimes he slid into rage. He would get his revenge. He'd knock Stern over the head and toss him into the sea. A life for a life. He'd give Larson a shove some moment and feed him to sharks. He'd bide his time and report this outrage to maritime authorities, put Stern in trouble. But time and toil and the sea dulled that, and he settled into sullen labor, his helplessness manifested in the rails that surrounded the main deck. That's where his entire world ended.

Sometimes he caught Stern, or Larson, watching him, amusement in their hard faces. They were cruel men, laughing at the misfortune of another mortal—misfortune at their own hands. Even as the nautical miles and leagues slid past the stern, he schemed and plotted. A knife! He'd steal one. He needed a weapon. Some of the seamen had taken to abusing him: a little shove of the shoulders when they passed, or crowding ahead of him in the mess line. They were daring him to do something about it, fight, bloody his nose, but White held himself aloof, saying nothing, not even when one or another seaman opened conversation about weather, or the porpoises playing off the bow, or the frigate birds in the rigging, or the dice games, or the tobacco that all the seamen, it seemed, cherished so much.

But overriding everything else in White's mind was black despair. He should be in Oakland, designing the new San Francisco, its boulevards and commercial buildings, its gracious homes and fountains and parks. He should be telling Marcia and the children about his magnificent future. But then his fantasies would halt, and he would see his claustrophobic new world, the foul heads he scrubbed, the decks he swabbed and sometimes scoured with holystone, the mountain of cracked white pottery he washed in the galley, the vats of foul clothing he scrubbed and rinsed.

Then they put him in the engine room, and he never saw daylight, or the mysterious horizons of the sea, or sun-sparked swells of the benign Pacific. He learned his mechanic's and fireman's trades fast. On those days when Stern chose to steam, White shoveled coal, carrying a heavy scoop of it from bunker to firebox, and dancing close, against blistering heat, to heap the fuel into the flaming maw. The roar deafened him. The fire roared, the steam-pistons thundered, the steam hissed, the bells from the bridge rattled his skull, and everything shivered and vibrated under him, so that oilcans and spare parts rattled on racks. He eyed the piston engines with contempt. The old boat didn't even have modern turbines in it. He wasn't a naval architect, or even a mechanical engineer, but he could show them a thing or two!

Feeding the firebox was even more brutal than scrubbing down the heads. The noise wrought swift and endless headaches, while the heat sometimes seared his eyebrows and scorched his face. He wore gloves against the ferocity of the firebox, but that didn't help the rest of his tormented body. If he slacked his work, the other fireman glared at him, or quit shoveling altogether, leaning on his scoop shovel, bemusement in his face.

He discovered purpose in Stern's conduct. The master used steam only when the wind failed him, and was bearing ever southward to reach the subtropics with their easterly trade winds. The day came when a soft, steady east wind blew across the sea, and then Stern unfurled the canvas, the *Manitou* rode ever west and south across the empty aching sea. During those times, he was assigned to work with the chief engineer repairing the twin engines, sealing leaks in the steam pipes, rebuilding salt-corroded valves, shoveling coal from one bunker to another. The crew stared at him, saying nothing.

He counted each bitter endless day. His bunkmates harassed him. He had disdained them, held himself aloof, and they had waited to see whether he would become one of them. And when he didn't, things began going wrong. One day something in his coffee made him sick, and Larson glared at him as if he were malingering. His clothes mysteriously fell apart, and White had to draw new ones from ship's stores—for a price against his wage.

He loathed them. They were all apes. They weren't even generous enough to leave him alone. But when he complained to Larson, he received no sympathy.

"White, a ship's a small hard place where men rub shoulders every moment. If you're not getting along, they'll let you know. You offend them. Maybe you'll learn something before you get into worse trouble. If not, no one can help you."

The beginning of his second month in captivity found him on the equator, sweating at every task. The *Manitou* had slid into the Southern Hemisphere, and something was stirring in White, seeking form. When it came to him at last, he gloated. He corralled Larson at the taffrail, in a moment when they were out of earshot.

"Mr. Larson," he began, "what I want to do is master every station, every position, on this ship. I have in mind making a future for myself in shipping, climbing the ladder. I'd like to become a helmsman, maybe a mate, maybe a master someday. I'm a man of ambition. What I'd like is for you to put me in each slot for a few days."

Larson studied him, and then stared at the bubbly wake boiling behind the stern. Then he faced White, his face a mask. "Takes years to become a seaman, much less someone skilled enough to be set in authority, or steer the ship. You know what a helmsman faces in a typhoon? Of course not. Benzel, up there, he's wrestled with more hurricanes and big blows than you'll ever know."

"That's just the point, sir. He's a great helmsman, and you're a fine officer, and if I can master these skills, then my future will brighten."

"Brighten, White?"

"Yes, sir. I can bring some skills and intelligence to this ship if I'm given a chance."

Larson smiled darkly, said nothing, and stared once again at the wake.

White wasn't discouraged. He would become a management man and escape that miserable forecastle with all its glowering apes. If that meant climbing the rigging for a day or two, learning how to riff a sail, he could manage that even though high places terrified him, and walking out a spar required the agility of a monkey. He just needed to know the routine so he could go on to better things. He wasn't set upon this earth to be an ordinary seaman. He'd turn himself into an officer, enjoy his own quarters, make Stern's responsibilities easier, and be someone. He had to be *someone*.

Larson did nothing. White continued to toil in the bowels of the *Manitou*, under the charge of the surly engineer, servicing the cranky engines and drive shafts, fighting the corrosion that could swiftly render the power plant useless. He despised the chief, who swore long and bloody oaths, snarled whenever he spotted the slightest sign of rust or corrosion, and treated White like dirt.

But White's plan blossomed within him. He had made himself useful to the Committee of Fifty, and knew he had valuable connections that would count when the city began to rebuild. Well, he could do that here, in this miserable world. He would make himself invaluable to Stern.

But the captain rarely was in sight. He and his officers ate separately. Sometimes a seaman could see the captain high up, in the pilothouse, his brass telescope peering one way or another, while one of his men ran the sextant.

That was it. He would ask Stern to turn him into a navigator. In a few days he would be able to plot longitude and latitude with perfect ease, and after that he could enjoy good company, pleasant meals, life among the elite, and probably a raise in pay.

But Stern was a hard man to approach.

Each day the ship plowed the tropical sea, white haze blurring the horizons, the heat murderous and unbearable. The forecastle turned into a furnace, and White retreated to the deck at night, preferring the hard teak and clean breeze to his hammock in the stinking hold.

Then, at last, he discovered the captain alone, peering into the green sea.

"A word, sir?"

"White, take it to Larson. He's your boss."

"I have some ideas that'd help you, sir."

Stern turned, that dangerous gleam in his eyes, his rawboned face squinted up in the tropical glare.

"Sir, I'm interested in rising. I think I can be of service to you. Helmsman, navigator, junior officer, senior officer someday. What I have in mind, sir, is learning the ropes. A few days doing this, a few days doing that. Now, of course, that doesn't substitute for experience. I'm sure than any seaman on board would be better in the rigging than I, sir. But you see, it's only necessary for me to know what it is all about so that I can make intelligent decisions when I instruct the seamen.

"Now as an architect, I acquired the broadest education. I had to deal with all sorts of complex and sophisticated matters, ranging from structural problems to aesthetics to movement of people, to providing good working conditions and comfort. And technology—wiring, boilers, windows, everything. And freight, sir. Office buildings require a means to move equipment, furniture, all sorts of things, just the way a ship does.

"I can do that on board, sir. Become a part of the management of this ship and make your life easier. I'm sure I could learn navigation. I've deep experience in handling people—and could command naturally and easily, whenever you're retired. I had staff under me in my offices. And when I was with the Committee of Fifty during the crisis, we directed hundred of volunteers, and I was a personal assistant for Mayor Schmitz in the sphere of planning. Or I could become a helmsman, sir, following your instructions. There's nothing I couldn't do, if you would just put me on a company advancement plan. Just let me work at your side, and absorb your wisdom, and you won't regret it. I could make the sea and shipping and profits my life, sir."

White rejoiced. The captain had heard him out. The argument was compelling, and probably White would find his life much improved in a day or two. That's how the world worked, whether it was the world encased in a large city, or the smaller world on a freighter. Get to know the right people and help them.

The master grinned malevolently. "You're an important man, White. But not to me." He laughed, softly, then uproariously, and then wickedly.

"Get the hell to work, you lobster, and don't ever brace me again."

CHAPTER 68

atharine Steinmetz discovered a few refugees camped in Sonoma's spacious plaza, but other than that the tawny Mexican mission village was little changed by the disaster not far south. She supposed there would be no rooms anywhere, but she had understood that risk when she departed from the security of the Presidio. She could not endure that awful place an hour more, and would take her chances here, in this sleepy place.

She had a name in mind: Gilberto Mendoza. She had seen several gallery exhibits of his harsh photographs of the last remnants of traditional Californio culture in the area. Women in rebozos, with seamed faces and gnarled hands; children on burros, a humble *obrero* hoeing a garden. Some of these had been printed in sepia, but most were richly printed with brilliant whites and shadows, slightly exaggerated to emphasize the painfulness of the life he was capturing.

He was her one hope.

She had come this far in a hack she had hired at Belevedere. It had been a long hard ride down dusty lanes arched by eucalyptus, but eventually the driver wheeled into the slumbering plaza. Katharine rejoiced at the sheer normalcy of the place. No crisis lurked here. What little damage she could see had mostly been repaired. Street vendors were doing a lively trade.

"Find me the photographer, Gilberto Mendoza, please," she instructed her driver, a moon-faced youth earning a few dollars from her for the long drive.

"How do I do that, ma'am?"

"I cannot walk. You must ask."

He did stop and inquire at two or three places, and finally drove her past the crumbling mission and north a few blocks to a venerable tin-roofed casa with a white rail around its veranda.

"Please wait for me," she said, easing slowly to the hard clay. "If he is not here, I'll have you take me back to the plaza, and I'll pay you there."

The four dollars would cut deeply into what she had left. But she was here, and she exulted.

Slowly, leaning heavily on a cane she had found among the Presidio's relief supplies, she walked up two steps, crossed the worn plank veranda, and knocked.

A slender gray-haired Mexican woman answered.

"I'm looking for Gilberto Mendoza," she said.

The woman eyed Katharine carefully, and then smiled. *"Uno momento,"* she said.

Mendoza appeared, staring at Katharine through a bulging screen. She beheld a pear-shaped man in a dark suit, as well-dressed as a deacon on Sunday, his dark smudged eyes hidden behind thick lenses of rimless spectacles, the whole topped by wiry black hair.

"Mr. Mendoza, I've admired your work. I've seen two of your exhibitions in San Francisco . . ."

"Yes, thank you."

"I'm a photographer. My darkroom was destroyed in the quake. I'm hoping I might rent yours, and pay for supplies. It's my only living. . . ."

He peered owlishly at her and shook his head. "No, I cannot do that," he said in a sandpapery voice.

"But . . ." Discouragement washed through her. "You're my only hope."

"No, madam, a darkroom is an intimate place, more intimate than a boudoir. My equipment is very—*viejo*—old. The enlarger, it has a will of its own, and I am its only master. I spend years subduing this equipment. This place where I work, it is an adobe shed behind the casa. It has no running water. Bits of adobe fall down and ruin my developer and then I have no-good prints. I cannot control the temperatures. Some days it is too cold, some days too hot. No, this darkroom is a place only for Gilberto Mendoza."

She absorbed that, not yet ready to surrender. "Mr. Mendoza, if I cannot rent it, can I hire you to print some salon photos? I have the negatives. You print. I'll just watch."

He shook his head. "No, it cannot be. Two people cannot make one picture. A negative and print must come from the same artist. And we would soon be unhappy, the two of us in one darkroom. I would say, more contrast, and you would say, more gray shades, and then where would we be? I make my own art. I see the world through thick lens, and the light is harsh. You make your own art."

She bit back despair. "All right. You print them to your standards and I'll stay away. All right?"

He shook his head.

"Would you know of any other place—anyone—with a darkroom?"

"Santa Rosa," he said. "Two others I know of."

She absorbed that. Tiredness stole through her like one of Mendoza's sepia baths. "Is there any place a woman can stay?"

He shook his head. "It is very crowded here because of the refugees."

She surrendered. "I will try to find someone in the plaza who'll help," she said, and turned away.

Mrs. Mendoza had reappeared at the door. "What is your name?" she asked. "I will send for you if I learn of anything."

"Katharine Steinmetz."

"*Dios mio,*" said Mendoza. "It is the Katharine Steinmetz of San Francisco?"

Katharine's heart lifted. She nodded, wearily. The boy in the hack looked restless.

"You are the *esposa* of Emil Wolff?"

"He died just after the earthquake. Our flat was destroyed."

"Emil Wolff is gone? There is a loss. I am sorry."

"It was what he wished. That is my only solace. Some of my negatives are the last photographs of him. They show his last thoughts. You can see it in his eyes. I'm so desperate to print them. . . ."

"My humble darkroom is not good enough."

"It is good enough for you to print some of the most beautiful pictures Emil and I ever saw. That is how I came to you. Let the adobe fall into your fixer. It does not matter."

"Would you like some tea?" asked Mrs. Mendoza.

"I mustn't keep the boy waiting, so I'll say no."

"No, no, you come in. I will tell him to go."

"I must pay him his four dollars," Katharine said.

"That is a lot of money."

"He drove me all the way from Tiburon."

Katharine walked slowly to the hack, paid the moon-faced youth, collected her bundle, and watched him drive down the lane toward the decrepit mission. She wondered what would come of this. Gilberto Mendoza had not said yes.

They opened the wobbly screen door to her, and she found herself in a dark parlor, the windowsills painted blue, the walls white-plastered adobe and irregular. She felt a warmth rise from these old walls. She settled into a sofa, grateful to get off her feet. The sofa was a miracle. She had been weeks without a chair and the pleasure of sinking into one engulfed her.

"This was once a part of General Mariano Vallejo's estate," said Mrs. Mendoza. "It is old. We love it because it is still in the fashion of our people."

Mendoza settled in a high-backed chair that reminded Katharine of a throne. "Would you print for me the best portrait of Emil Wolff?" he asked. "We have one of his etchings. Mission Dolores. It is better than what a camera can do."

Katharine hesitated, uncertain about what he wanted.

"I have paper enough. I will give you paper. I will mix the chemicals. I will show you how to coax the enlarger. It is worse than a mule. If you do not treat it just so, it will do nothing. Sometimes it will not focus. Sometimes half a picture is in focus and half isn't."

"You'll have your portrait of Emil," she said.

"And you would sign it?"

"Of course."

"You are smiling, Mrs. Wolff."

"I am sitting in a sofa. You cannot imagine what it is like to go for weeks without sitting in a chair or a sofa, or lying in a bed."

"None of those?"

"None."

"The children take up all of our beds. But we will move Adelita—our oldest—to the sofa."

Katharine nodded, too choked to speak.

They printed deep into the night, the pair of them magically seeing her negatives with a single eye, so much so that they scarcely needed to speak. Was a corner of an image too light? He picked up the dodger. Would this one be better cropped tight?

"Ah, ha!" he would say, lowering the lens. She had to stand, and her knees tormented her but it didn't matter. This was a sacred place, an altar, and the pair of them were high priests and acolytes, and one by one the prints emerged in the developer while she swirled them gently with tongs, and then dropped them into a stop bath, and then into the fixer.

"*Dios mio,* what an image here, this family, the little girl with the birdcage, the boy with his puppy! Mama carrying a baby in a bundle and expecting another and looking all worn-out. Papa carrying a hatchet. Ah!"

She thought so, too.

He worked slowly, fussing with the lens and bellows of the enlarger, studying each plate for specks of dust, imperfections, telltale streaks. They reprinted some, exclaiming when they had conquered a problem— a hand that needed to be seen, a water-spot on a plate that transferred to the print.

She grew faint, not having eaten since morning, but they didn't cease and she didn't wish to. They didn't stop for supper, in spite of Maria Mendoza's entreaties, but around nine, they put the last of the plates taken the day of the earthquake into his homemade dryer, a glossy drum with a heater within and a canvas wrap to pin the wet prints in place.

They ate rice and beans. No meal had ever been so joyous.

At ten, they retrieved the prints, and examined them in the glare of the Mendozas' kitchen light. They were magic.

"I am in the presence of genius," whispered Mendoza. "These are the true bricks and mortar of a city. I have seen only ruins. Now I see what destruction really is. Every face—every eye—is the face of grief and terror and dread and death."

Katharine agreed. They were much her best work. In the morning she would carefully wrap and express them to Alfred Steiglitz, at the Photo-Secession group's gallery, the 291, at 291 Fifth Avenue, New York.

That night she had the best sleep of her life.

CHAPTER 69

The hiss of steam and the clang of metal greeted Ginger Severance as she stepped off the conductor's stool onto the grim platform of Union Station in Chicago. It wasn't a sweet symphony, nor were the rank odors of oil and steel and tar and steam a pleasant introduction to a great city. The muscular metropolis on the shore of Lake Michigan provided no comforts for weary travelers; only a long hike through a train shed to the terminal building.

But that was Chicago. Ginger had been there before. She worked her way through the echoing station with vaulted ceilings so high she could barely see them in the haze, and climbed more stairs until she reached street level. The station was just west of the Loop, and much of its business was commuter trains to the northern and western suburbs. But that was not where she was going.

She paused in the chill, moist air of May, orienting herself a moment. She fought back fear. She had only a few dimes. The American Red Cross, one of the relief societies springing up in San Francisco, had given her a carpetbag for her few clothes, and three dollars to feed herself en route to her destination.

She always wondered about Chicago. It swaggered. It never seemed a proper place for females. It seemed to have unusual numbers of immigrants, many of them gotten up in strange costumes, speaking in tongues she couldn't fathom. In some vague way they alarmed her.

But it was the city where the Panhurst Bible Society had headquartered itself, and that was why she had come. It was also the end of the line, as far as free or discount tickets for refugees of the San Francisco quake were concerned. She told herself not to be afraid; God would provide. But she was.

She walked eastward on Adams until she reached La Salle, and then south until she passed Polk. The street grew gamier with every block, with saloons wafting acrid beer odors into the sidewalk, cheek by jowl with warehouses and commission agents and heaven-knows-what-else. The Bible Society occupied a venerable brick building tarnished black by soot. God's work was being done from a nondescript structure that had long since failed to attract commercial tenants.

But that suited her just fine. A society entirely rooted upon voluntary contributions shouldn't waste a penny. She pulled the grimy brass handle of a brown-varnished door, and entered a gray world of tired marble and more strange odors. Chicago seemed to be the smelliest city on earth, something dank rising from every iron street grille within sight of the Loop. The Society occupied a suite on the third floor, barricaded behind unmarked pebbled glass doors as if its mission required anonymity. She climbed worn stairs fretfully, aware now that her reception might not be cordial.

She pushed open the door, and closed it quietly behind her, not wishing to make a racket. The silence within engulfed her. Was no living mortal within its confines? Was this dead heart of a great evangelical society really responsible for shipping hundreds of thousands of little tracts, printed on virtual tissue, to be handed out by an army of God's workers, such as herself?

"Hello?" she said. "Hello?"

"Oh, yes, sorry, in here," responded a reedy male voice. She knew that voice and the bespectacled owner of it.

She passed through a gloomy corridor to a gray-lit corner office, embalmed with a desk, oaken file cabinets, two wooden swivel chairs, and stacks of pamphlets, of which there were a dozen, each considered a step toward salvation. The Society instructed its street-missionaries to gauge which of the tracts would be most effective in each case, and then to use their discretion.

L. B. Carlton, general secretary, peered up at the apparition, a bit flustered. "I believe it is Miss Severance. What a pleasant surprise," he said, unsurprised.

Carlton had an aesthetic face—as if flesh didn't count, nor eyes, nor lips, nor nose. But the lips smiled and that seemed to be a welcoming, so she settled in the hard wooden chair across his dreary desk.

"Mr. Carlton, yes, it's Ginger."

His eyebrows skittered upward. "You're a long way from your station, Miss Severance."

"I have no station, sir. No dwelling, no street corner, no people. Money's vanished since the quake. Not a dime in anyone's pocket. Nothing to support me. It's a wasteland. Burned buildings and rubble, entirely without human life."

"Yes, of course, but that isn't what I really meant. Your station is the entire wounded city, God pity them all, so in need of the Word. The parks, the camps, the courageous soldiers, the overburdened hospitals, the generous toilers who distribute the relief supplies."

"I had no pamphlets, sir, as I've told you. They were burned. And people—well, they're more concerned about physical well-being just now. So I helped people. I got them food, I carried their packages, I comforted them. I got them into the hospital."

She knew that would draw a gentle admonition, and braced for it. Man does not live by bread alone. . . . But he just nodded and smiled.

She thought to get right to it. "I need a new assignment. And money to get there. And tracts to give away."

He frowned, steepling and unsteepling his hands, and finally he shook his head. "But we have no money. We're quite in arrears to our printers. I wish you'd stayed there and helped us."

"I had reasons to leave."

"Well, I suppose you've prayed and meditated this, and so I must accept it," he said, magnanimously. "But it seems—a bit precipitous."

She sighed, not happy. She had hoped for some commendation. She had braved the tenderloin for years, introduced the most desolate and vicious people on earth to the Word of God. She knew God loved

her for it, but now she ached for just some small commendation from
L. B. Carlton.

"I'm in your hands, Mr. Carlton. What shall I do?"

He sighed. "I don't suppose there's free fare back; just away from
the disaster. We can't afford to send you back."

"I could work here, sir. This is a big and hungry city."

"You could. We need workers on every corner. But you'd have to
find means."

"I survived out there with an alms box."

He smiled. "Perhaps you could here, but I doubt it. What I'd suggest is that you find employment, and then work for us on your weekly
day off."

"Employment?"

"Yes, a shopgirl, something like that. Carson, Pirie, or Marshall
Field's or such a place. Get a room, share with others. Then you could
help us evenings and Sundays."

She felt somehow as if her life were sliding away from her, and her
options were narrowing down to nothing. "I see," she said.

"Now, if you lack means for a few days, I can arrange something
temporary. We're close to the rescue-mission people, you know,
They've a few cots set aside for women. No charge at all, and after you
get a pay envelope, you could find a nice little place within walk of the
Loop. I'd head south, myself. Lots of rooms just south."

"You won't send me anywhere?"

"The crop is ripe for harvest, but the workers are few," he said.
"Shall I call?"

"I didn't really wish to become a shopgirl."

"Ah, ah, Miss Severance. We should take our example from St. Paul,
who supported himself as a tentmaker all his evangelical life. And besides, you'll be an example and an inspiration to all the other shopgirls.
And as soon as you're ready, you pop in here and we'll set you up with
some tracts. I've had a hankering to put one of our people on the steps
of the Chicago Art Institute. These are godless people, you know. You'd
be embarrassed to see what hangs there, especially the exhibitions
from France."

"Yes, sir," she said.

"Here, now, let me ring up the mission," he said. He plucked up
his telephone, gave a number to the operator, and swiftly made
arrangements.

She should have felt relieved. She would have a cot in a small dor-
mitory. There would be soup and bread if she needed it.

The interview grounded to a swift, sad halt. She wondered why she
had come such a distance, and what she had expected. It had been un-

realistic to expect anything. She was one of only a handful of women who braved the streets to hand out literature. The Society didn't encourage women to do it.

She stepped into a sullen afternoon, weary from the long train ride—free passage didn't include Pullman accommodations—and felt the city clamp her in its jaws. Here her options had narrowed and her dreams unraveled. She knew that a shopgirl's life was a trap, the subsistence pay permitting nothing, barely even a phosphate at a soda fountain, and a shopgirl's only hope was being found and courted by some male customer, and whisked away to a better life.

The thought frightened her. She didn't know where all her fears had come from. They had always risen up, a stranglehold on her heart, in the presence of a desirable man. Paul had frightened her, and she didn't know why. He had been a model of decorum and decency, and yet he had looked at her with that male look—she always registered that certain look in the eyes of males—and then she fled. Why, oh why, had she fled him? She could scarcely imagine a kinder and more delightful man. But she had. He had only to touch her, peck her cheek with his lips, and something curdled within her, something she couldn't resist.

Was it her father? Had the well-driller inflicted something upon her? She knew he hadn't. But he had wanted another son to help him in his business, where brawn counted so much. And that sometimes made her feel useless. But that wasn't it at all. He had never made her afraid. She simply feared men who courted. No, that wasn't quite it either. She feared the courtship. She feared—intimacy? She could hardly imagine physical intimacy. But that wasn't it either. She didn't know what it was. She knew only that she had to flee Paul, that she couldn't bear his love, or her own for him. She wondered what it might be like to hug him, engulf him in her arms—but the very thought troubled her, and even wrought nausea within her. What on earth was the matter with her?

She couldn't fathom the unfathomable. Some facets of her soul were simply mysteries to her. She was a paradox. She had braved the roughest streets in the world, and yet tenderness with Paul Boswell alarmed her. This was not new. She had been disappointed in herself ever since growing up. And nothing had changed since then. But she would accept whatever came. She would start applying, and soon she would have a position. Shopgirls came and went; there was always a job.

She took heart. There was always reason to rejoice. Shopgirls fell into temptation, but she would be working beside them, ever ready to comfort one or another, joyously placing a tract in the hand of a woman who needed it. Yes! This, too, was God's will. She would find employment, and then bless each and every person she met. This was her life, and she would be true to her calling. She hurried along the streets of the Windy City, every step in the service of her Lord.

And yet every step drove her to the edge of an old, familiar abyss. She was so lonely. She had always been lonely. She had stood on the street corners of the world, awash in her loneliness. She had lived in her tiny room alone, made no friends in San Francisco, joined no church, attended no meetings, talked with no one at all—except to pass out a tract. She had fended off every man and woman who had tried to befriend her. And now she walked alone along a lonely street, amid strangers who didn't care, toward a lonely bed in a lonely rescue mission. She would find a lonely job, somehow live alone, shunning company, shunning men and courtship, shunning the shopgirls she would soon be encountering. She thought sometimes that she could not endure another day so alone, so starved for companions and love. If only someone would just hold her hand, just walk beside her so she wouldn't feel so desperately alone.

She trudged toward the Chicago Rescue Mission, where succor awaited, and hoped no one saw her tears. She should rejoice. She had done the right thing. She would toil in a department store, and toil for God, and pretty soon she would not weep for Paul Boswell anymore.

CHAPTER 70

The Devereaux family's way of celebrating the divorce was to throw a ball at the Shaker Heights Country Club. Let proper families regard divorce as a scandal; that wasn't how Marcia White's mother and father looked at it.

"Now we've something to celebrate," her mother announced. "A most valuable surgery. Cut the tumor out, that's what we did. The party will inform the world that the family is intact after a slight illness."

"He's the children's father, and we shouldn't be celebrating," Marcia said. She had misgivings about a party intended to celebrate a divorce. She regarded divorce as defeat.

"Tut, tut. Bad genes. I hope it doesn't ruin the little dears."

"I mean, they should learn to love and respect him. Someday he'll return and want to see them."

Her mother cackled.

Her father's approach was slightly different. "We've got to line up some beaux. About a dozen bachelors willing to pursue an experienced and attractive young beauty with a pair of cubs."

"But I don't really need any beaux. I'd be quite content just to paint a little and look after my babies."

Drake Devereaux stared grimly at Marcia. "No beaux, eh? This is worse than I thought. You are not yet thirty, and yet you pine for grass widowhood."

"No, Daddy, it's just that this takes getting used to."

"Well, try on a few men for size."

There were frequent moments among the Devereaux family when Marcia could either retreat or laugh. She laughed.

The divorce had slid through the court without the slightest impediment. Melvin Moulton, Esq., had presented His Honor with a well-wrought desertion case, evidence of scores of advertisements placed in periodicals all over California, evidence that the rascal had been alive and well after the quake and fire, and loitering around City Hall; evidence that the scoundrel had always neglected his pining wife, and had heinously abandoned her to her own devices the day of the quake; and evidence that what he so cavalierly called working for his family was nothing more than self-aggrandizement.

She got her divorce and a fat judgment. If she could ever collar the wayward architect, she could dig deep into his bank account. But until then, she owed a heap of legal bills—or rather, owed her father for them. That porcupine of a lawyer didn't come cheap.

The family made great sport of Harrison, and celebrated as if she had just won the Paris Grand Prix. She couldn't help but enjoy the tart comments and ribald humor—she had grown up with it—and yet it wasn't so easy. She had loved and lost, second fiddle to blueprints. His career had been the important thing. Wives and children were ancillary comforts, but nothing he couldn't do without—as he was now demonstrating. She knew the world was full of Harrisons, and next time—if indeed she did have a suitor—she would be alert and careful. She hadn't the foggiest idea of why he had abandoned her; she knew only that he had. She had not seen him since the day after the quake.

The party had progressed to the point of printing invitations, when Marcia put a stop to it. Celebrating the divorce was only half of what her father had in mind. The other half included inviting every eligible bachelor in Cleveland. He would put her on display, a sort of second coming-out, and hope some dandy would cart her off.

"Please stop this," she said to him in his lair. "I won't attend. I don't wish to celebrate a tragedy, and I don't wish to be put on display like some prize cow."

He feigned surprise. He was good at feigning whatever he chose to feign. She could always tell when he was pretending because his expressions and gestures would be exaggerated.

"Why! Marcia, what you need is a real man, and the party is just the way to let the world know. They don't come knocking unless you advertise. Wouldn't you say that Harry and Daisy need a real father?"

"Yes, they do. But I intend to take my time, and I don't wish to celebrate what I regard as a loss."

She knew there was something in her tone that told him she was an adult woman, ready to make her own decisions, and no longer was she an unmarried daughter whose will might be bent by the paterfamilias.

He set down his *Plain-Dealer* and peered at her gently. "Yes, of course, Marcia. If it doesn't suit you, we'll stop it."

"Please do."

"Have you anything in mind? I mean, by way of a miserable dried-up spinster life?"

She laughed at him, and he smiled slyly. "Yes," she said. "I think I was on my way to becoming a fine portraitist. I would like to find out whether I can, or can't, while my life settles down."

He nodded. "While you see whether Harrison'll be found and pay you the judgment."

She grinned.

"And that means a little interim financing."

One thing about Drake Devereaux, when he got the idea, he also got all the implications.

She nodded.

"Art is for Bohemians. You can't make a nickel at it, except now and then. But those flush moments are few and the long broke stretches go on and on. You'd be better off marrying. You have children to support."

"I'd like to finish my schooling. Then I could make a living."

He stared. "You're saying you wish to return to the Ecole des Beaux Arts."

She nodded.

"And live in Paris with your children, who would require a governess."

She nodded.

He set down the newspaper, glanced out the window at the cloudy sky, and finally addressed her.

"It'd be a pinch, but we could manage it. But I'd rather not. You've married and had children, who are your responsibility to nurture and bring up. That was all your decision when you married Harrison."

He looked uncomfortable, and she suddenly realized what was coming.

"I don't think I will," he said. "Not even if we could manage it. You know, we're pretty fortunate, always enough money floating around so that we all pretty much do what we wish. I make a pretense at being an academic, a lecturer. Your mother specializes in being scandalous, and I've picked up that vice. Bad habit, you know. We plunge into society to titillate it, which could hardly be a less rewarding enterprise. So I'm a poor one to be discussing wise living with you. I'm just an old fool, trying to manufacture quips.

"But, Marcia, money's serious. And so is remaining dependent on your parents. I just don't like the idea of shipping you and your children off to France for another bout of schooling."

"I would like to go."

"I'm sure you would, but that's the easy way out. Where will it lead? You'll have a grand time, of course. But will you become another Mary Cassatt? I certainly hope you will. But you have children to consider. Money is certainly the crux of the matter. You need some, and that may mean remarrying, even if your dreams are otherwise, even if you'd love to return to your youth."

She hadn't expected that. If there was one thing that characterized her family, it was the relentless pursuit of whatever was inspiring them at the moment.

"The ball was a bad idea," he said. "Atrocious and insensitive. That's what I've come to—anything to shock the world. I can do better than that. I'm glad you put a stop to it, Marcia. I think maybe you're right to wait and see what Harrison does. Ohio's writ doesn't run in California, and Harrison does not need to pay you a penny if he doesn't want to. When he surfaces, we'll see what sort of man he is. You're right to wait and see." He eyed her. "And while you wait, you might meet people. You mother and I have our little dinner parties two or three times a month. We could certainly include a few selected gentlemen. Ones with means, of course. And you could always take courses at the Art Institute."

She laughed, uneasily.

"You know, Marcia, you're a matron now, and your security must rank ahead of everything else. That, after all, is just what Melvin Moulton told the court. That is how Harrison failed you."

He was saying, gently, that her own impulse to return to Paris was, in a way, just as neglectful of her family as Harrison's single-minded pursuit of his career. She felt chastened.

"I would be happy to meet assorted males at your dinner parties," she said.

"I thought you might see it that way. Life is serious, and money is important. Much to my regret, we've tended to forget that in our family."

She thanked him and wandered outside, into an autumnal day,

feeling years older than she had just an hour before. Her father was right. Her idle dreams of a frolic in Paris, another bout at the Ecole, romping with all those Bohemians and enjoying the avant-garde, was no longer appropriate. She let go of it sadly, even as the trees were letting go of their leaves. She had veered dangerously close to Harrison's own peculiar vice, but her father had rescued her. Suddenly, as she strolled among the golden leaves, she felt a rush of gratitude toward Drake Devereaux. Her father had helped her to take the next step up the stairway.

The idea of the dinner parties sounded good to her. In addition, she would make her own contacts among old friends her own age. She would find an appropriate man. She knew she wasn't exactly the most attractive woman around, but if she looked, she would find someone. She would find love, security, a shared life, and a father for the children. What more could a woman ask?

C H A P T E R   7 1

Good news from the gallery. Katharine Steinmetz handed the letter to Gilberto Mendoza, who studied it carefully.

The New York gallery had accepted the twelve photographs of refugees she had sent them, and would mat and display them in a forthcoming exhibit on the earthquake, for a 20 percent commission. They would also display her portrait of Emil Wolff.

She rejoiced.

"Now you will be famous," said Mendoza.

"I'd settle for some money," she replied. She had lived upon the charity of the hard-pressed Mendoza family for weeks, but each time she had offered to camp in the plaza, they had protested. In truth, she was enjoying her stay with the Mendozas. Gilberto was so gifted in the special art of photographing people in their daily occupations that she blotted up everything he could teach her.

Then the reviews drifted in, and the first of them discouraged her.

"It is scarcely to be grasped why any photographer, surrounded by the greatest natural disaster in recorded history, should take pictures of ordinary people instead of focusing on upheaval, ruin, destruction, and fire. People are ordinary; the San Francisco quake was extraordinary," said Cantwell in the *World.*

"A side diversion, not the main fare," said Bartholomew in the *Sun.*

"Interesting family groups, fear in their faces, but of course an insignificant sidebar to the main story," wrote Jaquard in the *Herald*. "Mrs. Steinmetz missed a grand opportunity."

Mendoza studied those, too, with thickening anger. "They don't know a good plate when they see it."

Her spirits shrank. She began to wonder about her abilities. She would not change anything; she would take the same set of photos again, in those circumstances. But the world wanted fire and smoke and tumbling brick and bodies.

Then Alfred Steiglitz wrote her with a bit of good news. The Photo-Secession, he said in a brief note, had sold her portrait of Wolff to a forthcoming encyclopedia of American arts, and she would net eight dollars. "The critics haven't been kind to your plates, but the public is," he said. "They examine the ruins and flames with barely a glance, but when they reach your photos of fear-touched people, they pause. Perhaps they see themselves in the headlong flight from disaster. I myself think these are your finest work, both technically and artistically."

She beheld the eight-dollar postal money order with joy.

"Now I can pay you something, Gilberto," she said. "This is yours."

"No, no, you need it. We get along."

Getting along was all they did. Gilberto was not a man with business acumen. "Then let me do this," she said. "I owe you for paper and chemicals. The eight dollars barely pays for what I've consumed."

He sighed, stared out upon the silent blue sky, and nodded. The food and shelter proffered by the Mendozas would be charity; the darkroom expenses were something else.

She worried away her days in sleepy Sonoma. The refugee families camping on the plaza vanished, one by one, and the old mission town returned to normal. An inn on the plaza allowed her to display her photographs, but she sold none. No one had money in the aftermath of the quake. Some moments she despaired. She didn't know how to support herself. She lacked so much as a good camera, and had kept Charmian London's all too long.

She had not seen the Londons since the quake, but one day she received a note from Jack, with a five-dollar money order enclosed. They had sold another of the portraits of Emil Wolff, this time to *Collier's*. She was grateful. The trickle of money at least permitted her to pay Gilberto for the all the materials that she was borrowing.

Some days, when her knees didn't ache too much, she walked slowly to the plaza and sunned herself on a bench, enjoying the quiet. She had always been a city woman, and had never spent time in a village. But now this sleepy town beckoned her. She was getting old. Emil was gone. She liked to sleep. If she could find means, she would stay here.

But that was the catch. What could an old woman, a failed photographer without so much as a camera and a darkroom, do? She did not know. Life had passed by. Maybe there was a county poor farm where she might be sheltered and fed. Did it matter? She knew in her soul that it did. She had gifts to give the world if only she could.

She had come to love the Mendozas, and knew Gilberto would be a fine partner in a business. They could run a studio, take portraits, yearbook photographs, do weddings, capture fiftieth anniversaries and prize horses and babies. Yes, she could do that, and between them, keep a shop open. It was a good dream, but only that, for a woman living upon the charity of a hard-pressed family. Gilberto did several things for a living, the photography the least of them. He was a part-time teller, ran a coal and ice business, and cultivated an extensive garden that partially fed his family.

"Gilberto," she said one day. "Is there a small building where you and I might have a studio? Maybe an old carriage barn we might convert. Maybe a place with a room at the back for me? I am thinking we should have a studio. Maybe I could survive on wedding photographs."

He beamed. "I will look into it," he said. "But I don't know how . . ."

One September day Katharine received a thick envelope from the gallery, and a bank draft for two hundred thirty dollars. She stared at the fortune, stunned. A publisher doing a book on the quake had purchased single-use rights to all her photographs. The gallery had sold five more prints to private buyers. Magazines had purchased seven and wondered whether she had others she wasn't showing. A European collector had bought copies of her entire collection. And the gallery wanted more of her work.

She felt faint. She read and reread the draft, not believing the numbers.

"Gilberto, Gilberto," she cried.

"It is as I said," he concluded, after reading the letter.

"Now we can buy equipment. Now we can start!"

"You have reached the people, but the critics still ignore you," he said, restlessly.

"The money is what matters. It makes me whole again, Gilberto, don't you see?"

"No, Katharine. I don't see. I am waiting for just one blind critic to see daylight. Then I will rejoice. You make art! Art! And they don't know it."

She had an inkling what the trouble was. Her photographs weren't considered art. They were regarded merely as documentary pictures, no matter how carefully she composed and printed them, no matter how she controlled light. She had been thrown into the same boat as Jacob Riis and Lewis Hine, whose documentary photos weren't considered art in New York.

"Some day I will go to New York and show them what art is," he growled.

She liked having a champion.

Now, with cash in hand, they looked in earnest for a place to set up a business, and found one on the north side of town. She had to leave all that to Gilberto because her knees prohibited almost all work. But one autumn day, the Steinmetz and Mendoza photographic studio opened. He had insisted that her name should precede his, and she finally had surrendered to his whimsy. In the front was a studio, with a new Kodet on a tripod, several backdrops, assorted chairs and props, and floodlights. Behind was a darkroom with a used but excellent enlarger along with Gilberto's trays and chemicals and his old dryer; and at the rear, a small, sunny room for Katharine.

It seemed a miracle to her. She had her own bed, a chair, a kitchen alcove, and a small lavatory. And she wouldn't need to climb stairs to reach it. She needed little else.

CHAPTER 72

Nella wept. The little thing at her breast evoked no tenderness but only black despair. She felt worn and used up, though Mrs. Harkness said the delivery had been easy. If that was an easy delivery, then what was a hard one? The wizened creature she had given birth to was not the child she had dreamed of.

Mrs. Harkness had cleaned the infant and handed it to Nella without comment. Nella, sweaty and discouraged, beheld an infant with a twisted left foot, the heel high, the toes pointing down and inward. A clubfoot. A child marked for life, although doctors were learning how to straighten such deformities.

Grief washed through her. What sort of life would she have, raising a cripple? Would she ever want another child? She felt the infant squirm, and its small hands clutch and unclutch, and she ached to love it, ached for the flood of maternal love to release and engulf this little twisted thing. But it didn't. She held everything in, and it felt leaden within her.

What would Willis think? This wasn't even his child. He had bravely married her anyway, a gamble for both of them, and so far it had been a good marriage. But now? She feared this would tear their short marriage to bits, and he would take one look and begin to withdraw into his own world.

They had been living in Oakland in a flat the insurance company finally found for them, while Willis commuted each day on the ferry to the ruins of the city across the bay to examine insured properties and come to estimates of losses. It hadn't been hard. The losses were usually total, and in many cases the work crews had carted away the rubble before Willis could even get to the site. A web of temporary railroad tracks threaded the ruined area, enabling crews to load gondolas full of rubble, car after car, as San Francisco stripped itself down to bare earth and started over.

Willis was over there this day. The labor pains had started shortly after he had caught the ferry; she had no way of reaching him. He would come home to the bad news.

Mrs. Harkness, a peppery and superior woman, primly scrubbed and cleaned, rolling Nella this way and that while she changed sheets.

Nella's hands and arms instinctively coddled the infant she was rejecting, held it and caressed it while her mind reeled.

"I wish it had never been born," she whispered.

"It was the quake. Mark my words, it was the quake. That earthquake left its mark upon every child in every womb in San Francisco. I've seen it. I've delivered a dozen now, and I've seen it."

"What did you see?"

"The sign of the quake."

"Like a brand?"

Mrs. Harkness clutched her throat. "No, the mark on the soul. That quake released the devil from under the earth, and the devil put his mark on every child he claimed. That's why the earth cracked open— to let the devil out."

"Oh, that isn't true."

"Believe what you want," the midwife sniffed. "I've seen it. I know. This is just one more case."

"What were the other marks?"

"A baby still as death but breathing, his eyes staring into nothing. He had seen the devil in the womb. That's what I saw just last week."

"And what else?"

Mrs. Harkness frowned, hands on hips, and stared. "You wouldn't want to know. Even the ones that looked healthy and perfect were marked. Just you wait. Remember my words. The quake ruined their lives."

Nella sighed, wearily, too tired to resist. Maybe it was true. But if so, it wasn't anyone's fault. This little thing didn't ask for a clubfoot. She held the twisted foot in her hands, feeling its velvet softness, its high little heel, its downward thrust. Why couldn't it have been perfect?

She let it suckle, and with the tug on her breast she felt the infant seeking life, and she loved it a little, tentatively, grieving its deformity. Maybe the twisted foot had nothing to do with the earthquake. Maybe it was because Jeremy had his way with her, or more properly, she had her way with him, designing to take him to the altar one way or another. Yes, that was it. This poor baby bore the mark of her own sin. She wept. She lay there, feeling torn and used up and desolate.

"No one here so I'll stay until Mr. Hart comes back," said Mrs. Harkness. "See how dark that child is? That's the devil's hue. It sure don't look like his father."

The infant was too young to look like anything, but one thing was clear. Its flesh had a honey color, and its spidery web of hair was black.

"Oh, don't say that!" Nella cried.

Mrs. Harkness retreated into superior silence.

The assault on her infant only galvanized Nella's protectiveness. Now, suddenly, she realized this little thing was hers, and she loved it, and she wouldn't let this officious and bullying midwife wound her or disparage this child one moment longer.

"I want to rest now," she said.

"I'll wait in the kitchen. If your husband doesn't return soon, I'll have to charge an extra day. I'll leave the bill on your kitchen table. Ten days, cash only. Extra for return visits."

Nella nodded.

The bedroom door clicked shut smartly, and then Nella was alone with her sleeping babe, which lay in a flannel receiving blanket.

Willis would be home soon. It was after five. He had a twenty-minute walk from the terminal to their flat. He was going to get a cruel surprise.

She dozed, and then she opened her eyes and discovered him sitting on the edge of the bed, leaning over her shyly, his face wreathed in smiles, his hands running awkwardly around the rim of his fedora.

"Nella! You're all right! I didn't know!"

"There was no way of telling you," she said softly.

"It's a boy, that's what Mrs. Harkness said. But she was funny about it."

Nella fought back tears. She pulled the covering cloth away from the infant. She intuited what all this would come to: the end of a good marriage. Why would Willis Hart love and father this child? He had been a brave man to marry her, but he hadn't bargained for this.

"He's a fine child, a handsome child, Nella. We're blessed, you and me."

She shook her head and pulled the blanket farther away, until the naked infant lay exposed to Willis. She lifted the left foot and showed it to Willis, pushing back the tears.

"Something's wrong?"

"That's a clubfoot."

He sighed, studied the deformed little foot, and said nothing.

"And you're all right?"

She nodded.

"Were you torn?"

"No, apparently not, but I feel like I was."

"No hemorrhage?"

She shook her head.

"I love you, Nella. If I'd known—"

"I know," she whispered.

"There's treatment for this, you know. They put the foot in a series of casts."

"He'll never be right," she said. "It was the earthquake. That's what Mrs. Harkness said."

"That's superstition."

"No, it's all the things we don't know about."

He leaned over her, his hand caressing her face. "I'm glad you're all right. I thought it'd be another week or two."

"So did I."

"May I hold him?"

She handed the baby to him, and he took it gingerly. The child pawed the air, and then settled in the warm crook of his arm. She stared at the baby, and at Willis, her heart breaking. He was doing his best. He loved her.

"Have you given him a name?" he asked gently.

She couldn't meet his eyes. She had wanted to call him Willis Jr., but didn't dare. Not with another father, and not with this—clubfoot. "You name him," she said.

"We have to agree on something."

"I don't care."

"I think you do," he said, eying the little thing. "Do you love him?"

"I don't know."

"I know I can. This'll take getting used to, but all of life's nothing more than getting used to things we don't expect. What if I propose three names and you choose the one you want?"

"No, you name him."

"Is it because you don't want him?"

"No, I want him." She didn't want to say how afraid she was that he would flee.

"Well, how about Willis?"

"You would give him your name?"

"And yours. Willis Clapp Hart?"

Some logjam of emotion dissolved and floated away. She smiled up at her husband. "Oh, God, Willis, I love you," she whispered.

He laughed softly.

"Could we give him a nickname?" she asked.

He nodded, waiting.

"I want to call him Earthquake."

CHAPTER 73

Lieutenant Boswell received the posting he wanted, and moved to Washington where he would write military history for the War Office. It meant he would remain a lieutenant forever; the army could not afford to waste commissioned officers on such a task. But he could endure that if he had to. The posting would give him a chance to examine the role of armies in peace and war.

His most immediate task, requested by his new commanding officer, Colonel Dillwig, was to write an account of the military intervention in the San Francisco quake and fire. Boswell knew that the report would raise hackles, and probably result in explosive recriminations from his former commander, Frederick Funston, but the whole business needed airing.

The army had been best at relief, sanitation, and transporting vital and life-sustaining items, worst at policing and demolitions. It had also failed its constitutional obligations. It had no business marching into the stricken city without authorization from Washington, and General Funston's rationalization of that act, that an emergency required it, was dubious at best. Boswell knew he was going to deal with it. And he was going to deal with looting, the deaths of innocent civilians by armed troops, theft of property by army personnel, unnecessary destruction of property—especially the contents of saloons and liquor stores—by the army, and certain atrocities. The navy and marines had done better, providing valuable firefighting assistance, water, and waterfront patrols without violating the rights of civilians.

That was all hindsight. Officers and men did what they felt was needful in crisis. And he would say so. Emergency provided a degree of exculpation for any acts, just as the chaos of war often exculpated grave mistakes of judgment in heated battle. Historians all had excellent hindsight, and often failed to grasp how hard it was to make good decisions in the field, in the midst of chaos. Boswell knew he must guard against that.

The dynamiting had been particularly disastrous, and large portions of the city might have been saved but for the systematic demolition of whole blocks. Boswell knew he would have to make that case, perhaps in contravention of the self-satisfied reports that had been penned by General Funston and others.

His new posting was going to be a hot seat, and he wondered whether he would survive for long in the United States Army. If not, he would not imagine that his life was coming to an end.

He thought sometimes of Ginger, and felt oddly grateful that things had turned out the way they had. Marriage would have been a mistake, not because his theology was broader than hers—or so he believed—but because of the strange contradiction that lay in her soul. Ginger had turned out to be a paradox, a woman who could love humanity in the abstract, but not in the particular. She could respond to needs everywhere—it was she who had alerted him to the desperation of those Chinamen who had not fled to Oakland. But she could not respond to the promptings of her own heart. She could pass out tracts in one of the most dangerous and dark corners of the world, and brave whatever came. But this selfsame woman had fled from intimacy and friendship—and love. In that respect, every loving instinct within her had been ruthlessly bottled up, repressed by such fear and foreboding that he doubted she could ever love another, especially a potential spouse. Ginger was beset by fear in her intimate life, while a tigress braving life's terrors to love those she didn't really know.

He wished her well. He had fallen headlong for her, the lithe beauty galvanizing his senses, and her infinite caring and concern for the world's most oppressed and needful winning his admiration. Until he discovered how frightened she was. He couldn't ever know why, or what had bent the reed. Maybe her family, maybe not. Maybe theology. He couldn't imagine trying to live by a complex body of verses, some of them contradictory, that had been elevated to the status of absolutes, rules that were often in opposition and suited only for some other time and place. Such obedience would sap his own will, and must have had an enervating effect on hers. And yet, God love her, she was wonderful. Utterly a noblewoman. He hoped, devoutly, that life would be kind to her, that the terrors of soul that afflicted her would wither away, cleansed by God until no fear remained, and she was free to love.

But that was the past. Several hostesses in Georgetown had discovered his presence, and were inviting him to fill out their dinner tables and meet their daughters. That was the future.

Author's Note

. . . .

Immediately after the earthquake, many of the terrified citizens of San Francisco believed the world was coming to an end. Doomsday rumors were rife: great cities were burning, coastal cities were sliding into the sea, volcanoes were burying whole nations. That such rumors gained credence among the shocked victims of the quake is understandable. At every hand, they were witnessing utter disaster.

At the same time, both Protestant and Catholic clergymen were trumpeting their belief that the quake and fire were God's punishment upon a wicked city. Across the Bible Belt, ministers joyously proclaimed that the Sodom of the West Coast was succumbing to the long-delayed punishment of God. That view was not only a libel on San Francisco, but a libel on God. If these vindictive clerics had bothered to examine the account in Genesis describing the destruction of Sodom (around 1900 B.C., by quake and by fires rising from the oil and gas deposits there) they would have read of Abraham's lengthy bargaining with God about the forthcoming destruction, and God's promise to spare any city that harbored any righteous people. God made good his promise by sending angels to lead Lot and his family out of the wicked city, so that the catastrophe fell only upon the wicked.

Although San Francisco had a vicious quarter, and its rich lived in grotesque ostentation, and its citizens pursued relatively worldly lives, the city was no more wicked than any other seaport of the time, and its churches and temples were filled with devout congregations. It was, actually, a robust commercial city and the gateway to the Orient.

For decades, the common view was that the quake did not take many lives, probably about five hundred in all. This was the figure much bruited about by local politicians and businessmen anxious to allay fears about living there. But recent research by Gladys Hansen, emeritus curator of the Museum of the City of San Francisco, has radically altered that perception. Patiently, dwelling by dwelling, family by family, she has documented the deaths of nearly three thousand, six times more than the 503 dead that was the previously accepted figure. She believes the actual death toll was well over three thousand. Add the injured to that, and it becomes evident that at least one in every hundred of the city's four hundred–some thousand citizens was killed or wounded by the catastrophe.

Another of the myths about the quake is that Brigadier General Frederick Funston's swift assumption of responsibility, and deployment of federal troops in the city, greatly improved public safety and ensured the survival of life and property. The reality is darker. Funston, a genuine national hero, brave man, and Medal of Honor winner, actually behaved in a manner so erratic that the damage he did probably outweighed the good. His defenders argue that he acted boldly and bravely in a time of chaos, and he should not be charged with derelictions that arose in the midst of catastrophe.

But in at least two areas—the dynamiting and the military policing he inaugurated—his regimen was harsh and disastrous, not to mention utterly illicit and unconstitutional. It was only when his superior officer, Major General Adolphus W. Greeley, Commander of the Pacific Division, returned to the city on April 23, that the citizens of San Francisco were released from the draconian measures imposed by Funston. The number of alleged looters shot by the regular army, National Guard, and Mayor Schmitz's untrained vigilantes will never be known, but they were numerous. Certainly there were scores of citizens given drumhead justice, many of the executions witnessed. The troops made little effort to distinguish between actual looters and confused, frightened citizens searching for their own possessions in their own dwellings. Nor did Funston acknowledge or attempt to curb the wholesale looting by his own troops.

A veteran journalist, Henry Anderson Lafler, friend of Jack London, gathered these witnessed events into a nine-thousand-word indictment of Funston's odd behavior and published it in a small booklet after the editor of *Argonaut* refused to touch it. This was a response to Funston's own self-serving piece, "How the Army Worked to Save San Francisco," published in *Cosmopolitan* magazine in July 1906. Funston never responded, and for decades his version of events was the quasi-official one. Lafler's indictment simply gathered dust until recent times.

But it was clear to many at the time of the disaster, and not least Major General Greeley, that things were amiss. For one thing, Funston had turned Fort Mason into a fortress during the worst of the fire, building a defense perimeter bristling with troops, weapons, firefighting equipment and barricades around the innocuous post, apparently on the mad supposition that it would be overrun—by someone. For another, Funston swiftly grew autocratic and imperious, abandoned his promises of consulting with civilian authorities, and proceeded to blow up large tracts of the city over their protests. The leveling of the east side of Van Ness Street by Field Artillery was surely one of the most bizarre of his acts.

Funston, under pressure, finally acknowledged that there may have been some drumhead killings—two in all, and neither of those deaths ascribable to the regular army. As for the well-documented army looting, he said not a word, and went out of his way to praise his troops, and to announce that there was nothing better than the regular army for dealing with catastrophe.

Later, Funston was involved in the feckless pursuit of Pancho Villa, but never had another opportunity to pursue the action he always craved. He was promoted to major general, and died a national hero, which he was in spite of the aberrant conduct in San Francisco.

. I have used real people fictionally in this story. Jack and Charmian London did rush down from Glen Ellen to wander the fire-stricken city, and he immediately wired a superb account of the disaster to *Collier's Weekly*. Eugene Schmitz and Abe Ruef were indicted for graft, and in the ensuing months San Franciscans were treated to a bizarre series of events that included bribery of a juror, murder or suicide, and a great deal of maneuvering and plea bargaining. Ruef eventually served a brief term, but Schmitz, much loved even if corrupt, largely escaped punishment.

A badly frightened John Barrymore, arrayed in grimy evening clothes, stayed drunk during the entire period of the earthquake and fire, and used the cataclysm to evade an Australian tour of *The Dictator* by hiding in the Van Ness home of friends. He swiftly composed a colorful report of his experiences in the quake, and twenty years later confessed it had been a fraud. But it had won him the publicity he craved.

Enrico Caruso alternated between hysteria and gracious calm while he wandered San Francisco after the quake, sometimes alone, sometimes with some of his troupe. He was terrified of losing his voice. But eventually he made his way to Oakland on the ferry, and headed east, vowing never to return to San Francisco again. He used his autographed photograph of President Roosevelt as a sort of passport to make his way through the stricken city or move to the head of lines. The voice survived.

The central characters in the story are entirely fictional, and not based on any real people. Harrison White was not the designer of the Monadnock Building; Carl Lubbich was not the city engineer; Emil Wolff did not illustrate *The Call of the Wild*. My intent was to explore the ways various people react to disaster, especially the sort of disaster that cannot be ascribed to other mortals—disasters beyond the realm of blaming. Few people react rationally in such circumstances. Instead, they find direction in their own sense of self: Their guidance comes from family wisdom and folklore, their religious beliefs, and their impressions gained from education and experience through life, rather than from calculation during the crisis. The earthquake opens up the fault lines in their lives and marriages and relationships, and hidden truths lie exposed.

Thanks to the miracle of the Internet, I was able to download scores of primary documents from the Museum of the City of San Francisco. Other important sources include *The San Francisco Earthquake* by Gordon Thomas and Max Morgan Witts, and two remarkable books hastily published in 1906: *San Francisco's Horror of Earthquake and Fire*, and *San Francisco Earthquake and Other Great Disasters*. While neither of the 1906 books is very accurate, both brim with anecdotes, color, and the preoccupations of the times. My editor, Dale L. Walker, supplied me with valuable research material, including the Jack London account of the quake. I gratefully wish to acknowledge his able assistance, and the counsel of many others I consulted.

Richard S. Wheeler
December 1997